THE FROZEN RABBI

THE
FROZEN
RABBI

A NOVEL

STEVE STERN

ALGONQUIN BOOKS OF CHAPEL HILL   2010

Published by
ALGONQUIN BOOKS OF CHAPEL HILL
Post Office Box 2225
Chapel Hill, North Carolina 27515-2225

a division of
WORKMAN PUBLISHING
225 Varick Street
New York, New York 10014

Portions of an earlier version of this book have appeared in *Fiction* magazine, *Maggid,* and *Natural Bridge,* and portions of the final version have appeared in serial form in tabletmagazine.com

This is a work of fiction. While, as in all fiction, the literary perceptions and insights are based on experience, all names, characters, places, and incidents either are products of the author's imagination or are used fictitiously.

LIBRARY OF CONGRESS CATALOGING-IN-PUBLICATION DATA
Stern, Steve, [date]
    The frozen rabbi : a novel / by Steve Stern.—1st ed.
        p. cm.
    ISBN 978-1-56512-619-0 (alk. paper)
    1. Teenage boys—Fiction.   2. Rabbis—Fiction.   3. Memphis (Tenn.)—
Fiction.   I. Title.
    PS3569.T414F76 2010
    813'.54—dc22   2009047396

10 9 8 7 6 5 4 3 2 1
First Edition

for Sabrina,
who makes me almost human

THE FROZEN RABBI

1999.

Sometime during his restless fifteenth year, Bernie Karp discovered in his parents' food freezer—a white-enameled Kelvinator humming in its corner of the basement rumpus room—an old man frozen in a block of ice. He had been searching for a slab of meat, albeit not for the purpose of eating. Having recently sneaked his parents' copy of a famously scandalous novel of the sixties in which the adolescent hero has relations with a piece of liver, Bernie was moved to duplicate the feat. No stranger to touching himself, he hardly dared to dream of touching another, so inaccessible seemed the flesh of young girls. His only physical intimacy so far had been with his mother's Hoover, innumerable pairs of socks, and his big sister's orchid pink underpants retrieved from the dirty clothes hamper in the bathroom. Then he had come upon the novel he'd once heard his parents sheepishly refer to as the required reading of their youth. Not a reader, nor much of an active participant in his own uninquisitive life, Bernie had nevertheless browsed the more explicit passages of the book and so conceived the idea of defrosting a piece of liver.

Shoving aside rump roasts, Butterballs, and pork tenderloins in his quest, Bernie delved deeper among the frozen foods than he'd ever had occasion to search. That was when, having emptied and removed the wire trays, the boy encountered toward the bottom of the bin a greenish block of ice that stretched the entire length of the freezer. Scattering individually wrapped filets, tossing packages of French fries, niblets, and peas, Bernie was able to discern beneath the rippled surface of the ice the unmistakable shape of a man. It was an old man with a narrow, hawkish face, gouged cheeks, and a stringy yellow beard, his head wreathed in a hat like a lady's muff. His gaunt body was enveloped in a papery black garment that extended to the knees, below which his sticklike calves, crossed at the ankles, were sheathed in white stockings. His feet were shod in buckled bluchers that curled at the toes, his arms folded behind his head as if he were taking a luxurious nap.

Bernie's initial reaction was panic: He'd stumbled upon something he shouldn't have, and thought he ought abruptly to cover his tracks. He rolled the boulders of meat back onto the ice, slammed shut the lid of the deep freeze, and tromped upstairs to his room, where he crawled into bed and tried to still his galloping heart. A solitary, petulant kid, his chubby cheeks in their first flush of cystic acne, Bernie was unaccustomed to any kind of galloping. But the next day he returned to the basement to determine if he'd seen what he'd seen, and that night at dinner, ordinarily a somber affair during which his father related his business woes to an indifferent wife, Bernie muttered, "There's an old man in the meat freezer." He hadn't meant to say anything; if his parents were keeping some dirty secret in the basement, it was none of his business. So what had compelled him to blurt it out?

"Did you say something?" asked his father, unused to his son's breaking his sullen silence during meals. Bernie repeated his assertion, still barely audible.

Mr. Karp pushed his bottle-thick glasses back onto the hump of his nose and looked to his wife, who sat feathering her spoon in her consommé. "What's he trying to say?"

It took a moment for the fog to lift from her puffy face. "Maybe he found the thing."

"The thing." Mr. Karp's voice was level.

"You know, the white elephant."

"The wha—?" Mr. Karp grew quiet, his hands beginning to worry the loosened knot of his tie. "Oh, that."

"It's not an elephant," mumbled Bernie fretfully.

Mr. Karp cleared his throat. "That's an expression, white elephant, like a heirloom. Some people got taxidermied pets in the attic, we got a frozen rabbi in the basement. It's a family tradition."

Bernie retreated once again into silence, having been unaware that his family had any traditions. Then it was his sister Madeline's turn to be heard from. A voluptuous girl, exceedingly vain of her supernormal development, she condescended to inquire, "Like, um, what are you people talking about?"

Wary of his sister, who may have suspected him of stealing her underwear, Bernie slumped in his chair, avoiding her eyes. His father seemed to do likewise, for Madeline's looks could be oppressive in the matte gray Karp household; while Bernie's mother, still playing with her food, offered acerbically, "He's from your father's side of the family; they were always superstitious."

"He's a keepsake"—Mr. Karp's tone was defensive—"that they handed down from generation to generation." He squared his weak shoulders as he tried to summon some pride for an object whose existence he had clearly forgotten till now.

Annoyed, Madeline pushed her chair from the table, blew at a wisp of primrose hair that fell instantly back into her eyes, and flounced resolutely out of the dining room. Moments later a shriek was heard from downstairs, and Mr. Karp cringed. "He came with a book, the rabbi," he said, as if the literature conferred some official distinction. "Yetta, where's the book?"

"There was a book?"

Heaving a sigh, Mr. Karp readjusted his glasses and got purposefully to his feet, departing the room just as Madeleine emerged from the basement, her robust complexion gone deathly pale. "I, um, no longer want anything to do with this family?" she declared interrogatively.

"Here it is," announced Mr. Karp, squeezing past his busty daughter to reenter the dining room. "It was in the bottom drawer of the dresser, under my Masonic apron." Proprietor of a prosperous home-appliance showroom, Mr. Karp was a joiner, an affiliate of local chapters of the Masons, the Lions, and the Elks, his enrollment dating from a time when Jews were not always welcome in such organizations. His prominence and civic-mindedness, however, had earned him the status of an honorary gentile. He had even managed to secure his family a membership in an exclusive Memphis country club, which (with the exception of Madeline, whose endowments gave her entrée everywhere) the family seldom used.

Mr. Karp handed a limp ledger book of the type in which accounts are kept to his son, who began indifferently thumbing the pages. Instead of figures, the pages were covered in an indecipherable script that resembled clef signs and fishhooks.

"The book explains where the rabbi came from," continued Mr. Karp with authority. "My papa wrote it all down himself. Problem is, he wrote it in Yiddish." He may as well have said Martian. Then he added somewhat apologetically, "He's supposed to bring luck."

What kind of luck? Bernie wondered as he carried the ledger to his bedroom, a boneyard of aborted hobbies—the unpainted husks of model cars, the broken clear plastic trunk of a Visible Man, a PlayStation gathering dust. Though his only real enthusiasms to date had been a fondness for overeating and his late penchant for erotic fantasy, he idly perused the ledger's scribbled pages. When they refused to give up one jot of their meaning, he stuffed the book under his mattress alongside Madeline's panties and fell promptly into a dreamless sleep.

1889 – 1890.

When the holy man Rabbi Eliezer ben Zephyr, the Boibiczer Prodigy, wished to get closer to God, he would sit, or rather lie, by a certain pond in the woods outside his village. There, using techniques described in Gedaliah Ibn Yahya's *Girdle of Abimelech*, he would meditate on the letters of the Tetragrammaton until he entered a trance. In his youth he had been acclaimed for his public demonstrations of memory, his ability to recite passages of Talmud both forward and backward, and his feats of what the uninitiated called magic. But now in his twilight years he was far beyond such exhibitions, and preferred to exercise his powers in solitude. He would lie upon his back on the mossy bank of the pond, his clasped hands cradling his head as the *Girdle* prescribed, while his neshomah, his soul, ascended to the Upper Eden. There his soul sat in bliss among the archons studying Torah. Once, however, during one of his more intensive meditations — this was in the blustery month of Sivan, just after Shavuot — there came a mighty storm. With his soul aloft, his body, frail as it was, remained insensible to the moods of the terrestrial world; and so, while the storm raged and the torrents battered his meager frame, Rabbi Eliezer continued his meditations in peace. The drenched earth on which he lay turned to mud and the water of the shallow pond began to rise, inundating his legs to the waist, creeping over his chest and chin and ultimately submerging his hoary head.

Previously the sage had depended on the shulklapper summoning the faithful to prayer to signal the reunification of his body and soul, but the deluge had muted any noises from above the surface of what was quickly becoming a lake.

As their rebbe's retreats were fairly routine, Eliezer's small band of disciples had grown accustomed to the old man's frequent absences, but that he should stay away for so long in the wake of such a terrible storm seemed to them a distinct cause for worry. After several days, a party of Rabbi Eliezer's Chasidim, their earlocks streaming, gabardines flapping like crows' wings, began combing the pastures and thickets known to be the tzaddik's special haunts. Deracinated trees with roots like hydra heads, the bloated carcasses of drowned hogs, and roofless peasant huts were what they found, but no Rabbi Eliezer. Some of his followers even passed in the vicinity of the pond that had overnight turned into a considerable body of water, underneath which lay the Prodigy in his mystical transports. When weeks had passed without a rumor of their leader's whereabouts, the Chasids reluctantly called off the search; they tore their garments, beat their pigeon breasts, and sprinkled ashes over their heads but refused to say Kaddish, contending one and all that their rebbe would one day return.

The seasons changed, the russet and gold autumn supplanted by an alabaster winter, while Rabbi Eliezer continued his submarine meditations. The ground was blanketed, the trees stooped like peddlers under haversacks of heavy snow, and still the rebbe's body remained impervious to decomposition. It was the time of year when the industrious widower Yosl King of Cholera, accompanied by his feckless son, Salo, dragged his sledge across the snowfields to the banks of the Lower Bug to harvest ice. (He'd been an orphan, Yosl, whom the town had married off to another orphan during a plague in the hope of assuaging God's wrath—hence his name.) This year, however, Yosl had heard from the cheder boys, who skated the horse pond on Baron Jagiello's estate, that summer storms had increased the pond to the size of an inland sea. After investigating, Yosl went hat in hand to the baron and begged permission to carve ice from his lake in exchange for replenishing the estate's own supply free of charge. An agreeable man when it served his interests, the baron gave Yosl the go-ahead, and the ice mensch set out across the fields, trailed by his son.

When they arrived at the swollen pond, a few truant Talmud Torah boys were already there, their wooden skates describing wobbly spirals and arabesques on the jade green surface of the ice. Abandoning his sledge, Yosl trod the ice in his hobnailed boots to test its thickness and then, satisfied, began to cut a trench with his axe. He called to his son to bring him the double-handled ice saw, but Salo, as timid as he was lazy, ventured only to the edge of the lake to hand his father the tool.

"Amoretz!" Yosl complained to the iron gray sky. "He puts his shoes on backwards and gets from walking into himself a bloody nose." But that was the extent of his indictment, since Yosl had long since abandoned any real expectations of his son's usefulness. The boy's fear of almost everything in existence seemed to exempt him from life itself, let alone work, and sometimes his father wondered if Salo, whose mother had died in childbirth, had ever been entirely born.

While his father labored, Salo dawdled at the margin of the lake, ashamed as always to be hanging back but convinced that the ice would not support his lumpish weight. Occasionally, however, he might dare himself to rest the ball of a foot on the crusted surface, rubbing a circle as smooth as glass with the sole of his shoe. But rather than steal a glance through the polished porthole, lest it reveal something unpleasant, Salo usually turned away without even looking. At one point he did catch sight of a fish like a monarch's wing suspended in a sunless world where time stood still. And again, unable to resist a peek after rubbing another circle, he saw the face of an old man with a yellow beard.

"Papa!" cried Salo in terror.

In no particular hurry, Yosl trudged over to find out what his son was squawking about this time. "Gevalt," he exclaimed upon seeing the thing the boy had accidentally discovered, "it's the rebbe!" Shaken to the core, Yosl slapped his own face to collect himself, then rounded up the other boys (his own was too slow) and dispatched them to the Chasids' study house with the news. The rebbe's disciples came running, arriving breathless to find that Yosl Cholera had already set about excavating their long-lost leader. The ice mensch, his jaw working like a whiskered feedbag as he labored, was dragging a large block of ice containing the rebbe onto the shore of the lake with his rope and grappling hook.

Then the Prodigy lay before them on a mound of snow, and his gathered disciples, puffing like steam engines, were at a total loss as to what to do next. It was surely a blessing to have their tzaddik back in their midst again, apparently intact even if frozen stiff, but what now? In former days it was the rebbe himself to whom they would have applied for advice, but he was unavailable for comment. There were the texts of holy writ to consult, though even the most sedulous scholars among them — those who prescribed what portions of Torah one should consider during intercourse, or whether it was permitted to pee in the snow on Shabbos (which was tantamount to plowing, which was work, and so forbidden) — even they knew of no passages pertaining to the current quandary. Then one of their number, Fishel Ostrov, the shovel-bearded yeast vendor, proposed that they light torches to thaw the holy man on the spot. His theory was that Rabbi Eliezer, during his raptures, was proof against the depredations of time and the elements, and that once the ice was melted, he would be restored to them in all his prior vitality. There was a thoughtful buzzing among them until a wiser head prevailed.

"Know-it-all," accused Berel Hogshead, the teamster, insisting that the risk was too great, since, once thawed, the rebbe might begin to putrefy and his bones become — God forbid — food for the worms. Better they should put him somewhere for safekeeping, so that at least he would remain in one piece until he chose to burst forth from his repose of his own accord. More buzzing in the affirmative as Yosl King of Cholera, neither Chasid nor mitnagid but simple opportunist, stepped forward in his capacity as proprietor of the Boibicz icehouse: "Your honors, for a nominal fee . . ."

THE BOIBICZ ICEHOUSE was a windowless granite grotto dug into the northern slope of a hill at the edge of the village by giants or fallen angels in some antediluvian age. That was the legend, anyhow. All Yosl Cholera knew was that he'd inherited the icehouse after the death of Mendel Sfarb, its former owner, whose family claimed to have had it in their possession since the Babylonian Exile. The business was Mendel's guilty gift to the orphan who had been his ward and virtual slave from the age of six. From outside, the sunken structure with its domelike stone protrusion resembled an age-encrusted tomb, which made it a most suitable repository for the Boibiczer Prodigy; it was a place where his body could lie in state, so to speak, resistant to decay until such time as he saw fit to come forth again — or so his followers maintained. Much to Yosl's annoyance the Boibicz Chasidim insisted on honoring their rebbe's resting place as they would a sacred sepulcher: They warbled their prayers (excepting the prayer for the dead) at its entrance, placed messages in the cracks between its stones, and took turns inside cleaning the sawdust and flax that collected around the holy man's transparent berth. Though they cautioned one another not to diminish its mass, they discreetly shaved slivers from the block of ice, which they sweetened with dollops of honey and devoutly sucked. Since they refused to acknowledge the Prodigy as officially deceased, the Chasids were unable to elect a successor and thus came to be known for their veneration of the refrigerated rebbe as the Frozen Chasidim.

Diverting as were the antics of credulous fanatics, however, the inhabitants of Boibicz had other concerns to reckon with. Edicts and ukases were being issued by the imperial government in such dizzying succession that what was permitted in the morning was often forbidden by afternoon. The most recent stated that, for their own good, the Jews would be barred from leasing inns, taverns, and shops in the villages outside the Pale of Settlement.

In addition, no new Jewish settlers would be allowed in the villages and hamlets within the Pale, a decree that often stranded merchants returning from business trips or families from High Holiday worship in nearby towns. The Byzantine logic of these laws defied the understanding of even the most learned Talmudists, but as a consequence, many longtime citizens of Boibicz had begun to find themselves homeless, and for those still in residence the writing was on the wall. Eventually the Jews came to anticipate a wholesale exodus from a place that had been a home to their families for generations, though at that prospect they continued to drag their heels. In the end it took a delegation of their neighbors, chaperoned by a regiment of Cossacks dispatched by the government and operating under the blind eyes of the local police, to expedite their departure.

For all the chaos that erupted on that winter morning just after the Festival of Lights, the perpetrators went about their business almost mechanically, though the violence was no less savage for being deliberate. Without fanfare they entered the dingy Jewish quarter and smashed the shop windows, hauling out bolts of cloth, pedal-driven sewing machines, spirit lamps, unplucked chickens, anything that fell to hand. They defecated in the synagogue vestibule and wiped their goosefleshed behinds with the torn vellum scrolls of the Torah. Feivush Good Value, melammed and tradesman, they hanged from his own shop sign by his patriarch beard; they swung Shayke Tam, the idiot, by his heels, squealing because he thought it was a game, until his feeble brains were splattered across the shtibl wall. Those who fled to the woods were hunted down and beaten to splinters, though most who stayed put survived, among them Yosl Cholera's son Salo, who'd taken refuge in the icehouse.

The fact was, he had scarcely strayed beyond the shadow of the icehouse since the day he'd stumbled upon Rabbi Eliezer ben Zephyr suspended beneath the surface of the lake. Though the frozen rebbe was scrupulously looked after by his followers, Salo, having taken a surprising interest in his discovery, had conceived the idea that the holy man was his own personal charge. He kept his ears alert to the stories the disciples told one another of the Boibiczer Prodigy's wondrous feats of piety, and when no one else was about, the artless boy (in age already a young man) took his turn sitting vigil beside the block of ice. He admired the old man's tranquility while expecting, like his disciples, that at any moment the ice might yawn and crack open and the rebbe irrupt from his slumber. It was an event he had no desire to hasten, however, so easeful was the waiting. To show cause for his hanging about the ice grotto, the boy made gestures toward helping his father, but when the King of Cholera realized it was the frozen rabbi rather than the entrepreneurial impulse that enlivened his son, he dismissed the boy once again as a lost cause. Moreover, Salo's chronic attachment to the icehouse had been noted by his waggish peers, who gave him the nickname of Salo Frostbite, which stuck.

So it was that, on the morning of the pogrom, Salo was seated on a cabbage crate, gazing at Rabbi Eliezer's slightly distorted features, their beatific peacefulness having invaded his timorous heart. All about him the stacked slabs of ice were carved into shelves and niches, which contained fish, fowl, and barrels of kvass. In one recess Leybl the hatmaker's poker-stiff dog Ashmodai awaited the spring thaw for its burial. Rime coated each jar and jeroboam until it resembled a vessel made of spun sugar; ice stalactites hung from the vault of the ceiling like fangs. But the warmth Salo felt in the rebbe's presence (enhanced by his sheepskin parka, whose collar he pulled over his ears) practically deposed the arctic chill of the grotto in its subaqueous light, a light that seemed to emanate from the ice itself. "The Chasids sit shivah while you sit and shiver," Salo's father had complained, but in the rebbe's presence all the fearful chimeras of the boy's imagination were dispelled, and the world seemed almost an idyll, a winter pastorale. As a consequence, Salo never heard the cries of the tortured and defiled, the keening women and the breaking glass, nor did he smell the smoke from the burning synagogue. It was only when the sexton, Itche Beilah Peyse's, who'd lost his mind, began to howl like a hyena in the street that Salo's own peace was finally disturbed.

Bestirring his broad behind to go and see what was happening, he crawled up the slippery ramp and wriggled out of the hatch through which the large rectangular ice cakes were slid into the grotto. He stumbled down the hill into the village, past the Shabbos boundary markers where the snow was stained in patches with what appeared to be plum preserves. Outside the door of the smoldering timber synagogue a mother tried to revive her fallen son by pumping air into his lungs with a pair of bellows; a violated daughter begged her father on her knees in the ruts of the market platz not to disown her. The procession of wagons hauling bodies, already becoming rigid, to the cemetery vied with the jauntier parade of peasants carrying off samovars, chamber pots, a trumpet-speakered phonograph, a cuckoo clock. Plodding forward in his klunky topboots, Salo accidentally toppled the cantor Shikl Bendover, who had died of fright still standing, like Lot's wife. He paused to reerect the dead man, then realized what he was doing, and understood that the scene he had entered eclipsed any active fancies his mind might entertain. It put to rest forever his habit of ghoulish invention, for which Salo, who began then and there to grow up, was grateful.

He stepped into the smoky, slat-shingled dwelling that he and his father called home, where he discovered to his head-swimming sorrow that he'd been made an orphan like his father before him. Yosl King of Cholera lay on the raked clay floor in the stiff leather apron he'd donned for work, his head pincered by his own ice tongs. The handles of the iron tongs branched above his crimped skull like a giant wishbone, the blood streaming in crimson ribbons from his ears. Salo retched down his front and fell to his knees, leaning forward to touch those of his father's features that were still recognizable: a blue knuckle swollen from arthritis, a pooched lower lip like a water leech. For an indefinite time he lay prostrate without the least inclination ever to rise again, until he remembered that he now had a higher calling. Wiping his mouth and dabbing at his eyes, Salo crawled forward to wrench apart the ice tongs. He got to his feet and began to rummage in the debris of the ransacked hovel, eventually locating a pair of candles which he lit with a sulfur-tipped match and placed at either end of the murdered man's outstretched form. All the while murmuring Kaddish, he threw a cloth over the ancient mirror, its surface clouded with floes of mercury; then he squeezed himself behind the tile stove, scalding his tush in the process, and pried loose a wallboard in back of which Yosl had hidden his meager treasures—a handful of groschen and some ducats as worthless as slugs, an unsigned postcard with a sepia view of Lodz, a dented thimble that had belonged to his wife. Salo thrust it all into a capacious pants pocket along with the crust of black bread with dried herring that his father had laid aside on the table for his lunch. Stooping to right a toppled chair, he found himself gripping it tightly, swinging it into the stovepipe, which burst apart, releasing a naked tongue of flame that tickled the ceiling. He emerged from the cottage just as Casimir, a sooty-eyed Polish porter with hair like thatch, was tugging along Yosl's pussle-gutted mare by a frayed piece of rope; and though he knew the beast to be next to useless, Salo straightaway turned over his inheritance (minus the postcard and thimble) to the porter in exchange for redeeming the skewbald nag. Then, as the roof shingles of his former home began to curl upward, tugged at by threads of smoke, Salo took up the reins of the mare, whose name was Bathsheba.

He was aware, of course, that Rabbi Eliezer ben Zephyr, if he belonged to anyone, belonged to his worshipful followers. But the Frozen Chasidim and their families were packing up their belongings as was everyone else, and nowhere amid that doleful exodus of clattering barrows and carts heaped high with candlesticks and featherbeds did Salo spy any monumental block of ice. Ingenuity had never been his strong suit; indeed, Salo had never had a strong suit, but drawing from a fund of proficiency that he decided then and there was his father's legacy to his son, he undertook to replace the metal-rimmed wheel on Yosl's delivery wagon. When he'd managed over the course of an hour to unhobble the wagon, he hitched it to Bathsheba, whose sluggish forward propulsion seemed entirely owing to a chronic flatulence. Salo stopped at the old log prayer house long enough to appropriate the cedar casket that leaned against an interior wall beneath the half-collapsed roof. This was the single battered casket that the village had recycled for the funerals of the past hundred years. Loading it onto the wagon, the youth continued to lead the horse up the hill to the ice-house, where he studiously addressed the heavy mechanism of a block and tackle coiled at the threshold. He proceeded to snake the pulleyed device through the hatch and down into the stygian grotto, then lowered himself after it for the purpose of attaching the cables to the ice. Back outside again, awakening muscles that had slumbered for the greater part of his seventeen years, Salo hauled the rebbe by main force from his catacomb up the wooden ramp into the failing light of day. Then, sweating profusely despite the bitter cold, he slid the block of ice up a second, makeshift ramp of sagging planks onto the bed of the wagon. There he began to chip at the edges with his father's axe until he could shove the block, wrapped in burlap for further insulation, over a final improvised slope into the casket. Since Bathsheba's slack belly dragged the ground as if she were fed on cannonballs, there was no question of mounting the wagon; so Salo tugged at her reins and set off walking without further delay (as who was there left to say goodbye to?) in the general direction of the city of Lodz, which lay some leagues beyond the Russian Pale.

1999.

Finding an old Jew in the deep freeze did not at first alter Bernie Karp's routine in any measurable way. Overweight and unadventurous, he had no special friends to tell the story to even if he'd wanted, which he didn't: It was nobody's business. But even Bernie had to admit to himself that something had changed. It was still late summer and he continued, as was his custom, to spend most of each day in front of the TV, munching malted milk balls and digging at himself. Images passed before his eyes without leaving distinct impressions: In a comic sketch a failed suicide bomber was comforted by his veiled mother to gales of canned laughter; in another a little girl kept God in her closet; a heartwarming Hallmark drama portrayed a Navy SEAL romancing a mermaid; and a reality-based program dispatched a disabled couple on a blind date to Disneyworld. There were elections, massacres, celebrity breakups, corporate meltdowns — all of which tended to evaporate like snow on a hothouse window upon entering Bernie's brain. Still, he remained a passive captive of the flickering screen in the faux-paneled basement, which was largely his private domain. The only new wrinkle in the fabric of his days was that, while surfing the myriad channels, Bernie would also fan the pages of the ledger book in which the grandfather he'd never known had chronicled the history of the frozen rabbi in an alien tongue. He riffled the pages the way you might finger worry beads, and periodically he would rise and shuffle over to the freezer, where he rolled aside the game hens and packaged ground round to make certain that the old man was still there.

Then came the weekend his parents went to Las Vegas, all expenses paid, for a home appliance convention. They naturally had no problem with leaving the adolescent Bernie alone, since the boy had never demonstrated the least propensity for mischief, and at nineteen the headstrong Madeline, on vacation from college, would do as she pleased. It was Friday night around eight in the evening when the storm hit, one of those semitropical electrical storms with typhoon-force winds that often swept through Bernie's southern city in August. The television reported that funnel clouds had been spotted about the perimeter of the city, their tails corkscrewing the muddy ground like augers, sundering mobile homes. Lightning crackled and thunder rumbled like kettledrums, rain hammered the roof of the two-story colonial house, while Bernie sat more or less oblivious in the recessed cushions of the rumpus-room sofa. It wasn't that he was devoid of fear; it was rather that primary events had little more impact on him than events—save the odd Playtex commercial or his father's prime-time pitches for discounted appliances—on TV.

There was a violent sound like a fracturing of the firmament, after which the lights went out and the image on the TV shrank to a blip, then disappeared. Bernie continued sitting alone in the windowless dark, clutching the ledger, as what else was he supposed to do? His sister was out with one of her boyfriends, not that her company would have been much consolation; so there was nothing for it but to sit there listening patiently to the propellerlike drone of the wind and waiting for the floodwaters to rise above the eaves. When after some time had passed the storm began to abate, the boy was almost disappointed. The power, however, had still not come back on, and in the wake of the squall he could hear the sound of a hollow knocking nearby. Bernie listened awhile as if the faint but persistent rapping were an attempt to communicate by code; then he lifted himself from the depths of the sofa and groped his way to the shelves that housed the overflow of his father's framed civic citations and loving cups. Perspiring freely due to the shutdown of the central air, he stooped to open a cabinet beneath the shelves, foraging blindly among dusty wine bottles and photograph albums until he'd located the ribbed handle of a plastic flashlight. He switched it on and aimed its beam toward the source of the thumping. . . .

Standing over the freezer cabinet, Bernie slowly lifted the chromium handle that released the lid. Instantly the lid flew open, soggy steaks and tenderloins sliding onto the floor, as up sat a sodden old man like an antiquated jack-in-the-box, his fur hat stinking like roadkill. There was a moment when the old man and the boy with his hanging jaw were transfixed by one another; then the old man's scarlet eye grew narrow and gimlet sharp, and shaking himself, he asked in a rusty voice, "Iz dos mayn aroyn?"

Even had he been able, Bernie would not have known how to respond.

Groaning and soaked to the skin, his hands and face the consistency of wet papier-mâché, the old man endeavored to rise, only to fall back splashing into the freezer. "Dos iz efsher gan eydn?"

Again Bernie, his heart rattling the cage of his ribs, could only shake his head.

"A glomp," said the rabbi decisively, "a chochem fun Chelm," as he held out his scrawny arms for the boy to help him up. Bernie remained motionless with awe, but as the old man's anticipation had an air of authority, he took an involuntary step forward. The rabbi was no more than a featherweight, but his saturated ritual garments hung on him heavily, and, in attempting to lift him, Bernie felt as if he'd become involved in a wrestling match. When he'd managed to drag the old man from his sloshing sarcophagus, his decaying garments clinging to his body like bits of eggshell to a fledgling bird, the boy and the elder tumbled together onto the hooked rug. Just then the lights came back on and the TV began blaring, its screen displaying a smug master of ceremonies making a face as contestants held their noses in order to swallow the placentas of voles. The defrosted rabbi, lying sprawled atop Bernie, who had yet to release him, squinted with interest at the show.

"Voo bin ikh?" he inquired.

At that moment Bernie's sister, leading her escort in his Bermudas and crested blazer by the hand down the basement stairs, spied the half-naked old party in the process of extricating himself from her brother's embrace and screamed bloody murder.

1890 – 1907.

Since progress was slow along the czar's highway, glutted with so many displaced souls, Salo took to the less traveled back roads. This was the more hazardous course, for there was some safety in numbers, whereas alone he was more vulnerable to attacks by brigands and peasants who'd missed their chance to plunder Boibicz — or Shmedletz or Smorgon or Zhmirzh, all of which had also been emptied of Jews. But Salo, his head cowled in his filthy tallis and crowned by a peaked cap to protect him from the needles of falling sleet, preferred the risk to the ranks of his fellow refugees. He had grown impatient with the pall that overhung their caravan like the poor relation to a pillar of flame, their forced march toward some new oblivion that the Jews seemed born for. Should he feel guilty? Was he perhaps an apikoyros, a heretic, that he should experience such exhilaration on the heels of his father's homicide and the destruction of his hometown? But having spent the past seventeen years in nearly uninterrupted mooning about, he was thrilled, God help him, at having waked up to find himself at large in history. He was Salo Frostbite, self-appointed guardian of a slumbering saint, and while he might look like a schnorrer, his holey boots wrapped in rags to keep his feet from freezing, he felt he had become overnight a man of substance and parts.

It was a status corroborated by those who might otherwise have done him harm: the mounted Cossacks in their braided cloaks and astrakhan hats, who cantered alongside his wagon and threatened Salo with conscription, which for a Jew amounted to a life (if not a death) sentence in the army. They would lift his weak chin with their swagger sticks and accuse him of the Jewish trick of concealing treasure in unlikely vessels, then demand to know what he had hidden inside the casket. During the earliest encounters Salo wondered if he ought to refuse their request on principle, even if it meant imperiling his person; for wouldn't allowing these bullies to ogle the casket's contents amount to a type of desecration? But as his mission of maintaining the rebbe required his staying alive, he would concede in the end to raise the lid (the soldiers would have raised it in any case)—whereupon all questions would cease. Confounded by the revelation, the Cossacks would dig spurs into the shuddering flanks of their steeds and gallop away in a spray of mud. Eventually soldiers and peasants alike began to give the youth with his strange cargo a wide berth, a state of affairs Salo attributed to the gelid rebbe's disturbing effect on the goyim, word of which must have spread abroad in the land.

He had the conviction that so long as he took care of Rabbi Eliezer ben Zephyr, the tzaddik would take care of him. Meanwhile he starved, though occasionally some sympathetic old baba yaga would scuttle forth from her kennel to spare him a stale pierogen or a potato as soft as a powder puff. These he would dine on for days, storing the leftovers under the burlap in the refrigerated casket to extend their relative freshness. Lightheaded from hunger, Salo sometimes daydreamed: The river he had just been ferried across (for the price of reading scripture aloud to an illiterate ferryman) was the lost Sambatyon, on the other side of which lay the land of the immortal red-headed Jews. Or had he strayed off the map of the known world entirely and crossed the border into Sitra Achra, the kingdom of demons, which was beyond God's jurisdiction? But even as he indulged them, Salo recognized such notions as merely the shades of dead fancies, lingering vapors of the bubble-brained boy he had been only a short time ago. Moreover, with every meal he missed, a bit more of his vestigial baby fat melted from his bones, and although there were no available mirrors, Salo could feel that he was becoming somebody else: He was a young man transporting a sacred burden through a menacing winter landscape, the hero of his own unfolding story, who had no need of encumbering himself any longer with superstition and grandmothers' tales.

Sometime during the third week after the departure from his native shtetl, Salo came across a thickset peasant in sheep pelts shambling along the road, clutching one end of a rope that trailed over his shoulder. At the other end of the rope was a noose that circumscribed the neck of a woman whose haggard features—nose protruding like a cucumber from the folds of a ragged shawl—identified her as a suffering Jewess. Salo's first impulse was to nod deferentially to the peasant and pass by. The journey had taken a toll: His empty belly whistled to rival the flatus of his rattle-boned mare, and his feet ached as if he were trampling glass; to say nothing of how the relentless cold froze his brain. But prey to a stronger urge than self-preservation, Salo addressed the man in the Polish he'd heard since birth, and scarcely recognized his own brash voice.

"What's that you got there, friend?"

"Are you blind, friend?" said the peasant, giving the salutation a hostile emphasis as he continued to walk on.

At that Salo gripped Bathsheba's bridle to halt her, and turned to inquire in as diplomatic a tone as he could muster, "Beg pardon, but has no one challenged your right to the woman?"

The peasant abruptly paused and turned about, bristling, his flat face as flushed as a purple onion. "I found her in the village of Plok," he barked. "She's mine."

"Who's arguing?" said the young man, conciliatory, then gently submitted, "But isn't she, excuse me, a human being?"

The peasant peered at Salo as if he were a half-wit. "I knew she wasn't a goat."

Salo grinned, deciding to try another tack. He cleared his throat and assumed an attitude he thought of as strictly business. "So what'll you take for her?"

The peasant cocked an ear. "Is she for sale?"

Shrugging what he supposed was a mercantile shrug, Salo replied, "Everything's for sale, friend."

The peasant screwed up his doughy features thoughtfully; here was a language he understood. "Fifteen zlotys," he said at length, "and she's yours."

It was an astronomical sum, which the peasant was of course aware of, but Salo continued to keep up his end of the bluff. He sucked a tooth and gave the woman a once-over as if to assess her value. Then he was surprised to find that her spindly frame and sour face, furious despite her oppressed situation, engendered in him a mellow throb of desire. Here was a new sensation and, vibrating like a plucked fiddle string, Salo marveled at the range of passions the wide world afforded. He turned his head to spit an imaginary plug of tobacco.

Meanwhile the peasant had begun to eye the weathered casket in the bed of the wagon. Salo followed his glance, anticipating what would come next: how the man would ask to see what was concealed in the box, and Salo would comply to encourage further negotiation, after which the peasant would promptly cross himself and make tracks along with his captive. To avoid this eventuality the young man blurted, "Tell you what I'll do," and offered a straight swap. "This fine brood mare for your broken-down hag, what do you say?"

The peasant was caught off guard. He looked first suspiciously at Salo, then swiveled his head from the mare to the woman, as if torn between the audacity of such an offer and a horse-trading impulse he couldn't resist. "Which is more broke down?" he wanted to know.

"Why, just look at her," said Salo, beginning to find his stride. "What use can you expect to get from her? A few months, a year at the most, and she's finished—you'll dig her grave. Whereas, the mare will probably outlive you."

The peasant was incredulous. "The nag is more decrepit than the hag! It's already glue. Besides," with a simper that invited Salo's collusion, "women are better for fucking."

Uncomfortable with this turn in the conversation, Salo nonetheless rallied. "Are you crazy? The woman's bones will snap like matchsticks, while the mare will bear you a fresh foal every year." He was himself a little unclear as to the implied paternity of the foals.

"I'm crazy?" The peasant could scarcely believe what he was hearing.

"That's right," said Salo. "You would settle for a moment's pleasure with a tainted female whose pox I can sniff from here"—he was conscious that even in harness the woman was seething—"when you could enjoy the years of prosperity that only a good draft horse can provide?"

Amazingly, the peasant was beginning to waver, though he stiffened again when Salo began to lay it on a bit too thick, making claims for Bathsheba's thoroughbred bloodline. In the end, though, the youth moderated his tone, and the yokel, making a great show of reluctance, accepted the deal, handing over the tether in exchange for the reins of the unhitched mare. Once the bargain was struck, however, the peasant began to gloat, saying "Good riddance" to the woman as if he had suckered Salo all along: He had out-Jewed the Jew. Watching the man leading away his father's gangle-shanked jade, her tail raised like a mophead as she dropped a load in the muck, Salo felt sorry for the animal; her fate would not be a happy one. But life, though harsh, was full of unexpected gifts, and pleased with what he deemed (despite the peasant's response) a successful transaction, the young man turned to face his prize.

She spat at him, at first actual sputum, then a venomous stream of execrations: "Shtik drek! Gruber yung! I pish in the milk of your mother!" But Salo, as he endeavored to remove the taut noose from around her neck, took no offense. If anything, he felt a pang of nostalgia for the curses his father used to heap on his head.

"A finsternish, may your testicles soon toll your death knell!"

Then even as she continued spewing bile, she took up the traces, without prompting or inquiring as to what the coffin contained, and began to help Salo pull the wagon along the furrowed road. In the name of her martyred family and herself, Basha Puah Bendit Benchwarmer's, she denounced her rescuer as she did the God of Abraham for his discourteous treatment of Jewish daughters. She lamented her lost dowry—which had consisted of some pewter spoons, a milch cow, and an Elijah's chair—and reviled the world that had deprived her of her due. Enjoying the music of her wasp-ish tongue, Salo wondered how she might look with a little meat on her bones, though he expected that her raw bones would always shun flesh. But vinegar-pussed harridan that she was, at least a decade older than he, she was still a woman, and having never spent time in the society of women, Salo was greatly excited, his loneliness dispelled.

Warmed though he was by her litany of complaints, the young man begged leave to interrupt. "I respectfully submit," he said with a bashful formality, "that for the sake of decency we should marry as soon as we can."

Snarling as she resolved never to forgive him for the humiliation of having been traded for a horse, and for all the future offenses she antici-pated in his miserable company, Basha Puah ungraciously accepted Salo's proposal.

THEY WERE WED on the roadside beneath the tattered canopy of Salo's prayer shawl by a beggared Galitzianer rabbi in exchange for a glimpse of the Boibiczer Prodigy, of whom the rabbi had heard rumors in his travels. He'd heard that the Prodigy was encased in an immense blue sapphire, and was duly disappointed. For a witness there was the rabbi's dolt of a son, and in the absence of a goblet they made do with Salo's mother's silver thimble, which the groom stomped into the brittle mud with his heel. Nights on the road, the newlyweds slept wherever they could: on the splintered floor of an abandoned tollhouse, in the rafters of a sawmill with an ice-locked water wheel, and once, when they were stranded between shtetlakh, in the open wagon beside the cold casket, where they clung to each other desperate for warmth. And although Salo's termagant bride never left off upbraiding him — "From one degradation into yet another you thrust me!" — she was pregnant by the time they reached Lodz.

The city, which he'd journeyed so long and endured so much to reach, had assumed a golden aspect in Salo's mind. But the swarming Jewish district, called the Balut, rather than populated by saints, was a home to rag-pickers, organ grinders, professional cripples, prostitutes, and thieves, to say nothing of the legion of slogging automata employed in the silk mills and dye houses that bordered the banks of the sulfurous Warta River. The smoke from the factories hung a mauve miasma over the city, collecting in the twisting lanes of the Balut, whose citizens wore its permanent fetor in the folds of their clothes. Their working children, like human bobbins unspooling, trailed home sticky threads from the cocooneries, their pockets spilling caterpillars that continued to spin fantastic Jacob's Ladders in the attics of their dilapidated abodes. Slush steamed in the arcaded streets from the excrement of horses and the blood of the slaughtered animals that hung in shop windows or lay cloven and splayed across merchants' stalls. Malodorous sink that the ghetto was, however, you couldn't have proved it by Salo Frostbissen, who exulted in its carnival atmosphere, an attitude that incensed his wife all the more.

Nor was she impressed that Salo's reputation had preceded their arrival in the Jewish quarter, where a number of pious souls had gathered hopefully about the horseless wagon. They touched their prayer shawls to the rebbe's box, then kissed them as if the casket were a portable shrine, declaring that Salo's having survived the journey with the rebbe intact was a miracle, proof of the tzaddik's powers even at rest. Basha Puah, who had abused her husband throughout their travels for the bootlessness of his burden, let alone the added insult of having enlisted her assistance in conveying it, had thus far refused even to look inside the casket. Of a practical turn of mind, however, she was not above suggesting that those who wanted to take a gander might pay for the privilege. But Salo's stubbled head was a little turned by his hero's welcome, and while he feared that overexposure might diminish the rebbe's sanctity, he nevertheless revealed Eliezer ben Zephyr to anyone who asked. The dividends came in any case: Zalman Pisgat, proprietor of the turreted brick icehouse in Franciszkanska Street (beside which Yosl's was nothing, a hole-in-a-hill) requested the honor of installing the Prodigy in the bosom of his business; meanwhile the charitable members of the Refugees' Aid Society promised to locate some "cozy little nest" for the newlyweds. For a time it seemed that the orphaned bride and groom would be treated as dignitaries, the toast of the ghetto, and Salo, still caked in the shmutz of the road, basked in their triumphant entry into Lodz: It was the storybook finale to a great adventure. But as the misery of the quarter was in no way mitigated by his advent, and its citizens' short spans of attention were recalled to their daily woes, the son of the King of Cholera and his refrigerated tzaddik were soon forgotten, Salo's notoriety failing to survive his first week in Lodz.

They were installed in cheap lodgings in Zabludeve Street, a windowless cellar habitation that Salo praised for its favorable comparison to his father's grotto (it was certainly as dank and cold) and his wife cursed for the claustrophobic crypt that it was. Moreover, Zalman Pisgat's gratitude for having been allowed the mitzvah of preserving the frozen rebbe was also short-lived. He did, however, offer Salo the position of night watchman, though not without strings attached: A portion of Salo's wages would have to be exacted weekly to compensate for the rebbe's storage fee. That Salo willingly acquiesced to what amounted to his indenture, that he didn't toss the block of ice containing the holy man into the river and have done with it, were crimes Basha Puah added to the lengthening list of her husband's infamies. Salo was himself a little disappointed that his fame had so swiftly subsided, though he chided himself for his vanity. And after a spell in Pisgat's icehouse, dispersing shadows with a hurricane lamp as he navigated the crystal palisades under the glazed eyes of dead oxen, salmon, and hares, he was again reconciled to old Eliezer's unending incubation. He was content to spend his nights, between tours of the hyperborean premises, sitting vigil in his role as the saint's custodian, prepared to wait till hell itself froze over for the rebbe to hatch from his ice chrysalis.

So what if the ghetto was a pesthole in which he and his hatchet-faced bride lacked a pair of groschen to rub together, where they dined on hot water afloat with limp cabbage leaves and relieved themselves in a court-yard privy whose odor brought tears to the eyes? The Balut, in its unsleep-ing activity, was by Salo's lights a tonic to all who dwelled therein. And besides, didn't he enjoy the best of two worlds? By day he was a four-square householder who, with his expectant wife, fulfilled the commandment of marriage and multiplication; while at night, in retreat from the roiling streets, he was the solitary guardian of a legend that became more bur-nished the more it faded into memory.

For her part Basha Puah fulminated against their lot with every breath she took, cursing her husband's irrepressible spirits, though she was herself galvanized by the ghetto's raucous atmosphere. Despite her violated sense of entitlement, which she never ceased from registering with God and Salo, she was an enterprising woman. By the time their celebrity had expired, she had managed to parlay nothing into a couple of turnips and eggs, which she peddled in the Franciszkanska Street market—battling the other wives over coveted locations—for the price of another couple of turnips and eggs. Then a day came when she sold an egg at a profit and used the surplus capital to increase her inventory. Eventually, by shrewd reinvestment in the produce the peasant farmers sold wholesale from the wallow of their wagonyard, she established a modest pushcart business; she sold vegetables and eggs whose freshness her husband extended by storing them in the ice-house overnight. In a matter of weeks her market stall was a going concern, and full of admiration for his eruptive wife's industry, Salo helped her as best he could, though it meant that he seldom slept. He carted merchan-dise from the wholesalers to the marketplace and shlepped to and from the bakery the boolkies Basha Puah rolled at home and left to rise like inflating airships on top of the neighborhood oven. For gratitude Salo received his wife's habitual grousing that he was always underfoot. She also chafed at his solicitude with regard to her inconvenient condition, which she refused to let hamper her labors or leaven her poisonous tongue.

Then the twins were born and Basha Puah cursed the incontinence of her own womb, which she threatened, if her husband did not cease his mawkish cooing and fawning over the infants, to stitch shut. She savaged the mustachioed midwife for her complicity and Salo for having saddled them with more mouths to feed. Euphoric nonetheless, Salo bankrupted his expanded family by laying in schnapps and spongecake and inviting every ganef and teamster in their putrid trough of a street to witness the circumcision. He named the boys, in the face of his wife's indifference, Yachneh and Yoyneh after his ill-fated father.

Even as she carried them dangling from either udder to her market stall, Basha Puah excoriated the twins for their rapacious appetites. "Fressers, you suck like leeches and bite like asps!" Rascals that no one ever bothered to distinguish from each other, they were running wild in the unpaved alleys of the Balut before they were weaned. Early on they learned to ignore their mother's threats and jeremiads, or rather — following their father's blithe example — to be amused and even tickled by the lash of her tongue. From the first they were conspicuous for their cheek among the swarms of marauding ghetto urchins; they were foremost in teasing the blowsy whores who graced the windows and doorways of Žvdowska Street, and in tormenting the mendicant amputees till their flaring tempers enabled them to sprout latent limbs and give chase. From hanging about the slaughterhouses and tanneries, they brought home new varieties of noxious odors, and vile language that rivaled even their mother's. They rode the obsolete mill wheels and were baptized in the seething river that bubbled with acids like a sorcerer's retort. Basha Puah charged her husband to discipline the young savages, but in his eyes the boys, high-spirited and reckless, did no real harm. Besides, when did he have the time to be more than a benign spectator to the progress of his sons, whom (like everyone else) he'd never troubled to try and tell apart? He did attempt, for the sake of form, to see to it that they attended a local cheder, but the old melamed Yankl Halitotsis was unable to keep them (or their peers, for that matter) confined to an airless study house during the day. They were forgiven their truancy by their father, who harbored his own unpleasant memories of the village kloiz. To placate his wife, however, Salo assured her that, when they were old enough to appreciate him, he would introduce the twins to the Boibiczer Prodigy, whose aura had a moral effect on any Jew that beheld him. Basha Puah called him every manner of fool, then accused him of being a wanton beast as well for making her pregnant again.

"How did this happen?" she demanded to know. "When are we in bed, the two of us, at the same time?"

But the truth was that, while the marital mattress sagged between its creaking slats to the earthen floor and was only a few feet from the clay stove on which the twins slept, there were opportunities enough. And though Basha Puah would hiss at Salo for disturbing her much needed sleep and complain of a woman's travail, she never once refused her husband's advances.

This time the child was a rosy bundle of a daughter whom they called Jocheved, and Salo basked in the undiluted light of her countenance. "Give a look," he exclaimed, "how like the ner tamid she shines!" His wife asked him what did he know from an everlasting lamp, so rarely did he set foot inside a synagogue. This was not entirely fair: for a man who worked day and night, Salo had always kept Shabbos as best he could. If only from habit, he took the requisite ritual dip in the brackish waters of the Vlada Street mikveh and attended shul on high holidays. Deeming himself a most fortunate man, he had assembled a ragged minyan (its members as disreputable as a police lineup) to say the conventional prayers of thanksgiving at Jocheved's birth, and again at her naming ceremony. But while the prayers were ostensibly addressed to God, Salo reserved his real gratitude for the blessed Rabbi Eliezer ben Zephyr. It wasn't that he worshipped the rebbe—he wasn't so pagan as that; but after years of lifting the casket lid to ensure the security of its contents, after staring so long at the suspended tzaddik, Salo sometimes imagined himself staring back through the tzaddik's eyes (which remained tightly shut) at the swiftly aging watchman. Sometimes he felt as if he viewed the world from inside the block of ice, from a prismatic vantage that made everything appear lustrous and holy. Away from the icehouse, however, performing the tasks that bowed his spine and deepened the bags beneath his eyes, Salo wondered if perhaps he and the rest of the world were merely figments in the rebbe's dream.

With the passing years rumors of tottering empires and imminent apocalypse reached even the netherworld of the Balut. The graybearded alter kuckers, as usual, predicted the advent of Messiah (waiting for whom was their principal vocation), and the worse conditions became for the Jews, the more convinced were they that Messiah's arrival was at hand. But the young tended to read the signs differently, and many were fed up with a religion predicated on anticipation and the suffering one must endure in the protracted meantime. In cellar coffeehouses and shtibls where printing presses had replaced the ark of the Torah, they whispered sedition and conspired to carry it out. The Frostbissen twins, Yachneh and Yoyneh, were among those infected by the revolutionary fever. They had never bothered to assemble separate identities, and despite their tender years they were already sated with the stew of vices the ghetto afforded — they'd shared women with the same cavalier indiscretion with which they might have shared a bottle of contraband cognac or a wager in a game of shtuss; and now, susceptible to loftier passions, they had become enamored of the doctrines of radical change. They joined the socialist labor Bund and, barely literate themselves, distributed Marxist pamphlets on the streetcorners of the Balut. They mouthed the prevailing rhetoric, inveighing against the capitalist cockroaches among their own people. "The Jewish bosses, once they cease their blood-sucking exploitation, will be regarded as equal partners in the proletarian struggle for an independent Poland!" and so on. While they'd scarcely lifted a finger to alleviate their parents' ceaseless toil, they now took unskilled jobs throwing silk and stirring the vats of synthetic dye in the fabric mill, where they attempted to organize the workers into unions. Their efforts and those of their comrades resulted in havoc, sparking strikes and subsequent lockouts that led to battles between protesting workers and hired thugs, to beatings at the hands of police and mass arrests, which the twins only narrowly escaped. And lately, though they had only a nodding acquaintance with their own mother tongue, they had begun to disparage Yiddish as *zhargon*, espousing the revival of Hebrew as the official lingua franca of the Jews.

Between working and dreaming, Salo was unaware of his sons' political activities. On those infrequent occasions when he saw them, he could only marvel at how much they had grown; he admired them for having turned into some rare new breed of Jew, no longer anemic and long-suffering but muscular and purposeful, while Basha Puah grumbled that they were becoming so gentile she wondered if they were still circumcised. She couldn't help but hear the news that percolated throughout the marketplace: There was a failed revolution in Russia, and dozens of Lodz citizens sympathetic to the insurrectionists had built barricades and been wounded in clashes with the police; after which both Polish and Jewish youths, sentenced without trial, had begun to vanish from the city streets by the score. Then all of a sudden the twins came in from the cold; they were back in the cellar, looking over their shoulders, stuffing clothes into canvas knapsacks and informing their mother and baby sister that they were off to found a Jewish state in Palestine. They referred to Zion as if it might have been their original home, which they'd have argued that in a sense it was. For the opiate of religion they of course had little patience, their reasons for going having nothing to do with "holy" lands; nothing was sacred in this unjust world, they contended, but the human will. Full of the zeal of their righteous new ideology, they neglected to say that they were wanted by the authorities.

Basha Puah marched to the icehouse to fetch her husband, insisting—when she'd managed to pry him loose from his post (an increasingly difficult operation due to his stiffening joints)—that he do something to prevent the boys from leaving. But Salo was perplexed; hardly conscious of the passage of so many complacent years, he still thought of the twins as impish little pishers incapable of serious mischief. As for their newly minted ideals, their father never presumed to discourage them, though he wondered why anyone would want to go elsewhere when life was so unquestionably headquartered right there in Lodz.

"Yachneh, Yoyneh," he appealed, "I mean, Yoyneh, Yachneh. What return? You were born in the Balut, which may I remind you rhymes with galut — the Diaspora. What business have Jews got in Jerusalem?"

But when it became apparent that there was no dissuading them, Salo, to his wife's profound vexation, fell to regarding his husky sons as figures of romance and grew excited at the prospect of their formidable journey. Before they left, though, they must first come to the icehouse: He had something to show them; and if only to get him off their backs, the twins promised to stop by Pisgat's on their way to the Promised Land. But arrangements had to be made, smugglers of human beings to be contacted, old gambling markers called in to gather money for bribes — all this while Salo waited in vain in his far corner of the cooling room beside the aged cedar casket. In the end, instead of his sons in their broad-belted tunics and visored caps, the watchman was visited by the police in their helmets like blackened lamp chimneys, who bullied him to no avail with questions and threats. In time the twins sent back letters from Palestine, recounting Herculean labors. They were formal epistles written by scribes to be read aloud by scribes ("To our esteemed and virtuous parents, long life!"), standard propagandistic accounts of draining swamps and irrigating deserts that bloomed with date palms and tamarind, of triumphant battles with mosquitoes and hostile Bedouin tribes. While his wife dismissed these chronicles as pure fabrication, Salo thrilled to their letters as if his intrepid boys had entered the pages of *The Book of Legends* itself. But the letters, sporadic at best, eventually ceased to come at all, and Basha Puah, eyes brimming with tears she refused to acknowledge, raged against her husband with an unprecedented vitriol for having lost their sons.

Meanwhile Jocheved had grown apace, her vibrant presence a perpetual reminder to her mother that the twins were gone. Still, Basha Puah was relatively frugal with her rebukes to the girl, who was after all an obedient daughter and a help in the market, her comely figure and natural charm an abiding inducement to commerce. But though she spent her days at her mother's side hondling with the wives and rolling dough for kreplach, Jocheved was finally her papa's girl. It was she that brought to the icehouse in the evenings his covered dish of lukewarm pupiklekh and sat beside him on melon crates in the arctic cold while he ate. Though she had grown too old for them, Salo continued to regale her with the stories he'd told her when she was a child: preposterous tales of his pitched battles with the ice pirates who raided Pisgat's repository (which, please God, was deadly quiet at night), of his adventures and narrow escapes on the long and arduous road from Boibicz to Lodz. The stories often had a soporific effect on the teller, who sometimes nodded off, and Jocheved was amused at how her heavy-lidded papa's narratives sedated him like self-inflicted lullabies. They created such an air of unreality in the lamplit chill that the first time Jocheved lifted the lid of the casket while Salo dozed, the frozen rebbe seemed no more authentic to the girl than her father's extravagant tales.

"Our family has been elected," Salo once solemnly informed her, meaning they were chosen to be stewards of a sacred trust he would reveal to her when the time came. (The time came shortly after the twins' departure, but by then Jocheved had long since preempted the revelation.) "Elected to what?" the girl had replied, brushing crumbs from her father's beard—because, didn't her family live in an unrelieved penury due to the universal injustices that her absconded brothers had made the girl so keenly aware of?

But while she paid lip-service to her brothers' sentiments, she never invoked their anger, for like her father she was possessed of an amiable disposition, and like her mother she had a practical turn of mind. What interested Jocheved most about Pisgat's establishment, with its goggle-eyed heads of herring and carp staring out of their frozen cataracts, was the ice itself. Early on in her visits she'd begun to cultivate the idea that there were more things one might do with ice than cool drinks and preserve the carcasses of dead animals and old men. Taking a cue from a moon-struck anecdote of her father's about how the rebbe's disciples had chipped "saintsicles" from his lucent block, the girl brought with her to Pisgat's one evening a sealed tin cylinder acquired from a rag and bone man. While her father slept, she shaved slivers from the stacked ice cakes and packed them into the container, which she tucked away among the demijohns of chilling schnapps. The next morning on the way to the market, under cover of the hectic loading and dispatching of wagons, she retrieved the tin drum from the icehouse. She had a scribe scratch GEFROYNS in charcoal on a piece of bunting and flew the banner from a pole over her mother's stall. Then for a grosz she scooped the crushed ice into paper twists and flavored it with treacle and nutmeg, with powdered ginger, vanilla syrup, and lemon juice. In subsequent days she began to sprinkle the ices with almonds, raisins, and runny fruit jams as her customers desired.

Once she had determined that there was a demand for her product, Jocheved ended her furtive activity at the icehouse. Unbeknownst to her father, she sought an audience with Zalman Pisgat in his office, its walls plumaged in orange invoices. She offered him a most reasonable percentage of her profits in exchange for the few kilos of ice upon which her business daily relied. As impressed with the maiden's pulchritude as with her ingenuity, the grizzled old ice mensch suggested a salacious arrangement of his own; but, a little ashamed of himself, when the girl seemed not to know what he was talking about, the old lecher agreed to her generous terms. In this way Jocheved was launched in her career as merchant and manufacturer.

These were the dog days of the month of Tammuz and, impoverished as they were, the citizens of the Balut stood in line to shell out a few coins for a taste of Jocheved's flavored winter. They queued up, according to the goyim (who queued as well), with their tongues lolling as if they were waiting, God forbid, to take communion. The thriving progress of her business venture fueled the girl's ambition, and seeking to improve her product, she obtained some recipe pamphlets from the local book peddlers, which (as unread as the rest of her family) she nevertheless set herself to decipher. When she'd laid by a little extra capital, she bought from a general merchandise catalogue an item called a Fuller's freezing pail. This was a wooden bucket with a zinc interior and a rotating central handle for mixing the preparation of egg yolks, cream, and sugar, and whatever exotic ingredients (jasmine, musk) she might wish to add. The operation involved surrounding the vessel in an azure moat of ice and sal ammoniac, churning with one hand while scraping off the crystals as they formed on the pail with the other. It was strenuous work, to which Jocheved was of course no stranger, and she thrilled at the alchemical process of converting her raw ingredients into sweet confections—a transformation as stupendous as the wonders in her father's tales. As she expanded her repertoire, so did she increase the volume of her production, crowding the cellar flat with vessels like paint pots filled to the brim, the entire stock of which she sold every day.

Soon she was able to contribute significantly to the family coffers, but rather than simply turn over her profits, Jocheved preferred to present her parents with gifts they would never have purchased for themselves, such as a clothes wringer, a tea urn, a rotary flour sifter, and a japanned coal hod for her irascible mother. Then there was the controversial mohair walking skirt with a flounce and the pair of mercerized lisle stockings, which Basha Puah complained were an insane extravagance and must be returned—though she was seen wearing both skirt and stockings with a touch of hauteur in the women's gallery of the Vlada Street shul on Tisha B'av. In that same shul her husband, relegated to the rear of the congregation in the pews reserved for the common laborers, could be seen sporting a new pair of knee-high chamois boots. In addition, Jocheved had begun seeking more salubrious accomodations for her family. The Feuchtwanger clan, about to depart for America, would soon be vacating their apartment, which consisted of two cramped rooms in the same reeking hive of a tenement. Still, their flat had a window overlooking the courtyard, which, foul though it was, was at least a few yards removed from the blight of Zabludeve Street.

Among Basha Puah's catalogue of grievances was the complaint that her daughter was working too hard and, while she bestowed her bounty on others, did nothing for herself. But for Jocheved the success of her labors was reward enough, and as for the absence of personal ornamentation, her beauty shone all the brighter in contrast to her drab apparel. It was a winsome beauty that seemed almost her own invention, since neither of her herring-gutted parents could have taken credit for it. They could never explain the luxuriant black curls with their auroral lights, or the skin like the clarified cream from her freezing pail, the satiny eyes that flickered with a lambent green flame. Sometimes, despite her modest attire, perspiration in the heat of the day revealed certain contours of her slender form; then the dovelike breasts beneath her coarse linen bodice looked as if they yearned for release. While the girl, in her industriousness, was only vaguely aware of her tantalizing appeal, this was far from the case among the ghetto lads, who fell over each other in their eagerness to purchase her frozen custards and sorbets. They flirted with her, the bold ones, inviting her to go for strolls along the river or accompany them to the cafés; but borrowing a text from her mother, albeit tempered with humor, she would admonish them not to waste her time, there were customers waiting. A couple of the more persistent had even tried to present themselves as bona fide suitors, assuring her that they expected no dowry and promising her a comfortable future. But while a husband and children did seem an inevitability, for the time being, clearly prospering without them, Jocheved only laughed at the young men for the nuisances they were.

Most accepted her chastening in the good-natured spirit with which it was given, though some of her more fervent admirers became bitter. Basha Puah, on whom little was lost, noted their truculent attitude and cautioned her daughter that looks such as hers could be more of a curse than a blessing. But although Jocheved humored her mother, she dismissed her warnings, so preoccupied was she with an undertaking that promised to lift her family out of their long-standing wretchedness.

In the climate that had followed the failed revolution, however, the ghetto remained apprehensive. Jews, daily accused of collaboration and betrayal, were shipped in increasing numbers to the salt mines and labor camps; others fled to America, the Golden Land, from which stories were heard of limitless possibilities and untold wealth. But Jocheved, happily engaged in her flourishing trade, was unaffected by the millennial currents that had swept her brothers away. She'd recruited the services of a couple of neighborhood girls to help prepare her product and peddle it farther afield, and in rare idle moments she might even indulge the dream of expanding her cottage industry into an empire—though it alarmed her somewhat, the extent of her own aspirations. Then, miragelike, the promise of prosperity began to recede. Crackdowns and layoffs in the wake of more textile strikes, plus the purges of so-called undesirables, had left many families unemployed; and as the Jews liquidated their savings and pawned their valuables in exchange for shifscarte passages to America, there proceeded a creeping exodus from the ghetto. Who, in the face of such circumstances, could justify even the slight indulgence of a sugarplum sorbet? Meanwhile the first biting blasts of the coming winter also did their part to undermine Jocheved's energetic marketing endeavors. But for her would-be suitors (whom she should perhaps not be so quick to dismiss?), the girl had difficulty finding customers in Franciszkanska Street, and after discharging the assistants she could no longer afford, Jocheved herself began to seek business in other neighborhoods.

One late afternoon, under a sky leaking the tapioca-thick flakes of the season's first snowfall, Jocheved, enveloped in shawls, wheeled her clattering handcart through a part of the ghetto she generally avoided. But she was tired, having spent the day in the more genteel districts from which she was returning nearly empty-handed, and thought she would take a shortcut home. The unfamiliar streets with their anarchic angles and blind alleys confused her, however, and as she veered beneath an arcade to avoid a fallen truck horse whose putrescence stained the icy air, she realized she was lost. Turning a switchback corner in an effort to retrace her steps, she was accosted by a hollow-cheeked youth whose temple curls dangled from his ears like convolvuli. In his short alpaca jacket and the further affectation of a pair of lemon spats, he looked like some half-caste creature, part yeshiva bocher and part swell.

"You should have in these unsafe streets an escort," he offered in a sibilant voice, taking her arm.

She abruptly reclaimed the arm and replied, shakily, "I never needed one before."

"You're the hokey-pokey girl," as if assigning her the role she had already assumed, "the one that won't give the boys a tumble." He ungloved a hand to dip his middle finger into a tub of parfait on her cart, stirring slowly before licking the finger with a tongue Jocheved half-expected to be forked. Then closing his eyes to smack his sensuous lips, he tugged down the leather bill of his cap and grabbed her arm again, this time with a firmer grasp. She tried to pull away and, for the first time in her memory, Jocheved was afraid. At that point another man in a ratty fur ulster and hat, his face like cracked crockery, appeared from nowhere to grab her other arm. He pressed a piece of damp cheesecloth with a sickly sweet smell to her nose, which caused Jocheved to shake her head violently, snorting to clear her nostrils of its fumes. But the more she struggled to resist the almondine odor, the deeper she was forced to inhale, her brain careering free of its axis. Houses whose listing walls were propped up by warped timbers reeled about her like beggars on crutches, and the sun showed its guttering flame just in time to expire.

1999.

The evening after their return from Las Vegas, Mrs. Karp served
a dish of meatloaf whose fetid taste no one could stomach.
"Don't blame me," she said, still woozy from jet-lag and the phenobarbitol
of the night before. "I'm not the cook." Nettie was the cook, a hard-bitten,
church-going woman with swollen ankles, who had once barged into the
bathroom where Bernie sat in flagrante with a lingerie ad torn from a
newspaper. "I ain't seen nothin'," she assured him, and slammed the door,
though she tended to avoid him ever after, as Bernie did her. Sometimes
she could be heard muttering under her breath about the trials of working
for "Jewrish" folk—though there was nothing especially Hebraic about
the Karp household unless you included the old-world relic in cold storage,
which Nettie, if she knew anything of it, never mentioned. But she was
familiar enough with the deep freeze, and had taken out the ground beef
for the meatloaf that very morning, still (as Mrs. Karp attested) frozen
solid.

Mr. Karp tugged at a drooping earlobe as if to aid his powers of deduc-
tion and asked his son, "Bernie, was there any kind of an electrical failure
during the storm?" For he and his wife had returned from their weekend
trip to find evidence of the tempest's damage strewn all over town.

Bernie replied that yeah, there had been a kind of an electrical failure, then immediately had second thoughts.

"Eureka!" declared Mr. Karp in full gloat. "The meat in the freezer must have thawed, then spoiled, and froze again. Mystery solved." He showed horsey teeth, then frowned at the realization that the family trove of turkeys and roasts, now tainted, would have to be jettisoned wholesale. "Tell Nettie to clean out the freezer bin in the morning," he advised his wife, who told him to tell her himself.

The next morning, having complied with orders, Nettie toiled up the carpeted staircase to report the outcome of her appointed task to the missus, who was reposing in her aerosol-scented bedroom with the curtains drawn. Mrs. Karp, still in her dressing gown at half-past eleven, looked up vacantly from the steamy pages of a novel by Arabesque Latour, as the bull-necked servant informed her, "He gone."

"Who gone?"

"The man in the ice box."

Mrs. Karp raised a tweezered brow, let it drop, and resettled herself on her chaise to continue reading. "Good riddance," she was heard to say to herself.

But Nettie was unappeased. Having apparently mustered all her tolerance to abide the old man in the freezer over the years, she was past consoling now that he was at large and possibly dangerous. Grumbling that it was more than her job was worth to remain in their employ, she plodded down the stairs and out of the Karps' haunted house forever.

That night Mrs. Karp served her family a meal of canned applesauce and pork 'n' beans that she had been compelled to prepare herself.

"What's this?" asked her husband.

"It's called dinner," replied Mrs. Karp.

"Maybe at the county penal farm," said Mr. Karp, pleased with his riposte, "but on Canary Cove" — which was their bosky residential enclave — "we call it something else."

When she was satisfied that her husband's patience was sufficiently stretched, Mrs. Karp plumped her frosted shag and explained that Nettie had quit.

"That's impossible." For Nettie had been a fixture in the family for nearly a decade.

Mrs. Karp gave her signature shrug, as if to imply that the impossible had become the order of the day. Then she let it drop that the maid was upset on account of the disappearance of the frozen old man.

"What's that you say?" exclaimed Mr. Karp in disbelief. His wife asked languidly if he were deaf and repeated the information, which her husband challenged. "Do you think he could just up and walk away?"

Mrs. Karp shrugged why not.

For the second time in as many months, Mr. Karp was moved to interrupt his evening meal with a peevish harrumph. He rose, removing the napkin from his collar, descended the stairs to the rumpus room, and returned after some moments to announce, "This is a calamity," though without much conviction. He sat back down and heaved another sigh, which seemed to signify (along with his puzzlement) a measure of heartfelt relief. Because if the heirloom had truly vanished—never mind how—it was now somebody else's responsibility, for a change. Of course, as head of the family, it was incumbent upon him to get to the bottom of this enigma, wasn't it? He couldn't in good conscience simply let the matter drop. "Bernie," he asked, "you don't know anything about this business, do you?"

Since his father's words were more statement than question, rather than contradict him, Bernie assured Mr. Karp that he knew nothing about anything—a response nobody would gainsay. Then he darted a glance at his sister, whom he had silenced with threats of revealing her late-night basement trysts. Clearly counting the minutes until she could quit this bughouse and return to college, Madeline took the cue from her loathsome little brother and volunteered her ignorance as well.

Mr. Karp made an authoritative moue, which his wife parodied with a lopsided face of her own, and that seemed, for the moment, to be that. Then it was as if the thing in the basement had never existed at all. Bernie, too, was greatly relieved, feeling that he now had a license to continue his sub rosa relationship with the defrosted old gentleman he was harboring in the guest-house apartment behind the family domicile.

Bernie himself would have been hard pressed to explain why the secret had to be so diligently guarded, but aware that one person could not technically belong to another, he nevertheless felt that the rabbi belonged to him. It was an attitude he'd conceived almost from the instant the old man had emerged from the freezer, when Bernie had overcome his initial repugnance to swaddle the rabbi's frail bones in bath towels. Then he'd outfitted the creaky old party in a pair of his father's flannel pajamas before installing him in the guest house out back. This was the independent efficiency unit that had remained unoccupied (excluding Nettie's periodic dustings and Madeline's romantic rendezvous) since the death of his Grandpa Ruby soon after Bernie was born.

During his first few days in the world the hand-me-down holy man had remained in a relatively stuporous condition, stunned and cranky after his sudden awakening, while his convalescence stirred the boy to action as nothing in his experience ever had. At first he'd brought the rabbi table scraps, which were meager during the period between Nettie's departure and the hiring of a new maid-of-all-work. Later, squirreling away portions of his own meals in napkins, Bernie was able to smuggle the old man more substantial fare: a sparerib, some boiled shrimps in cocktail sauce, a nibbled ham and cheese omelet, cookies rich in butter and animal fat. Weak from having fasted for over a century, the rabbi could at first only manage to pick at the food, but soon his appetite returned with a healthy gusto and he began to gobble up everything the kid set before him. Bernie, whose religious education was limited to a few Bible verses from his forgotten Sunday school days, nevertheless sensed that these offerings might be in violation of some primitive dietary code. Feeling he ought perhaps to research the rabbi's care and feeding, he made an unprecedented excursion to the library at the suburban temple his family attended on high holidays, where he checked out an illustrated volume entitled *To Be a Jew*. Perusing its pages, the boy came to understand that he'd been sustaining the old man on filth. Though his vocabulary even in his native English was not extensive — conversation was never his forte — Bernie made an effort to apologize to the rabbi for his trespass in the droll language he had begun to pick up snatches of.

"Ich bin nebechdik, rabbi," he offered in an unusual foray into humility, and further testing the water, "Hab rachmones?"

"Moychl," responded the rabbi dismissively, slouched in a morris chair examining the piping on the lapel of Mr. Karp's cotton batik bathrobe. "A deigah hob ich." And as he was himself a quick study: "Takhe, think of it nothing."

After that Bernie tried assiduously to separate meat from dairy in the dishes he smuggled to the old man. Viewed suspiciously by the lady volunteer at the temple library, who was unaccustomed to borrowers of any age, least of all adolescents, Bernie checked out several kosher cookbooks and, despite having never made anything more ambitious than toast, expressed his readiness to attempt broiled udder, stuffed spleen, tripe, liver, lungs, and pupiklekh. The recovering rabbi suffered the kid's good intentions with a minimum of irritation but asked when he might have the opportunity to taste again "the insects from the sea."

These were the great days for Bernie Karp. Nothing in his listless history (or anyone else's he knew of) had prepared him for such an event, and it seemed to him that prior to the rabbi's resurrection nothing of note had happened in his life at all. It was as if he'd only been marking time, waiting all his fifteen years for the rabbi to come forth from his retirement. While the old man lay in bed regaining his strength, or sat sunk in his chair by the window in a shaft of sunlight that made his paltry bones appear as nearly pellucid as the ice he'd emerged from, Bernie would coax him to converse. Normally reticent if not downright fractious, the boy was at times a little stymied by his own uncharacteristic behavior, but his newfound curiosity had acquired a momentum that would not turn around. It was an awkward process in the beginning, since neither understood the other's spoken language; in addition, the old man, who appeared perpetually vexed from his rude awakening, could be moody and not always inclined to indulge Bernie's efforts to draw him out. But in the end he tolerated the kid's graceless gestures and crude indications and with a little persuasion would return them in kind, until they'd commenced an exchange that passed for communication. At length, each had gathered enough scraps of the other's mother tongue to allow for a tentative dialogue. Bernie was delighted by his gradual acquisition of his guest's fruity idiom, but even more than with his own, he was impressed with the rabbi's rapid and seemingly effortless progress. Of course Eliezer ben Zephyr—it had taken the old man a while to recall his own name—had the added advantage of exposure to the TV, which had captivated him from the moment he'd tumbled out of the freezer.

It had been Bernie's inspired idea to lead the rabbi, once his stick legs were ambulatory again, back across the covered walkway into the basement whose ground-level entry was at the rear of the house. Not only did the television in the rumpus room give the old man a leg up on the language, but it also introduced him to a culture he might have been ill equipped to apprehend at first hand. It was a culture that seemed to intrigue him as much as his own murky origins interested Bernie, who pestered the rabbi for information about his past at every opportunity. Such opportunities had to be taken more often than not during commercial breaks, though commercials could provide their own brand of entertainment, discouraging interruptions. But over time the two developed a kind of quid pro quo, as Rabbi Eliezer put more questions to the boy about America, which he'd come to understand was the place in which he found himself.

It seemed to fascinate him, this America, or at least the part of it that he viewed through the bowed window of the cabinet that was the centerpiece of the rec room, the passage to and from which was Eliezer's only exercise. Having initiated the rabbi into this passive orientation to his new world,

Bernie was a little chagrined that, fresh from an immemorial slumber in one box, he was so quick to be transfixed by another. But whatever pleased Rabbi ben Zephyr (and subdued somewhat his crusty exterior) was also gratifying to the boy. In the omnipresent news broadcasts the old man showed little interest: The relentless advance of the Horsemen of Apocalypse was already a stale subject on earth even before the rabbi had entered his suspended condition. But about the splenetic woman who conducted a daily din toyreh, splitting hairs over laws concerning two-timers and clip artists with the perspicacity of a Daniel; about the smug gentleman who encouraged public loshen horeh (gossip) and orchestrated encounters between parties guilty of mutual betrayal; about the portly schwartze who invited intimate confessions from her guests and wept openly over their Job-like afflictions; about antic surgeons, garrulous chefs, faithless couples, deceitful castaways, teenage exorcists, and the Jew repeatedly duped into fornicating with shikses, old Eliezer was deeply inquisitive. He was especially interested to observe the willingness of citizens to air their indiscretions in public forums.

"If a man to other men will sell his wife," he might ask in the crossbred Yinglish to which Bernie was starting to grow accustomed, "is not obliged Reb Springer to cleave open his breast and tear out his farkokte heart?" "When they shimmy, these daughters in their supple skins in the orgies of the MTV, do not their fathers say already Kaddish for them?"

Such questions and a score of others Bernie was hard put to answer; the permissiveness of his culture, from which he felt himself unfairly excluded, was something he and everyone else took for granted. But what struck him most about the rabbi's inquiries was that, prickly as the old man could be, he seemed more interested in than outraged by what he witnessed on television. In fact, there was an empirical tone to Eliezer's interrogations, as if he already acknowledged the old judgments to be obsolete and was anxious to learn the nature of the new in a depraved western world.

After several weeks of this routine it was clear to Bernie that the rabbi had recovered sufficient strength to leave his confinement and walk abroad. But despite an intermittent restlessness, the old man showed no inclination to travel farther from his bed than the paneled basement across the way, and the boy, happy to prolong their present circumstances, did not encourage him to do more. Meanwhile Rabbi ben Zephyr continued his acculturation on the sofa in the rumpus room (where Bernie's parents never ventured), absorbed by the parade of assumed infidelities that turned out to be misperceptions; the heated embraces in which the lovers were most certainly not thinking of Torah; the ads for depilatories, male enhancement, and bladder control. Mostly the old man watched with an owlish objectivity, though once there came a moment when something in the hysterical nature of the canned laughter, provoked by a German coinage, clearly disturbed him. This was when the Jew who fornicated with shikses made a joke about his girlfriend's gaudy earrings, which clattered like a Kristallnacht.

"Vos iz Kristallnacht?" the rabbi asked Bernie a bit rhetorically, since he was unaccustomed to receiving satisfactory information from that quarter.

And it was true that only a few weeks earlier the blockish Bernie Karp would not have been able to provide an adequate answer; but owing to the Judaica that the rabbi's venerable presence had prompted him to bring home from the Temple library, the boy was now prepared to marshal a response. In fact, he had a large book with shadowy black-and-white images, which he showed the old man. Eliezer studied the book as intently as he might once have pored over holy texts, and Bernie thought that here was the rabbi in a posture that bespoke his authentic past. Of course, the rabbi was unable to interpret the English captions, but while he seemed enthralled by the documentary photographs, he declined with a firm shake of his head Bernie's offer to read to him. Then, without a word, he closed the book and shoved it aside, turning back to the TV, which he gazed at as one might look toward a sunrise from the prow of a ship. It was at this juncture that Bernie chose to ask once again how the rabbi had survived so long in a block of ice.

Appearing at first to ignore the question, Eliezer scratched a cheek whose skin flaked into his beard like blistered paint, then said, "I was fed on visions that even *The X-Files* and *Extreme Makeover*, l'havdil, couldn't touch them." But having admitted that televised fare fell short of the spiritual reaches of his once glorious meditative flights, of the life of the spirit he claimed now to have had his fill. Just then there came on the screen a commercial in which a man in a sharkskin suit, eyeglasses sliding down the slope of his needle nose, earnestly promised not to be undersold. Opening the doors of refrigerators and ovens to display their spacious interiors, he intoned, "Don't be square; be sharp, shop at Karp's . . ."

The rabbi groaned oy and switched channels with the remote, in the use of which he'd become quite adept.

Surprised at his own unwillingness to let the matter go, Bernie pressed the old man for details of his visionary experiences. Without deigning to look at his questioner, Eliezer answered in due course, "Maybe on TV you don't see them, the Merkabah or the Throne of Glory; you don't see the divine ponim—which it is the face of God—but I seen already the face of God, and I can tell you it ain't that pretty."

A little chilled by the old man's disparagement, Bernie nevertheless remained single-minded. He persisted in his haphazard reading exclusive of the rabbi's supervision, feeling that, in his sallies into the world the rabbi came from, Eliezer ben Zephyr was still his mentor and guide.

From the well-endowed library in the prairie-style synagogue a shady half mile walk from his home, Bernie checked out the standard Weinreich Yiddish grammar. The volunteer from the Temple Sisterhood, a maiden lady whose helmet of hair was riveted to her skull by plastic barrettes, seeing that the book had not been checked out in living memory, gave him a regular third degree.

"It's not for me," Bernie assured her, concocting a story about his father's wanting to get back to his Jewish roots—getting back to one's roots being a fashion frequently touted in celebrity interviews. Why he didn't confess his own desire to decipher what his dead grandfather had scribbled in his ledger book, he couldn't exactly have said, though his instinct was not to arouse suspicions. Besides, embroidering the truth was a talent for which Bernie had only just discovered he had a knack, and it was bracing to realize more of his hidden potential. His answer had merely elevated the inchworm of the librarian's brow. Once home he was frustrated by the grammar's initial inscrutability and thought he would never get past the alef-bais, but with dogged perseverance he eventually began to make some progress. While he still got nowhere with the spiky cursive in Grandpa Ruby's age-yellowed ledger, Bernie was at least able to reconstruct in his mind the night the rabbi had tumbled forth from the freezer—when the old gent wondered aloud, on looking about at the beaverboard paneling, the beanbag pouffes, and the bowling-pin lamps, whether he was dead and the insulated cabinet was his casket. Had he arrived at last body and soul in gan eydn, in paradise?

And was Bernie, he had inquired, a zaftige malech?

"Nisht kayn malech, Rabbi," Bernie would have apprised him if the scene were repeated. "I'm no angel. Ich bin a yiddisher kind, a Jewish kid."

Now he was a little sorry that the old man had been disabused of his original illusions. He almost wished he could take back the information that, rather than paradise, Rabbi Eliezer was in Tennessee.

Never more than a mediocre student, unmotivated and lazy, Bernie was becoming daily more driven in his pursuit of the knowledge that would help him understand old Eliezer's provenance. Seated beside the rabbi on the harvest plaid sofa adjacent to the squawking TV, he read his parents' copies of *The Joys of Yiddish* and *The World of Our Fathers*, books that were standard issue in Jewish households but appeared never to have been opened in this one. He read their coffee-table edition of Abba Eban's *Heritage*, a profusely illustrated history of the Jews that was a companion book to a TV series, videos of which were available in the Temple library. But Bernie never bothered viewing them: there would have been little opportunity to watch them on the downstairs VCR without interrupting the rabbi's programs, and besides, he was coming to prefer the printed word to the video image. Unsatisfied by the generic texts on his parents' sparsely populated shelves, however, he lugged home from the Temple library (to the librarian's tacit disapproval) several moldy volumes of Heinrich Graetz's comprehensive history of the Jews. These Bernie entered gingerly at first, feeling like an interloper in their forensic pages, then impressed himself by devouring the books as greedily as the doughnuts he'd habitually bolted in the days before the rabbi's defrosting. In fact, his desire for physical nourishment seemed to have been deposed by his burgeoning intellectual appetite.

In the Graetz history there were references to other books of dubious repute, with bizarre titles such as *The Cockscomb of Rabbi Yahyah* or *The Book of the Face* that gave Bernie a peculiar itch. They were books the author of the magisterial history derided as hokum, though the boy, whose association with the wayward rabbi had given him a taste for maverick perspectives, couldn't help but be curious. They were books of hermetic mysteries and forbidden knowledge, some of which — *The Book Bahir, The Sefer Yetzirah* — Bernie was astonished to find in abridged translations in the Temple library. Only, this time when he tried to check them out, the librarian sniffed her displeasure and told him to wait, then marched out of the glaringly lit room and returned after some minutes with Rabbi Birnbaum himself. He was a man in his middle years with a hairpiece and an artificial tan, his heliotrope shirt open at his slightly crepey throat to reveal a gold mezuzah.

"So . . . Bernie, is it?" placing a ring-laden hand on Bernie's shoulder. The boy nodded. "What seems to be the problem?"

"There's a problem?" asked Bernie, somewhat disingenuously.

"Miss Ribalow here says you want to check out the *Zohar*?"

Bernie repeated his refrain, "It's not for me," resisting an urge to pry the rabbi's jeweled fingers from his shoulder. Again he explained that his father wanted to "get in touch" — that was the phrase he'd heard bruited about — with his Jewish heritage.

The rabbi exchanged meaningful glances with Miss Ribalow, both of them familiar (as was the entire congregation) with Julius Karp's aggressive TV marketing campaign, which seemed incompatible with the notion of a spiritual quest. But in the end the rabbi delivered some sanctimonious banality about the function of a lending library in a free society, and issuing a transparently breezy caveat—"Tell your daddy not to conjure up any whatchamacallem, any golems, heh heh"—permitted Bernie to check out his heretical volumes. Back in the basement the boy opened them with the same palpitating excitement he'd felt when opening Madeline's underwear drawer, but even in their abbreviated English editions, the books were impenetrable, full of sphinxlike symbols and cryptic diagrams. Bernie assumed that the books contained recipes for spells and incantations meant to result in supernatural effects; and though he'd never been especially superstitious, he wondered whether, if you followed the recipes, it might be possible for a person to enter a trance that would allow him to, say, survive a hundred years undisturbed in a block of ice. But his ignorance of mystical discipline prevented him from exploring further, and Bernie was mortally frustrated at having arrived at such an impasse. The keenness of his frustration amazed him, and he could scarcely believe that his desire for the flesh (and intimate garments) of young girls had been so readily replaced by a hunger for obscure learning.

He appealed again to Rabbi Eliezer. There was a joke among the congregants of the Reform synagogue the Karps annually attended that their temple was so progressive it closed its doors on Jewish holidays. While an exaggeration, it was true that the time-honored traditions of the Jewish people, largely expunged from the synagogue liturgy, had scarcely left a dent in Bernie's consciousness. But the unlighted past, as represented by the fusty rabbi, now consumed the boy's waking hours, and though most of Eliezer's tutelage consisted of unhelpful remarks made during the less sensational TV ads, Bernie credited the rabbi with the responsibility for all his new knowledge, and thought of himself as the holy man's protégé.

When the preoccupied Rabbi ben Zephyr waved away his solicitations, however, Bernie made a deliberate pest of himself. While the old man was absorbed in watching *Your Money or Your Life* or *The Killing Machine* or the yeasty sitcom *Menage à Melvin*, Bernie would station himself next to the sofa and practice religion. Experimentally, he donned the accessories he'd obtained for Eliezer, who seemed to have no use for the stuff. These included a silk kippah, a striped prayer shawl, and a set of leather phylacteries with whose complicated straps Bernie wrestled as with serpents — all items purchased with several installments of his allowance from the gift shop at the orthodox shul in its crumbling downtown quarters, to which Bernie had made a Saturday-morning sojourn by bus. Thus attired, the boy would take up a borrowed hymnal and, nodding as he'd seen the men nod (like bobble-headed dashboard figurines) in the shopworn shul, recite the phonetically transcribed Shmoneh Esreh, a prayer intended to be said silently. The rabbi managed for the most part to ignore him, so long as he stayed out of his direct line of vision, but when Bernie began showily attempting to read in their original the Hebrew books that had already defeated him in English, an irked Eliezer was finally distracted. Provoked by the kid's clumsy progress, the old man reluctantly disengaged himself from *Love Bytes*, a soap opera he followed religiously, and condescended to advise Bernie regarding a few shortcuts to enlightenment.

He bade the boy to sit on the carpet between him and the TV, whose volume he turned down but not off, and admonished him, "Everybody that don't stop searching after things too hard for him, or seeks things that from him should be hid, it's better he should never be born." That said, he told Bernie that the criteria for studying the mystical texts were three: one must have at least forty years, a wife and family, and a paunch as a hedge against involuntary levitation. "To my knowledge only the belly you got." And it had begun lately to shrink. Then Eliezer told the cautionary tale of the four rabbis who entered paradise: how one dropped dead, one went meshuggah, the third forswore his faith, and only the sage Rabbi Akibah escaped in one piece — "and you, sweetheart, are no Akibah." But as the boy remained rapt, showing not the least inclination to heed his warnings, the rabbi emitted a sigh, then proceeded to explain the notion of the Etz

Chayim, the Tree of Life — each of whose branches, called sefirot, corresponded to the rungs of Jacob's Ladder, which corresponded in turn to their respective astral realms.

"The rungs for all I know are shoyn farfoylt. Nu? they're rotten already. The nimble can still ascend, but they break from under your weight every rung, which it means you can't come back again down. . . ."

Eliezer's nasal voice, despite the jumbled syntax and foreign phrases, was melodious to Bernie, who hung on every syllable, oblivious to the TV dialogue that filtered through. In this way, over a number of days he lost count of, the boy was initiated into certain mysteries. He was introduced to the kabbalistic concepts of kavanah and devekut, intensity and cleaving, techniques that enabled you to swing with a simian grace from limb to limb of the Tree of Life. He was told of the tzimtzum, God's retreat from His own universe, like a landlord who, disgusted with the tenants who had trashed his premises, rather than evict them, exits slamming the door. The noise of his withdrawal is the big bang, the shevirah, behind which the whole house of cards collapsed, the dust from the rubble rising to heaven where it caused the Lord to sneeze. The shower of sparks that ensued from his divine sternutation lodged in crannies throughout the detritus, and it is our lot, saying endless gezundheits for the gift of God's luminous snot, to retrieve those sparks from their hidden places. Then fanning them into flames, we make sufficient light by which to begin restoring the fallen world to its former splendor.

"Such is on Earth our task," said Eliezer, with more than a hint of boredom.

Of course, this world was only one of several alternative worlds, not the least of which was the Yenne Velt, the Other Side, populated by creatures at once more feral and more complex than ourselves. It was a realm that intersected our own, its denizens sometimes invading our very beings in the form of dybbuks, malign spirits that take up residence in the organs and apertures of the living, or ibburs, which inhabited the recently deceased in order to complete the mitzvot they'd left unfinished on earth.

There were dizzying categories of demons, including jester demons that played tricks on the soul during its posthumous journey toward Kingdom Come: They turned the laws of reincarnation, the gilgul, helter-skelter, giving false directions to souls already bewildered by the mapless thoroughfares of the afterlife.

"It's from below that the yetser horeh, the yearning," revealed Eliezer, suppressing a yawn, "brings about the completion above."

Listening, the boy understood that all his reading to date had been mere amateur dabbling. He was told of the true significance of Torah, which had spawned the seraphim. It was through Torah that all worlds were sustained, though no one could have beheld the Law if it had not clothed itself in the garments of this world. Those garments were composed of fine-spun Hebrew characters that contained God's essence, and by shifting the letters anagram-fashion — Bernie pictured swapping sleeves for pantlegs as if to fit impossible beings — you could alter the course of galaxies. When he was fairly bursting from a surfeit of magical wisdom, the rabbi told the boy to be still already.

"Concentrate now on the Hebrew word for 'I', *ani* (אני)," counseled the old man, explaining that the word should then be reconfigured in the mind to form another word: *ayin* (אין), "nothingness." When he'd meditated on this awhile, Bernie began to grow light-headed and uncrossed his eyes to regain his bearings, only to have the rabbi introduce another exercise. He should focus next on the Tetragrammaton, the four-letter name of God, whose characters, once visualized, he should then rearrange. He was given the numerical equivalents of the four possible spellings of the written letters, which comprised the rainbow threads of the garment of Torah with its 231 buttonholes, called, since the destruction of the Temple, the Gates of Tears.

Even as he followed the rabbi's instructions, Bernie wondered what such arcane practices had in common with his unspoken desires, whose object he could no longer identify. But he could not deny the tingling that had commenced in his brain, which felt as if the lid of his skull had been raised like a convertible's roof to expose its contents to the elements. Then, as if borne on the warm breeze from an open window that invaded his simmering brain, the visions started to come. He could hear the voice of the rabbi, syntax no longer scrambled; but though he comprehended fully, the boy was uncertain what language the old man spoke: "As the hand before the eye conceals the mountain, so does our little life hide the mysteries of which this world is full." He heard the riddles the rabbi put to him: What eagle has its nest in maidenhair, where its young are plundered by creatures not yet created and taken to places that don't exist? Who is the beautiful virgin with two left breasts? And Bernie thought he knew the answers! He saw connections everywhere: how, for instance, the redbreast on the honeysuckle just outside the window had its own appointed star and each star its designated celestial being, who represented the bird according to its rank before the Holy One, blessed be He. He saw how certain stars trailing peacocks' tails held sway over certain herbs called "delirious elixirs," not to mention certain bodily discharges and women's hairstyles; that the diameter of one's penis and the circumference of one's third eye were influenced by the phosphorescent trajectories of comets across the firmament. Bernie saw the Throne of Glory, which, though vacant, resembled a giant La-Z-Boy in need of dusting, and the Divine Chariot with its tractor tread; he saw the Shekhinah, the celestial presence in Her female aspect, wearing a schoolgirl's uniform. When She lifted her kilt, Bernie felt his flesh ignite, his sinews blazing, retinas turning to embers, eyelashes flashing lightning, follicles sprouting flames. He was surrounded by hybrid beings, with cloven hooves and ivory wings, so that he cried out the words of the patriarch Jacob that he had not known he knew: "They compass me about, yea, they compass me about like bees . . ." When the creatures had finished collectively urinating on the conflagration that was Bernie Karp, they vanished, leaving him a smoldering heap. Then, as his senses began gradually to return to the mundane world, he saw again the old man in an outsize bathrobe watching reruns of *The Dating Game.*

Rabbi Eliezer cackled and pointed at Bachelor Number Two, a teetotaler, who had just expressed a wish to drink prune juice from the bachelorette's shoe.

CAME THE EVENING MEAL when Mr. Karp asked his son if he knew anything about certain books that had been checked out of the library at Congregation Felix Frankfurter. It seemed he had had a phone call from Rabbi Tommy Birnbaum expressing concern about some volumes of "mysticalism" (the rabbi could scarcely contain his distaste at pronouncing the word) that Miss Ribalow had brought to his attention, which had yet to be returned.

"He wanted me to know I should always feel free to talk to him, called me Julius, this Rabbi Whosits who don't know me from Adam. Then he asks me do I think it's appropriate that I should send a boy to fetch such books. Son, you got something to say to me?"

There had, of course, been other clues to the effect that all was not as it had been in the Karp household. For one thing, while Bernie continued to clean his plate each night and ask for more, the kid had begun to lose weight, his amorphous body assuming a more recognizably human form. Moreover, his pimples had started to retreat like a defeated army from his forehead and cheeks, leaving behind a pitted visage revealing rudimentary traces of character. But Julius Karp and his wife, otherwise engaged, had never been especially sensitive to changes in their son's physiognomy. What Mr. Karp was aware of, however, was that certain items of his own sartorial wardrobe—a bathrobe, a shirt, a houndstooth jacket, a pair of Dacron slacks—had gone missing, an absence he attributed to the newly hired schwartze's presumed kleptomania; and he had duly ordered his wife (who ignored him) to confront Cleopatra, the maid.

"Well, young man," pressed Mr. Karp, slightly uncomfortable in the role of interrogator, "I'm all ears." Which he flapped Dumbo fashion to ease the tension. "So what's the story?"

Bernie assured him there was no story, then muttered some excuse about researching a social studies paper on the Jews.

"Jews?" Mr. Karp made a face as if sampling some foreign dish. Bernie's school, whose season had recommenced, was in any case largely run by Southern Baptists who gave short shrift to the very idea of Jews, let alone inviting papers on their habits and mores. "Isn't that an awfully broad topic?"

"Yessir," said Bernie, which was a bit of a give-away, since nowhere in memory had he ever said "sir" to his father. "But I only have to name the main attractions," digging himself a deeper hole. To try and climb out of it, he began to cite highlights from the Judaic tradition in both its normative and antinomian aspects, remarking upon the influence of various saints and religious geniuses. In the midst of a discourse that threatened to run away with him, he realized that his parents' mouths were hanging open in response to their son's unnatural erudition, so Bernie shut up. Still the jaws of Mr. and Mrs. Karp remained mutually agape, though their eyes had shifted from the boy to the middle distance beyond Bernie's left shoulder. Bernie swiveled in his seat to follow their gaze, which lit upon Rabbi Eliezer ben Zephyr himself, standing squarely beneath the dining room's proscenium arch. He was wearing a felt fedora and a houndstooth jacket several sizes large, a burgundy shirt with a parrot necktie fastened about his wattled throat (visible now beneath his unevenly trimmed beard) in a combination of a Windsor and a Gordian knot.

"I think," announced the old man, his flesh as translucent as beeswax, marsupial pouches beneath his rheumy eyes, "I will like now to see for mayn self the Golden Land."

Oscillating between horror and disbelief, Mr. Karp turned again to his son. "You knew all the time he was still around?"

"Uh-huh," replied Bernie, surprising himself by his utter lack of contrition. "Can I keep him?"

His father exploded: "He's not a pet!"

Upon which Mrs. Karp, who seldom concerned herself in domestic matters, for once made to advise her husband, "The responsibility might be good for the kid."

"Who asked you!"

"Touchy, touchy."

Bernie twisted his head back toward the rabbi in the hope of gaining some show of support, but the old man was already gone. It was three days before he turned up again. In Bernie's late addenda to the annals of the Boibiczer Prodigy that Grandpa Ruby had detailed in his ledger book, old Eliezer's absence is referred to as "the three lost days."

1907.

Jocheved awoke on her woven-rope cot after a terrible dream. In the dream she had been in a strange house full of unfamiliar women and men — the women mostly stationary in loose kimonos and wrappers, lounging on moth-eaten divans in an ill-lit parlor, while the men came and went, came and went; though what their purpose was in the house she wasn't sure. Her father had figured in the dream in a frightful fashion, bursting with an unwonted fury into the parlor where she reclined. The years of sitting vigil in the icehouse and patrolling its frozen merchandise had replaced the marrow of Salo's bones with rime, leaving his joints stiff and his back as curved as a shepherd's crook. But in the dream he charged like a bull into the parlor, wielding a crowbar of the type used to pry apart ice cakes, which he swung at the head of a man who was pawing a disheveled Jocheved. Other men assaulted her papa, bloodying him with dirks and blows, since, having dropped the bar in order to lift his daughter, he was now defenseless. In fact, he seemed almost to welcome the knife blades, turning this way and that to receive them, protecting the girl from injury in an improvised waltz. This vision of her papa shielding her as the blood jetted from his wounds seared Jocheved's brain like a signet in hot wax, the wax losing the vision's imprint as it seeped into her breast and bowels. She was aware of her lantern-jawed mother hovering over her in their cellar flat, bathing her forehead with a compress and babbling complaints, but this did not seem to be part of the dream. She was also aware of the half-drawn patchwork curtain and beyond it the featherbed, a deflated cloud in its enameled iron frame, on top of which lay the naked body of her father. His ivory-white limbs were chevroned with gashes the size of open mouths, which a gathering of dour men endeavored to stitch closed, swabbing him with sponges dipped in brine. Jocheved thought it curious how her father's lacerated body had been transported out of a dream and into the cellar crowded with milk churns in cobweb skirts; then having observed as much, she groaned aloud and sought the deeper, dreamless depths of sleep.

When she woke again, her mother was still attending her, wetting her lips and insisting she take a spoonful of barley broth, against which her stomach rebelled. Alongside her mother stood the midwife with her hussar's mustache, the same old crone who had presided at the girl's nativity nearly two decades before; but the bed where her father had lain was now empty. Jocheved took this as proof that the bad dream was finally over and she was awake indeed; it was a conclusion corroborated by the ache in her heart and vitals, which yearned for something her murky mind could not name. The pain spread until it was general throughout her body, whose very skin seemed to plead for an even greater portion of hurt. Her skin invited further punishment while her brain, as if swathed in damp gauze, remained at a distant remove. Although she recognized that she was in a state of authentic agony, the agony was itself as remote as the memory of her dream, images of which reemerged only to retreat back into their fog. But some of the images persisted, assuming more clarity, and again she saw her naked father with his gorse-like clumps of hair and beard, his concave chest, his genitals like eggs in a nest. It was a picture that did not square with the ferocious image of the watchman in the dream parlor, where he behaved as he had in the stories he'd told of laying waste to the enemies of the icehouse, stories that even as a child she'd understood to be lies. Again she saw him swinging his crowbar in those tawdry rooms, smashing the skull of a character whose name she seemed to recall: Wolfie, it was, the walleyed famulus of Zygmunt the Yentzer, the Pimp. Then Wolfie went down, though not before he'd delivered a slash or two to the intruder's chest and cheek. Her injured papa had nevertheless gathered up his daughter from the sofa where she lay in her rucked chemise, just as Zygmunt himself stormed into the room yammering scripture and attacking her papa, who bled already from a dozen wounds. Still, he had managed to carry the languid girl out of the brothel and down the stairs into the slushy streets, stumbling past a thousand witnesses: the poulterers and lottery-ticket peddlers, rusty-eyed millworkers and market wives, the pimp himself in his earlocks and lemon spats, who followed but dared not assault the watchman further before the gawking audience. Thus did Salo stagger with his burden all the way back to Zabludeve Street, where he deposited the girl, wrapped in his bloody sheepskin, on the cot behind the stove, drawing the curtain to give her some privacy. Then, while his wife excoriated him for a hopeless ninny and threatened to increase his wounds, he lay himself down on his own bed and slipped away.

Or had he been a walking dead man all the while he was carrying his daughter home from the shandoiz? For that was the version that evolved in the ghetto, a story that thrilled its citizens, some of whom still recalled how Salo had entered their city preceded by legend; he'd been the guardian of a celebrated tzaddik's remains, hadn't he? though there was still some controversy as to whether the holy man was actually deceased. This was all long ago, but the memory, vague though it was, supplemented the perception that Salo Frostbissen was a holy warrior, come forth from his dormancy in Pisgat's icehouse to do battle with the evil element. So emboldened was the local population by the tale of Salo's martyrdom that, when Zygmunt the Pimp returned to claim his stolen property, he was met by a party of implement-brandishing neighbors standing outside Jocheved's door. Zygmunt swore on his hip-pocket siddur that he would come back with reinforcements and proved as good as his promise, returning with a cadre of crime-syndicate shtarkers to break the heads of those who'd dared to defy him. But as he'd been in no special hurry to stage his reprisal (and was himself not exactly a popular cause), by the time he reappeared Jocheved's mother had already followed her husband's lead: Having hounded him throughout his days, she had apparently no intention of allowing death to come between them, and so pursued him into the hereafter with a stinging fund of leftover abuse that she'd neglected to unload on him in life. She had expired (this was the coroner's diagnosis) of a ruptured heart that few gave her credit for having, and her daughter had since vanished without a trace.

But that was sometime after Jocheved had woken from the nightmare that trailed her like the raveled train of some spectral gown into consciousness. Her body ached from what she now understood were injections — the subcutaneous pinpricks and intravenous invasions of the hypodermic syringe — that Zygmunt the Pimp had administered to break her spirit and render her his virtual slave. Over the indefinite weeks of her captivity, almost no part of her anatomy had remained unpenetrated by needles, and her arms, legs, and buttocks bore the angry cipher of those marks. Now the inflammation of her flesh had infected her insomniac mind, which could no longer confine the horror of her waking to a faraway dream; and in her increasing awareness the horror grew until the dream took dominion everywhere, supplanting the mean interior of their basement flat. In the throes of her morphine withdrawal, Jocheved thrashed and flailed, fighting her exhausted mother, who was forced with the aid of the midwife to tie her daughter with leather straps to the sides of her cot. It was during this period that the girl, recalling another instance of being bound, came to realize that the worst she could imagine was true.

The facts revealed themselves by degrees through her mother's running rant. "Oy, your papa, the yold, the mule," keened Basha Puah. "I tell him go to the authorities, but he says they don't care, the police, what uses the Jews put their daughters to. Your daughter's lost, I tell him, so why's he got also to lose himself? But he don't listen, di zikh onton a mayse, the suicide; he sets out all alone for Gehenna, to hell he goes alone to fetch you back." The tears she refused to release scalding her eyes.

And so the thread of her mother's piecemeal narrative provided a logic that strung together the fragments of Jocheved's dream, an awful logic through which she understood that she no longer belonged in the broken bosom of her family. She was a fallen creature, soiled and defiled, and must return to the sty whence she'd been snatched. Her whole body affirmed the urgency, though she was too weak to act on her need, and during the occasions when she attempted to rise from the bed, her mother and Shulamith, the vartsfroy, tightened her bonds. Then it was as if the girl had to be lashed to this world lest she escape to another — though it was paradoxically to another world, a new one, that Basha Puah in the end enjoined her daughter to flee.

For the time being, however, she and Shulamith kept the girl fastened to the cot, force-feeding her broth, herbal decoctions, and purgatives, examining her stools as though they were auguries. They applied leeches to her armpits, heated cups in whose glass globes (or so the midwife maintained) homunculi drawn out of Joheved's soul had been trapped, until after a couple of weeks the girl began to calm down. When the several levels of wakefulness she was straddling started to resolve into one, Jocheved looked in her infirmity across the cellar to where her mother, beyond weariness herself, had taken to the bed from which her husband's corpse had only recently been removed. Then there was just the old hag in her florid babushka emptying slop pails and stoking the stove, while Basha Puah cried out in her fever for her daughter to leave this place: "Gay avek! Go already to the Golden Land." For America was the place her mother had fixed upon as her daughter's salvation. But as her father's girl, wasn't it Jocheved's duty to follow her papa whither he had gone? Though her mama's own manifest determination to do the same made her reasoning seem somehow redundant, almost as if the crossgrained Basha Puah were physically blocking death's door. Besides, it wasn't so easy to die, and while she tried to resist the nourishment the old vartsfroy prescribed, her body (whose craving for narcotics had been gradually replaced by an appetite for solid food) overcame her mind's obstinacy. Then a literal death seemed frankly not worth the trouble, since she judged herself already as good as kaput. But self-pity aside, her physical survival was a haunting reminder of the dreadful journey her father had made to recover her, barging into an underworld from which he'd shuffled back in his mangled body only, while his soul had perhaps departed along the way. The girl had the mad impulse to return the favor by setting out in search of her father's lost soul, at which point she remembered the old artifact on ice.

He'd been included in her mother's injunctions that she leave behind the slough of the Balut. "And don't forget to take with you your papa's farshlogener rebbe, it should be for you a blessing."

Jocheved was amazed to hear such a thing from her mother's cracked lips, which before had only cursed the icebound ancient as evidence of her papa's narishkeit. Now her insistence that the girl take him with her seemed to signal the extremity of Basha Puah's condition. Jocheved herself had demurred, recalling her father's laughable assertion that all the family's blessings came from the frigid saint. "What blessings?" she would have asked him now. "Our life is an abomination." She remembered how he'd alleged that, if you took care of the rebbe, the rebbe would take care of you. He was convinced that the refrigerated relic gave meaning to their spare existence, as if the old man's rotting crate were not a casket at all but the Ark of the Covenant itself and Salo Frostbissen the high priest charged with its maintenance. It was all claptrap, of course. Moreover, if you had a mind to, there were other means by which you might atone for your sins; there were rituals of purification, scape-beasts you could heap your trespasses upon. But the frozen rabbi was Salo's sole bequest; it was his legacy, and having sullied the name of her family beyond redemption, there remained only one gesture left by which the unclean girl might honor her papa's memory.

HER FIRST OUTING after having risen from her convalescent cot was to attend her mother's funeral. Still muzzy and unsteady on her feet, bundled in a beaver shawl that covered her desolate head, Jocheved was astonished at how many mourners were gathered at the gravesite. This was especially surprising given that Basha Puah's burial followed so hard upon the heels of her husband's, to say nothing of her reputation as an incurable shrew. But in death both Salo, the working stiff, and his joyless widow were transformed respectively into hero and helpmate, the wife so devoted she was unable to endure the cruel demise of her spouse. It was a story worthy of the improbable tales that Salo had told his young daughter long ago in the arctic environment of the icehouse. The morning of the funeral had dawned blustery and overcast, the ground still hard in the cemetery behind the textile factory walls, but here and there a crocus had broken through the crust of the earth. Having been so long away from the natural world, Jocheved almost resented how it persisted without her, squeezing the clod of dirt she was meant to drop into her mother's grave until it crumbled in her palm and was scattered by the wind. After the ceremony the mourners, some of whom were strapping teamsters and bare-boned yeshivah scholars, escorted the girl back to Zabludeve Street. They were solicitous of her frailty, protective of her personal safety; and letting her guard down, Jocheved felt that, for the daughter of her parents, there would always be a place in the ghetto. Perhaps she might yet revive the halcyon satisfactions of her ice-making enterprise. But as the teamsters crowded about her with a brazen forwardness and the scholars kept their distance as if from a contagion, the girl remembered the shame that could never be erased, let alone the lingering danger. She was appalled by her selfishness, that her grief over her own corruption should have displaced, if only momentarily, the grief for her family, for whose deaths she was in large part responsible.

In Jocheved's absence old Shulamith had dusted and cleaned the cellar, having removed (no doubt as her due) some of the luxury items—the Tuscan bronze egg beater, the enameled douche pan—that the girl had lavished on her mother in more prosperous times. May they serve the old ganef well, thought Jocheved, noting that in exchange for what she'd taken the woman had also contributed, beyond her labors, some pot cheese and a bottle of schnapps for the guests. The stench of the cheese helped neutralize the stench of sickness and death that still pervaded those recessed rooms. After the chalk-faced men of the Chevra Khadisha had finished saying Kaddish, the guests departed and Jocheved was finally alone. Utterly spent, she slumped onto a wooden stool, laid her head on a noodle board, and slept a while, dreaming of a despondent child with wings too heavy to flap. When she awoke she heaved a ragged sigh, got slowly to her feet, and took down the large copper kneading trough that hung from a ceiling beam. Since the apartment's single mirror was turned to the wall, she gazed at her distorted reflection in the trough's tarnished surface and saw only a ghost gazing back at her. Having already ritually torn the pongee collar of her mourning dress, the only store-bought frock in her wardrobe, she tugged at the lapel until she'd ripped the bodice from her shoulders. Then with both hands she tore the cambric corset cover underneath, wrestling herself out of her ravaged garments until she stood naked and shivering on the cold flags of the cellar floor. Further compelled by the tattoo of her pounding heart, the girl located her mother's teak sewing box, extracted from it a pair of tailor's shears, and with only the ill-defined reflection in the copper pot to guide her hand, she clipped off her mane of crow-black hair. Thus shorn, she flung the pot and kicked at the fallen hair that encircled her, releasing a sob that collapsed her chest as would a wrecking ball. This was her sorry state when the door to the hallway scraped open and Shulamith, midwife, rootworker, and sometime enema lady, crept in.

Without a word — had they ever exchanged a word? — the hag took in the situation. Jocheved looked on sniffling, hugging her bare breasts as if she meant to stifle them for good and all, while the old woman went straight to the clothes press and in a gesture that had about it something of the miraculous (she was regarded by many as a kishefmakherin, a sorceress) lifted the lid. From its camphor-reeking confines she withdrew a man's suit of clothes—the dark navy worsted with an alpaca lining and rolling lapel that Jocheved had purchased for her father during better days. Salo, who slept in his peasant smock and sheepskin, had never found occasion to wear it; though he took pride in possessing the suit and pledged to put it on when Mashiach finally arrived, or on the day the rabbi disenthralled himself from the ice, whichever came first. His wife sneered that he was waiting to be buried in his gladrags and, seized with a sentimental urge that he realize that end, had quarreled with the burial society, which pronounced such off-the-rack apparel a desecration.

Passive after the energy she'd expended in cutting her hair, Jocheved looked on with detached curiosity as Shulamith laid out the garments on the sagging featherbed. Nor did she resist as the midwife helped her into first the warm woolen gatkes, then the short-bosomed white dress shirt with its upstanding collar. Next came the hair-line trousers with their double-sewn buttons at the crotch and the single-breasted, round-cut sack coat. There was also a pair of leather bluchers, several sizes too large, whose interiors the old woman padded with newspaper whose headlines described the stewpot of Europe building toward a boil. Still relatively benumbed, Jocheved supposed it was fitting that the vartsfroy who had supervised the girlchild's delivery should also attend at her rebirth as a pallid young man. Though the clothes hung somewhat baggily on her slender frame, the girl had the odd sensation that she would grow into them. An alien in her own skin, she experienced a composure she hadn't known since before her abduction; it was a feeling that, while it had little in common with a homecoming, gave her the sense of having been liberated from her outworn self.

Shulamith, notwithstanding her smoky eye and hirsute upper lip, had once had a husband, and with gnarled fingers she meticulously knotted the ash gray cravat at Jocheved's throat. Then she took up the shears and trimmed the uneven edges of the hair the girl had so recklessly hacked off. Afterward they stood gazing at each other with the sodality of coconspirators who together have defied the law; for even unread women knew the Torah's prohibition against wearing the clothes of the opposite sex, how it deceives not only others but oneself, confounding the soul that finds itself trapped in a stranger's body.

"Azoy," said the midwife in a voice whose girlish lilt was chilling for its incongruity, "now you are again brand new?" From the pocket of her calico apron she fetched the couple of gulden she'd received for pawning Basha Puah's embroidered challah cloth and porcelain cuspidor, plus the curio of a cedar ice cream freezer. In return the girl bestowed a kiss on the kishefmakherin's wrinkled brow, who (for an instant in Jocheved's vapory imagination) was a maid again.

After the old woman's departure Jocheved dropped onto her cot to take account of her circumstances. She was clearheaded enough to realize that the pittance Shulamith had given her would not begin to defray the expense of her project. It was barely enough to bribe a customs official, never mind purchase a passport or shifscarte ticket. And even had she had the funds for the journey overland from Lodz to the port of Hamburg, then on across the North Atlantic, how would she manage to drag along with her a box containing a saint-size block of ice? But these questions, rather than overwhelm her, seemed to pose a merely abstract problem, just as in her uncustomary attire the girl felt the weight of her grief reduced to an almost hypothetical burden. What was more, beyond the lightening of her leaden heart, her masquerade offered obvious practical advantages. For one thing, it would be easier to deal with the perils of travel as a man . . . as, say, Max Feinshmeker. She pulled the name out of thin air and immediately warmed to it, how its jaunty consonants mocked her own somber aspect, lifting her spirits. If not quite a perfect fit, it was a name that, like her new suit of clothes, she would eventually grow into. She would be Max Feinshmeker, nephew of the deceased Frostbissen couple on the family's distaff side, a young man for whom the complications of the journey to the Golden Land would constitute a great adventure. Jocheved felt the slightest twinge of excitement at the prospect.

Of course, one could argue there were any number of favors that might be more easily obtained by a woman—a notion that turned Max Feinshmeker's stomach and filled him with disgust. This early evidence of her dual disposition prompted a fluttering in Jocheved's breast: She was Max, a skeptical, forward-thinking youth, a staunch adherent of Haskalah, the Jewish enlightenment movement, and disdainful of the outdated tradition the girl had been raised in; though that tradition, like the persistence of the girl herself, still cramped his modern attitudes and worried his bones. Jocheved's thoughts then returned ruefully to the matter of capital, to the documents that might have to be forged, the unfriendly world that must be navigated between her ramshackle ghetto street and America. With all this in mind she rose from the chair and propped the stiff-crowned derby at a gallant angle on her handsome cropped head. Then she set off in the direction of Pisgat's icehouse without a clue as to how she would proceed but with a lightness of step that the defeated daughter of Salo Frostbissen would never have been capable of.

SHE RAPPED AT the wire-glass window in the door of Zalman Pisgat's disordered office, while behind her porters in leather aprons shouldered sides of beef like wounded comrades and wheeled trolleys stacked with leaky produce crates.

On being admitted Jocheved announced tentatively, "I'm Max Feinshmeker," and inspirited by her own declaration, "a near relation of the Frostbissen clan on the maternal side. I've come to relieve the proprietor of this establishment of the casket and its contents abandoned by my Uncle Salo at his demise." It was the speech she'd rehearsed all the way from Zabludeve Street.

The ice mensch scratched the prickly pear of his jaw. Like everyone else he'd heard the tale of Salo's bloody quietus; he'd even been questioned by the police concerning his employee of some twenty-odd years, though as long as Jewish crime didn't spill beyond the confines of the ghetto, such investigations remained largely a formality. Salo's death had reminded

Pisgat, first, of the existence of the watchman, a timeworn fixture who barely earned his keep, and then of a long-forgotten item stored on his premises; he'd been half-expecting that someone might turn up to reclaim it. Old goat that he was, he had hoped it might be the girl, the story of whose fall had also reached his ears, and he was visibly disappointed that another representative of the family had come in her stead. Turning up the flaps of his plush cap to release his jug ears, he wondered aloud what had become of Jocheved.

Agitated, the girl nevertheless managed to keep Max's sober façade from cracking apart. "The daughter is indisposed," was all she was willing to say.

"A shame," said old Pisgat, finally too busy to pursue the subject further. He was glad at any rate of an opportunity to rid himself of an incommodious object that had taken up precious space in his icehouse these many years; though on the other hand he was reluctant to engage in any transaction without realizing a profit.

"So what do you want the thing for?" he inquired cagily, as if he might have designs of his own on the relic.

The girl shuffled in her outsize shoes. Why indeed was she so intent on making herself the curator of her father's archaeological curiosity? "I want," she squared her shoulders, expanding her straitened chest, "to give the rebbe a proper resting place."

Pisgat took a pinch of snuff from a briar box, stuffed it into a hairy nostril, and sneezed, wiping his nose on a sleeve. "What's wrong with here?" he asked, batting his red-rimmed eyes, for it had occurred to him that he might extend an imaginary lease on the storage area.

"I want to put him someplace," her answer framed itself as a question, "more permanent?" She winced internally at her own lack of conviction.

The proprietor raised a shaggy brow. "Pisgat's icehouse is going away somewhere?" No reply from the lad forthcoming, he leaned back in his swivel chair and grew thoughtful: It was indeed a scandal that the frozen tzaddik's remains had been kept above ground for such an unconscionable time; he should have been interred long ago. "But you, excuse me, don't look like a religious; takhe, you don't even look like a Jew. So what's the old fossil to you?"

"He's . . . ," the girl floundered, then rallied, recalling her mother's mandate, her father's blind faith; the rabbi was, for better or worse, her destiny too. "He's a sacred trust of our family that I owe it to my Uncle Salo to take care of him."

"Hmph." Pisgat shrugged, reassuming his professional demeanor. "Call for the legacy, you pay for the funeral. Naturally there's a fee to convey the thing from my place of business, plus the outstanding rent on the space it's occupied since your uncle's passing." He named an extortionate sum.

The girl was momentarily taken aback, but despite all she'd been through Jocheved still had an instinct for fair and not-so-fair trade, and where her shrewdness left off, Max Feinshmeker's (she felt) began. "On second thought," she said considering, "forget it," and started to turn on her heel.

"Wait a minute!" Pisgat shouted. "What's a matter, you never heard from negotiation? Or maybe you mean to bluff a bluffer?"

Jocheved turned again, searching her mind for more leverage; she was after all doing the old fortz a favor — but just as she was about to offer that insight, another man shouldered his way through the office door. This one wore the sealskin reefer that was a common livery in the twilight world of which the girl had some bitter knowledge.

"I got outside in my wagon a shipment beluga caviar, three-quarters pood fresh off the boxcar from Vilna," the man informed the proprietor, who told him shah, couldn't he see they were not alone? Tapping a sharpened tooth with the handle of his horsewhip, the man continued to disregard the youth as he issued his ultimatum: "You want it, you don't want it? I got other customers standing in line. The g'vir Poznanski, him with his palace on Piotrkowska, is prepared to pay top zloty, no questions asked. Make up your mind, the stuff won't wait."

Snapped Pisgat: "Didn't I tell you I have already a buyer with an order from the millionaire Belmont in America, USA? This is guaranteed. Only a few arrangements I got first to make."

Pisgat's visitor, heavy-set, with greasy hair like matted seaweed straggling from under his cap, chewed impatiently on his braided whip. "I gah arery arraymum uh my om." Unclamping his teeth, "And don't think I don't know what happened to the sevruga that got seized at the border last month."

"Then why you even came here?" barked Pisgat.

The middleman relaxed into irony. "Think of it as a courtesy call."

Kibbitzing, Jocheved was only just able to catch the drift of their discourse, while the worldlier Max seemed to comprehend more. By "arrangements" the ice mensch meant contacts for smuggling contraband undetected over an obstacle course of customs agents and border guards. In this instance the shipment involved a case of black market caviar transported by land to Lodz from the Gulf of Riga. The legal export of such a luxury item was apparently out of the question: International tariffs and duties would be prohibitive, and the taxes alone on imported delicacies — or so Max assumed — could be excessive to the extent of canceling one's return on the initial investment. There might even be a loss of revenue. You could camouflage the caviar along with other less levy-heavy perishables, but those items would still warrant transport by sealed boxcar and later in a ship's refrigeration hold, thus inviting careful scrutiny. Besides, since the aforementioned seizure, Pisgat's network had by his own admission broken down.

In an effort to stall the middleman, the ice mensch allowed that things were difficult, but he needed only a couple of days to reestablish his connections and pave the way for the shipment. Until then the sturgeon roe might be kept safe from spoilage in his icehouse.

"A couple days and Poznanski returns to his Black Sea dacha," said the middleman, taking another bite out of his whip.

The ice mensch sputtered that the rich man should burst from pleasure. "May disease enter his gums!"

Meanwhile Jocheved, her confidence increased several fold by Max's ingenuity, had concluded that here was a chance that would not come again. The idea she'd hit upon and refined while giving ear to their felonious exchange was this: It would be more economical to facilitate the legal transport of a dead relation for burial in a family plot overseas than to finance a clandestine consignment with all the elaborate palm-greasings that entailed. And what better cover for the fish roe than the rigid rabbi (his casket reinforced and lined with lead, or better zinc), whose frozen condition would ensure the freshness of the merchandise upon disembarkation in the Golden Land? As the self-possessed Max Feinshmeker, Jocheved stepped forward to present her alternative.

"Gentlemen," she began, clearing her throat, lowering her voice an octave or two. "Gentlemen, perhaps I can be of service."

1999.

Bernie was beside himself with relief at the rabbi's homecoming, though the delinquent holy man scarcely acknowledged him, brushing past the open-mouthed boy in his haste to talk with Bernie's father. It seemed that in his three days of wandering, the old man had seen a lot of life, and returning bug-eyed and bathed in sweat — the fedora battered, the sportcoat soiled, the loud parrot necktie hanging from his throat like a noose — Rabbi Eliezer ben Zephyr had reached a stunning conclusion about the world he'd recently awakened to.

"Shopping bazaars it's got, and Dodge Barracudos and Gootchie bags made I think from the skin of Leviathan, churches from Yoyzel it's got big as Herod's Temple, but it ain't got a soul."

All this he communicated breathlessly — less judgmental than plainly impressed — to Mr. Karp, who, relaxing in his postprandial recliner, appeared confused at first as to just who the intruder was. He was doubly disturbed, once he'd recalled the prodigal's identity, that the old man should have planted himself directly between his chair and the wide-screen television — on which he was viewing his favorite program, a comedy called *Nobody Likes Larry* about a harassed family man. When his wife, looking up from a novel whose cover featured a woman swooning into the arms of a grenadier, reminded him that this was the fugitive from the deep freeze, Julius Karp snapped that he knew perfectly well who it was. On that note Mrs. Karp popped a Spansule from her heart-shaped pillbox and rose to tiptoe exaggeratedly out of the room. Meanwhile the bedraggled rabbi kept on reporting his reconnoitering of latter-day America, or at least the representative slice of it he'd seen.

"The people, they are such chazzers, all the time gobbling: gobble gobble; they feast on everything that it's in their sight. They eat till their bellies swell by them like Goliath his hernia, and shop till their houses bulge from the electronic Nike and the Frederick of Hollywood balconette brassiere, but they ain't satisfied."

Jerking a lever as if shifting a gear, Mr. Karp brought his Stratalounger to an upright position. He was mightily irked at the way the old freeloader added insult to injury, compounding the crime of his return with an uninvited lecture on ethics. A firm believer in free-market economy, Mr. Karp resented the notion, tired as it was, that there was any higher principle on earth than goods and services. How dare this phantom of the ice box presume to instruct him, Julius Karp, citizen merchant—and in his own borrowed finery yet.

"Riches they got would make a Rothschild blush," continued the rabbi, who seemed more gleeful than provoked; in fact, he seemed intoxicated, "but they ain't got what makes them happy."

"So?" said Mr. Karp, trying to keep a lid on his impatience. He'd heard the same commonplaces from Rabbi Birnbaum in his High Holiday sermons, though Birnbaum had the discretion to qualify his assaults on mammon so as not to offend the comfortable congregation who paid his salary. But from the perspective of his thronelike recliner, in front of which the wizened petitioner stood hat in hand, Mr. Karp (subvocally groaning) felt obligated to hear the old man out. "What exactly are you getting at?"

"I'm proposing," the rabbi humbly submitted, "to restore to the people their soul."

"Oh," replied Mr. Karp. "I thought you might have something really ambitious in mind." He sniggered over his witticism.

Unfazed, the rabbi went on. "A betmidrash, a study house I will establish, that they can come in it, both yehudim and goyim, and be born all over again. I got already my eye on a little place by the Rebel Yell Shopping Plaza . . ."

"Take it easy!" cautioned Mr. Karp, raising his hand like a traffic cop. "Now let me get this straight: You want to open up some kind of a religious institute where people come to study? Study what?"

" 'Study' I don't use in the traditional sense. More like, what you call them, exercises."

"You mean like those Plottie classes my wife took once and went to bed for a week? Aren't you a little out of shape for that sort of thing?" Again he chuckled.

"I'm talking spiritual exercises," said the rabbi, with dignity. Then he complained that his feet were sore and asked if Mr. Karp would mind if he took a load off.

"Be my guest," said the appliance merchant, though the invitation resonated unpleasantly in his gut.

The old man lowered himself with a grunt into the armchair that Mrs. Karp had vacated, so that both men now sat facing the TV. On its screen the put-upon family man, importuned by a marriage counselor to get in touch with his feminine side, had been moved to don his wife's apparel in secret. An invisible audience guffawed like honking geese.

" 'There shall not be a man's garment on a woman, nor a man wear a woman's gear,' " cited the rabbi, like a wistful reminiscence; then returning to the matter at hand, he offered Mr. Karp the once-in-a-lifetime opportunity to invest in his enterprise. "On the ground floor I'm willing to let you."

Mr. Karp turned down the volume with his remote, shoved his glasses back over the hump of his nose, and swiveled his chair in the direction of Rabbi Eliezer. "Whoa," was all he said.

"You can take out from the bank a loan so you ain't got to spend a shekel, and will come back to you the money in spades."

The retailer was frankly dazzled by the rabbi's command of the vernacular, let alone his loquacity. "Let me get this straight. You want me to risk my capital, to say nothing of my good name, so that you can start up a . . . whadidyoucallit? "

"A betmidrash."

Mr. Karp took a breath. "Look, Rabbi, I'm not an unreasonable man. If you wanted to open a little shop, say a mom-and-pop sundry, then maybe we could talk. But let's face it, you're maybe what, a century and a half past the age of retirement? And even if you weren't, this idea of yours, excuse me, is pretty screwy."

"Julius," began the rabbi. "May I call you Julius?" His ingratiating air fooled no one. "I ain't talking your zayde's study house. I'm talking Rabbi ben Zephyr's House of Enlightenment, where I'm dispensing on demand ecstasy."

Mr. Karp went livid. "You mean like drugs?"

Now it was the rabbi's turn to sigh. "Julius," there was the patronizing note again, "today religion is good business. Give a look by the gentile revivalist with his double-breast polyester in the stadium, and even the Jewish boys and girls, that they sacrifice to some barefoot swami all their possessions, who tells them, 'Go dress in shmattes and dance in the street.' And it ain't even Simchat Torah! Wants to acquire everybody, along with the BVD and the satellite dish, a bissel the living God, but for the years discipline they ain't got time. So now comes a tzaddik ha dor, which it's yours truly, to give them in a few easy steps a taste sublime."

"Are you trying to tell me that you intend to peddle . . . ," Mr. Karp searched without success for the word, which the rabbi supplied:

"Be-a-ti-tude," tasting every syllable on his glaucous tongue. Then he allowed that he might also sell a few specialty items on the side — books and talismans, red string to ward off the evil eye, everything marked up and elegantly repackaged of course . . .

"Slow down!" said Mr. Karp. "What's a two-hundred-year-old greenhorn know about markup?"

"You would be surprised how much business deals is in Talmud. Take for instance the Tractate Baba Batra, which it tells us from dinei memonot that it is permitted to be given for a gift cash money." He began to cite the avot, the principle categories, concerning partnership, sales, legal documents, and so forth. Judging himself a canny man of commerce, with a level head and an eye for the main chance, Mr. Karp cursed his own creeping credulity: How could he entertain for even an instant that such a cockeyed proposition might in fact have some sound fiscal basis? But the old man was relentless, rubbing together the dried kindling of his palms as he described the plans for his ecumenical prayer and meditation center where, for a fee that might be adjusted along a sliding scale, he would provide the tools by which his clients could obtain the practical means to regenerate their wretched lives. And if in the process the rabbi should himself make a tidy profit whose dividends his prudent investors would share, then where was the harm? All he needed was a little seed money that might be readily acquired by Julius Karp's signature on a loan application from the bank.

Disinclined to relinquish an ounce of his native skepticism, Mr. Karp nevertheless had to admit that he was impressed with the rabbi's mercantile savvy, so much so that he forgot he was talking to a freak of nature. Trying his best to rein in his own entrepreneurial instincts, he put it bluntly: "So you want me to put my reputation on the line to bankroll an illegal immigrant that don't even have a green card?"

Flashing his few remaining teeth, the rabbi was unctuous. "You're a man of integrity, Julius. Du farshteyst, you understand how it works, the system; you can put to the squeaky wheel the grease."

Resist as he might, Mr. Karp found himself succumbing to the rabbi's blandishments. Wasn't this after all a way to kill two birds with one sharp bargain? He could get the seedy old specimen out of his hair while at the same time enjoying the benefits of a scheme that just might be crazy enough to work. Turning back toward the television, he tried to recover some vestige of his reasonable doubt, but aware that the rabbi (asking,

"Have we got a deal?") had proffered a talonlike hand across the end table, Julius Karp extended his own without looking. As they shook, the beleaguered TV husband, still dressed as a woman, had ventured into the street, where he was solicited by a very butch lady dressed as a man.

You couldn't have called it eavesdropping, since Bernie was standing by the open French doors in full view of his father and the rabbi in their parallel chairs. Still, he felt as if he were listening to things not meant for his ears. The experience revived the sense of being invisible that had plagued him for much of his life, though the self-inflicted curse seemed lately to have been lifted. Now, however, ignored by both father and mentor, he was hurt, resentful at being excluded from a project concerning which the two of them appeared to be suddenly as thick as thieves. How had this happened? And for that matter, how could Rabbi Eliezer plan to give away (for a price) the secrets that Bernie had struggled so hard to learn? He realized he was being selfish: The old holy man was a resource whose wisdom should be available to all. Certainly Bernie appreciated that the tzaddik was a repository of worldly as well as sacred learning, his knowledge recently expanded to include a lively critique of the modern age. Still, he couldn't shake his attitude that Rabbi Eliezer ben Zephyr belonged to Bernie Karp alone and that the worshipful spiritual program he'd imparted to the boy should stay in the family. Moreover, though he couldn't put his finger on it, Bernie felt there was something unkosher about marketing enlightenment in the same way a person might trade in used automobiles.

Days passed, and in the face of the frosty treatment by his mentor, Bernie fell back on old habits. Slothful again, he took to the rumpus room sofa; he abandoned his reading and thought often of abusing himself, though the admonition against Onan, who had "threshed on the inside and cast his seed without," stayed his hand for the time being. But now that school had resumed, he was eyeing the girls with a fish-eyed yearning, as fearful of them as ever. He was more fearful, in fact, since, now that he'd lost his flab and his acne had subsided, his face had taken on a little definition, and the girls for whom he'd been beneath contempt now looked at him with only mild disfavor. Now, when he stared at their blue-marble thighs beneath the hems of kicky skirts, their midriffs and jeweled navels, the butterfly tattoos fluttering out of low-slung waists, they might look back with a measure of curiosity. They noticed him in a way that caused Bernie to feel he'd finally shed his mantle of nonentity, which made his condition all the more disquieting and aggravated the desire, which in turn increased the ache.

Though Bernie's high school was situated in a tree-lined suburban neighborhood, its population comprised mostly of white kids from affluent families, it was nonetheless a purgatorial place. Neanderthal bullies built like brick incinerators body-checked you into lockers without warning, while preppies sporting the heraldic insignia of fraternal orders skewered you with a look. There were golden girls with their coteries of drab hangers-on; hipsters with dreadlocks and tie-dyed accessories reeking of weed, with spiked hair in primary colors, hardware piercing nostrils and lips like fish who've been caught and thrown back again. Young seductresses lured willing boys into the stalls of lavatories whose mounted cameras were rendered sightless by chewing gum; fledgling satyrs, their mouths shredded from entanglements with orthodontia, dragged dewy girls into the office of the guidance counselor, she herself having been sacked for inappropriate behavior with students. Having sleepwalked those chlorotic corridors from his tenderest years, Bernie, now in the eleventh grade, was alert to menace everywhere.

He no longer sought the company of those sad cases who fastened their belts just beneath their armpits and, belonging nowhere, belonged by default to each other; there was no refuge for an unaffiliated type such as Bernie Karp—not in homeroom, where the frazzled teacher's imminent breakdown was the subject of wagers, nor in the library study hall, where monitors patrolled the aisles like prison guards. On this particular afternoon in the library not long after the rabbi's return, Bernie was browsing—for want of Mosaic texts—aboriginal photos in a National Geographic magazine to avoid his Household Mechanics homework. (Tracked as a dullard on account of his feckless academic performance, he'd been sentenced to the gulag of vocational training.) As he glanced about in his boredom, careful not to make eye contact, Bernie's gaze lit on the notorious Patsy Bobo, seated at an adjacent table chewing the segmented tail of her peroxide braid. Her legs were slightly splayed under the table's surface to accommodate the spidery fingers of Scutter Eubanks, which were inching up her tender thigh beneath her skirt toward the juncture that was mystery incarnate. Bernie felt himself begin to shudder and grow dizzy at the sight, felt the familiar thrumming in his loins, the pressure building toward a seismic discharge. He fought helplessly against the coming release, imagining the subsequent stain he would try to conceal with an unavailing shirttail. But in the moment when his whole body was braced against the inevitable convulsion, the pressure reversed itself, and Bernie was catapulted clear out of his skin. In the quiet that ensued, he viewed the study hall, which included his own inert self, through the eyes of his soul from the vantage of eternity.

This was the first of several such experiences, each of which had the result of projecting Bernie into an element of radiance compared to which his sexual longings seemed incidental. Nor was sex the only spur to these ethereal sojourns: A phrase of music from an open window, a candy wrapper borne on a breeze, a red ribbon flickering like a serpent's tongue out of a knothole in a twisted tree—any of these might serve as the trigger for a spontaneous out-of-body experience. Of course, while in his transports, there was the matter of the body that Bernie had left behind, which would appear as dumb and insentient as a stroke victim to the ordinary observer. It left him wholly unresponsive to a teacher's questions and vulnerable to the malign scrutiny of his fellow students, for whom he was both an object of suspicion and a figure of fun. As a result, his abandoned corpus might be subject to abuse, to being graffiti'd with Magic Markers or plumaged like a bird in yellow Post-its bearing unkind messages. He might be carried in his cataleptic state to the urinals and his head flushed in a function called a "swirlie," after which he would exude an odor no shampoo could dispel. Not that Bernie, when in the throes of rapture, cared much about what became of his physical self, though on his return—and always he had to return—he felt pity for the offenses his body may have suffered in his absence. Rather than feeling injured in spirit, however, he tended to view the abuse more as a persecution that lent poignant meaning to his extramundane flights. Still, this occasional absentee relationship to his own mortal form required skills he had yet to master; and the shell of his forsaken self was a spectacle that had prompted more than one teacher to recommend medical attention. In the event, resolving to learn how to manage his flights with more dexterity and tact, Bernie swallowed his pride and set out to seek the counsel of Eliezer ben Zephyr, the Boibiczer Prodigy, in his place of business.

BERNIE HAD THUS far studiously avoided the strip mall where the rabbi had established his House of Enlightenment. In truth, he'd felt completely abandoned by his mentor and bore him a petulant grudge, just as he did for his greedy father who was guilty by association. Bernie had even stopped watching TV for fear of seeing the rabbi's puckered phiz smeared across the screen, reading awkwardly from a teleprompter as he guaranteed his audience that the wisdom of the ages could be theirs for only pennies a day. All this had galled the boy to the verge of disaffection, though his recent transcendental experiences had put him in a forgiving mood, and in the first brisk breeze of October, he walked the mile or so from his school to the Rebel Yell Shopping Plaza.

The House of Enlightenment, with its six-pointed star dangling like a neon watch fob in the plate-glass window, was sandwiched between Uncle Ming's Chinese Take-Out and Layla's Little Piggies Pedicures. Bernie pushed through the door to the sound of tinkling chimes and stepped into a vestibule that was equal parts gift shop and doctor's waiting room, with a nod toward a Carpathian study house. There were framed testimonials from satisfied customers on the paneled walls, though Bernie wondered that the place had been open long enough to satisfy customers. The testimonials were flanked by mounted diagrams of the Sefirot, the kabbalistic Tree of Life, resembling the configurations of painted Tinker Toys. An air-brushed portrait of Rabbi ben Zephyr himself, the bronze plaque beneath it reading simply The Rebbe, loomed above bookshelves bowed from shrink-wrapped sets of the Zohar in its Moroccan binding. A glass display case presented an assortment of Judaic kitsch: ceramic hamsas and amulets with labels advertising their occult powers, bobbins of red thread for warding off demons, Heroes of Kabbalah trading cards and drinking cups—everything tagged for sale at inflated prices. There was also some standard religious paraphernalia: prayer shawls and kippot, phylacteries hanging from hooks like gauchos' bolas, all marked up exorbitantly. Seated on a stool behind the display case was an attractive middle-aged lady, wisps of iron gray hair peeping from under a lavender turban, her matronly figure enveloped in a matching kaftan like a vestal gown. She looked up from a graphic-novel edition of *Tales of the Baal Shem Tov* when Bernie came in.

"Can I help you, dear?" she asked, squinting over her bifocals with a simper that seemed to assume he was in the wrong place. Oriental elevator music dribbled from a quadraphonic sound system.

Feeling suddenly self-conscious, the tail of his T-shirt poking from under his windbreaker like a skirt, Bernie hesitated; there was something very wrong about this place. "I'd like to see the rabbi," he muttered.

The woman informed him in a tone of honeyed condescension that she was sorry, the Rebbe was conducting a transformation-of-self-through-dynamic-stillness session at the moment. "Would you care to wait?"

The answer was no, but Bernie held his peace and continued to shuffle in place. Beyond a paisley curtain he could hear the master's amplified voice, exhorting the faithful with words and images that the boy already knew by heart: He was citing the significance of each of the four rungs of Jacob's Ladder, the four faces of Ezekiel's angels, how the student must concentrate on the letters of Torah until they appear like black fire upon white; there were words whose pronunciation ought to be growled like a lion, others meant to be cooed like a dove. The rabbi told them, himself croaking like an asthmatic frog, to "Be still like the wife of Lot when with salt from the Dead Sea she was encrusted; be lit up like Moses his ponim when he came down from Sinai . . ." They were the same visualization exercises the rabbi had dispensed so offhandedly to Bernie; only now he uttered them with an emphasis that (whether earnest or feigned) made the boy jealous. Why jealous when he knew that Eliezer ben Zephyr was a certified tzaddik, and the tzaddik's mission was to function as God's go-between, a conduit between heaven and earth? Bernie ought to be ashamed of himself. But while the receptionist had assured him that no one was allowed to enter or leave the "sanctuary" during a session, he couldn't stand the suspense. As the turbaned lady resumed her reading, Bernie edged toward the curtain and parted it a hair.

The low-ceilinged room on the other side, most likely a former dance studio, was surrounded by mirrors. In it, sitting on yoga mats before the rabbi, were a score of women, mostly in their middle years, though there were younger ones as well, some as sleek as greyhounds, a couple in the final stages of pregnancy. There were also a handful of men who may have been uxorious husbands dragged along against their will, though they and the ladies seemed equally engrossed. It was an altogether impressive turnout (multiplied to infinity by the wall mirrors) given that the medita- tion center's grand opening had been only weeks before—a testament to the success of the marketing campaign underwritten by Julius Karp. Rabbi ben Zephyr himself was seated on a raised dais in one of the Karps' surplus Naugahyde armchairs, its creases reprising the furrows of the old man's face. He was wearing a belted white satin kittel, wielding the scepter of a cordless microphone, a fancy pillbox kippah cocked like the cap of an organ-grinder's monkey atop his dappled gray head. In place of a prayer shawl, a lei of tropical flowers draped his turkey neck; stray flowers en- twined the weathered whiskbroom of his beard. The women were dressed in tracksuits and gym shorts, a few in spandex leotards with gauze skirts, their eyes closed in concentration as the rabbi began to warble various prayers. Bernie recognized the prayers as a hodgepodge of penitential slichot, with lashings of the mourner's Kaddish and the El Molay Rachamim. Then the rabbi broke into a singsong, chanting the Ani le-dodi ve-dodi li ("I am my beloved's and my beloved is mine") refrain from the Song of Songs, repeating it over and over like a mantra while encouraging his would-be intitiates to do the same. Bernie, for whom such prayers had become second nature, wondered if the others knew what they were parroting. But while there were one or two faces of a darker Semitic cast, the assembly as a whole didn't look particularly Jewish. Not that it mattered, since the rabbi's hypnotic chant apparently required no comprehension to inspire a collective euphoria—as was evidenced by several women who appeared to be in transports, a few showing shadows under their tushies that revealed them to be sitting in midair.

The receptionist came forward to draw the curtain back into place, tugging it with a prim gesture as if to cover up an indecency. But no sooner had she admonished Bernie once again with her zipped smile and returned to her post than the curtain was reopened from the other side. The session was over and the rabbi's disciples began streaming into the vestibule, most of them still looking half-entranced like an audience leaving a cinema. Some, however, had the presence of mind to pause and browse the display case, purchasing items from the receptionist who doubled now as salesclerk.

"But Hepzibah," pleaded a pie-faced woman whose tights above her leg warmers appeared to be stuffed with cottage cheese, "you know I don't read Hebrew."

Hepzibah, clearly well rehearsed, assured her customer that such knowledge was overrated, if not entirely unnecessary. "As the Rebbe says, 'Power is in the hands and the eyes.' You have only to trace the letters with your fingers for their healing power to enter your soul." When another asked if the outrageous price of a prayer shawl could possibly be correct, she was told that its ritual fringes were colored with an indigo dye derived from the rare purpura snail found only at the bottom of the Aegean Sea. "You can read about it in Numbers 15:38."

Now that Hepzibah was preoccupied, Bernie took the occasion to duck through the curtain into the so-called sanctuary, which was hung with banners bearing Hebrew characters like an array of military standards. With the aid of a couple of women at either arm, the rabbi was stepping down from the platform, where he was immediately encircled by more adoring ladies, some of whom bore votive offerings in the form of homemade peanut brittle and casseroles. The rabbi rewarded their grateful indulgence with intimate touches, caressing one's shoulder while pinching another's cheek, paying special attention to the younger students—such as the ingenue in her red Lycra body stocking, who asked the holy man to please interpret her aura.

"You were in your last life a flower," croaked old Eliezer, pressing her forehead with bony fingers, "that plucked it the prophet Elijah, may his name be for a blessing, and stuck in his buttonhole."

The girl turned the color of her costume.

Overcoming his customary reticence, Bernie hailed the rabbi, hoping that once the master set eyes on his erstwhile apprentice he would shake off all his hangers-on. But Rabbi Eliezer merely acknowledged the boy with a nod, then turned back to his admirers.

"Rabbi," called Bernie, who didn't like drawing attention to himself, but he was convinced that his predicament called for an urgent audience. "Rabbi, I need some advice."

The rabbi glanced over his shoulder. "Get why don't you a pair long pants," he replied, and upon reflection, "also maybe a haircut." His sarcasm incited titters among his devotees, who assured him he was a rascal and a scamp. Bernie stood rooted to the spot, cheeks burning, as he watched his mentor borne off on a tide of worshipful women toward a door marked PRIVATE at the far corner of the sanctuary. They were squeezing his pasty flesh (which stayed squeezed) and teasing his sparse hair, the ladies, who appeared to Bernie like devils tormenting a saint—though in this case the saint seemed to be greatly enjoying their petting. Always surprised by the way bits of scripture came back to him now at odd moments, Bernie recalled a verse from Deuteronomy, the one in which Moses says, "Just as I learned without payment, so have you learned from me without payment, and thus you shall teach without payment in the generations to come." Feeling it was incumbent upon him to remind Rabbi Eliezer of the patriarch's decree, Bernie charged after the holy man to apprise him accordingly.

"Boychik," said the rabbi, serene in the midst of the women, "they pay by me only for the time that I lose which I would otherwise devote to earnink a livelihood. As it is written, 'Torah is the best of merchandise.'" Then assuring the boy he would ask if ever he required his advice again, he passed through the doorway along with his entourage.

Mortified, Bernie slouched past the curtain and out the front door of the House of Enlightenment. But on the way home, still crestfallen, he observed the shadow of a day lily shaped like a jester's cap on the side of a house, and the image propelled him straight into the realm of the sublime.

1907.

When the ferry from Ellis Island deposited Shmerl Karpinski (his name recently shortened by a harried customs official to Karp) on the bustling wharf, he shut his eyes to keep out the stimuli that threatened to overwhelm his brain. But the hastening crowds into which his fellow immigrants had already begun to dissolve, the clangor of horse cars and the rattle of the elevated train, assaulted his ears; they upset the peacefulness of the "laboratory" back in Shpinsk, which he was trying to reconstitute behind closed lids. Opening them again, he waited for his gaze to light on something that made sense, and saw the young man from the ship seated beside the driver of a dray whose bed contained a worm-eaten wooden casket. Shmerl had seen the youth before through waves of nausea while clinging to the splintered rail of his berth in steerage, trying not to roll off into the broth of vomit and slops. The atmosphere below decks was suffocating from a multitude of private functions made public, but while the whole of the steerage class groaned in time to the drumming pistons of the SS *Kaiser Wilhelm der Grosse*, the young man—perched on a barrel and peering out of a porthole at the sawtooth sea—seemed to retain a meditative poise. Shmerl saw him again in the crush of passengers who, mutinous after their long confinement, had emerged from their quarters to overrun the lower deck once the promised city hove into view. Some had shinnied up a mast and climbed into the rigging, where they became entangled like bugs in spider webs. All craned their necks for a glimpse of the Statue of Liberty in her verdigris robes and the glinting towers at the foot of Manhattan Island, itself appearing to float like a low-lying argosy. Everyone looked toward New York, America, all except the staid young man with his handsome face and the worsted suit he seemed never to remove; leaning on the taffrail, he gazed across the expanse of chartreuse ocean the ship had just traversed, as if less interested in where he was going than where he'd been. Lonely since being dispatched by his family to save him from conscription (and to distance him from a community grown ever more censorious of his behavior), Shmerl Karp envied the youth his apparent self-containment. Since they were about the same age, he might have introduced himself, but Shmerl didn't like to impose, and his slight humpback tended to make him rather shy.

The driver cracked his whip and the wagon bearing the casket drove off, leaving Shmerl to assume that the young man's aloof demeanor had its origin in his grief for a loved one who'd passed away (as had perhaps a dozen others) during the voyage. But that was all the time he could spare for contemplating strangers now that he had his own welfare to negotiate. Still reeling from an ordeal that had left him barely ambulatory, he was unable amid that head-splitting Babel to grasp the concept of terra firma. After weeks of seasickness, during which he felt he'd regurgitated his very soul, Shmerl had been shunted from steamship to steam launch to the turreted fastness of Ellis Island. There he was made to suffer through stations of functionaries asking bewildering questions in pidgin Yiddish, checking his answers against the ship's manifest with the severity of clerical seraphs verifying his name in the Book of Life. Doctors thumped his chest, testicles, and gibbous spine, inverted his eyelids, labeled him with chalk, and festooned him with paper flags; then they directed him back into the pitching ferry, where he scarcely understood that, instead of being detained in a holding cell reserved for undesirables, he'd been given a license to enter the Golden Land — which swirled about him now in a flurry of internal combustion engines and clopping hooves. But while the other immigrants, met by family or landslayt, had disappeared with their duffels and eiderdowns into the chasms between the commercial towers, Shmerl still tottered on the dock among pecking seabirds, wondering how best to proceed.

What did he really know of America anyway, outside of the rumors that on arrival everyone became an instant millionaire, which had already proved to be patently untrue? Only a few phrases in New Yorkish such as "awpn der vinder" and "kosheren restoran" were familiar to him; he knew also the address of an aunt and uncle who, when informed of his coming, had responded in a letter that was the equivalent of a grunt. Also he understood that in these turbulent streets the distance from heaven was even greater than it had been in his impoverished and pogrom-ridden Ukraine. Beyond that Shmerl knew little and had nothing besides a carpet bag containing a few scraps of clothing and some designs for inventions that had no practical application whatever. It wasn't much to begin a new life with, though standing there on that alien shore he felt that his old life, such as it was, was already lost to him. Of an essentially retiring disposition despite the nuisance he'd made of himself back in Shpinsk, Shmerl believed that the person he was meant to become had yet to be born.

For a time he'd been a model yeshiva student who, since his bar mitzvah, had dutifully accompanied his father, Reb Todrus Karpinski, a junkmonger, to morning and evening prayers, and to the oily pool of the ritual bath on Shabbos. Shmerl was well versed in scripture, fluent in the 613 mitzvot, able to cite hair-splitting discrepancies between the Babylonian and Jerusalem Talmuds. His specialty had been parsing knotty halakhic conundrums, such as: What is the degree of defilement to a house cleaned for Passover when a mouse brings in a crumb of chometz? During his adolescence, however, when Scheuermann's disease began to deform his spine and his fellows started making fun of him, Shmerl became more remote. At the same time he was wracked by physical discomfort, not necessarily restricted to his back, which he sublimated into an intensely pious streak.

Its symptoms included periods of dreaminess during which he might be seen wandering alone with his peculiar stoop among the moss-mantled stones of the cemetery. He lingered, as well, beside the waterwheel that powered the lumber mill, where he became possessed of the notion that the wheel was for propelling the earth through time. Then it was all he could do to suppress an impulse to plunge an axe handle into the gears that turned the wheel, thus testing his theory and perhaps preserving his town from further aging.

Though he'd always had a healthy respect for traditional religious prohibitions, Shmerl began to look furtively into mystical and alchemical texts. In a corner of the mildewed study house he pored over books reserved for householders past the age of forty. Grown restless with the thorny dialectics of pilpul discourse, Shmerl secretly attended the third meal at the home of a local Chasidic rebbe, a rancid old gentleman whose beard was sprinkled with fried groats. In his homily the rebbe declared: "Is not a figure of speech, God's longing for His feminine aspect, his Holy Shekhinah, which since the destruction of the Second Temple is exiled along with the Israelites." It was an ongoing drama with regard to which the sage exhorted his disciples to play matchmaker to the reunion of haShem with His better half. Seized with a desire to participate in this cosmic romance, Shmerl began to research ways of actively promoting the reunion, which would bring an end to Diaspora and raise the fallen earth to the height of the celestial Jerusalem.

Using as his handbook a volume called *Sefer Sheqel ha-Qodesh* by the medieval kabbalist Moses de Leon, he began to clear cobwebs from the interior of the tumbledown storage shed behind his father's junk shop. In lieu of the called-for crucibles, alembics, and bird-beaked vases, he culled from among items deemed too shoddy even for the shlockmonger's shop an array of patched pots and dusty bottles. Discovering in himself a heretofore unrealized knack for construction, he stacked broken bricks in an inverted funnel to approximate an open-hearth stove. Raw materials such as copper and zinc lay around in abundance, but for the substances he would need as catalysts in his transformational processes, he appealed to the barber and chemist Avigdor the Apostate. A freethinker with a cynical view of his community's naïveté, Avigdor nevertheless stocked his shelves with jars of leeches and quack remedies to humor his superstitious clientele. Accustomed as he was to strange requests, however, the fox-faced apothecary (known to have eaten shellfish) was unused to yeshiva bochers inquiring after quicksilver, powdered lodestone, and cinnabar, to say nothing of rare herbs such as ypericon. When asked what he planned to do with these items, Shmerl was prepared with a story about a correspondence chemistry course, a pursuit he thought the freethinker would approve of. It was in any case easier than explaining that he meant to perform, in microcosm, processes that the universe might then repeat writ large. Naturally Avigdor was not deceived, but sensing mischief on the part of the boy (and curious to see where his activities would lead), he accepted an oxidized flatiron and the skeleton of a parasol in exchange for the desired ingredients.

"In the interest of advancing secular education," said the apothecary, with a wry tilt to his lips.

Of course, Shmerl might simply have prayed for change as the Jews had done for generations. But in heated competition with his fanciful nature was a pragmatic temperament that refused to make hard distinctions between the miraculous and the purely technical. And now that in adolescence the scales seemed to have fallen from his eyes, he saw clearly that the Jews of Shpinsk, and by extension the whole Pale of Settlement, were in urgent need of salvation; there was a compelling demand for heroic action on the part of some passionate young idealist. Everywhere he looked Shmerl saw men and women compared to whom his own affliction was negligible. There were boys his age who'd hacked off digits and wrecked their insides from drinking lye to exempt themselves from the draft, old men who'd been kidnapped as children by agents of the czar from whose army they returned decades later like hungry ghosts. Malnourished infants whimpered while their mothers went mad from the vermin that swarmed in their sheitl wigs. The centuries of persecution and degradation had left the Jews physically and morally depleted, their prayers ineffectual. What was required now was yichud, a conjunctio, the union of heaven and Earth that would transform the Jews of Shpinsk into a robust and beatific species, their constitutions as hardy as those of Russian muzhiks.

His initial efforts were inauspicious. In an attempt to extract the Fifth Essence, called the Elixir of Life, from a mixture of ground antimony and dog waste distilled in a battered samovar, Shmerl produced instead a drizzle of vile gray liquid afloat with crescents like cuticles. He took a cautious sip and puked, then waited in vain for his spine to straighten and his mind to expand in boundless clairvoyance. His disappointment was accompanied by vertigo and a weakness in the knees, which buckled under him, leaving him in a heap on the cold clay floor of the shed. That was how his father, come to investigate the rumor of a trespasser in his storehouse, found his oldest son. With a host of other sons too numerous to keep track of, Todrus and his wife, the footsore Chana Bindl, were generally too preoccupied with making ends meet to concern themselves with the shenanigans of their spawn. A crafty type with an eye for the favorable prospect, Todrus took in at a glance the condition of his son, along with the furnace and the urn spouting copper tubing, the jar of cloudy liquid resting on an anvil. His nose twitched at the scent and, dipping a pinkie into the jar, he dabbed his tongue then lifted the jar to quaff its contents, after which he breathed fire and pronounced Shmerl's elixir ("Batampt!") a perfectly serviceable schnapps. He cuffed the boy's ear for engaging in unlawful acts, then ordered him to begin the immediate manufacture of his potion by the barrel, and later Todrus hauled in a squiffy rabbi to bless the distillery. This was the beginning of Shmerl's temporary enslavement to his father's bootleg operation, on the merits of which Todrus converted his junkshop into a provisional tavern. It was a short-lived venture, however, since his son's mephitic cordial turned out to have debilitating side effects, such as temporary blindness.

In the meantime Shmerl persisted in his experiments, whose results

remained unsatisfactory. While he would have preferred to work in solitude, now that his labors were popular gossip, he was often surrounded
by inquisitive siblings eager to offer themselves as guinea pigs. Though he
tried to discourage them, his little brothers made a game of snatching up
his decoctions fresh from the still and swilling them neat. One of them,
the web-toed Mushy, was confined to the outhouse for hours during which
he lost his baby fat and the ability to laugh; whereas the eight year-old
Gronim was seized with a steely erection that kept his little petsl stiff for
a day and a night. Then came the explosion that formally concluded the
alchemical phase of Shmerl's investigations. He had been hoping to recre-
ate the esh m'saref, the refiner's fire that transmuted base elements into
a liquid philosopher's stone, which insured strength, health, and eternal
youth and postponed death indefinitely. (It was a process also said to render common metals into gold, though Shmerl had no interest in that particular consequence.) He was cooking sulphur together with charcoal and
saltpeter in the brick furnace, and had a pulverized rind of ethrog on hand
to feed the growing flames, when a blast occurred that blew out the flimsy
wall of Todrus's storeroom. Burning debris sprayed a salvo of torches over
the swayback roofs of the Jewish quarter, causing the shingles to catch fire.
The whole shtetl might have been consumed in a single conflagration had
not the Water-Carriers Guild been summoned to form a bucket brigade
from the town pump. Shmerl himself emerged from the rubble uninjured
but black as pitch, his hair and eyebrows in patches where they hadn't been
singed away; his clothes were in shreds, his modesty protected only by
the remnant of his knitted tallit koton. Appearing like some cacodemon
hatched from one of his own makeshift retorts, he frightened the children
and reinforced the general opinion that he had become a dabbler in the
black arts, one to be shunned for looking into things he should not.

Around that time a maskil, a self-appointed representative of the Jewish
Enlightenment, appeared in Shpinsk. He drove into town in an awning-
covered caravan, a rattletrap conveyance run by a windy mechanism trailing fumes, which he parked on the market platz beside a vendor of cracked

eggs. Then climbing onto the caravan in his frock coat and natty beard, he rolled back the awning to reveal a gallery of modern marvels as yet unseen in the Jewish Pale. He introduced to a skeptical crowd, among whom the young Shmerl Karpinski stood riveted, a gas turbine engine which he jerked into motion by revolving a dogleg crank. The resulting din caused babies to squawl and a draft horse to bolt in its traces. He exhibited neon gas in vacuum tubes linked together like glowing wurst, and an electromagnet entwined in a copper helix that pulled cutlery from a knife-sharpener's sack several yards away. For a pièce de résistance he used his own ramrod body to conduct a direct current between a live wire in his left hand and a glass bulb in his right, thus challenging the light of the sun in an overcast sky. The crowd of mostly peasants, tradesmen, and truant children watched in rapt fascination, while the local Chasidim spat "Kaynehoreh!" against the evil eye. But for all the maskil's disclaimers to the effect that the items he demonstrated had exclusively practical purposes, Shmerl — never keen on the distinction between science and magic — thought the power in these contrivances might be harnessed for more spiritual ends.

Banished from what was left of the storehouse and forced to keep out of his ill-tempered father's sight, Shmerl had since reestablished his base of operations in the vine-tangled ambience of Yakov Chilblain's abandoned flour mill. This was a spongy structure, nearly reclaimed by the surrounding vegetation, that the Shpinskers generally regarded as haunted; imps, it was said, rode the windmill's ragged sails, and vampire bats flew out of the sack loft at night. But Shmerl was undeterred. A rationalist, he knew that imps and demons, though real enough, were merely pests that could be vaporized with the proper apparatus — such as a coil heated by electricity generated from a Voltaic pile composed of a stack of magnetized coins. (The coil also generated a hearthlike warmth, which was incidental.) He read about this phenomenon in *The Book of Wonders* that he'd obtained from the maskil along with a sheaf of diagrams in exchange for some waste product (a pearl?) from one of his former experiments. It was the first profane book that Shmerl had ever owned, and while initially he resisted opening it out of guilt, he was soon immersed in its illustrated descriptions of the technological revolution that was so late in arriving in Shpinsk. Then, rather than being put off by the book's lack of a doctrinal bias, the boy set about discovering ways to render that catalogue of utilitarian inventions supremely impractical.

There followed a period of feverish industry. With a sense that he was doing work for which he'd been divinely ordained, Shmerl gathered tools and materials, and what he couldn't locate in the detritus behind his father's shop, he dispatched his little brothers to find. Natural scavengers (some might have called them thieves), they brought back to the mill odds and ends that might double as crankshafts, pistons, and connector rods; they hauled their acquisitions up the ladder into the creaking loft, where Shmerl hammered them into shapes that ultimately evolved into engine parts. From Kabbalah he'd learned of the peculiar faculty of the Holy Ari of Safed, who could liberate souls that in the course of their gilgul, their metempsychosis, had become trapped in random objects on earth. With that in mind he girded a railroad spike in an armature of brass, mounting it between the poles of electrified magnets, which caused the spike to spin like a dreidl. His little brothers scrounged horsehair brushes that Shmerl looped about a length of pipe, explaining as he worked the concept of a "pressure drop." This was the inhalation that would occur between the rotating brushes and the vacuum formed from the effect of the spinning spike. He fastened the entire gizmo onto a blacksmith's bellows, whose accordion frame he replaced with a canvas nose bag, then mounted the reverse bellows — dubbed di neshomah zoiger, the soul-sucker — on a garden cart, which he and his brothers pulled in broad daylight over the ruts of Sheep Dip Alley to the doorstep of the Karpinskis' crumbling abode.

He'd determined that his family's dwelling should be the first to be sanctified by scourging it of the souls wedged in its various fissures and crannies. Even before he'd said the appropriate blessing and connected the wires to the alkali cell, inciting a mechanized uproar, before he'd begun to aim the articulated stovepipe into the room's obscurer corners, Shmerl had attracted a sizeable audience. Neighbors looked through the rag-stuffed windows and word soon reached the junkman and his wife, who came scurrying over from Todrus's shop on the market square. What they saw when they joined the other rubbernecks was their son wrestling a fat silver serpent that dove beneath the hulking clay stove from which a hen was sent packing; it nosed among pickle casks, rattled the garlic braids, and burrowed into every recess of that cluttered house. Chana Bindl, high-strung and perpetually pregnant, swooned in a heap of dimity skirts, so that Todrus had to send to Avigdor's for smelling salts. Then Shmerl, with an extravagant gesture, yanked the wires to break the circuit and removed the equine receptacle from the bellows, wrenching it open in the hope of setting free a cluster of imprisoned souls. He didn't know exactly what such souls would look like, but was reasonably certain the dirt that spilled from his contraption onto the floor was not their residue. Chana Bindl, having been revived, grew distressed again at the revelation that the rooms she so scrupulously scoured had remained full of grime, while her husband stood chewing his whiskers, conflicted in his kippered heart. His son had become on the one hand a figure of derision whose notoriety extended even to the goyim, while on the other he'd conceived a machine that cleaned a house in a manner your besom or feather duster couldn't have touched. Even as he lurched through clouds of dust to furl his fingers about Shmerl's scrawny throat, the junk dealer asked him what it would take to construct a fleet of similar carpet sweepers.

But the downcast inventor judged his machine a failure of no redeeming metaphysical value, and assuring his father through a pinched windpipe that he could do whatever he wished with di neshomah zoiger, Shmerl was already contemplating a new direction for his research. *The Book of Wonders* in its outline of the history of aerodynamics declared that recent developments had taken technology to the very threshold of manned flight. Shmerl envisioned a wholesale exodus of the Jews, enabled through innovative engineering to make aliyah to the Upper Yeshiva without having to die. His own mistake, however, was to fix his propeller—fashioned from the windmill stocks whose shredded sails were replaced with taut muslin—to the interior rafters rather than the roof of the family's hovel. He'd feared that instead of waking up in Paradise, his parents would open their eyes to a house with its roof torn asunder and midnight pouring in. As it was, the unholy racket roused Todrus and Chana Bindl from their rude mattress, whence they staggered forth in rumpled gowns to gaze blearily upon the thrashing blades. But even as the junkmonger sputtered and fumed, his wrath was checked by the breeze that cooled the room and fanned the brow of his agitated wife, who went directly into labor.

Shmerl, however, was disconsolate. He vowed to build another engine powerful enough to raise the roof of the entire planet and stir the stars into wheeling spirals, but his faith in his own abilities was severely impaired.

He returned to the mill to find that the combined weight of the various machinery parts had finally collapsed the rotting floor of the loft. A shambles, the place was the outward expression of Shmerl's internal despair, the perfect analogue—he judged—to his arrogance and grand designs. Bereft of illusion, he concluded that all his efforts were suspect, all merely in the interest of distracting himself from another kind of yearning; though despite his intrepid investigations, he was shy of the maidens, who were put off for their part by his reputation and the bell-shaped curve of his spine. No self-respecting marriage broker would ever approach him. Consumed by remorse for his own vanity, Shmerl languished in the millwright's wrecked quarters beyond the Shabbos boundary and the reach of a father who sought to turn a profit from his blunders.

"Every day is Yom Kippur," he declared to his little brothers, who'd grown bored with his misery and were happy to leave him alone.

The summer wore on with a soupy heat that set the lice seething, which in turn bred an epidemic of typhus that swept through the shtetl of Shpinsk, sparing neither goyim nor Jews. There were so many funerals that the processions trotted back and forth in relay fashion from cemetery to shul. The wailing of women along the route could be heard all the way to the ruined mill, where a passing installment peddler left word that one of Shmerl's brothers—Pinya, was it, or Melchizedek?—had fallen prey to the plague. Said Shmerl, ripping the lapel of his jerkin, "It should have been me." The younger brother had been taken in retribution for the sins of the elder (this was his logic) and though other siblings had from time to time perished in the starveling Karpinski household, this death harrowed the conscience of the inventor as no other; the pain was acute and ineffable. While it was too late to sacrifice himself in his brother's stead, there was still another course of action that lay open to him; yet for what he considered, Shmerl was sick with apprehension. Though the ancient texts strongly decried necromancy, he located an obscure passage in *The Book of Bosmath bat Shlomo* that included the prayer: "Baruch mechayei hameitim, blessed is he who raises the dead." But however often he repeated it, Shmerl could never quite believe it was true.

Still, there was no time left to tarry; tonight was the watch night and tomorrow the dead boy's body would be committed to the earth. Working full throttle according to certain principles of Faraday and Clerk Maxwell detailed in the journals his brothers had pilfered from Avigdor, Shmerl electrically magnetized a horseshoe. He surrounded the shoe with a halo of wooden spools bundled in soft-iron wires and insulated copper coils, further equipping the device with a notched lead gadget called a commutator, like a viper with a rubber boot heel in its jaws. Then he lowered his completed dynamo into the case of a mahogany coffee grinder and hung it around his neck by a barber's strop. As he crept into the house in the small hours of the morning, Shmerl discerned among the usual odors— petroleum, onions—another smell, tart as citrus, which he determined as death. It was not an unfamiliar odor; death was practically a member of their family, but tonight, as he stood watching his father and mother at their vigil, seated on tea crates at either side of the corpse, Shmerl experienced a sadness beyond words. Slumped in his threadbare tallis, Todrus Shlockmonger snored fitfully, while his mobcapped wife, even as she suckled the newborn at her breast, also nodded in sedentary slumber. The dead boy, cocooned to the chin in his miniature shroud, was laid out on a mat on the floor between them, a flickering havdalah candle at his head.

The Karpinskis had mourned a number of children in their time, and wasn't Chana Bindl already nursing the dead boy's replacement? (Though this one was a daughter, which hardly counted as a replacement at all.) But despite the repeated incidence of expiring offspring, Shmerl detected a unique oppression in the atmosphere, a pall of centuries that was his duty to dispel. Kneeling, his joints creaking from the weight he carried, the inventor inserted the electrodes into the florets of the dead boy's ears, then stood again to turn the rotary handle attached to the handmade dynamo. No sooner did the whirring begin than a visible reverberation of dancing sparks traced an outline around the entire corpse, which sat abruptly upright, jiggling as if to shake off the torpor of rigor mortis. Then either the whir of the machine or the delirious knocking of Shmerl's heart at the walls of his chest — or perhaps it was the clattering of the coins ejected from the corpse's eyes — frightened the baby, which began to bawl, rousing in their turn the junkmonger and his wife. Chana Bindl looked, shrieked, and passed out again, while Todrus sat gazing with eyes on stems at his dead son, who jerked like a monkey to the tuneless instrument played by the demonic organ-grinder standing over him.

Though he and his wife had enjoyed the chance benefits of Shmerl's inventions, this time the outraged junk dealer could see nothing at all redemptive in the boy's experiment, nor was he inclined to forgive him his monstrous crime. Neither, when the word got out (as it always did) of Shmerl's iniquitous tampering with God's decree, were the Jews of Shpinsk, their tolerance exhausted, willing to indulge him further. "For whoever doeth such things," they quoted Deuteronomy on the subject of sorcerers, "is an abhorrence unto the Lord," and not a week after his sacrilege the inventor received notice of his imminent induction into the army of the czar. The timing suggested some meddling on the part of the community, especially since, when Todrus protested that his son was a hunchback, the townspeople assured him that the government was willing to make an exception in Shmerl's case. The junkman railed that the boy had dug his own grave, but in the end there was nothing for it—short of giving him up to a military that would purge him of Jewishness and separate him forever from his tribe—but to appeal to the services of the smuggler Firpo Fruchthandler. Thus, with the sale of Shmerl's soul sucker and celestial elevator to Ben Tzion Pinkas, the local shylock who'd grown rich from a spate of recently pawned nuggets and gems, the Karpinski family raised the money to hire Firpo. The bibulous smuggler then spirited Shmerl in the back of a donkey cart, rolled up in a rug under cages of fantail pigeons, across the border into Poland, whence he could make for the coast and from there book passage to America.

As the *Kaiser Wilhelm* steamed into New York harbor, Max Feinshmeker, standing amid the throng of immigrants at the bow, twisted his neck toward the stern. He looked back toward the titanic green lady and the broad bay's narrows into the open sea, to make sure that the past was keeping its distance. There had been several occasions during the month-long journey from Lodz when he felt that the past had not only overtaken him but had invaded his very being in the form of the whore Jocheved, who sometimes wanted to die. She constantly reminded Max that he had no family, no home, that his soul was so ravaged it could no longer cushion him from the insults of a hostile world. "This is news?" Max would reply, but Jocheved was a malevolent dybbuk, and there were times when she had encouraged the young man to throw himself overboard. Then he would imagine himself bobbing in the steamship's wake, watching its great bulk diminishing as it churned toward a blood orange horizon, while he sank into a dark and distinctly un-Jewish element. In truth, the vision had a certain consolatory appeal, and there were moments when Max, in his loneliness, might have succumbed to the dybbuk's urging, were it not for the aged Chasid encased in a block of ice atop three quarters of a pood of beluga sturgeon roe.

For the sake of the contract with his patron Zalman Pisgat, Max was obliged to keep himself in one piece. He was sworn to deliver the goods safely into the hands of the agent of an American financier, who despite his fabulous wealth enjoyed a bargain, especially if it involved a little risk. (Although, to the novice smuggler's mind, the risk was entirely his own.) Upon receipt of the caviar the agent would hand over an agreed-upon sum that Max would then wire in its entirety back to Lodz. He was to take no percentage for himself, his compensation having been the investment that the ice mensch had already made in his journey, an investment for which old Pisgat expected a tenfold return. And if that sum were not remitted by a certain date, Zalman Pisgat would then be forced to inform parties less magnanimous than himself, whose operatives would track Max down and tear out his spleen. Max appreciated the forthright simplicity of the arrangement and admired how the humble icehouse proprietor was connected to a criminal network whose reach dissolved the distance between Europe and America. Such was the nature of Max's motivation; while Jocheved, when she wasn't feeling suicidal, had her own reasons for making the trip, which involved an allegiance to her frozen inheritance that remained largely inscrutable to the smuggler. Not that he didn't try to fathom her attitude, as he sat beside the reinforced casket under hanging flanks of beef in a railroad reefer car, or later on in the steamship's refrigerated hold. But Max preferred his own practical incentive: that he was enlisted in a mutually beneficial business covenant, which footed the bill for the journey across what was left of Poland into Prussia and farther on.

Without Zalman's endowment the trip would have been out of the question, an unimaginable hardship given the added burden of the cedar box and its outlaw freight. As it was, Max had traveled in relative comfort, looking out of boxcars and wagon-lit windows at a countryside whose beauty his consciousness, bred in the ghetto, was ill prepared to take in. There were purple meadows spattered with crimson poppies from which clouds of finches started up at the sound of the train, fields of sunflowers, cherry orchards, linden groves that were the remnant of a primeval forest cleared for pastures. Peasant cottages like overturned longboats bordered the rivers and canals; thatched hermitages protruded from grottoes, and onion domes sprouted like toadstools amid the rolling plains. The roads meandered like the unraveling threads of the old regimes, from whose frayed fabric a million poor Jews had tumbled. They clogged the highways and station platforms, the Jews, trudged the gauntlets of inhospitable villages, lugging their chattels and scrolls and trailing goosedown like surf. Periodically their ranks were swelled by the youthful fusgeyers tramping with their tents on their backs and singing hymns: "Go, yidelekh, into the wide world . . ."; then the tattered company would march in step with them, expanding their chests until the young people had passed them by, after which their weary feet would drag again.

It was the continuation of a trek that had started in Egypt, then passed through Jerusalem and Sefarad into Eastern Europe, where it took a breather for a brief millennium—a long slog during which many fell, and even those who could afford to ride were not immune from humiliation: like the boy Max had witnessed in the crowded rail car mocked by soldiers who clipped off his sidelocks. How resigned he had been, as if the abuse were an initiation he had to endure in order to enter America—for they were all (with only marginal Zionist exceptions) on their way to America.

All this Max observed with a certain detachment, buffered as he was by Zalman's stipend, which is not to say that the excursion was without peril. The rail leg of a journey that should have taken only a matter of days took instead a fortnight, and there were constant interruptions when officers carrying weapons came aboard to inspect documents and passports. (Forged by Pisgat's associates, his papers consolidated an identity to which the smuggler still had only a tenuous connection.) Sometimes they were accompanied by physicians threatening the spot examinations Max dreaded. Then he would have to dip into his funds and hand over another installment of the sweeteners that Pisgat had settled on him. But the funds were limited, and at the rate he'd had to dole them out along the route, oiling palms at every juncture, Max knew he would arrive on the other side with empty pockets. Still, bureaucratic obstacles notwithstanding, he owed Pisgat a debt of gratitude for partially clearing the way for him, because at each depot and border crossing he would be called upon once again to present his papers and explain the frozen stiff he was transporting (this was his story) to his bereaved family across the sea for burial. It was an anxious trip at every turn of which suspicious officials had to be silenced with zlotie, then marks, dissuaded from their insistence that the young man submit to disinfection and quarantine. No wonder that by the time the train reached the coast Max was fresh out of sops for insuring the secrets that lay beneath the ice and his own increasingly fusty suit of clothes.

In the louche North Sea port of Hamburg, sailors with their painted doxies and passengers on board electric trolleys ogled the invasion of the Jewish unwashed—who were hounded through the city as far as the seawall by a corps of money changers and bogus ticket agents, cheapjacks and impostors. Speaking a Yiddish he could scarcely make understood, Max once more asserted to officials that his papers were in order and the deceased already approved for transport, its ice-bound condition a guarantee against putrefaction. While all the time he thought: Azoy gait, so be it, I've done what I could; let them confiscate the box and everything it contains. Let them discover the contraband payload and fling me into a dungeon; it's immaterial to me. Or were these the thoughts of Jocheved, with whom Max was so often at odds? In the end, though, the ticket was validated, the bill of lading stamped, and the casket carted by porters up the gangplank into the bowels of Rolling Billy, as the crew called the gargantuan flagship of the Hamburg-Amerika Line. Max straggled behind them into the ship's yawning hold to make certain that the rabbi was well situated among the racks of splayed and gibbeted mutton, the crates of perishables and cases of brut champagne.

He was assigned a berth in the third-class section, where he slept alongside the retching masses in a stench to which Max himself, stewing in Salo Frostbissen's funeral suit, contributed. Two days out the ship hit a storm, and the steerage passengers, pasted against the bulkheads when not tossed into one another, declared that the vessel was lashed to Leviathan's tail. In fair weather they fought over the gruel ladled from the common kettle into their dinner pails, only to spew it later on into the aisles, creating between bunks a moat in which the pious stood davening. Compromised laws of kashrut aside, Max was unable to eat in such an environment, though he might occasionally nibble a bit of fruit or dried fish that some shy maiden, blushing vermilion, would press upon him. Such overtures, however, made him as uncomfortable as did the viscid-eyed victims of nausea and dysentery gulping air whose oxygen was usurped by foul gases. The toilets were bogs, the showers briny trickles that Max had anyway to avoid for fear of revealing his secret anatomy. Every bodily function involved an irksome covert procedure, often in the presence of men whose exposed parts were abhorrent to the girl concealed beneath Max's apparel, which was why he kept as much as possible to himself.

When not trying to inhale a salty breeze through a porthole below decks, he preferred to keep company with the rabbi, during spells in which he established an uneasy intimacy with his charge. In the polar climate of the ship's capacious meat locker, Max would plunk himself down on an asparagus crate, shivering in the dense air from the ammonia compressors that was scarcely more breatheable than the Sheol of steerage. Still he preferred the solitude, where he was seldom interrupted in his meditations concerning the past that he hoped to outdistance. Picturing the basement flat back in Zabludeve Street, as vacant now as a plundered crypt, he would make an effort at shoring up his new identity, though Jocheved invariably kicked out the props. He thought about his bedfellows in third class and wondered what, aside from their shared rootlessness, they had to do with him. What had become of the faith that bound him to his own kind? He wondered as well about the assertion of Jocheved's father, Salo Frostbissen, for whose sake his daughter had been willing to shlep an ungainly impediment halfway around the world. How could the watchman have believed that the rabbi (who would be carrion were it not for his artificial preservation) was still somehow alive? It was a conviction to which Jocheved also paid lip service, if feebly, though Max could only disdain her credulity with a scorn that she assured him was mutual.

The smuggler had to exercise stealth during these visits, since the storage hold was technically off-limits to passengers—especially third-class passengers admonished not to stray from their confines, their very presence constituting an offense in the better quarters. But as the route through the ship's entrails was lengthy and circuitous, Max could scarcely avoid the occasional confrontation with a purser or ordinary seaman. Then he would try through gestures and snatches of fractured German to explain his unauthorized presence, while the crewman, who already knew him by reputation as the lad with the refrigerated relation, would wave him past without further interference. At first Max couldn't account for their leniency, though ultimately he came to understand that his looks were a factor in their favorable disposition, just as they had been for the railroad officials and border guards. And while Jocheved had only contempt for the comely features she shared with the smuggler, Max was, himself, not above exploiting them for the sake of survival. Of course, his face could just as easily have become a liability, particularly in steerage, where the girls were forever finding excuses to approach him, which was all the more reason not to bathe.

Once, having taken a wrong turn in the depths of the vessel, he descended through an open scuttle and found himself in a brass and lead jungle among grease monkeys swinging from exposed ducts and flues. Bare-chested toilers caked in ebony dust wielded shovels from atop a hill of soft coal, feeding the maw of a belching boiler whose flaming tongue set the dials on the pressure gauges spinning crazily. Giant turbines whined a counterpoint to the shooshing of screw propellers ploughing the unseen waves, while Max stood nailed in the hatchway by the glowering of the stokers, which chilled Jocheved's blood. Their attention, however, was abruptly recaptured by a crookbacked immigrant in a shabby jerkin, his neck craned like a turtle peeping from its carapace. Appearing to have stumbled out of a jet of steam expelled from a whistling slide valve, he commenced asking questions he seemed simultaneously to answer, in a Yiddish the stokers couldn't have understood. "So does it make by you a difference, the quadruple expansion of your twin-screw propulsion engine, which requires 560 tons coal a day . . . ?" The stokers peered at the interloper with uncordial bloodshot eyes while Max made his getaway.

Another time Max climbed an unfamiliar companionway that turned a corner into a carpeted staircase, emerging into an opulence like nothing he had ever beheld. Still aboard the windward-riding steamship, he had entered a palace where lounges and plush smoke rooms bordered a grand saloon, a chandelier like a diadem dangling from its ceiling. There was a baroque dining room appointed in ornate carvings, gilt-framed mirrors, bas-reliefs, and stained glass; a library with a blazing fireplace and a marble mantel, Tiffany gas lamps the rich relations of the hurricanes that scattered shadows in the benighted quarters below. Trespassing amid all that splendor, Max could scarcely believe that such a place occupied the same planet as steerage.

In a palm court luxuriant with potted orchids beneath a vaulted glass dome, a bushy-haired man in a boiled tuxedo shirt, his rolled sleeves showing powerful forearms, was performing card tricks before an audience in evening dress seated in white rattan chairs. There followed a round of polite applause after which a slight, bird-breasted woman in puce tights appeared bearing an assortment of properties. She proceeded to manacle and straitjacket the solemn magician, then helped him into a steamer trunk, which members of the audience were invited to encompass in chains. The darting assistant then drew an ornamental screen about the trunk and, gravely pronouncing the name of the presentation, "Metamorphosis," disappeared behind the partition. Mere seconds after she'd vanished, however, the magician himself stepped forth to universal gasps and riotous applause. Folding back the screen, he unlocked the locks, removed the chains, and lifted the lid, as out popped the lady assistant, straitjacketed and handcuffed.

So spellbound was Max by the performance that he'd forgotten what a

distraction his unlaundered presence might be in such genteel surround-
ings. He could have retreated unnoticed had not a filigreed matron with
terraced chins, seated at the end of the row of chairs, pointed at him to
exclaim in a piping contralto, "You're bleeding!" He looked down to see
that the dampness which had seeped through the crotch of his pants had
leaked a droplet of blood onto the bottle green carpet. Fleeing toward
the promenade in a frantic search for the hatch that would lead him back
to the ship's kishkes where he belonged, Max felt a renewed disgust for
the female body he was forced to accommodate. Didn't the men in shul
thank God daily for not having been born a woman? Nor did it assuage
his humiliation to recall how the gentiles of Lodz clung to the age-old
belief that male Jews had monthly emissions. Still, there was the consoling
afterthought that Jocheved, having had no womanly discharge since her
abduction, had at least not been impregnated during her ordeal.

Looking over his shoulder for the rest of the voyage, Max was scarcely
aware of their proximity to the New World until the ship, escorted by
spouting tugs, nudged into its berth at the flag-bristling Hamburg-Amerika
wharf. The first- and second-class passengers streamed down the gang-
planks to be absorbed by welcoming crowds, while the rabble of steerage,
teased by their close encounter with the mainland, were unloaded onto
launches that ferried them to Ellis Island. Max had held out the hope
that the special circumstances of his alleged funereal mission and the burden it entailed might somehow exclude him from diversion to the Isle
of Tears. But the casket with its licit and illicit contents was lowered by
cargo net along with the baggage of the other prospective greenhorns, then
transported to the island and dumped in a cordoned area pending further
inspection; nor could it be reclaimed until its owner had been admitted
through customs. This prompted a period of forced separation from his
property that caused Max his greatest anxiety thus far.

On the island the candidates for immigration were herded through red-
brick portals into the cathedral-size echo chamber of the receiving hall, the
sunlight slanting down from high windows like crossed swords. Tagged

with numbers and letters, the logy assemblage were made to wait hours on hard wooden benches, then rousted from their languor and hustled into stalls according to nationality, driven between the paint-chipped railings as into an abattoir. Stations of uniformed examiners awaited them, as Max dredged his empty pockets for the bribes that no longer remained. He steeled himself to face the first inquisitor, at whose shoulder stood a spade-bearded gent—apparently there to act as interpreter—with the Hebrew Immigrant Aid Society insignia stuck in the band of his bowler hat. A relentless battery of questions ensued, designed to determine whether Max were a lunatic, convict, anarchist, polygamist, or otherwise potential parasite and threat to the state. Encouraged by subtle jerks of the interpreter's head to answer every query (how else?) in the negative, he was then shoved along toward a doctor in a dirty smock, who ordered him to open his shirt just short of revealing the tender buds of Jocheved's breasts. Thankfully inattentive, the doctor concluded that Max suffered from neither leprosy, consumption, nor any other "loathsome or contagious disease," then passed him on to yet another doctor seated on a stool surrounded by a circular hospital curtain.

This one, with a cigarette dangling from fleshy lips, was in the process of lifting with one hand the sagging belly of a burly peasant in order to inspect his external genitalia with the other. The sight of the big man standing there with his trousers about his trunk-like ankles made Max rigid with panic. All the accumulated tensions of the journey revisited him with a gathered force that rocked his entire frame, until he had no way of measuring whether his fear was proportionate to the situation. Flinging madly about in his brain for some reason that might exempt him from the examination, he fixed on the gory excuse of an injury inflicted by rampaging hooligans during a ghetto episode. Perhaps the tale might inspire a sympathy that would stay the doctor's hand from exploring the conspicuous absence in Max's pants.

Then just as the physician dismissed the balagoula (who'd farted like a horse as his parts were handled) and summoned Max with his rubber-gloved fingers to step forward, a disturbance erupted in the next line over. Even above the surflike cacophany of the hall, urgent voices could be heard calling out for assistance—as coincidentally a hospital screen crashed into Max's, which toppled domino fashion, the wreckage revealing a knot of officials kneeling over a fallen woman. Wearing a headscarf and several layers of skirts despite the heat, she had the look of an open umbrella tossed in the wind as she writhed on the floor in the throes of a seizure. Yellow sputum bubbled from her lips, her upturned eyes as blank as boiled eggs. Heaving a sigh, Max's doctor got leisurely to his feet and toddled over to the aid of his colleagues, one of whom was struggling to prevent the woman from swallowing her tongue. In the doctor's absence the HIAS man assigned to him, one half of whose face was contracted in a wink, took up a piece of chalk from the box beside the physician's stool and made a mark on Max's sleeve. Confused, Max had yet to budge from his spot when the man yanked him roughly forward by the lapel and, looking both ways, beckoned to the fellow behind him in line. Faint with relief, Max pushed through a turnstile back into the discordant hall, past the quarantine cages where men and women who had failed their examinations were detained.

Reunited with the rabbi and once again aboard the launch, he allowed himself to appreciate for the first time the cloud-banked perpendicular city ahead of him, believing that the worst was surely over. It was an optimism that, for once undisparaged by Jocheved, was borne out by the expedition with which events began to fall into place. Pisgat, who'd assured Max that arrangements had been made at the other end, proved as good as his word. The poker-faced agent of the financier (whose name was not to cross the smuggler's lips) was there to meet him on the North River docks in the molasses-thick afternoon sunshine. Recognizing him by the plank sarcophagus beside which he stood, the man spared the new arrival no more than a nod before seeing to it that a couple of porters transferred the casket with swift dispatch into the waiting wagon. All fortitude spent, Max was content to climb aboard the wagon himself and place his fate in the hands of his tight-lipped convoy. There was of course much to see as all around him disembarking immigrants were beset by long-lost relations or confidence tricksters posing as such, by labor gang contractors and sweatshop recruiters. There were omnibuses whose rooftop passengers had to remove their hats as they passed beneath the Elevated trestles, kiosks that invited pedestrians to descend into rumbling catacombs beneath the earth, a gothic tower on the side of which frolicked a lady fifteen stories tall in a bathing costume. But Max preferred to keep his eyes fixed straight ahead, as blinkered in their way as the nag's that hauled the wagon, which might now be mistaken for a hearse. The streets of America, he resolved, would offer him no distractions until he had first attended to the business of collecting his wits.

Gebirtig & Son's Ice Castle on Canal Street, give or take its crenellated turrets and galleried façade, was a bookend to Pisgat's overseas operation, the two establishments bracketing the whole of Max's journey. It was true that the present structure was the more imposing, its breadth spanning a whole city block. A fleet of mule-driven delivery vans was parked in the furrowed thoroughfare outside and an army of laborers wheeled dollies and barrows up and down a ramp through the wide warehouse doors. But once he'd stepped over the Ice Castle's threshold, passing from the torrid month of Tammuz into a frosty Shevat, Max relaxed in the chill environment familiar from a former life. Vertical lifts containing bales of salmon and pyramids of artichokes rose in the chromium light to the upper lofts,, where the freight was slid along tramways on sledges, stored in niches carved out of the frozen ramparts like shrines; and Max, unlettered but for the Yiddish romances that Jocheved had browsed on the sly, had the reverent sensation of having entered an archive of ice. Deflated as he was, he was glad to be behind these vault-thick walls leaking sawdust like sand from a thousand hourglasses; he was glad of the business that gave him a reason for being there, acutely aware that, when the business was over, he would be left entirely on his own.

The casket was rolled upright on a handcart into the building's deepest sanctum, a pine-floored locker where wheels of cheese large as millstones, beer barrels with ivory spigots, and various imported delicacies were stored. There the proprietors, Gebirtig Junior and Senior, welcomed their guests to the Castle's keep. Well-fed burghers both, wearing identically striped galluses and with fat cigars plugged into complacent grins, they seemed happy to defer to the brisk direction of the financier's agent. At his command the mammoth green lozenge of ice with its dormant occupant was hoisted by workers from its box by means of a winch suspended from an overhead gantry. Max held his breath as the dripping block dangled in the frigid air from a hawser-thick noose, dipping left and right like the arms of precarious scales. Then the flannel-wrapped pillows of fish roe upon which the ice had rested, smelling surprisingly fresh, were removed from the casket and placed on a butcher's slab, after which the block was thankfully lowered back into its crib. But what made Max even more ill at ease than had the thing's visible exposure was the way the two Gebirtigs had scrutinized the ice-entombed rebbe almost as covetously as they had eyed the caviar.

The agent plucked from the lapel of his cutaway a tiny silver spoon with which he proceeded to sample the goods, chewing with methodical concentration before declaring the morsel satisfactory; then removing an envelope from his pocket, he tossed it to Max, who snatched it out of the air like falling manna. He supposed he was expected to count the money, which he had just enough presence of mind left to do, feeling the eyes of the proprietors upon him all the while. Stammering that all was in order, he stuffed the money back into the envelope, tucked the envelope into his inside coat pocket, and bowed to the agent with a slight spillage of raven curls. The fish eggs were then loaded into the wagon and buried in straw, on top of which were nestled, as a further decoy, sacks of groceries and bottles of vintage Sauterne. Then the agent departed without ceremony, leaving Max to the good offices of the Gebirtigs, who insisted he call them Asher and Tsoyl.

Obviously well compensated for their part in the relay of merchandise, they seemed also well informed concerning Max's commission on behalf of the glaciated old man. "Be assured," they told him in a homey Ashkenaz idiom, "will be looked after respectfully, your zayde, till you return from making his funeral arrangements."

"I have first to visit the office of the Western Union," Max announced, as per Pisgat's instructions (and lest it be thought he had other plans for the cash). This too the Gebirtigs seemed to anticipate.

They gave him explicit directions as to how to reach the telegraph office on Delancey Street and described the procedure for wiring the money back to Poland. Feeling as if the cash in his pocket were a hot potato he must promptly dispose of, Max set off with a purpose into the jostling unknown. He had been told his destination was only a few blocks away, but the welter of the Lower East Side streets was immediately disorienting, and alone he remembered that, notwithstanding his pocketful of ill-gotten gains, he was without a sou to his name. Of course, once he was rid of the money, his empty pockets would at least preserve him from the risk of robbery, but despite his apprehensiveness he couldn't help entertaining other possibilities. Given all Max had endured during his journey, would old Pisgat begrudge his skimming a scant few bills from such a thick bankroll, just enough to tide him over till he managed to secure a foothold in America? It was safe to say he would never be in possession of such a fortune again, and how, when it was gone, would he support himself, never mind see to the perpetual care of the ice-girt oddity? Thinking of which: Temporarily liberated from that weighty encumbrance, Max had the sense that his task was done. So what was to prevent him, other than Pisgat's threats (and Pisgat was very far away), from taking the money and disappearing into the country's interior, where he might perhaps purchase a kingdom and rule over a tribe of grateful savages? What, in any case, was the alternative? He supposed he would have to appeal to some benevolent society for a few dollars with which to rent a hole in the wall, then take a job in the rag trade—the industry in which he'd been told all greenhorns were employed—thus insuring his indenture to pisher wages for the rest of his days. On the other hand, already a smuggler, why not a thief? But still in the process of inventing himself, he decided somewhat grudgingly (nudged by Jocheved) that Max Feinshmeker was a man of his word, and anyway he just wanted to put this nerve-racking chapter behind him.

He paused on the corner of an avenue congested with market stalls, carts sporting garlands of tinware, trussed and flapping geese, bins piled with alps of eyeglasses, felt slippers, and celluloid buttons, wing collars like a nest of albino butterflies. Garbage choked the gutters, creating swamps into which women in brogans chased shoplifting urchins who ducked under the bellies of draft horses dead on their feet. From every fire escape hung the doubled-over carcass of an airing mattress, from every storefront an illustrated placard boasting a giant scissors or molar, its legend inscribed in holy and unholy tongues. Max paused to look left and right, realizing that in weighing his options he had forgotten the Gebirtigs' directions, if indeed their directions were accurate; he'd lost all track of his whereabouts. Everyone around him was in motion as if desperately searching for something they'd lost, or leastwise bent on their next purchase or sale—everyone, that is, but the lanky golf-capped character in his patched plus-fours lounging in the doorway of a nearby bakery. Hadn't Max seen the very same character lounging in another doorway a few blocks back? Or was it half a world away? Because, while any comparison to the Balut was invidious, the faces among this coarse congregation might have been the same ones he remembered from Jocheved's native slum. It was as if, minus the mired motorcar or the manhole cover rattling above a subway like a gyrating coin, he'd traveled this far only to wind up where he'd begun.

In any case, despite Jocheved's better judgment, he approached the loiterer, inhaling the aromas of baking strudel that reminded Max of how hungry he was, and inquired, "Zayt moykhl, reydstu Yiddish?"

"What other mother tongue would have me?" the loiterer responded in the vernacular, breaking into a grin that threatened to burst the pustules stippling his downy cheeks.

Subduing a shudder, Max asked him please the way to the Western

Union. The young man instantly hopped down into the street paved in herring bones and broken glass, taking hold of Max's arm to point him in a southerly direction. But no sooner had he done so than another youth, a bulkier one with a buzzard's beak poking from under the bill of his cap, slammed into Max from behind, spinning him like a compass needle one hundred and eighty degrees.

"Klutz!" Max's companion shouted at the youth, who forged ahead through the press of pedestrians without stopping. He let go of Max in order to make an exaggerated show of straightening his new friend's disarranged coat. Then issuing somewhat mystifying directions ("You'll want to turn left at Purim then pass on through the valley of dry bones"), he saluted with a click of the heels, about-faced, and took off like the other into the market melee. Over his shoulder he flung a proverb: "Eyner hot dem baytl," letting loose a fusillade of laughter as he broke into a run, "der tsveyte hot dos gelt." One has the wallet, the other the cash.

Max knew before he checked his pocket that the envelope containing the money was gone.

He realized also that he was lost, famished, exhausted, and now a marked man on a foreign shore where he hadn't a notion of where to turn. Tears welled in his eyes—Jocheved's tears, of course, but trailing through that dingy quarter it was he that was too reluctant to appeal to another stranger for advice. Regarding exactly what? There seemed nothing left to do but carry on trudging aimlessly until he dropped, which was surely imminent. So this was the Golden Land—this wagon rut where the setting sun was reflected in the beer spilled from a growler by the child sent to fetch it? Across the way a fishmonger spread the gills of a carp until it resembled a striking cobra; an evicted family surrounded by a drift of bedding lit a yahrzeit candle on their front stoop. And again Max had the feeling that he'd been here before, an impression corroborated by the reappearance over the road of the Gebirtigs' place of business, to which he'd come full circle. It comforted him somewhat to remember that he was expected. Entering through the Ice Castle's gas-sconced arcade, he located the joint proprietors at adjacent bill-laden desks in their mezzanine office, where he asked if they would mind extending his zayde's storage a little longer. "A few days yet I need to find a funeral plot. . . ."

Father and son exchanged a look, then turned to Max as if he were certifiable. "What are you talking a frozen person?" wondered Asher Gebirtig, and Tsoyl, who'd clearly not fallen far from his father's tree: "Eyz-kugel he thinks we sell here made from human beings." They had never heard of such a thing. And truly, as he stood there before them in desolation, Max himself was almost willing to believe that the rabbi was a fantasy hatched by the demented Jocheved under the influence of her meshugeneh father; her family, the Frostbissens, they were always a peculiar brood. But stuck in a charade whose motions he felt helplessly condemned to go through, he demanded to revisit their treasury, and finding it bare of the reinforced wooden casket with its frozen occupant, threatened the proprietors with the police. Asher laughed heartily and reminded him he was in no position to make threats, while Tsoyl said that if he wanted to play that game, they would see his threats and raise him a couple more. Although Max had little idea what Gebirtig Junior was talking about, in the end he understood there was no recourse left him but to depart the premises and seek solace elsewhere.

Outside, the strange and the familiar tended to cancel one another out, so that Max looked upon the multitudes escaping the brick kilns of their tenements with an undiscriminating eye. He had strayed into a dark street under the El train stanchions, where red lanterns hung from the lintels of narrow frame houses on whose doorsteps women in dusky dressing sacques displayed their ankles. Despite his diminished condition, they nevertheless called out to the pretty boy to follow them upstairs, while other boys, men, and even a nervous, bearded patriarch clutching his phylactery bag heeded their enticements. It was then it occurred to Max that Jocheved might be similarly turned to good use. Perhaps, given his predicament, it was time to end the masquerade and admit defeat: the attempt to become Max Feinshmeker had failed. Max was at any rate a man who, due to his carelessness, would be fingered now by his former employer for retribution. So what better disguise could he assume for his own protection than that of the girl he had disguised himself to protect in the first place? But Jocheved was more stiff-necked than that; for all her indifference to her own extinction, she still reserved in her breast a flicker of something like pride. Max was sui generis; he had no forebears and could not be expected to share her sentiments. But while her sympathy for him made her waver, she owed it to her father to recover the by now melting contents of the family's eroded hope chest.

2000.

Floating somewhere outside of time and space, Bernie heard his name called from a corner of a distant planet.

"Mr. Karp," asked Ms. Drinkwater, his biology teacher; "Bernie Karp," she asked in the throaty voice that irreverent kids would impersonate to her face, "can you shed some light, so to speak, on the process of photosynthesis?"

From his disembodied vantage, Bernie knew many things. He knew the Shi'ur Komah, the measurement of the body of the Creator, whose height was 236,000 leagues; he knew that the measure of a league was three miles, the mile 10,000 cubits, the cubit three spans, and that a single span filled the entire world. He knew that heaven was full of windows through one of which he had glimpsed the hindquarters of the deity Himself and that the vision was as real as it was imaginary. This was a paradox that could not be translated into any earthly tongue and would evaporate upon his reentry into the earth's atmosphere. But of photosynthesis he sadly knew nothing at all, having neglected his Biology homework, just as he had his Remedial Hygiene and Small Engine Repair, to say nothing of his failure to con the square-dancing diagrams for his Phys Ed class. Viewing himself from such an awful distance—an empty husk with kinky hair in a navy sweatshirt, his textbook on the desk before him tented over a compact edition of Ginzberg's *Legends of the Jews*—Bernie felt suffused with pity. He no longer saw the classroom with its laboratory paraphernalia through the lens of Paradise; instead he saw the room in all its dreariness, the air riven by desires trapped within its phlegm-colored walls. It was an ill-starred environment that touched off the compassion that signaled the moment when his free-floating essence, lonely for the clueless youth he'd abandoned, reinhabited the stoop-shouldered body of Bernie Karp.

He was welcomed back to Olam haZeh, to the ordinary world, by the uncontrollable sniggering of his peers over his inattention to Ms. Drinkwater's query—though his abrupt animation prompted a universal intake of air. No sooner had he returned to himself, however, than he experienced a painful sense of contraction, the cosmos once again confined to the narrow dimensions of his protuberant skull. He could still recall the concept that sparked his transports: how the stories of Torah, as retold in *The Legends*, functioned as templates for locating the coordinates of a vast hidden world, but all that was reduced to foggy abstraction now. And as to the definition of the process of photosynthesis—A nechtiker tog, as the rabbi would say: Forget about it.

"What was the question?" asked Bernie, in an attempt to buy time.

The teacher, in her sensible serge, her face bleached from the chalk dust that earned her the nickname The Abominable Snow Woman, rolled her eyes, which was the cue for the class to resume its sniggering. Bernie understood the strategy; other teachers had employed it as well: They ingratiated themselves with recalcitrant classes by making themselves complicit in the mockery of Bernie Karp. The butt of much humor herself, the elephantine Ms. Drinkwater was taking the opportunity to deflect some of it in Bernie's direction. "Photosynthesis," she repeated, "the subject of the experiments we've been conducting all week. What is it?"

He made a stab. "It's got something to do with chlorophyll." And on second thought: "Or is it fluoride? Something they put in the water so you can't have babies?" More laughter, though some of it cautious, as if he might after all be correct.

Realizing she'd given the class too much rope, Ms. Drinkwater tried to reel them back in, calling on a pet student who could be relied on for a rote response. But the damage was done and the class remained ungovernable, passing notes and tossing parts of dissected crayfish until the bell rang, when the teacher asked Bernie to please stay behind. By now he knew the drill. She would express an obligatory concern for his pathological woolgathering and send him once again to the nurse's station, from which the flinty Ms. Bissenet would pass him on to Mr. Murtha, the school's resident psychologist. Mr. Murtha, whose years of dealing with troubled adolescents had left him a little unhinged himself, would welcome him back like a long-lost nephew. Prefatory to nothing, he would lecture him on the significance of the new millennium and the need to be prepared for the coming apocalypse; then having sown sufficient confusion, he would conclude that their talk had done them both a world of good. That was how it had gone after the day in study hall when a coalition of jocks and preppies had consigned an oblivious Bernie to the top of the library bookshelves; and again after he'd been found in the trash compactor by the janitor, Mr. Spiller, who came that close to turning him into bonemeal. So the boy had no reason to believe that today would be any exception.

"What's new, Bernie?" inquired the psychologist with an immoderate grin, as if a melon slice had been wedged between his cheeks. "Still having your," making rabbit ears with his fingers to signify quotation marks, "out-of-body episodes?"

Bernie allowed that that was the case.

Mr. Murtha licked a pinkie to plaster a cowlick that refused to lie down, giving his unruly hair the look of ruffled feathers. He loosened and tightened the clasp of his string necktie as if playing a slide trombone. "Why don't you describe again in your own words what you think is happening to you?"

Bernie scrunched his face in thought. Gone was his wary impulse to keep everything secret; and there were times of late when he felt almost reckless, almost ready to tell the world, while on the other hand he suspected he may have already confided too much in this dickhead. "I think," he said after some consideration, "I'm starting to outgrow myself."

"Uh-hmm." The psychologist nodded before letting his grin expand beyond the diameter of his freckled face, the melon slice becoming a canoe. "Looks to me like you're shrinking." And it was true that, since he was no longer tempted by the greasy diet that had sustained him since infancy, no longer particularly interested in food at all, Bernie's physique had become almost angular. The psychologist leaned back in his chair, twining his fingers behind his head. "Y'know, Bernie, I get all kinds in here—kids that whittle their own arms to bloody stobs, kids that want to blow us all to hell, bad seeds with eyes like lizards and no conscience to speak of. I see girls who soak their tampons in liquid methedrine, boys who can't keep their peckers in their pants, but I never had one yet that couldn't keep his soul in his body. You know what I think, Bernie?" He seemed to be waiting for Bernie to venture a guess.

"You think I'm a wack job?"

"Did I say that?" gasped Mr. Murtha, capsizing the canoe. "I never said that." Fluttering his eyelids. "But now that you mention it . . ."

Then he let the boy know, entre nous, that he viewed Bernie's spontaneous fugue states as good practice for the Rapture, that maybe there was hope for at least some Jews in these final days. "However," said the psychologist, "much as I've enjoyed our little sessions, let's face it, we're getting nowhere." Raising himself to a posture of official rectitude, Mr. Murtha then declared that, in his capacity as protector of the emotional welfare of the students of Tishimingo High, it behooved him to notify Bernie's parents of his disorder.

If in agreement about little else, Mr. and Mrs. Karp showed a solid front in their antipathy to the school psychologist. It was inexcusable that he had dragged them away from their busy schedules (Mrs. Karp had had to cancel an electrolysis treatment) to inform them of what they already knew, that their son was subject to daydreaming. But despite their obvious resistance, Mr. Murtha, in his ex cathedra mode, delivered his diagnosis with unfazed equanimity.

"It's my opinion that your son," shooting Bernie a sidelong grin that the boy expected to spread out of all proportion, though today the psychologist managed to keep it in check, "your son is suffering from a rare strain of what might be termed static epilepsy—that is, epilepsy minus the grand mal seizures but still a variety of what we call saint's disease . . ."

Mr. Karp looked to his wife (who told him, "Don't look at me") to confirm that the man was speaking nonsense, wasn't he? He had enough on his plate with his own affairs, which had lately come to include Rabbi ben Zephyr's increasingly demanding commercial initiatives. Seldom deliberately rude, since you never knew who might be a potential client, Julius Karp thought that in this case he could make an exception.

"The kid's what?" he protested, turning again to his wife who perfunctorily supplied him with Bernie's age. "Sixteen? Who's normal at sixteen? So he sometimes drifts away to cloud cuckoo land. This is so bad?" He appealed once more to Mrs. Karp, whose blasé nod seemed to imply that narcosis was a Karp family custom.

Mr. Murtha reminded them that, as a consequence of his condition, Bernie was also flunking out of school. It was the first his parents had heard of it.

"What's the matter with you?" his father sharply asked his son.

Still marveling at the psychologist's ability to control his quirks, Bernie was not altogether engaged in the dialogue. "I'm a dunce?" he offered reflexively.

His father seemed to accept this as an adequate explanation, though he was aware that his son's academic performance, never impressive, had reached its nadir since the thawing of the formerly cryonic old man. But since Rabbi Eliezer's burgeoning fiscal empire had become (beyond the appliance emporium) Mr. Karp's chief concern, the tzaddik was now above reproach in his mind.

"It's a phase," insisted Mr. Karp. "He'll grow out of it."

"That's what he says," replied Mr. Murtha, who, turning to share the private joke with Bernie, could no longer suppress a crescent grin that threatened to eclipse his face.

Eager to escape, Mr. Karp conceded that some manner of professional attention was probably in order.

BUT DR. TUNKELMAN, the family physician—the Tic Tac on his tongue failing to hide the brandy on his breath—gave Bernie a clean bill of health and pooh-poohed the idea that the boy might require psychotherapy. He assured the Karps that all the kid needed was a little more meat on his bones. Bernie was almost disappointed that they weren't going to lock him up; he'd imagined himself chained to the wall of an asylum where paying visitors would view him on Sundays. It was an appealing image in its way, since he'd become partial of late to the notion of ascetic deprivation: Fasting, he'd decided, made him more responsive to transcendental phenomena. But at home the issue of mental imbalance, a taboo subject in polite households, was never mentioned, the prevailing attitude being that any problem if ignored long enough would simply go away. Besides, in view of his mother's taste for sedation, the son was a regular chip off the old block. Meanwhile Bernie's father was more distracted than usual, keeping (with the help of Mr. Grusom, his cagey accountant) the books for Rabbi ben Zephyr's House of Enlightenment, which had recently moved to more ample quarters in a former Baptist tabernacle on a manicured knoll fringed in lilac trees. Julius Karp and Ira Grusom were working overtime to itemize the rabbi's God-realization packages, from the economical fast-track to cosmic consciousness to the costlier but more scenic route to self-illumination.

What had lingered most in Bernie's mind since the family meeting with Mr. Murtha was the reference to his recent birthday (for which he'd requested a subscription to *Commentary* and received instead a new watch), because sixteen was three years past time for the bar mitzvah he'd never had. Suddenly he felt duty-bound to remedy the oversight. Unmissed at home, he took the hour-long bus ride downtown after school to the old Anshei Mishneh shul just off North Main Street. A rundown brick-and-mortar building flanked by vacant lots, it contained an authentic cheder Torah, a stuffy room with a coughing radiator, water-stained walls, and shelves crammed with moldering volumes of Talmud and Midrash. Acutely self-conscious at first, Bernie soon grew accustomed to seating himself at the long table, where he traced with his finger the Hebrew letters whose shapes left corresponding vapor trails in his brain. He liked poring over pages as brittle as autumn leaves while recalling the Talmudic dictum: "Turn it and turn it, for everything is in it." The old men, often short of a tenth to make a minyan, welcomed him, inviting him to daven with them at their ma'arev prayers. A skeleton crew of old-timers fanning the dying flame of tradition in an otherwise assimilated Southern community, they made much of the serious young man come to study and pray. But while he enjoyed the liturgy, liked crowning his head with the dome of a kippah, Bernie felt himself to be a dissembler in their midst. His guilt was exacerbated by the silence he kept when he overheard complaints about the old fraud who'd set up a Kabbalah center in the suburbs, for Rabbi Eliezer had become a subject of much indignant chin-wagging among local Jews. And who, after all, was the party responsible for having unleashed on a gullible public the musty savant?

But on the other hand, when Bernie thought about preparing for his belated bar mitzvah, Eliezer ben Zephyr was still the only adviser he cared to apply to. While his cool reception from the rebbe on his single visit to the center did not augur well for their future relations, Bernie had never developed the habit of holding a grudge. Besides, he still retained a blind belief in old Eliezer's sagacity, and was determined to make another trip to see him in his new quarters, where they could perhaps start over from scratch.

Then an unforeseen incident caused him to postpone the trip. It happened when, after hearing what he'd perceived as the music of the spheres over the school cafeteria's public address, Bernie came back to himself inside a locker along an upstairs corridor. Light invaded the cramped space through a louver in the metal door that put him in mind of gills, so that he felt, due in part to the unnatural position into which his body was squeezed, that he might be inside the belly of a fish—albeit one with a Fiona Apple poster plastered to its innards. It was a peaceful notion and, done in as he was from his celestial navigation, Bernie made only a half-hearted effort to jimmy the mechanism that would have released the door from inside, had it not been locked in any case from without. Able at times to escape his own skin, he lacked the wherewithal to free himself from his present confinement, or even to bang on the interior till he was heard. Instead he adjusted his bones into a snug fetal tuck to await his discovery: Eventually caught, the fish would give up its prey. He was awakened from his brief nap when a crowbar jarred loose the padlock and the locker door sprang open, revealing the same prune-faced janitor who'd extracted him from the garbage compactor. A black man in a skullcap fashioned from a lady's stocking, his querulous expression suggested it was more than his job was worth to have to attend to such affairs. He accepted with a brusque nod the thanks of the girl who'd apparently engaged his services, then departed, leaving her to ask Bernie, antagonistically, "How did you get in there?"

Bernie confessed he hadn't the least idea.

The girl exhaled a puff of air that lifted the dark fringe of her bangs like a wave. "You're that loser kid who's always tuning out," she accused, her accent bordering on a hillbilly twang.

He saw no reason to deny it.

"Of all the lockers in the whole damn school, why'd they have to stuff you in mine?"

Again he was without a ready explanation. She stared at him another beat as if inspecting a rare insect, then demanded, "Well, get out!"

He explained apologetically that he didn't think he could move; he'd been in one position so long that his muscles had seized up. "What muscles?" she sneered, then reached into the coffin-size space, grabbed his arm, and yanked him until he tumbled onto the scuffed linoleum floor. From there he began the painful process of unfolding himself, looking up at the girl as he did so, noting that, no thanks to her makeup and scruffy attire, she was almost pretty. She wore torn jeans and a bulky, black leather jacket over a cameo-pink T-shirt, her feet (turned out like a dancer's) shod in hooflike yellow clogs. Coltishly skinny, she'd converted a perfectly pleasing mouth into a crooked cupid's bow with violet lip gloss, and her eyes, an aqueous jade, were made aggressively feline by her shadowed squint. Harlequin bangs framed her forehead like a bouquet of parentheses. Her outfit was the kind some girls affected as a punkish fashion statement, though on her the clothes looked as if they might have come by their wear naturally. And while her accent typed her as working-class, the kind of poor girl who was automatically classified a slut in the high-school pecking order, her attitude dared you to classify her at all.

Seeing that he was still having difficulty with his stiffened limbs, she took his arm again and hauled him to his feet. Bernie thanked her, registering the shock of prehensile female fingers on his flesh. Then the blood suddenly left his head and the girl had to support him once again lest he swoon, and when she removed her hands from his arm, he was a little regretful to find he could stand on his own. He waited for her to depart; she'd done her bit, shown him a kindness beyond the call that should make her feel pleased with herself—Bernie winced at his own cynical observation. Why didn't she just walk away?

Biting her lip as if literally chewing on a thought, she asked him—while passing students gawked at the girl who condescended to speak to Bernie Karp—in a voice just above a whisper, "So where do you go?"

"Eh?"

"Where do you go when, y'know, like when you go off the way you do?"

Bernie suffered a tremor whose source was either the bowels of the earth or his own, he couldn't have said. No one other than Mr. Murtha, who merely taunted him, had ever bothered to ask. He told himself it was intrusive; she had no right to pry; his exaltations belonged exclusively to him. But here was a girl his own age weathering the stares of her peers to inquire about his experience, and what he felt despite his best efforts to resist it was gratitude.

"Heaven, mostly," he replied. And there it was: the answer fluttering from his mouth like a moth he hadn't known was trapped inside.

"Cool." Pronounced with the requisite nasal diphthong to rhyme with *cruel*, though from her it sounded a touch ironic.

A silence ensued during which Bernie shuffled in place, wondering if she, too, were only mocking him. Feeling altogether too vulnerable, he was ready to walk away from her but found that he lacked the will; maybe the janitor would have to pry him loose again. Accustomed as he was to being the butt of jokes and abuse, what appeared on the surface as honest curiosity unnerved him. Yet he, who considered escape his signature feat, was helpless to devise a convenient means of extricating himself from her gaze.

"So what's it like?" she wanted to know, and Bernie felt as if he were being drawn out onto thin ice.

"I can't really describe it," he stammered.

She frowned. "What do you mean? You're not allowed to describe it or you don't have the words?"

"Whatever," was his witless reply.

Her fierce squint returned. "Then what's the point of it? What's the point of going where you go?"

This sounded downright combative. What's the point of breathing? he wondered. What's the point of being born? "What's the point of anything?" he answered, marveling at the hint of anger in his tone. Did a thing have to be described to make it worth doing? Though he knew that his irritation at her for asking was only the corollary to his irritation with himself for his inability to explain; and it frustrated him to the point of tears that in the face of the great adventure of his previously uneventful life, he remained tongue-tied. Then the bell rang, signaling the end of the lunch period, and Bernie took the opportunity to say so long forever to the girl.

But she was dawdling there in the glass brick vestibule amid the after-school stampede, the students dispersing toward their various clubs, cliques, and satanic cabals. Pretending not to see the girl, Bernie sloped toward the exit and nearly reached the threshold, where she managed as if by magic to plant herself athwart his path.

"So who do you read?" she asked, adjusting the bulging book bag slung over her shoulder.

He paused, looked askance at her, then recited a catalogue of immortals: "Abraham Abulafia, Moses de Leon, Nachman of Bratslav . . ." Thinking, *That should shut her up*; though why should he want to shut her up?

Digesting the names without blinking, she inquired, "Do you ever read Herman Hessie?"

He was unfamiliar with the author.

"What about Carlos Castaneder or *Autobiography of a Yogi*?"

"I can't say that I have."

"They write a lot about altered states of consciousness."

"Really."

"Yeah."

There followed an awkward silence the complement to the one they'd shared earlier that day, during which Bernie found himself wishing—though not as hard as he might—for another bell to ring. Still he could think of nothing to say.

"You ever took LSD?" she asked.

He shook his head. "You?"

"Oncet." It was a syllable from a foreign tongue. "I looked in a mirror and saw cottonmouths crawling out my eyes and nose, which is like pretty cliché. I can do better than that without drugs." She sniffed disdainfully and Bernie involuntarily sniffed along with her. Who was this person, anyway, with her pudding-bowl hairdo and tomboyish manner, the green eyes that looked, despite the heavy hand with which she laid on her mascara, as if their severity were in the service of resisting tears? Her single earring was a silver ankh dangling from a safety pin, and Bernie wondered if her body bore strange markings in secluded places. He felt as embarrassed for her sake as for his own: since whatever her reputation, it would be compromised from now on for having been seen in conversation with the major laughingstock of Tishimingo High.

But anxious as he was to part company with her, he was equally aware of the fact that she had waited for him; no one had ever waited for him before. He couldn't linger, though; there was the bus to catch to the downtown shul, an afternoon ritual on its way to becoming routine. After a day in uncongenial classrooms, never mind Dumpsters and lockers, he was eager to return to the pages whose antique code he hoped, with the help of broken-backed grammars, soon to crack. Then the words, once he'd determined their meanings, would acquire the weight of the thing itself, words that didn't so much denote as embody whatever they spelled. He was about to make his excuses—he had places to go—when she volunteered her name.

"I'm Lou." Her expression challenged him to make a remark. "It's short for Lou Ella which sounds like Louella but it's really Lou Ella." Bernie was perplexed. "Two names," she explained, her humorless lack of inflection coming on as provocative.

"Right," he said. Then to make up for not having asked, he asked her, "Lou Ella what?"

"Tuohy."

He tried to wipe from his face the look that had congealed there—too late. "Excuse me?"

"Sounds like somebody spit, don't it? It's a real trailer trash name because, hey, trailer trash c'est moi." Again she seemed to be waiting in defiance for some remark. When it didn't come, she added as if by way of vindication, "It's Irish. The name, it's Irish."

"Uh-huh," was all Bernie could manage, thinking: This is getting out of hand. Here he was being shmoozed by a creature (make that critter) from a South he knew only from hearsay, the unreconstructed South of tarpaper shacks and cotton-eyed sharecroppers with teeth like potsherds. She seemed a misfit even in a school full of every variety of freak, but she was also a girl. She had legs, however gangly, and breasts, if barely developed, and no doubt what the rebbe would have called oyse mokem, a you-know-what. What's more, she dared to talk to him even as she dared him to talk to her. Then before he could decide which of them was the more jeopardized by their mutual commerce, mirabile dictu, they were walking together into the cloudy February afternoon.

IF SHE'D BEEN homely maybe he wouldn't have felt so squeamish. But pretty trumped trailer trash, and he knew that if she'd wanted she could have run with the semipopulars; in her case outcast was something she seemed to have elected to be. As it was, while Bernie never sought her out, she continued to turn up, and though he told himself she was a nuisance who distracted him from more pressing concerns, he was flattered by the attention she paid him. During lunch in the turd-green Nutrition Center where he was used to sitting alone over half-eaten fishsticks, or after school in front of the flagpole from which a disturbed student had once hanged himself, she would corner him. Usually she was on her own, though once or twice he'd seen her peel away from girls even more stateless than herself to catch up with him. She had followed him to the bus stop and on one occasion, when he'd foregone his afternoon trip to the downtown shul (on her account?), part-way home. He thought about telling her flatly to leave him alone, then thought better of it when he realized that he would miss her; yet he never felt quite at ease in her company. After their initial conversation concerning his trances the subject was never broached again, though Bernie knew it was always on her mind. Why else would she hang around? He could feel it in her vigilance: She wanted to be there when he lapsed into rapture again. But when they spoke, always sporadically—for

neither seemed able to find a topic beyond the elephant in their midst—
they talked mostly about neutral matters: the pathologies of certain teachers and classmates, the utter pointlessness of going to school.

She never smiled, though once, acting on an erratic impulse, Bernie
had tried to make her. "Two cannibals are eating a clown," offering the
single joke in his repertoire. "One says to the other, 'Does this taste funny
to you?'" Nothing, not a snicker, though his delivery wasn't all it might
have been; still, she needn't have looked at him as if he'd passed gas. Occasionally she would volunteer some unsolicited piece of information about
her past: She had come to Memphis from the Arkansas Ozarks when her
mother landed a clerical job at Federal Express that had somehow fizzled,
leaving her consigned thereafter to manual labor. She had no idea where
her worthless-as-tits-on-a-boar father was, nor any interest in finding out.
She missed the mountains and the piney woods, though she liked living
close to the Wolf River, a minor tributary of the Mississippi which to
Bernie's mind was little more than a glorified drainage ditch. She didn't
actually live in a trailer, though their tract house—a shotgun affair in a
treeless subdivision the other side of the interstate—was no more commodious than a double-wide. It was largely empty but for some sticks of
rented furniture and the teething toys of her baby sister, Sue Lily, whom
she adored and cared for while her mother was at work. Her room she described as if it existed in another dimension: how it was littered with books
you had to pick your way through like "the fallen bricks of Jericho." (She
could be fanciful.) She recited their titles: *Women Who Run with Wolves*,
The Celestine Prophecy, *Thus Spake Zarathustra*, *The Mists of Avalon*; she
mentioned the divas she admired: Lotte Lenya, Avril LaVigne; the journal
she kept; the poetry of Rumi and Arthur Rimbaud. Then, as casually as
she might have asked him the time of day, she invited him to come see her
room for himself. But that was later on.

In the meantime she continued to ration the biographical tidbits that
Bernie felt ashamed of not having requested in the first place. He knew she
wasn't naturally talkative, and her confidences, not easily rendered, were

meant to provoke similar utterances from him. But he couldn't get past
the fact that she was a girl, and regardless of how dramatically his own life
had been altered since the Great Thaw (his term) Bernie Karp had never
mastered the knack of talking to girls. Of course this one was different;
this one followed him around. He'd spent his years in a virtual sleepwalk,
his small joys derived from spasms of passing interest that, always a secre-
tive kid, he kept to himself. Now an immeasurable joy had awakened him
to another reality and, friendless as he was, he had a desire to relate what
he'd learned, but the vocabulary for communicating that information was
unavailable. Once in a while, however, he might submit apropos of nothing some crumb of dogma gleaned from his reading:

"Did you know, there are 903 different kinds of death? The most difficult one is the croup, which is choking, and the easiest is death by kiss,
which is likened to drawing a hair out of milk. This is from Tractate
Berakhot, and from the medieval *Sefer Yetzirat* we read . . ."

She would look at him expectantly, but when the words, detached as
they were from emotional moorings, petered out, her anticipation turned
to disappointment and even scorn. So they walked primarily in silence
along suburban streets, strayed through the thickety woods behind the
school, and strolled beside the banks of the septic river through the remnant of a slate-gray February into an even bleaker March. Having abandoned his trips to the downtown synagogue and shelved for the meantime
his plans for bar mitzvah, Bernie would sit with her in a booth at a coffee
bar in the very strip mall from which the rabbi's academy had decamped.
It was clear to him that Lou was making sacrifices to be with him; he knew
that even her lusterless friends now snubbed her, that those who'd written
him off as a wing nut (which included all and sundry) now banished her
to the same category. He felt he owed her something and resented that she
should make him feel that way. At the same time he was thankful that she
no longer interrogated him, though once as they sat nursing cocoa amid
the strumming of a lank-haired folk singer to whom no one was listening,
she had the temerity to ask him,

"So when do you reckon on leaving your body again?"

She might have been inquiring after his adherence to a railroad time-table. Bernie assured her he didn't know, that anything might trigger an involuntary departure though he remained unable to take flight at will. Clearly impatient with his response, she said almost testily, "Let me know when you feel one coming on again." Then prey to an apparent change of heart, she softened, hastening to add coquettishly, "And when you go, maybe you could take me with you?"

The question surprised and confounded him. Who did she think she was? Who, for that matter, did *he* think she was? It was enough that she pried into the private domain of his spiritual life; now she aspired to enter it physically as well? Again, as upon their first meeting, he wanted to flee. A sudden deep distrust of the girl stung his heart. Okay, so here on earth he was a dweeb, a regular kunyehlemel, but aloft he was something else: like in that tale of Rabbi Eliezer's about the country that contained within it all countries, and in that country was a city that contained all the cities of that country that contained all countries, and in that city a house that contained all the cities of that country that contained all countries, and in that house a man who bore all this within him — and that man was he, the boy Bernie Karp, when he was enraptured. Nothing in the world he'd inhabited these sixteen years was as real as his extraterrestrial for-ays; everything else was phony: his neighborhood, phony; the houses with their plantation colonnades and lantern turrets, phony; his family was phony. Nothing could touch the places he'd ascended to for authenticity. While on the other hand, nothing on earth — he had to concede — was quite as real to him as Lou Ella Tuohy. But nobody could accompany him on his excursions, and if he had been able to take her with him, which was impossible, wouldn't he be depriving the planet of a precious natural resource? It was a sentiment he could no more articulate than he could explain where it was he went.

What was abundantly clear, however, was that while she kept him teth-ered to the terrestrial (for he'd yet to make an ascent since he'd met her) you couldn't really blame the girl. After all, she'd never inspired in him the kind of appetite that had consumed him in the days before the rabbi's unfreezing. This was a good thing, for as the *Shulchan Arukh* stated unequivocally, he who gazes at even the small finger of a woman in order to enjoy its sight commits a sin. Not that Bernie set much store by such prohibitions, but if life happened to comply with them, then so much the better. Lou, of course, tended to mask her looks more than augment them, though her soft features were never totally obscured, and even without the subtler cosmetic embellishments of the popular girls, she was fetching. But preoccupied with loftier concerns, Bernie felt no carnal itch for her whatsoever, and since desire was not an issue between them, he had lately begun to relax in her company. But that was before this afternoon, when she'd gone and spoiled their friendly relations with her invasive request. And then, compounding the outrage, she made another, inviting him in her annoyingly offhand manner to come see her room.

IT WAS MUCH as she'd described it, if a little less otherworldly: the wilderness of dog-eared paperbacks — some draped in mildly gamy castoff garments — scattered about the floor, the Matisse dancers thumbtacked to the wall, the ancient marmalade cat with its molted tail resembling a fishbone, the peacock feathers in a Mason jar. To get there they had traversed the living room, its walls as flimsy as a Japanese teahouse, where her mother, a faded woman in Capri pants and hair curlers, sat on a ruptured sofa in front of the TV. She was dandling on her knee a sticky-faced infant with eyes as dull as Orphan Annie's, watching a game show. Lou had introduced a fidgeting Bernie, whom her weary mother ignored, reminding her daughter that her shift at the Hub started in an hour. Lou said yassum, then hustled Bernie into her bedroom and locked the door behind them, inviting him to sit on her bed between the cat and a family of pretzel-limbed sock monkeys. (He would have preferred to sit elsewhere, but there was no chair.) She put on a CD of a singer with a French accent, whose adenoidal trill sounded as if she were strapped to Julius Karp's vibrating recliner. Bernie looked toward the locked door as the girl settled herself beside him, opening the clasp of a quilted diary filled with crabbed writing, from which she began hesitantly to read.

"He comes back to me from the outer reaches of the galaxy like Rimbawd the poet, who come home with one leg to his mama and baby sister telling stories about crossing deserts with a caravan of guns and slaves. I give him tea with opium and look after him like that other Lou, which is my namesake, who looked after Nitchie, Rilkie, and Frood. . . ."

Bernie was just beginning to realize that the person to whom she was ministering in her fantasy was him, when she abruptly left off reading to announce, "It's all a crock, id'n it? Truth is, Bernie Karp, you don't really know shit from Shinola."

He had started to tremble, feeling never so out of place. What did she mean by making him the captive audience to her flaky journal? Did she think she was casting some kind of a spell? He was all for exploring the heights, was himself a veteran of celestial altitudes, but this girl contained unplumbed depths that frightened him. Also he noticed—all right, so he'd already noticed—that she was wearing a skirt today, a short, tiered denim mini, and her spindly, criss-crossed legs were encased in striped woolen warmers pulled above the knee. Bernie had never been so conscious of her legs, and when she caught his eye, he became aware that she was aware.

In the face of what he took as her flung gauntlet, he understood it was now his turn to make some reciprocal disclosure. "It all started," he began, working hard to overcome his diffidence, "when I found an old rabbi under the frozen foods in my parents' deep freeze—" But no sooner had he embarked on the tale than she interrupted him.

"It's okay, Bernie, you don't have to make up stories on my account. This ain't a competition." Having said which, she tucked her knees under her chin, allowing the skirt to fall back, revealing the blue-veined underside of her thighs above the stockings and the scallop-shell gusset of her ribbed underpants. Bernie grew dizzy, and as Lou watched the blood depart his head for nether regions, she grinned. It was the first time she had smiled in his presence.

"So," she said speculatively, "if you can't carry me to heaven one way, maybe you can take me another?" Then she pulled up her sweater to expose her small breasts with their nipples the size of pink catkins. Her ribcage framed the hollow of her belly like a pair of wings in whose shadow the tattoo of a tiny scarab crawled from her navel.

Bernie straightaway lost his head. Before his brain could intercede to insist that he had no interest in the girl's bare anatomy, he lurched forward to embrace her, his nose and lips nuzzling her breasts. Her rapid breathing fueled his own, which chuffed like a locomotive as he felt her hands caressing his spine; then she was yanking at the waist of his jeans, overlarge since he'd lost so much weight, pulling them down along with his shorts over his bony hips without bothering to unzip them. Now they were tussling, embroiled in a heedless roughhouse while trying to stifle each other's nascent hilarity, rolling about as if caught in a wildfire that tickled rather than burned. More clothes were shucked in the process, though Bernie, swept into a near delirium, couldn't have said exactly how. During the fracas the cat was displaced, rearranging itself in its lassitude among the monkeys, themselves upended like bodies tumbled under a steam shovel's plough. (The image reared up as a last desperate damper to passion, then just as quickly dissolved.) When she touched him at his root, the first intimate touch he'd ever received from another, he sprang to such rigid attention that he thought his organ would pop its cork and fizz like a Roman candle. She canted her hips to remove her powder blue panties with one hand while holding onto him with the other, guiding him toward the bow-strung sinews of her parted thighs. He almost wept to realize what was happening, how she was about to introduce him to the waking world's premier mystery; but just as he was poised to enter the flesh of a living girl, feeling himself more present on the material plane than ever before, his soul brimmed over and was launched clear out of his body. Looking back from the stratosphere with a thousand eyes, Bernie glimpsed the frustrated diminution of his desire and heard the girl saying before he surrendered himself to eternity,

"If you can't take me with you, at least bring me something back."

1908.

Until he was thrown out on his ear from his Aunt Dobeh and Uncle Zaynvil's apartment, Shmerl Karp had no leisure to enjoy the clamorous streets of the Jewish East Side. The eviction itself did not particularly distress him; worse things could have happened: He might for instance have remained shackled to relations who used him for a Hebrew slave. But the circumstances surrounding the eviction left him confirmed in his belief in the inherent evils of technology.

For a time Shmerl was satisfied that the innumerable tasks he was assigned throughout the working day—a day which began at dawn and continued into the evening—were a fitting penance; they were the chastening he deserved for the arrogance of his messianic pursuits back in Shpinsk. So he never complained on discovering that he had ceased to be a guest of the Oyzers in their handshake tenement, a discovery that became apparent after his first cup of tea. Childless, the choleric couple had welcomed him into their home with the assurance that he would be the son they never had, then promptly set him to work. He dutifully accepted his role as scullery boy and swabber of slopjars; he swept floors, fetched coal, baited rat traps, hung flypaper, and swatted cockroaches the size of tortoises. In the parlor sweatshop to which the apartment was converted every day of the week, Shabbos included, he functioned as general factotum. He received the bundles of piecework the infant shleppers delivered regularly from an uptown contractor and tied the finished waists and vests into bales slated for a retail jobber, also uptown. He kept oiled and in prime running condition the loop-stitch sewing machines that his Uncle Zaynvil, chewing the wet stub of a cigar, rented to the weary-winged operators who arrived with their greasy lunch bags at daybreak.

Though his tasks kept him largely fettered to the tenement, Shmerl never complained; America was as intimidating as it was enticing, and the unventilated apartment was a safe enough harbor for the time being. The streets, his dour Tante Dobeh assured him with a husky "Feh!" were fleshpots; they were places of pagan amusements in cruel contrast to the surrounding squalor. This much Shmerl could see from the Oyzers' fire escape. But the city was also a showcase of marvels: the telegraphs, rotary engines, safety hoisters, electric chairs, moving pictures, and elevated railroads that were conveying the New World into a revolutionary new age. Despite having yet to set eyes on all these prodigies, Shmerl was aware of them, his very blood purling along with their hum. But something was missing from the rush to mechanize everything in Creation, he concluded (on the evidence of instinct alone), and that something was, well, the yetser tov, the good intention. The machines of America, he was persuaded, were inspired by Moloch rather than the holy spirit, which seemed to be strictly an Old World phenomenon. Wonder rebbes, lamed vovniks, and every species of hallowed figure that had presided over his youthful imagination remained behind in the Russian Pale. Nor did this new world seem to offer a natural environment of the type that nourished such souls, let alone the denizens of Yenne Velt, the Other Side; for scarcely a tree or a blade of grass could be found in the ghetto, or at least that part of it viewed from a window on Rivington Street. This left only the man-made environment and the harried men and women, worn to shadows by need and greed, who inhabited it. Shmerl supposed on the one hand that, with his intuitive knowledge of the way things worked, he was eminently suited to his new situation; while on the other he had no wish to employ his skills in a place where they could never come to a sanctified fruition—even should those skills result in his being admired by the opposite sex.

So he kept his nose to the Oyzers' grindstone, picking threads from the finished shirtwaists, wrestling mattresses like recalcitrant drunkards onto the fire escape to be aired; he even learned to operate the eight-pound pressing irons attached by extension springs to the ceiling hooks that rendered them mobile. These had salubrious benefits, increasing the wiry musculature of his upper body (crooked spine notwithstanding) in the manner of the scientific weight-training methods of Eugene Sandow. Meanwhile Shmerl picked up more snatches of the American language—*cockamamie, mishmash, bumerkeh, ayeshdworry*—from the whispered conversations he overheard among the Oyzers' otherwise taciturn employees. They were men and women of an indeterminate age, their ashen faces and arms stained liver brown and madder blue from the fabrics they worked with. With eyes leached of light, they seldom looked up from their labor, only to check the time on the clock whose hands Aunt Dobeh moved craftily forward or backward to regulate their progress.

Confusing his deformity with dimwittedness, Shmerl's aunt and uncle had assumed that operating a sewing machine was too complex an exercise for their greenhorn nephew to master, at least at this early stage of his apprenticeship; and it was true that, while he had grasped the concept of the mechanism at a glance—as well as acquired its nomenclature: shuttle hook, bobbin winder, needle bar, presser foot, feed dog—sewing hems, plaques, and darts involved an expertise he had no special desire to learn. Still, he attended to the machines, as shapely in their fashion as ladies' calves; he folded them affectionately into their wrought-iron treadles to convert the factory back to a parlor for the couple of hours before the Oyzers (in identical pear-shaped union suits) went to bed. But by day the parlor was once again a beehive of unremitting activity—"a choir of Singers," quipped Uncle Zaynvil, an inflexible taskmaster not ordinarily known for his humor. Nobody laughed; nobody ever laughed or turned their head or left their work unnecessarily, preferring to suffer from chronic constipation rather than have their movements interpreted as slacking from the task at hand. Because the least unsanctioned action could result in having your wages docked or worse. Nor could Shmerl, despite his blood relation — a connection the Oyzers sometimes called into question — expect any privileged treatment from his bosses.

Sometimes he saw the romance in his drudgery. He thought of Jacob toiling seven years only to be double-crossed by his future father-in-law, of Joseph's patience in Egypt before attaining his nobility. But Shmerl's labors were merely for the purpose of lining the pockets of his miserly aunt and uncle, and while he disdained the ambition of a Joseph, he found himself, after some weeks had passed, entertaining a subversive thought or two. Lately his Tante Dobeh's potted meat and rubbery farfel had seemed small compensation for the long hours of mindless toil; nor did their table talk, which mostly concerned the markup on the needles and scissors they sold their employees, keep him amused. He was made further restless from browsing the personals column of his uncle's discarded *Forverts, The Jewish Daily Forward.* In them, young men represented themselves as exemplary candidates for matrimony, spinsters advertised their dowries, and marriage brokers guaranteed prospective bridegrooms a "zivug hashomayim," a match made in heaven. Wasn't it time, thought Shmerl in his lonely hours, that he should consider starting a family of his own? Didn't the Talmud state that a man without a wife was without joy or blessing? And the Zohar went even further, declaring that the unattached individual is not yet a whole being. But as long as he remained in thrall to the Oyzers' grinding gesheft, he would never have the opportunity or the means to become his own person. At length his frustrated thoughts sought an alternative outlet. Running the irons over a swatch of calico or hauling up a bucket of coal in the dumbwaiter, he might wonder: What would happen if the sewing machines were harnessed to, say, a single enormous dynamo? There were a thousand such sweat factories in the ghetto, each with their pallid operators pumping their treadles with a grim tenacity; yet the whole collective endeavor remained stationary. But combine their efforts and the machines were a potential source of energy that could at the very least electrify all of Manhattan Island, and perhaps elevate this modern Babylon to exalted heights.

Shmerl told himself that such thoughts were foolish and dangerously out of place, but he could no longer ignore his own discontent. There came a night when, lying in his nest of scraps in front of the stove installed in an empty fireplace, he couldn't sleep for his rampant imaginings. Despite the cold weather that gripped the city, the tenement remained close and stale from the lingering vinegar odor of the departed laborers. Eyeing the machines, Shmerl decided that he'd suffered his servitude long enough to warrant a holiday. Not that there was anywhere in particular he wanted to go, not on the planet at any rate, since his fancies tended toward more empyrean destinations. With his latest brainstorm brewing, he reasoned that a minor experiment would hardly disturb the fabric of the universe, and try as he might to resist what he regarded as an impure impulse, he nevertheless succumbed in the end to temptation. He rose after midnight and stole out of the apartment, braving the wind in his thin Prince Isaac jacket to venture beyond Rivington Street for the first time since he'd arrived in New York.

What surprised him was that the sleepless city, even at that small hour, was less menacing to walk in than it had been to descry through a filmy third-floor window. In fact, Shmerl was so distracted when passing the all-night coffee saloons and dancing academies, the stalls piled with fish like segmented rainbows lit by blue carbide flares, that he nearly forgot his mission. On a corner a soapbox orator exhorted a phantom audience concerning the crimes of the idle rich; a puppeteer walked a gypsy marionette around a circle of lamplight; a quorum of Chasids gathered beside a hoarding to bless the new moon. Remembering himself, Shmerl began trolling the construction and demolition sites that interrupted the tenements, delighted at how readily available were the scraps of aluminum, copper wire, and iron nails he required for his bricolage construction.

Back in the apartment he blew on his stiffened fingers, then removed from his carpet bag the electromagnet complete with alkali battery he'd brought with him from across the sea. That and his *Book of Wonders* were the only vestiges of his shameful old life he'd permitted himself to take along on his journey.

In truth, it was not a complicated operation; he'd undertaken more ambitious procedures back in Shpinsk, and his uncle's tool chest was more replete with precision instruments than any he'd previously had access to. But by the time he'd assembled the mechanism and fastened it to the curlicued struts of a sewer's treadle, looping the elastic belt around the flywheel, Shmerl was too fatigued to see his experiment through. It was still dark out and there was time for a catnap to restore himself before testing the success or failure of his motorized Singer; dawn, he assumed, was still hours away. He crawled onto his piecework pallet lulled by a sweet suspense, ignoring the window shades turning from gray to a pale lemon hue. Nodding off, he saw a swarm of raggedy wage slaves pedaling their machines across the face of the moon on their way to celestial ports of call. He awoke to screaming, and only later, after the Oyzers had sent him packing, was he able to piece together what had happened.

"Jews, give tzedakah," crooned an old man with a flowing beard and helical sidelocks stationed beneath an awning on Christie Street. "For the righteous of Palestine, give halukkah, your pennies for the destitute of Jerusalem . . ." His voice a touch too mellifluous for his wasted face, he rattled the soup tin that served for a pushke in the failing light of day. The tin rattled from the buttons and pins that citizens lacking spare change had dropped in, believing no doubt that something was better than nothing. Did they think that because he was ancient he was also blind? (Though blindness had sometimes figured in his arsenal of afflictions.) Finally someone deposited an actual coin, and the old man muttered a blessing barely distinguishable from a curse before retiring to a drafty cellar nearby to count up the day's take. There he removed the false beard and earlocks, peeled the crusted putty from his cheeks and nose, and hung up the mud-daubed caftan and the shtreimel that resembled an ermine babka. He sat down at a table covered in an oilskin on which puddles of wax had congealed, spilled the coins and other items from the tin can, and with slender fingers protruding from ragged mittens totted up the negligible amount he'd collected. Max Feinshmeker, née Jocheved Frostbissen, was growing tired of this particular ruse and would soon feel compelled to adopt another, a transformation he had repeated several times throughout that frigid winter.

He could see his breath in the cellar storeroom beneath Tzotz's Dairy Restaurant on Delancey, where he kept company with barrels of pickled sturgeon and tubs of sour cream. Tzotz the proprietor, for charity's sake, had agreed to let the mendicant kip there awhile before he returned (this was his story) to the Holy Land. Over the long winter months he'd slept in an assortment of cellars, three-cent lodgings, and detention cells, assuming a variety of disguises in his effort to remain elusive. Uneasy with each new incarnation, however, Max had tried on and discarded a dozen impostures, employing them a week or so before rejecting them for good. It was a sound enough strategy, he reasoned: Before his enemies had time to unmask him in one guise, he would already have taken another—though Jocheved sometimes insinuated that, in donning and doffing these serial personae, altering his character with each new subterfuge, he was looking in vain to find his own true self. She needled him that way persistently, urging him to continue the search for Rabbi Eliezer ben Zephyr in his zinc-lined casket, which quest was all that seemed to matter to her.

"We're alone here without a pot to pish in," was Max's routine complaint, which he was sometimes observed by passers-by to mutter aloud. "We're hungry and dirty and even if I had the pittance for a shvitz, I couldn't use it for fear they might discover you—and all you can think of is a corpse on ice?"

"He's not a corpse," Jocheved would reply through Max's own mouth, making him feel like a ventriloquist's dummy.

"Then what is he?"

"Asleep."

At this Max would sock his brow with the heel of his hand. "Farvos?" he asked. "Why why why is the old kucker so important to you?"

And here Jocheved always chose to keep mum, as if the answer should have gone without saying. It did go without saying as far as Max was concerned, because it made no sense. But discordant agendas aside, there was the real and present danger of Pisgat's threat hanging over his head.

At first he'd considered becoming the girl again, if only temporarily—that would have been the most practical disguise; but Jocheved wanted nothing to do with herself, nor was she willing to assume any other version of a female, neither maiden nor balebosteh, and Max couldn't battle her. "You don't want anymore to be yourself," he complained, "yet you snipe at me for staying under wraps," a point her silence suggested was well taken. And so, disguised as Ig Smolensk, who welcomed greenhorns fresh off the boat, soliciting their dues for an imaginary landsmanschaft; or Chaim Fut, who received alms for a rare and disfiguring skin disease; or Reb Itzik Saltpeter (sometimes the Blind), who sold Jerusalem dirt for sprinkling on stiffs and begged remittances for the saintly Jews of Palestine, Max Feinshmeker remained incognito. But all these assorted masks came later, after he'd pledged himself to vigilance and stealth and then set about failing miserably at both.

Having wandered the dense streets around Division and East Broadway during the first night after his arrival, bone-weary, mortally dispirited, and ravenous, Max had snatched a solitary orange from a bin. His inaugural theft, it was an act prompted as much by his hypnotic attraction to a fruit he'd never seen as by extreme hunger. He was caught red-handed. The grocer, whose wizened frame belied his dogged strength, grabbed the thief's wrist with both vicelike hands and wouldn't let go. He hailed a cop on the beat, who handcuffed the thief, then flagged a hack-drawn black maria, which transported Max in disgrace to the well-worn back steps of the nearby Essex Market Courthouse. There he was frog-marched by a pair of gin-soaked warders through a corridor and down a ringing spiral stair into a subterranean cell block echoing with the cries of unseen prisoners, where he was locked up for the night. It was a three-by-seven stone cell with built-in iron berths and a noisome slop bucket, but so played out was Max that he took some solace in simply having a roof over his head. He might even have slept, had not a slit-eyed cellmate, leaning against his upper berth and boasting of petty swindles in an underworld patois, kept finding excuses to touch his person: "Used to I fenced your fawneys which the tiny forks would hoist for Red Augie, him that flashed a rare handle to his physog . . ." Reclining on his pallet, Max of course had no clue as to what the fellow was talking about, though he winced every time the man rested a clammy hand on his shoulder or arm; and once, as Max began to doze off in exhaustion, his cellmate squeezed him between the legs, pincering air. So horrified was Max by the intrusion—which equally shocked the intruder, who shouted, "You ain't a cove, you're a tum-tum!"—that his bladder let go; it was that long since he'd had access to a private facility. Ashamed of the dampness and the ensuing odor, abused by the leering speculations of his cellmate, and afraid of giving vent to Jocheved's outrage, he lay in a tight fetal ball throughout the remainder of the night. In the morning, despite his long fast, Max could scarcely face the bowl of glutinous gruel delivered through a slot in the door; though for the sake of his enfeebled condition (and indifferent to the dietary laws he'd already abandoned), he forced himself to choke it down.

Hauled into the dock at the Essex Market tribunal, he understood nothing of the proceedings. The courtroom was a circus of aggrieved and bedraggled humanity, the pews swarming with professional criminals—pickpockets, prostitutes, firebugs, horse poisoners, two-bit confidence men—as well as drunks and vagrants guilty of a clumsy desperation. Court reporters slouched in the casement windows; runners colluded with jackleg lawyers squirting tobacco juice between their teeth into brass spittoons. All appeared oblivious to the pounding gavel of the judge issuing pleas for order from the bench. Beet-faced, the judge dispensed draconian punishments — this one for the water drop cure at Blackwell's Island, that one to the treadmills at Ludlow Street — which a wry-necked shorthand stenographer conscientiously recorded in her log. When it was Max's turn, the arresting officer stood to recite the immigrant's alleged offense, but in the absence of the greengrocer, for whom the affair had apparently ended with the apprehension of the thief, there was no one on hand to press formal charges. Nevertheless, the judge was reluctant to let such an obvious felon go scot free. "How do you plead?" he demanded, careless of legalities, while Max shook his head in incomprehension, anticipating the worst. Then a spruce, brilliantined young man in silk suspenders stepped up to offer his services in Yiddish. Max was ready to accept help from any quarter, when the man was interrupted by another, this one in rumpled attire, with a doleful bloodhound face, who explained that the pushy fellow was an opportunist and had not the greenhorn's best interests at heart; whereas he, clutching a battered briefcase bound with twine to his threadbare vest, was the true voice of the oppressed. Having said as much, he set down the briefcase, hooked his thumbs in his sweat-ringed armpits, and began to declaim in orotund fashion; but the speech, despite its repetition of catchwords — "bourgeois toadies," "bloated plutocrats" — was entirely lost on Max.

The judge had begun banging his gavel again, ordering the attorney to keep silent, when a brash voice whispered in Max's ear that "nisht gedey-get, don't worry," she would look after him. She was — when he turned — a plump woman in her middle years, acrid with the fragrance of rose water and perspiration, her grin slightly predatory, her coral wig shaped like a ziggurat. In the brief hush that succeeded the curtailment of the lawyer's peroration, she spoke up, informing the judge with all due respect that she would stand surety for the greenhorn. "Give to me in custody the boy, and I will guarantee he should behave himself and personally put him in the way of gainful employ." Impatient to move on to cases of more moment, the judge agreed to remand Max into her care.

IT WAS EASY enough for Shmerl to guess what had happened: the cutter, the baster, and the finisher, along with the three lady stitchers, had come in early that morning as usual, and as usual had avoided any friendly chitchat preceding their work in his uncle's shop. (Chitchat was discouraged as leading ultimately to guild socialism.) They all removed their coats, the stitchers grumbling under their breath that only one machine had been returned to its operational position; then they rearranged the machines and sat down to work. The pasty-faced Pearl Voronsky sat at Shmerl's customized Singer and started without preamble to stitch a hem. Leaning over her machine to position the fabric beneath the needle bar, she began to pump the pedal, only to find that the pedal, activated by the elementary friction-drive engine that Shmerl had installed in the undercarriage, pumped away on its own. The needle began its rapid pecking, the pedal its automatic seesawing motion, the improvised fan belt rotating at an ever increasing speed. Then a loose strand of the girl's mousy hair was caught in the sewing mechanism and was itself sewn in a literal "lock" stitch into the fabric, yanking Pearl closer to the treadle platform with each tick of the needle. Finally her head, as if leaning nearer to hear a secret, was yanked to the level of the metal platform and her scalp torn loose with a sickening pop from her skull. The bleeding was profuse, her screaming shrill, general chaos having erupted in the parlor. The noise awoke Shmerl whereas a kick in the behind from his uncle, making his customary entrance after the arrival of his workers, had not. There was no question on the part of Zaynvil, squinching his brow above the tufted bulb of his nose, as to who was responsible for the disaster; he'd had advance notice from abroad of Shmerl's monkey business and had been warned that he should be on guard against it. Nor did Shmerl deny his part in the debacle. Without protest he accepted his uncle's hasty justice, seconded by a scowling Tante Dobeh handing him his bag, and allowed himself to be bum-rushed out the door.

On the street it was winter, the banked snow peppered with soot, and now both homeless and penniless, Shmerl considered his options. He might present himself to Messrs Westinghouse and Edison, whose new patents were announced almost daily in the *Forward*, which had assumed the task of educating its subscribers in scientific as well as political revolutions. It outlined in detail the uses of the labor-saving and pleasure-giving devices that these elui, these modern Prometheuses, had begun to conceive in rapid succession. Surely such venturesome men had need of a lad with Shmerl Karp's gifts. But this latest fiasco was the final straw, and beyond contrite, Shmerl found himself actively deploring the notion of secular progress, which clearly led only to disaster. "What place is there in the Golden Land for a wizard who's sworn off wizardry?" he asked, then felt instantly ashamed of the self-pity implicit in the question. Sorry as he was for the pain that his runaway sewing machine had inflicted on an innocent, Shmerl was in any case relieved to be away from Rivington Street. His pauper's status served him right, he supposed, though recalling Sholem Aleichem's Motl Peyse's, the happy orphan whose adventures were serialized in the Yiddish dailies, he was secretly a little thrilled by his situation. For all around him thrummed America, which he still didn't approve of, though he had to admit that, barren as it was of holiness, its streets had spectacle and drama to spare.

So buoyed was he by the sights of the neighborhood, in fact, that he knocked about its streets a day and a night before realizing how tired and hungry he'd become. Everywhere the hucksters and pullers-in, warming their hands at ashcan fires, beckoned you to step with them behind the scenes, though the streets outdid their most eloquent come-ons. At a bookstall an arrogant peddler snatched a volume from a potential buyer and informed him that "this one ain't for you," while on a fire escape above them a blanket-bundled prodigy played a mournful rhapsody on a violin. A scribe with a fiddlehead beard squatted on a bucket, offering to pen salutations to your ancestors "that I promise will stink from Isaiah"; a city editor emerged from a basement press festooned in teletape aflame from an ash that had dropped from his cigar. These were attractions that Shmerl could afford, whereas he lacked the means to enjoy even the cheapest cafeteria fare—a fact he remembered once his eyes and ears (gone numb from the cold) were sated, leaving his stomach to make its own demands. That's when he applied to a storefront Canal Street mission for a bowl of soup tasting of solvent, and in the mongrel tongue he'd been refining over his weeks in the sweatshop, inquired through still chattering teeth after a job. He knew there were factories of every type in the ghetto, foundries and tool and die shops, garment factories, of course, by the score; but Shmerl thought it best to keep his distance from machinery, and he'd had enough of the rag trade to last him the rest of his days.

A couple of luckless Litvaks in the mission, both of whom had submitted to baptisms for the sake of nominal cash rewards, exchanged confidential winks as they advised him concerning a situation. Taking Shmerl's malformed measure, the more talkative of the two remarked, "It's a job I think maybe this one was born for," scribbling a Pitt Street address on a scrap of paper. Locating the street number only a few blocks away, Shmerl found there a small clutch of men milling about outside a wagonyard gate, stomping their feet and rubbing their hands to promote circulation—a dance the greenhorn found it natural to fall in step with. Around midnight the wooden gate of Levine's Livery Stable swung stridently open, and grizzled old Levine himself appeared in his mangy mackinaw. He began without ceremony to count heads, then told the men in the mixture of zhargon and English that was a standard Tenth Ward parlance to line up. A motley bunch that included a pair of scarified Negroes and a monkey-jacketed Chinaman, they seemed familiar with the routine, forming a single file for the purpose of receiving long-handled shovels from the toothless contractor. Falling in with them, Shmerl asked the chap in front of him, the bill of whose cap was pulled over one eye, "What are we?" and was informed in a Galway brogue, "We be night scavengers." Without comprehending, Shmerl had the impression he was participating in a mysterious rite.

The wagon, a storm lantern swinging from its rear axle, trundled out into the ghetto streets, as the men alongside it began shoveling horse manure from the pavements into the maggoty wooden bed. Sometimes the shit stood in pyramids like cannonballs, sometimes in delicately balanced coproliths, or in mounds like brittle meringue and fresh paddies spread over the cobbles and trolley tracks. Where the stuff lay on the macadamed roadway, it could be scooped up efficiently and tossed onto the growing heap, but often the more obstinate turds had to be prized from fissures and sinkholes and flung into the wagon like clay pigeons sprung from traps. A few of the men, between shovelfuls, pulled slab bottles from their reefer pockets and took deep drafts to stave off the cold; then they would reel and occasionally break into sentimental song ("She is more to be pitied than censured . . ."), some teetering and falling face forward into the slush where they were left to lie. Without the benefit of spirits, Shmerl neverthe-less found the exercise bracing, itself sufficient to warm his bones, and the stench of excrement, mitigated by the frosty air, was no worse than the odor of anguish in the Oyzers' shop. Hauled by a brace of stilt-legged plug horses that Old Man Levine had constantly to cajole, the wagon rolled as far as the East River wharves, where its contents were unloaded onto freight scales before being dumped into a garbage scow. The skipper of the scow exchanged some salty small talk with the contractor, handing him his commission as a gang of sparrowlike urchins crept from the shadows to leap atop the piles of drek. Hovered over by mewling seabirds, they picked through the shit in a futile search for trophies worth salvaging.

When the night cart returned near dawn to the wagonyard, Levine dis-mounted his squeaky vehicle to dole out their token wages to the stalwarts who'd survived the dung circuit. The laborers dispersed in their several directions, leaving Shmerl to totter alone in the odorous yard, chewing his chapped lower lip. "What's a matter, you froze?" asked the shambling old contractor of the greenhorn, who replied with unguarded candor, "I dunno where I should go," just before he crumpled to the ground from exhaus-tion. Examining him with a blood-rimmed eye, Levine grunted it wasn't his problem; then, a soft touch for both animals and oddballs, he relented, scooping up Shmerl and half-walking, half-dragging him to an uninsu-

lated tarpaper shack where he could sleep. The shack, hung with horsetack
and bridles, abutted the stables, and in exchange for cleaning them, for
watering the crow-bait horses and strapping on their feedbags, for delivering the tribute money to the Jewish Black Hand in their headquarters
behind Sam Schnure's saloon, and for shoveling shit, Shmerl could have
the run of the rickety outbuilding. On top of that (and depending on the
weekly levy imposed by the Yid Camorra) he would receive a salary of
around two dollars a week. With his wage plus the chickpeas and potato
peels he foraged from the Hester Street market—he was, after all, a seasoned scrounger—Shmerl was able to keep himself alive and relatively fit,
as well as to sock away a little something for a rainy day. In most respects
the wagonyard regimen was even more punishing than the sweatshop, but
unlike the sweatshop it had its rewards.

For instance: Shmerl would sleep through the mornings and wake to
perform his appointed duties, which were generally completed by early
evening. Then his time until the dead of night was his own. He would
stroll into streets whose mercantile tenor had begun to take on by that
hour a more recreational mood, the cafés filling with drones from the
factories who shed their torpor on the spot, transforming themselves into
poets and firebrands. Among their ranks were the artistic young ladies
in their tulip-shaped walking skirts, whose ordinarily drawn faces appeared flushed with public and private passions. Admiring them through
plate glass, Shmerl thought that, given his own double life (for he was a
drek shlepper with the soul of a dreamer), he had much in common with
these zealous young people, though he lacked the self-assurance to mingle
among them. Besides, temptation was itself a form of idolatry—or so he
told himself before finally turning away from the cafés and dancehalls to
go meet the nightwalking crew.

Once, during a twilight constitutional, lonely and full of a yearning
he dared not name, Shmerl ventured as far afield as the Bowery, amazed
as always that he could see so much of the world in the space of so few
blocks, that he needed no stamped document or visa to travel from one

district to another. Here was Babel all right, though he seemed to have lost the capacity to judge it; predators and victims alike now appeared to him as merely the naturalized citizens of the urban landscape, just as the borderline between the spirit and the flesh was virtually indiscernible in this corner of the globe. The storefront chapel rubbed elbows with the hot-sheet hotel, the oyster bar with the Yiddish theater, beneath whose bulb-studded marquee a band of Chasids had gathered to exorcise the abominations within. Sandwiched between a music hall and a shooting gallery, with the Third Avenue Elevated roaring overhead, was a gasoliered façade with an ornate triple M painted above its arched entryway: The Museum of Miracles and Misfits, admission one thin dime. It was no doubt wasteful to spend a whole dime to see "miracles" when there were sights enough along any city street, but lured by the garish monstrosities depicted on the banners outside the building, Shmerl impulsively turned over a coin to the man in the booth and entered the hall.

Inside was a great gaslit firetrap of an exhibition hall hung with cheap tapestries, smelling of peanuts or broken wind, where human curios sat beside here a water pipe, there a gramophone, on raised tinsel thrones. There was a fat lady with chins spilling glacier-like toward her fardel-size breasts, her proscenium skirts lifted slightly to reveal a boy with leopard spots peeking from underneath. There was a living skeleton with cheese-straw bones, the bearded girl in crinoline billed as an "infant Esau," a pair of wild Patagonian children said to be the link between the orangutan and man. A giant in a military tunic held an identically uniformed dwarf in the palm of his hand; the two-headed Liesl-Elise, Siamese twins joined at the buttocks, obligingly showed their point of juncture without (as the high-flown barker assured the families) any infringement upon their modesty. There was a leather-skinned Indian who claimed to remember Captain John Smith. They were all a little unnerving, not so much for their abnormalities as for their frank and accomodating manner, more than willing as were most to impart their singular histories. More disturbing to Shmerl than the breathing oddities, however, were the inanimate ones:

the monstrous so-called mermaid abob in a jar of formaldehyde, the cabinet containing the head of President Garfield's assassin, the four-legged rooster, the man encased in a block of ice.

The barker, a tiddly gent in shop-soiled evening dress who called himself Professor Nimrod, with a monocle and a permanently flexed brow, explained the attractions that couldn't explain themselves. But despite his extravagant claims for their authenticity, the pickled grotesqueries—the "mermaid" resembling the hybrid of a fish and a marmoset, the ice man scarcely visible in a berg the green of rancid milk—remained less popular among the spectators than the vital and articulate exhibits. Still, Shmerl saw no reason to disbelieve: The Professor's ballyhoo ("This frozen phenom is your actual corpus of a medieval Israelite mage preserved *en glace* like a fly in amber, imprisoned by the curse of a rival sorcerer . . .") was certainly arresting. And if you peered hard enough into the cloudy ice, its edges ebbing away from the box that enshrined it, you could just make out the lineaments of a beard and belted caftan, the prayer shawl and courtly fur shtreimel of a rabbi or holy man. Then there was the canted, half-rotten casket the specimen was displayed in—which hadn't Shmerl seen somewhere before? It troubled him that he couldn't place it, as did the fact that, notwithstanding the frigid temperatures outside, the museum's interior, warmed by steam heat and the legions that passed through it, was causing the ice to melt slowly away. Which was why, after the Professor had completed his narrative, Shmerl approached him cap in hand, rehearsing a hesitant proposal in his head.

The room was emptying out as the crowd, to make way for a new influx of patrons, was encouraged to pass through a curtained portal toward a melodrama entitled "Mazeppa's Last Ride" that was about to commence in the little theater beyond.

"The ice that it's melting," Shmerl humbly volunteered, "I can for you restore."

The Professor studied the immigrant a moment, as if he were an item presenting itself as a potential exhibit. Then, in a voice that gained volume as he spoke, he let the young crookback know that his offer had indeed struck a nerve. He told Shmerl that frankly nobody was much interested in the old back number anyway and it was a fact that the ice would soon deliquesce, leaving him with nothing but a moldy Hebrew cadaver on his hands. The truth was, he continued, increasingly exercised, that the thing wasn't really worth the trouble of its upkeep; the museum was doing just fine with its live curiosities. Then having reached the height of his dudgeon, he relaxed his features, allowing the monocle to drop out of his eye and dangle medallionlike from its cord.

"You want him?" he said at last to his petitioner, "he's yours."

ON THE TROLLEY ride over to Norfolk Street she introduced herself, holding forth a pudgy palm: "Mrs. Esther Weintraub, widow," as if being relict were her occupation, "but please you can call me Esther." Then shouting over the lurching horsecar and its yammering passengers, she qualified her title: She was a grass widow, actually, her husband among the multitude of the missing whose photos were posted daily in the gallery of farshvoondn menschen in the *Forward*. She'd been in court as her landlord's witness in a suit against a defaulting tenant and had stuck around to watch the nogoodniks receive their due, when she'd taken pity on the bewildered immigrant. "To my own big heart I am a slave," she declared, squeezing an ample breast. She was a dressmaker by trade but admitted to an arrangement with her landlord, Mr. Opatashu, a fine gentleman and scholar who like herself was a native of Velsh. In his magnanimity he'd allowed her to remain in her apartment free of charge in exchange for her services as "janitress." She gave the word a certain dashing cadence, then immediately assured Max he shouldn't get ideas; there was nothing improper about their relationship. She chattered on, a bit hysterically, Max thought, about what a useless lump of suet was her husband and how well rid of him she was; in fact, she was doing fine on her own, a sheynem dank, and therefore in a position to lend assistance to a newcomer such as . . . What was his name again? "Oh yeah, *Max*; don't worry, Max, I will waive for you your first month the rent till you make a salary," grazing his cheek with her fingertips. "Connections I got with a certain garment manufacturer. What you mean, you got no skills? Everybody gets off the boat is lickety-spit a Columbus tailor . . ."

They arrived at her second-floor walkup, where the broad-beamed widow bustled about rattling coals in the grate and removing baggy undergarments from a line strung across the kitchen, while Max sat in a slump at the deal table. She continued nattering about how she'd yet to take in a boarder herself, but surely Mr. Opatashu would not begrudge her the extra income. Still, she paused to speculate while primping her wig, there was the landlord's potential jealousy to consider . . . Weary as he was, Max was alert enough to feel squeamish at finding himself in the woman's charge; this wasn't what he'd had in mind. But the apartment was warm and he was glad to be out of jail and off the street, doubly grateful for the stuffed chicken neck and lokshen noodles that Mrs. Weintraub (he couldn't bring himself to call her Esther) served him with his tea. She also boiled a cauldron of water on her cookstove, fogging the windows, tooting her horn all the while about what a resourceful lady she was. "Agunah they would call me in the Old Country, but here the husband leaves, you are free to find another, no?" Max didn't think so but held his peace, realizing it wasn't necessary for him to speak at all. The widow poured the steaming pot into a large tin washtub, then carried a basin out to a common spigot in the stairwell, returning to mingle the cold water with the hot, testing it with her fingers as she might have done for a child. When she was satisfied that the temperature was tepid enough, she told Max to go ahead and wash himself; afterward, while she laundered his own (pinching her nostrils theatrically to indicate them), he could change into some of her husband's old clothes. Then she retired to the bedroom to give him his privacy, humming a music-hall air as she departed.

Looking warily over his shoulder, Max shucked his filthy garments, then couldn't help remarking the satin-smooth contours of Jocheved's body, graceful despite its sour pungency, hateful for its latent provocation.

He lowered himself with a deep sigh into the tub, his inky hair (badly in need of a trim) fanning the surface of the water, the cares of the moment seeping out of his pores along with the rising steam. So relieved was he for this respite from his trials that he began to think of Mrs. Weintraub as a godsend. But no sooner had he relaxed in the luxury of his bath than the widow herself waddled back in, and snatching up a loofah mitten from the washstand set upon Max.

"Don't worry," she assured him, "I'm a old married lady; you got nothing I ain't already seen."

When he felt the sponge stroking his neck and shoulders in fluid figure-eights, Max practically swooned, so soothing was it to be touched by another; but when the mitten began to slide over his collar bone and down the gentle slope of his chest, he came to his senses and, crossing his arms in front of him mummy-fashion, abruptly submerged himself. Under water he supposed there were worse things than revealing his true gender to this wanton woman, which surely would have discouraged her overtures. But Jocheved was more resolute than that; she thought she might prefer to drown. Opening her eyes under the sudsy water, she was almost wistful, imagining herself sinking to her rest in a watery grave where wrecked galleons were guarded by undulant octopi. But despite the seductive submarine vista, the girl's eyes were smarting, her lungs rebelling in their hunger to breathe, until Max resurfaced with a huge gulping intake of air. He found himself alone again in the kitchen, Mrs. Weintraub having apparently taken the unsubtle hint. Climbing hurriedly out of the tub, he snatched up the absent husband's clothes that the widow had left folded over a chair, and without stopping to dry himself pulled them on as he fled the dumbbell flat.

Looking back, Jocheved mourned the loss of her father's mossbacked funeral suit, which Max had left behind.

After the relative calm of the apartment, the street seemed even more riotous than before. A milk float collided with a beerwagon, the drivers climbing down from their respective vehicles to pummel each other's ears.

The bitter wind whipped the pantlegs and flapped the coattails of Mr. Weintraub's ill-fitting garments, and a steam-driven motorcar, braking too late for an alley cat, sounded an unearthly horn. America was tohu-bohu, a madhouse, and it galled Max that he had endured such an arduous journey to reach it. Surely there must be more to this country than met the eye; there must be places scoured of sweaters and shmeikelers, with room to breathe. But the Lower East Side of New York was where the Jews were, and given the mameloshen that was his sole means of communication, Max saw no alternative but to lose himself in the melée of the ghetto. He decided, as what choice did he have, to rededicate his energies to survival, but when he tallied up the talents he might call upon to that effect, he found himself wanting. He could make ice cream, couldn't he? though Jocheved was adamant in her contempt for the profession that had led to her downfall, and Max had already proven that he had no gift for sneak thievery. Of course, there were any number of menial jobs, but to remain at a single occupation over time would leave him exposed in a way that would put his life in further jeopardy.

On the other hand, cold and bedeviled as he was, Max also felt some-what revitalized; he had a full belly and was reasonably protected from the elements by the errant husband's hand-me-downs, the shell coat and the large bowler hat that jugged his ears. Maybe, thought Max—though the thought flew in the face of his better judgment—things would work out after all. Perhaps Pisgat's operatives would never find him on this side of the Atlantic, in this roistering district where everyone strived to rein-vent himself. Who knew but that the old so-and-so was bluffing with his threats, playing on the youth's gullibility; surely prospects would present themselves to such a well-knit lad as he.

It was then that the character in the turned-around golf cap and tatty plus fours drew alongside him. "You're so pretty," said the fellow, dressed as if for the links of Gehenna, "you just got to be Max Feinshmeker. My Uncle Zalman ain't too pleased with you that you didn't send him his cash."

In an instant the broad world shrank to the size of a slum, the Balut having overtaken the Tenth Ward, and Max understood precisely what had transpired: how this raffish character with the lazy eye had lain in wait for him from the outset, betraying the old ice mensch by snatching the money that was owed him and leaving the greenhorn to take the blame for the theft. Now the fellow, recalled by loose ends, had come back to complete what he'd begun, and if Pisgat never recovered his cash, at least he would be avenged.

Suffused with a fatalism that nearly neutralized his fear, Max responded, "So why you didn't send him the money yourself?"

"Who, me?" The fellow feigned indignation. "What do I know what happened to my uncle's money? Maybe in a game of chance you lost it? You greenies do get fleeced so easy. Shtrudel," nodding in the direction of a sizable crony who had closed in on Max's left flank, "ain't this the one made off with Uncle Zalman's gelt?"

But Max didn't wait around for Shtrudel's verdict. Spurred by Jocheved's memory of assault and abduction, he shrugged off the hands that attempted to grab him and broke away, making a headlong dash around a corner and diving into the first alley he saw. The alley was blind, with a slat fence at its terminus, which Max hit at a dead run and scrambled over, dropping into an unpaved courtyard on the other side. Afraid to look back, he flung himself over a low brick barrier, crossed another yard, and climbed another fence into yet another alley, fueled in his flight by equal parts exhilaration and terror. The alley debouched into a doglegged defile of a street that smelled of the river, in which a few stolid residents were roosting like teraphim on their wooden stoops. The slate roofs of the narrow houses leaned conspiratorially toward one another, so that only minimal sunlight was admitted into the street, where a small party of pedestrians were making their way toward the end of the block. Distinctive for their shared disabilities, they progressed with a will: a man with a single leg who swung himself along on a pair of crutches like a fugitive pendulum; another in an opera cape, wearing opaque spectacles, flailing left to right with a Malacca cane. A woman veiled in a woolen shawl emerged from a tributary alley hauling a wagon containing a quadruple amputee, his face like a prow, his trunk a fat bowling pin decorated with medals. All were advancing in the direction of a decrepit brick building with a tin-plated door and no sign.

Wherever those poor souls were headed, Max figured it was a place no healthy citizen was likely to go, and so he followed. He reached the tin door, got a foot in just before the door slammed shut, and squeezed inside, where he nearly tumbled into the wagon that the cowled woman was dragging behind her. Its wooden wheels clanked loudly down the short flight of ill-lit stone steps, and Max, once his eyes adjusted to the dimness, marveled at how the little sack of a man managed to remain so steadfastly erect in his bouncing conveyance. At the foot of the stairs there was a windowless catacomb lit by flickering sconces, where patrons in various stages of affliction were seated at tables and milling about a whiskey bar mounted on wood-staved kegs. Having hopped on his good leg to the bottom of the steps, one of the cripples who'd preceded Max hung up his crutches and unfastened a leather harness to release his stump, which he unfolded into a perfectly serviceable limb. The blind man had meanwhile cast off his cane and smoky glasses with a flourish to elbow his way toward the bar, where a couple of customers took turns sucking beer from a tube protruding out of a bunghole. In his wagon the limbless veteran, wriggling on his back like a bug attempting to right itself, had also begun to regenerate missing arms and legs; while his female attendant dropped the shawl and peeled away the festering sores stuck to her cheeks, revealing herself as a woman of tolerably pleasant features.

Where some recovered lost appendages and faculties, others were busy pruning and abrading themselves, applying jellies and scabs, rubber bald caps with wens, prostheses that simulated bone diseases and malformations. Some worked with straps and trusses to achieve amputations, while others hunkered around a woodstove heating fixatives and gels for sculpting artificial wounds. A bird-breasted gent with a pedagogical manner demonstrated on his own person before a small circle of students how to counterfeit furuncles, lesions, stigmata, and gangrene. Those not involved in inflicting or healing mutilations admired their own handiwork in murky mirrors; some inspected a well-stocked wardrobe rack or contented themselves with conversation over needled beer.

Max recalled having heard of places where the blind were made to see and the lame to walk, but those were holy places, and this dank dungeon didn't seem particularly sacrosanct. Of course, there'd been any number of phony beggars in Lodz, but who knew that they were the products of such elaborate industry? Having edged wide-eyed down the steps into the cellar proper, Max could overhear English spoken all about him in a variety of broken dialects and accents, including Galitzianer. He made bold to inquire of a landsman with a bleb the size of a cupping glass on his forehead, "Where am I?" and was told in stagey Daytshmersh, "This is what is known as a cripple factory." Grinning with a show of black-capped teeth, his informant continued: "A western franchise, if you will, of what in Europe they call a court of miracles, though some would say a court of last resorts."

It was further explained that the customers might have the use of the costumes and props that the beer cellar provided gratis, so long as they signed a contract, notarized by the proprietor, promising to share a fixed percentage of their supplicant's proceeds. This guaranteed that the majority of patrons would return the fruits of their mooching to the cellar as to a company store.

That was how Max initiated the series of impersonations that would see him through the lean winter months. Panhandler by day, he took shelter by night in a shadow Manhattan, sometimes sleeping in the Municipal Lodging House on its barge locked in North River ice, or in the faded opulence of the HIAS quarters in the old Astor Library. There were hapless periods when, lacking the price of a flop, he slept outdoors with one eye open on top of a steam vent or a heating grate; nights when his daylight appeals had gone well and he might rent a closet-size crib above a bar-room, the company of mice being preferable to the public sanctuaries that left him vulnerable to deviants and thieves. Occasionally, sick and tired of dissembling, he might briefly forgo the accessories that rendered him maimed or blind to take an unskilled job: once as a buttonhole puncher, another time a suspenders peddler—the latter activity affording its own style of camouflage, adorned as he was in galluses like a willow tree. With each new occupation he assumed a new name: Chaim Fut, Itche Grin; but mostly he remained under cover and hustled. Every so often he was granted a holiday, as during elections, when the Tammany bosses provided free lunches to anyone who voted repeatedly for their candidates, but even then Max was afraid to lower his guard. Of course, as a girl, as Jocheved, he would have been eligible to take shelter in more benevolent refuges such as the Daughters of Rachel Home for Wayward Jewish Girls, a place of tender mercies or so he'd heard. But Jocheved had as good as drowned in Mrs. Weintraub's washtub, so little was her voice heeded anymore in Max's affairs; and Max himself was so lost in his Igs, Chaims, and Abednegos that he'd forfeited the memory of precisely who he was supposed to be.

As a consequence, Jocheved's pleas that he should continue the quest for Rabbi ben Zephyr, which alternated with her disturbing indifference to her own fate, fell on deaf ears. Doubly disguised, Max tended to forget about the submerged Jocheved altogether, except during those functions whose privacy Max had to make no end of degrading efforts to secure. Then there were the fiddles, his expanding rag-bag of deceits, the latest involving the sale of little sacks of sand scooped from the gutters, which he pitched as Jerusalem earth. Still, it was only a matter of time before the current ruse was discovered: the charities that dispatched their itinerant ambassadors—some begging alms for the outworn parasites of Jerusalem, others for the young pioneers of the Yishuv—often clashed with each other, while both factions were on the lookout for impostors. So on this particular night Max had decided to retire old Reb Saltpeter. Then, unthinking in his marathon weariness, he put on the shell coat and bowler of Mrs. Weintraub's absconded husband without resorting to any cosmetic effects. Only half conscious of having returned to his original disguise — though aware enough of having missed it — he ventured out into Delancey Street to purchase a bit of kippered herring or maybe a piece of fruit. It wasn't lost on him either that the evening's weather showed signs of a warming trend, or that he was lonely.

As he strolled toward a produce stand beneath the shuddering uprights of the Second Avenue El, a fellow in a floppy golf cap turned about jockey style stepped up to greet him familiarly: "You're so pretty," he said, "you just got to be Max Feinshmeker."

IT WAS THE young man from the ship. Despite his dowdy apparel, Shmerl was as sure of his identity as he had been of little else during that long cold season of carting dung. He was amazed at how relieved he was to see him, though they had yet to exchange a word, but while Shmerl thought he might now have much to say to him, his anticipation left him timid and reticent. So rather than cross immediately over the road to accost him, he followed the yungerman awhile from the other side. There was, after all, no particular hurry; hours remained before he was scheduled to make his rounds with the shit patrol, and it calmed him somewhat to observe the lad from a distance; saddened him as well to see how the intervening months had taken a toll on his former dignity. After a block or so along Delancey, Shmerl noticed that another, a lath-legged character in knee breeches and a turned-around caddy's cap, also seemed to be dogging the young man's heels. Then the caddy cap accelerated his pace, drawing alongside the yungerman to speak to him, upon which the youth, who had paused at a fruiterer's bin, took off like a streak. Shmerl's heart kicked at its cage as he watched the lad hotfooting it down the sidewalk, trying madly to dodge the passersby. In flight he looked over his shoulder, then turned around just in time to run smack into the arms of a big fellow in an ankle-length duster who had planted himself athwart his path. Thus embraced, the youth from the ship was manhandled by the duster — along with the caddy cap, who'd bolted forward to grab his collar from behind — into an alley off the crowded thoroughfare.

Shmerl was not the only one who had witnessed the abduction; others behind stalls and in horsecars saw the young man, a hand clapped over his mouth, struggling with his captors as they dragged him off. But while those who'd stopped to watch resumed their business as soon as the unpleasantness was out of sight, Shmerl recognized the event as the fateful moment he'd been waiting for. Confident in the strength that pressing irons and dung shovels had imparted to his stooped physique, he straightened his shoulders as best he could and drew forth from the walking stick he carried a slender metal wand. "Shemhemphorash!" he cried aloud, which was the name of the magic hat of Moses as mentioned in the *Sefer Sheqel ha-Kodesh*. It was as good a Hebrew battle cry as any he could think of. Zigzagging through heavy traffic, he crossed Delancey and charged the alley, where he began to thrust here and there in the gloom. The stock prod, which he'd devised on the principle of Aaron's rod (it was a cane with a serpent's sting) quivered like a fencing foil in his hand. He'd fashioned it with a trigger that sent a six-volt charge from a carbon battery to the platinum spikelet at its tip. The thing was designed for the purpose of encouraging horses in the livery stable to behave, but the nags were already so docile that he'd as yet had no occasion to try it out. This was his invention's debut, and judging from the response of the young man's attackers, it worked to good effect — especially now that Shmerl's eyesight had adjusted to the halflight and he was aiming his thrusts with more accuracy. Both the duster and the caddy cap yowled as if they had fallen into a nest of electric eels; they dropped the blackjack and the naked shiv respectively to clutch at their parts, doubtless as shocked by the bent creature wielding his stinging weapon as they were by the weapon itself.

Having rendered the two assailants temporarily hors de combat, Shmerl sheathed his prod in order to raise their intended victim from the flags and hustle him out of the alley. The young man from the ship gripped his forehead, a thin trickle of blood leaking from between his fingers, but allowed himself to be led at a stumbling dogtrot behind his rescuer. Holding his stick in one hand, Shmerl pulled the youth along by the wrist onto Delancey, where after a short block he turned abruptly into another alleyway. Together they threaded a concatenation of puddled passages, emerging now and again to cross a noisy street only to duck straight-away back into the maze. Eventually they found themselves in a vacant lot strewn with refuse and bed frames dragged outside in the hope that the sun would lure the bedbugs from their slats. The lot was surrounded by a high wooden fence, one of whose boards Shmerl swung aside to usher his friend—Was it premature to think of him as a friend?—into Reb Levine's wagonyard. Breathing the foul air with relief, he invited the stunned youth into his shanty, where he sat him down on a bed covered in horse blankets, which was lowered from the rafters by a system of pulleys and weights. Then kindling a lantern, Shmerl began without hesitation to attend to his guest's wound, which amounted to little more than a shallow abrasion crowning a nasty bump on the kop.

HOLDING HIS ACHING HEAD, Max counted it as an aspect of the stupefaction brought on by his injury that the furniture in his host's modest quarters appeared to be floating in midair. A table and chair, stove, workbench, and thunderbox all hovered above them amid dangling horse tackle, as if waiting for the shack's occupant himself to levitate. As his rescuer dabbed at his forehead with the putrid-smelling poultice he'd pre-pared in a porcelain basin, Max also wondered at the swiftness with which he'd been spirited from the ghetto streets to this peculiar cell; though, accustomed as he was by now to uncommon places, he understood that the ghetto must still be close at hand. He supposed that under the circum-stances he ought to introduce himself to this curious figure who had after all saved his life, but the problem was, he seemed for the moment to have misplaced his own name. Itche Fut? Chaim Grin? He felt his face for any artificial asymmetries (the irony of an authentic wound notwithstanding) and recognized its velvet contours.

"Feinshmeker," he tendered rather formally, offering his hand. "Max."

"Shmerl," replied his host, with a hint of familiarity that made Max wonder if they'd met before. "Shmerl Karp," which may have been the first time Shmerl had pronounced his abbreviated surname aloud. Eagerly he cranked Max's extended palm with his right hand while continuing to dab with his left at the swelling goose egg on Max's bare head. "I saw you already on the same ship we come over from the Old Country on."

Max tried to square this information with the immigrant's odd environment, such a far cry from the sweatshops and pushcarts and shuls. His gaze strayed again from his host's smiling face and his shock of upstanding auburn hair toward the items suspended above their heads, and following his glance Shmerl folded the poultice into Max's own hand. He stepped over to a console containing what looked like a rudimentary keyboard, a bellringer's assemblage of wooden handles from which ropes of varying widths fanned upward like a web of ratlines on a sailing ship. Then he began with closed fists and a sudden startling show of energy to hammer the individual handles, which caused the airborne objects to begin descending in concert: the lit stove shaped like a cast-iron pig with a percolating coffee pot on top, the laboratory bench laden with frothing beakers full of incandescent purple gas. There was a large construction like a miniature refinery at whose center was an inverted milk can caged in perforated metal strips, surrounded by brackets, gears, belted bicycle wheels, and nodes of fairy lights — the whole contraption coated in a fur of polar rime.

"The machine," explained Shmerl, giving one of the rimless wheels a spin, which caused coils to glow, an engine to hum, and steam to rise, "that it duplicates the prophet Ezekiel his vision of wheels within wheels. 'Wherever the spirit wished to go, there the wheels went, for the spirit of living creatures was in the wheels.' It makes, the machine, a perpetual motion that makes also, when is liquefied under pressure ammonia gas, eppes an everlasting winter."

On cue the machine belched into a chute, with a tin pan attached to receive it, what was either an enormous multifaceted diamond or a large chunk of ice.

Max gaped in fascination for a full minute before his eyes were again drawn irresistibly toward the ceiling, where a narrow cedar box remained aloft. Once more noting the object of his guest's curiosity, Shmerl depressed another couple of beveled handles, this time with an outright bravado. Chains ratcheted over iron sprockets as the casket began to descend until it rested on the earthen floor, its lid springing automatically open. "This I think belongs to you," submitted the crookback.

Max got to his feet of his own accord but allowed Shmerl to assist him as he shuffled over to the box, where, pressing the poultice to his forehead as if to cushion the clapper in his skull, he looked inside. There was Rabbi Eliezer ben Zephyr, the Boibiczer Prodigy, resting comfortably in a clear block of ice that looked remarkably none the worse for wear. In fact, unlike the eroded green boulder that Max remembered, this one was pristine, showing the old recumbent tzaddik with his beard and gabardine to fine advantage. Turning back to Shmerl, Max asked him pointedly, "Who *are* you?" though he could as well have put the question to himself. In his fuddled brain he tried assembling what might pass for current articles of faith: that he was in a shack in a stableyard at the end of March, entertained by an outlandish person quite possibly escaped from an institution or storybook; though this did little to relieve his profound disorientation or to explain how the girl Jocheved could feel so perfectly at home.

2001.

On his way to see the rebbe, Bernie Karp observed the elongated shadow (his own) that preceded him along the dappled
sidewalk. He'd transferred to a crosstown bus in order to reach a neighborhood on the city's southern periphery, which was not unlike the one he
lived in, a recent subdivision of overblown houses in a medley of architectural styles, none distinctive enough to allow the eyes any real purchase on
the past. The streets were bordered by mulberrys and forsythias, oaks and
elms in their scrawny infancy, peppered by fusillades from sprinkler jets.
Approaching Rabbi ben Zephyr's New House of Enlightenment, Bernie
noted that his shadow was becoming shorter, and his feet, as he proceeded,
seemed to have advanced from the shadow's base to its knees. Then he
stepped over the waist, chest, and shoulders, trod upon the head, and
walked away from the shadow—which, when the boy turned around,
was no longer there. Grown accustomed to the uncanny over the past few
months, Bernie said to himself, "Easy come, easy go."

These days the physical world was forever inviting incursions from
zones that did not always conform to the laws of cause and effect. Such
phenomena, he suspected, owed something to the influence of Lou Ella
Tuohy, whose ministrations helped to integrate Olam haBa, the beyond,

into Olam haZeh, the here and now. Her presence in his life was an assurance that, when he returned from his mystic adventures, some of the sights still clung like thistledown to his brain. As a consequence, Bernie found that his affection for Lou was often indistinguishable from his affection for Creation itself. There was sorrow in this loss of a particular focus, of the tension between his desire to ascend to celestial heights and his longing to be near the girl.

"You make it too easy for me to leave you," he complained, if only because Lou Ella herself was so uncomplaining. Not only did she lend a literal hand in facilitating his spiritual leave-takings, but she patiently guarded his physical well-being when his spirit was not in residence, and welcomed him home again as a hero.

The girl, who had recently dyed her hair the green of pure Mercurochrome, thought this over. "It's the truth," she agreed without acrimony. "I'm an enabler of the most selfishest smuck in the world."

"It's shmuck," corrected Bernie, apologizing once again for having returned empty-handed from his sorties into hidden dimensions.

Meanwhile, although the old man was virtually AWOL from Bernie's life, the boy still regarded Rabbi Eliezer ben Zephyr as the progenitor of his expanded consciousness, a figure of unimpeachable authority. This despite the monkeyshines allegedly taking place within the confines of his New House of Enlightenment. For Rabbi ben Zephyr and his popular spiritual center had become something of a lightning rod for media attention in the Bluff City. Having hosted the birth of rock 'n' roll and the martyrdom of a black messiah, the city of Memphis was no stranger to controversy, but the antics of the unfrozen holy man had drawn the interest of a populace divided on the subject of his authenticity. Those who weren't among the growing numbers that attended his instruction and meditation sessions were inclined to denounce him as a charlatan and imposter. It was an accusation that might have been viewed as a species of old-school anti-Semitism had not so many Jewish institutions lent their voices to the chorus of disapproval. In fact, the synagogues were more vocal than most in their righteous hostility. But if anything, controversy added spice to the rabbi's ministry and heightened the profile of his media campaign. Commercials advertising the House of Enlightenment's promise of the cosmos on demand were frequently broadcast on local radio and TV. Billboards featured the hoary head of Rabbi ben Zephyr in a coonskin shtreimel, declaring, "Feel good in yourself is the whole of the law," and an Internet website posted a menu of New House programs.

It was sobering to consider how meteorically the old man had risen from his inauspicious beginnings in the Karp family rec room; but while Bernie attributed to the rabbi's influence his own transformation from slug to apprentice adept, he also reserved the right to believe that the indebtedness was mutual: The rabbi owed him something for having attended at his reawakening. After all, it was he who had introduced the rabbi to the New World, easing his acclimation via TV shows such as *Few Are Chosen* (in which wealthy teens anguished over maxed-out credit cards) and *America's Funniest Videos* (in which kids were caught on camera interfering with their pets). With this debt in mind, Bernie had set off once again to seek an audience with the rebbe, for the sake of asking him questions he'd yet to formulate.

He'd given up on the idea of studying for bar mitzvah with the Boibiczer Prodigy, not that he considered himself above the Law; no one was above the Law. But while he continued his delving into sacred texts, Bernie confessed to Lou that for him ritual was not an imperative. He tried in his daily life to keep the commandments according to the *Shulchan Arukh*, but while not averse to structuring his days along the lines of strict observance, the varieties of experience available to him tended to steer the boy in a less doctrinaire direction. The letter of the Law, he admitted, was sometimes superseded by its mercurial Spirit. But because his inconstancy (as Lou Ella saw it) did occasionally weigh on him, it remained unclear to Bernie exactly where responsibility lay. Surely the rebbe would have something to say on this score. Never mind that Rabbi ben Zephyr himself, if the newspapers could be believed, had compromised every positive value he claimed to embody. Bernie knew enough by now about crazy wisdom and the crooked paths to enlightenment along which artful sages led their disciples to understand that the rebbe must have his reasons. Still, he was aggrieved that the tzaddik's calling had taken him so far beyond the sphere of their original intimacy. He understood that Eliezer ben Zephyr belonged to the world and had little time for indulging private relationships; nevertheless, he thought he might prevail on their shared history to speak with the great man just this once.

"So you think you got a claim on the old momzer?" Lou Ella's vocabulary had grown exponentially during their acquaintance. "But truth is he's got a wicked claim on you."

Bernie allowed this was probably the case but argued that it wasn't necessarily a bad thing. It disturbed him, though, that Lou Ella seemed to have developed a testy attitude toward a holy man she'd never met, and that she remained a confirmed agnostic concerning the rabbi's icebound résumé. He suspected her of jealousy; but as her jealousy also flattered him, he couldn't be angry with her; he could never be angry with her. It was summer and, school being out (Bernie felt that for him it might be out forever), they were spending much of their time together. Between Mr. Karp's preoccupation with his own and the rabbi's affairs and his wife's newfound interest in self-realization (she attended New House sessions after which she went straight to bed, exhausted from a surfeit of quietude), Bernie's parents hardly remembered they had a son. (Or a daughter, for that matter, since Madeline had taken an art-school modeling job and resolved never to come home again.) Mrs. Tuohy worked nights and slept days, leaving her daughter to mind her baby sister, which left Lou Ella and the Karp kid virtual orphans. When Bernie wasn't riffling his copy of *The Ethics of the Fathers*, which he carried about everywhere, or traveling outside of time, the two of them would cruise—on nights when she got a lift from her carpool—in Mrs. Tuohy's rustbucket Malibu coupe.

Taking in tow the vapid Sue Lily, over whom Lou Ella never ceased fawning, they tooled along Delta roads south of the city, past the gambling mecca that had sprouted among the cottonfields like some lurid Emerald City. They drove downtown on Lou's insistence that Bernie be introduced to the world he was forever in the process of leaving; though Bernie suspected he was merely her excuse to see the sights—the honky-tonk where W. C. Handy had penned "The St. Louis Blues," the movie palace where Elvis Presley had ushered—which, to her disappointment, had vanished long ago. They even added to their itinerary, at Bernie's recommendation, a deserted North Main Street from which the old Yid immigrants (excepting the holdout of a single synagogue) had long since departed.

"The past is a lost continent," declared Lou elegiacally, which to Bernie's mind made the present even more of an irrelevancy.

They were hard put to define their relationship, not so much because it remained unconsummated; they were after all only sixteen, and sexual congress, even in the new millennium, was not necessarily a precondition for calling each other sweethearts. Or so Bernie reasoned. In fact he would have been happy to call Lou Ella his girlfriend had she not eschewed the label herself. "I'm your handler," she quipped, taking a word out of the show business lexicon that she claimed was more accurate. It troubled Bernie to hear her talk that way, and he often felt he'd let her down, though she assured him he shouldn't feel guilty on her behalf. "Just do me proud," she charged him, leaving him to interpret what that might mean. Still, they fooled around, if gingerly due to the presence of Sue Lily, who was often wedged inertly between them. At first the tot made Bernie uncomfortable, but ultimately he learned to ignore her, an attitude that earned him Lou Ella's displeasure. "Please to respect her personhood," she scolded him, and when he complained, "I can't win," Lou would cluck her tongue in mock sympathy and consign her baby sister to the backseat.

Knowing that she was waiting for him gave Bernie the courage to travel further in his ecstasies than he'd previously dared; although, when he returned, he was often met with a terse: "Wha'd ya bring me?" When he showed his empty hands, she sullenly remarked that the earth was on its last legs, Armageddon was nigh, and still he came back from the nebulae with nothing new. "It's the beginning of the end of the world or ain't you noticed? and doofus that you are, you keep on hoarding all the grace for yourself." Suggesting that she may have overstated the case, Bernie nevertheless resolved to seek the counsel of the teletzaddik Rabbi ben Zephyr, whose example he hoped to observe again at first hand.

THE NEW HOUSE of Enlightenment was situated in a stadium-size structure surrounded by crepe myrtle and lilac, atop a knoll carpeted in shaggy grass slabs like an igloo made of turf. Originally a Baptist tabernacle whose pastor had fallen from grace in a sex-for-prayer scandal, the hulking, flying saucer–shaped building had undergone few alterations since changing hands. Coming upon the place through the humid morning haze, Bernie found himself transposing it in his mind to the Temple Mount in Jerusalem, with the rabbi's followers dragging trussed and bleating animals up its steps for sacrifice. There was a big sign out front of the type that ordinarily proclaimed Jesus as Lord, its changeable letters now declaring LIVE ALREADY LIKE THE DAY IS HERE! What day? wondered Bernie, skeptical as to the imminence of a new age. Confronted with the sheer square footage of the rabbi's institution, however, Bernie had to admire his ambition. His own path was so solitary by contrast. Which was why, at Lou Ella's urging (though she may have been only joking), he had begun to think that he too, despite his tender years and lack of credentials, ought perhaps to consider starting a ministry of his own — concerning which he would also seek the rabbi's advice. He'd come at an early hour, hoping to beat the heat and catch the old man before his day began with its busy round of self-ultimate classes and motivational talks.

Finding the glass doors to the foyer still locked, Bernie rapped on the panes, which rattled like distant thunder. Presently a broad-shouldered black man in a suit and mirrored sunglasses arrived to unlock the doors, releasing as he opened them a chilly blast from the air-conditioned interior.

"Can I hep y'all?" he asked in a voice that seemed to emanate from the bottom of an oil drum. When Bernie said he was there to see the rebbe, the man—a Bukharan kippah riding his shaven head, a walkie-talkie gripped in a hand wrapped in leather like a cestus—inquired if he had an appointment. "No," said Bernie, "but we're practically related," and gave his name. "I'll see can he see you," said the security, looking askance at the boy, who caught his own reflection in a lens of the man's glasses: a shnoz-heavy adolescent with a head of sprung curls, his T-shirt bellying about his much diminished frame. He checked the other lens in the hope of glimpsing a more imposing countenance, but the image was identical. The man spoke into his mobile instrument, which crackled affirmatively, after which he beckoned Bernie to follow his rolling gait past a gift shop stocked with an inventory of extravagantly priced books and arcana. They stepped into a glass-walled elevator that resembled nothing so much as a colossal ice cube. The elevator rose past the mezzanine, whose wide, sunlit corridor encircled the auditorium, to a third level, where a catwalk stretched over space to a vaultlike door. Exiting, Bernie's escort crossed the resounding steel span and knocked. The jellyfish eye that winked from a peephole was made redundant by the sentinel camera mounted above the door, which rolled open on metal casters to reveal a zaftig woman in her middle years. She was wearing a floral print muumuu and smiling a ruddy-cheeked smile, her hair spooled about her head like pink cotton candy.

"Bernie!" She greeted him as if they were old acquaintances. "Our rebbe has told us so much about you."

Delivered into her hands by the myrmidon (uttering a deep-toned "Peace be wicha" as he departed), the boy thought he might have recognized the woman from the old Kabbalah center in the shopping plaza, but in his memory all the ladies at the center looked alike. That impression was reinforced when another woman, similarly clad and with a face stretched tight from cosmetic surgery, took his other arm and also made over him as if he were kin. They conducted him into a commodious, cork-paneled room, the hybrid of a press box and an air control tower. Seated therein, yet another caftaned lady, headphones clamped over Medusa-like hair, manned a blinking computer terminal from which she too looked up to grin sweetly at Bernie. In front of her a row of thick windows overlooked an arena the size of a circus bigtop, its steep tiers of theater seats surrounding an Astroturfed paddock. A bank of video screens hugged the curve of the wall above the windows, each displaying a different aspect of the auditorium below. "Behold the pulsating nerve center of the House of Enlightenment," announced the woman with the cotton candy hair in her role as tutelary spirit. Bernie had just begun to peer through the tinted glass into the amphitheater, where a trickle of devotees were beginning to assemble for the morning session, when he heard behind him a once familiar voice,

"Boychikl!" it croaked.

He turned to see Rabbi ben Zephyr himself entering from a private chamber off the control room. He was wearing a cap like a truncated mitre and a summer-weight suit of iridescent leek-green, while yet another female, trim in her tennis skirt, trailing a chestnut braid the length of her vertebrae, was placing an embroidered ephod over his head. There was a ruff of tissues stuffed into his collar to protect his suit from the makeup that the woman (really a girl) with the braid had begun to rub into his rutted brow.

"Hartzeniu," he greeted, actually pinching Bernie's cheek as he shuffled forward, "the prodigal returns. Looks like he could use something to eat, the prodigal. Messy . . . ?" The cotton candy lady—whose name, the rabbi offered in an aside, was Messalina—snatched a tray of fruit danishes from a conference table in the center of the room and presented it to Bernie, who declined; his stomach was too skittish for food. Still, he was grateful for the exuberant welcome that had replaced the raillery he'd encountered on his prior visit.

"How are the folks?" asked Rabbi Eliezer, waving away the hand of the girl wielding the powder puff. "Don't tell me. Your papa's got up his sleeve another investment scheme, and your mama, she comes to the noon minchah meditation. A dedicated lady, is raised now her conscious almost to the third degree. Soon she don't mind no more the hot flash or the droppéd womb. How do I know? What don't I know," wriggling his crooked fingers spookily. "Also, they had me last night in their house to supper. And where was you that ain't never at home? You still with the knee-jerk assumptions to glory, or did you go back to touching yourself all the time?"

Speechless in the face of such a barrage, Bernie concluded that celebrity had improved the rabbi's disposition. When he found his tongue, he admitted that, yes, he did seem to be living in at least two worlds at once. "I keep, y'know, stumbling into paradise." He chuckled self-consciously, wanting suddenly to tell the old man everything: how conventional reality now seemed to him almost negligible, except for the existence of the girl; but the rabbi was wagging a finger like a windshield wiper in front of his nose.

"Barney—"

"Bernie."

"Bernie, paradise is where already you are."

Uncrossing his eyes from their fix on the ticking finger, Bernie wondered if the rabbi were speaking to him in earnest or in his capacity as peddler of commercial illumination; then he scolded himself for thinking that there was such a distinction. "Still," he submitted in a lower key, "I keep having these, y'know, experiences."

"Hust," exhaled the old man, and there was the finger again, this time pressed against his desiccated lips. "There's physics you can take for them, the experiences." Then he cackled with a hilarity that was seconded by his ladies.

A good sport, Bernie nevertheless responded with a touch of defiance. "The visions, when they come, they swallow up every part of me but my body."

"Nu," replied the rabbi patronizingly, his eyebrows opposing slopes, "visions." The ladies also looked on with undue fondness. "Sweetheart," said his mentor, "visions I dispense here like shalachmones at Purim; it ain't so special, the visions." Then sotto voce, "But don't tell to my congregation this."

The note of confidentiality heartened the boy enough to ask the first of his laundry list of questions: Did the rabbi's "congregants" ever bring back any, um, like gifts from their meditative flights?

"What are you kidding?" The rabbi was incredulous, or anyway pretended to be. "What you think, dveykuss, which you call it conscious, is a cruise ship to the Bahama? Conscious . . . ness? is the end of the line; you get yours and you're a satisfy customer, end of shtory." One of the women had stuck a lit cigar in his mouth, which he clenched between rows of shiny new ivories.

"But" — Bernie was thinking of the wisdom that the masters would retrieve from their excursions to the celestial academies — "the tzaddiks . . ."

The old man harrumphed. "What tzaddiks? There ain't no more tzaddiks. I was the last one and I drownded in the century before the century before this."

"But Rabbi," Bernie begged to differ, though the rebbe's painted fetish of a face posed a weak argument, "you're still alive."

"In a sense," said old Eliezer mysteriously.

"What do you mean?" asked Bernie, perplexed.

"Rabbi," Messalina respectfully interrupted, "you shouldn't tire yourself out. It's time to go down and meet your flock."

The old man lifted and let fall his scant shoulders, as if to say, I'm a martyr to my public, and took a last puff of his cigar before handing it back to the buxom lady with the reconstructed chin. As his attendants escorted the rabbi out the door, Bernie thought he resembled in his vestments an oversized playing card: The joker, he said to himself before guiltily banishing the thought. He stood wondering what to do next, when the snake-haired woman at the computer terminal, removing the headset to introduce herself as chief technician, invited him to watch the rabbi's performance from the skybox. She explained that the holy man's words would be videotaped for uploading onto his website, where his wisdom could be disseminated throughout cyberspace. Bernie pressed his nose to the bulletproof windows to view the assembly, which, if not quite the multitudes the papers had reported, was still an impressive turnout for a weekday morning. The gathering was composed primarily of young and not-so-young women arrayed in stylish exercise outfits, with here and there a fey young man, similarly attired, while the remainder of the crowd—wives in Capri pants, husbands in wife beaters and industrial caps—might have been left over from the Baptist evangelist's era. Had they returned through force of habit? Seated on a raised dais in a thronelike armchair, a tiny microphone appearing to orbit his jaw like a fly, Rabbi ben Zephyr began his pulpit discourse. It was a case history, really, about a Mrs. Kissel, whose caterer had had a coronary on the eve of her son Sean's bar mitzvah. The event was to have been followed by a theme party inspired by the video game Grand Theft Auto, its centerpiece a cake in the shape of a car raised on a hydraulic lift.

"Mrs. Kissel, who is here today?" A squat bruin of a woman got awkwardly to her feet and was roundly applauded. "Mrs. Kissel that she might have blew a gasket, but instead of to react she becomes . . ." The rabbi invited the word with a come-hither gesture, which the congregation shouted as one: "Pro-Active!" "On the names of the Unnameable she meditates," he continued at an amplified pitch, "which it allowed her to see better the essence instead of the sorry substance from young Sean's bar mitzvah. She sees how on the higher plane he is readink already his portion Torah in the presence of Rabbis Hillel and Shammai." Behind the speaker enormous power-point images of the ancient sages were projected onto a screen, juxtaposed with snapshots of Sean in his tallis among action figures from the Grand Theft video game. "The next day, the caterer, olav hasholem, is dead, the reception after the bar mitzvah a train wreck," another image of guests in a rented hall looking bewildered over the absence of food, "but in her proactive bubble Mrs. Kissel is tranquil, aware of by Heaven and Earth the con-tig-u-i-ty. So what is the lesson? What looks like it ain't exactly the Garden of Eden, with a little adjust from the focus, it's the Garden of Eden."

Unsure of what he'd heard, Bernie shook his head as if to rid it of a flea in his brain. Meanwhile cantorial music was being piped into the amphitheater, and the assembled, profoundly moved, were on their feet swaying ecstatically with upraised hands. Their rebbe went on to assure them that the Light was no more hidden than the Passover afikoymen a papa hides for his children in plain sight; they should keep their eyes peeled. Then beckoning one and all to come down from the stands and sit on the artificial turf at his feet, he explained in a pseudoscientific jargon the power of the Ben Zephyr system to increase CO_2 in the lungs, thereby lowering the efficiency of the cerebral reducing valve . . . and so on. While visual prompts were flashed on the screen behind him — mansions with satellite dishes, food processors, digital cameras, and handguns, along with fat cherubs out of Currier & Ives — he led them in a laughing meditation, during which Bernie's own special perceptions began to come into play. He saw all about them a carnival of auras ranging the spectrum from Technicolor to snot gray, souls shaped like bagpipes shedding period costumes to arrive mother-naked at this particular station in time. The session ended with a penitential prayer, the gathered beating their chests with their fists responsively as if in a martial salute. Then a brief benediction after which the rabbi was ushered by his thick-necked sergeant-at-arms through a gauntlet of the faithful, all wanting to touch him.

When he reentered his communications aerie on the arms of the women, his few remaining tufts of hair were plastered in spit curls to his sunken temples; his face was runneled in sweat, which the girl with the braid (who looked frankly not much older than Bernie) was busy mopping from his forehead and cheeks. The braid tickled her buttocks, which in turn lifted the pleats of her skirt like a partridge tail, as she dabbed at the makeup staining his beard.

"You still here?" he inquired a bit hoarsely of the boy.

There was a moment when Bernie was unable to equate the sage, so composed on his podium as he orchestrated a spiritual debauch, with the runny-eyed scarecrow shuffling into the room.

"What did you mean," Bernie still needed to know, "by 'in a sense'?"

"Means?" the holy man knitted his parchment brow in an effort to recall where their conversation had left off. Then nodding his head he remarked offhandedly, "Means I'm dead already and in heaven."

It took Bernie the better part of a minute to respond. "Excuse me, Rabbi, but this isn't heaven."

Messalina was pulling the linen ephod over his head while the girl ("A dank, Cosette") helped him off with his suit jacket and loosened his collar. The wash 'n' wear shirt was wringing with perspiration, clinging to his skeletal frame, inciting Cosette to flutter about him with a church fan emblazoned with an aleph in a cake of ice — presumably the House of Enlightenment logo. The lady with the chin tuck offered him a glass of tea with lemon.

"La chayim, Rosalie," said the old man, popping a sugar cube into his mouth, his carmined lips forming a fishy oval through which to slurp his tea; then he returned to the subject of Bernie's repudiation: "Is as good as."

Taken aback, the boy nevertheless stuck to his guns: "No, it isn't." He was startled by the aggressiveness of his own rejoinder; where did he get the gumption? But he was thinking of Lou Ella's daily catalog of disasters, the body counts she gleaned from the radio and insisted on reciting to Bernie to keep him informed. It was the ballast she provided to help tether him to his home planet — though didn't the ills she listed also compound his reasons for drifting away? "It's time for your catechism by cataclysm," she would jauntily announce, to which Bernie might add for good measure various khurbanim, the horrors that had uniquely afflicted the Jews.

The rabbi had assumed a smug expression. "Ketzele, you can't sit on two pots with one toches. Gib a keek on my boudoir over there." Bernie glanced through the open French doors at the circular bed beneath its soft track-lighting, surrounded by velvet draperies, electronic monitors, and various gadgets on whose purposes he preferred not to speculate. "You'll see I got your home theater complete with the ZipConnect CD stereo, the Sony subwoofer and digital tuner; I got your liquid crystal plasma TV and the webcam for broadcasting to my followers Rabbi ben Zephyr his intimate moments, so under their rebbe's bed they don't have to hide to get carnal wisdom. I got here your robotic massage chair." Lowering himself with a deal of grunting into a padded swivel chair at the head of the conference table, as Rosalie, donning a pair of cat's-eye glasses, pressed a button that made the chair vibrate. "In the p-parking lot I g-g-g-got a Ch-chevy Tahoe and the P-p-p-porsche car which my bodyguard Ch-ch-ch-cholly Side-pocket will learn me to drive." Rosalie switched off the chair. "I got in the basement a infa-red shvitz, a frigerator stock full with smoked Nova and import schnapps; I got the ladies" — blushes all around — "to spoon-feed me and give to me the pills that will make to stand up again little Yankl. Takhe" — whispering, though what was left to be discreet about? — "they even change by me mayn vikele should I pish myself." Bernie was close to clapping his hands over his ears. "I got students that like Messiah ben David they worship me. If this ain't Gan Eydn, what is?"

The boy opened his mouth to object, something wasn't right, but found no ready reply.

"I got also scheduled the Botox injection and the vein removal treatment to make me again young. This way will I live forever."

"Wait a minute," inserted Bernie, his head spinning. "I thought you said you were dead."

"In a sense," replied Rabbi ben Zephyr.

At that point Bernie groaned aloud: Was the rabbi playing with his mind? As if to confirm it, the old man grinned, scattering wrinkles like jackstraws over his hollow cheeks as he changed the subject. "Hey, Moishe Kapoyer, Mr. Upside-Down, you got yet a girl?"

Bernie made a mighty effort to respond in kind. "In a sense," he said.

"Mazel tov," said the rabbi, though whether congratulating him on the girl or his ironic faculty (touché), the boy couldn't tell. "Are you shtupping her?"

"Pardon me?"

"What's a matter," the old man seemed concerned, "you ain't with her yet a man? You're old enough to pull your putz, you should be already a man. So boychik, you want maybe to borrow my pills?"

Trying to regain some perspective, Bernie asked his mentor in all seriousness, "Is that what's important? The shtupping?"

"What else?" said the rabbi breezily. "Sex is for the poor man his davening. Of course, there's the eating and drinking and the chutzpedik movement of the bowel, but ah, the shtupping! I'm shtupping almost every night, almost on Monday, almost on Tuesday . . ."

The ladies tittered like glockenspiels.

Feeling bludgeoned, Bernie endeavored to remind himself that this was his own Rabbi ben Zephyr, the wonder rebbe he'd salvaged from the deep freeze and in whom he placed his implicit faith. "Lou Ella . . . ," he tendered, and immediately wished he could take back her name.

"A shiksa?"

"Does it matter?'

The rabbi grinned again, his false teeth glistening like eggs in a nest, and rolled his eyes to indicate the diversity among his attendants.

Cautiously appeased, the boy proceeded with his confession. Was this what he'd come here for? "I think I love her," he stated under his breath, aware that the ladies were cupping their ears, "but I can't, like, y'know"—he nodded in a way that caused the rabbi to nod in sync—"because every time we start my spirit takes off for points unknown."

"Hmm." The old man frowned like a doctor hearing doubtful sounds through a stethoscope. "Then maybe with the sacred you should break already your connection, so you ain't no more torn."

Bernie looked at him with incomprehension. "But isn't torn what I'm supposed to be?" For this, as the texts agreed, was the human condition.

"Not at all," replied Rabbi ben Zephyr, dismissing, as Bernie saw it, the fundamental tenet of his creed. "Look at me, how at peace I am with the world."

"Which world?" wondered the boy, all at sea.

Up went the crooked finger again. "That is the question."

Again Bernie groaned as the rabbi chortled and took from a tiny gold pillbox a pinch of snuff—at least the boy presumed it was snuff. "Rabbi," he submitted, "you'll forgive me, but these things are easy for you to say. You're" — Did he still believe it? — "an enlightened saint."

"Nifter-shmifter," said the rabbi, and sneezed into one of several proffered hankies, "I finished with all that saint business when I was alive."

"But you *are* alive," insisted Bernie.

The rabbi grinned, and Bernie waited for the words he was thankfully spared, though variations — *in no sense, innocence* — resonated in his head all the same.

"You see," the old gaffer continued, "the rebbe that I was never waked up from on ice his dream, which it's a long nightmare I don't have to tell you. His neshomah that it never returned to his breast. But me myself, Eliezer ben Zephyr, what I realized, I am born again in heaven like I was on earth. Here, nothing is written, everything is permitted. Feel good in yourself is the whole of the law."

It occurred to Bernie that such heterodox pronouncements might be merely for the benefit of shocking him, though he rejected the notion as precisely the kind of self-centered thinking that Lou was forever upbraiding him for. "What about the mitzvot?" he asked, knowing the question probably no longer applied.

"When I was alive in my life," came the refrain, "all six hundred thirteen precepts I observed; I was tamim, a perfect master. Tiqqun ha-kelali I practiced to preserve the sex continence, and all my years I never looked once at my shwantz. I would read in a flash your tzelem, what you call the genealogy from souls. Were legendary also my disciples for their piety; about us tales were told all over Galut. Did you hear the one how I hired a person just to keep the names of God before me? How I outwitted the Angel of Death and captured the devil Samael, but let him go so there would still be in the world evil and therefore free will? Then in the flood I died and woke up in Paradise, where it's my reward there's nothing I got to observe anymore. So I'm telling the gantser klal, gentiles included, this is heaven already on the planet of Earth. It's all in my book."

Bernie reflected that the exploits the rabbi alluded to bore a marked similarity to those of the masters in Martin Buber's *Legends of the Hasidim*. "This is what you teach your students?" he asked.

"Peace of mind I give them to trade in the gilt-edge security and refinance the adjustable mortgage, that they should feel good in themselves and not guilty that they beat der kinder, cheat on the wife, or betray the friend. Then I give to them a bisl divinity so as to leave with them a little bliss. Praise God who permits the forbidden. Live like the day is here. 'Hide not thyself from thine own flesh.'"

"What about"—Bernie was conscious of sounding a tad sanctimonious—"'Do not unto others what is also hateful to you?'"

"I don't like to embarrass with too much Jewish stuff the goyim," repined the rabbi, "though speaking of Hillel, what about 'If not now, when?'" squeezing the broad behind of Messalina, who giggled gamely.

"This is not helpful," Bernie admitted to himself.

"Bubbie, you're all farmisht because how you suffer from the blue beytsim." He touched his own scrotum sympathetically. "Relax and deposit in the appropriate female orifice your seed. This is nature. Myself, I never had on earth no wife and kids; like the Karaites that would make from themself a eunuch, I was pure. Till the afterlife I waited to be a man so that I'm makink up for it now the lost time. So stop kvetching and start yentzing; this is my advice that I give to you free of charge, plus a first edition of my book that it's called *The Ice Sage*, adventures of Rabbi Eliezer ben Zephyr and God. Rosalie, ziskeit, fetch for me a copy the book, which it's twenty-nine ninety-five retail."

Bernie received the self-published volume with its glossy cover portrait of the rabbi in his shtreimel with the snap-on raccoon tail. "Thank you," he said uncertainly. Here was at least something palpable he could bring back from his visit. Wasn't that what Lou was always bugging him about, that he should bring her back something of value from his travels? It wasn't enough just to tell her about the unity which is the redemption of all things, and so forth; redemption you could get for a pro-rated annual "tithe" at ben Zephyr's New House of Enlightenment. For a reasonable fee the rabbi would restore your soul. What more could you ask? Which was precisely the question that the still frustrated Bernie put to the rabbi, who sighed impatiently.

"H'omer . . ."

"Bernie," the boy corrected.

"I know by you your name. H'omer means matter; the material world, called also pardes, the Garden, which it is all that here concerns us."

"But," Bernie felt himself succumbing to exasperation, "isn't it pretty hopeless, I mean, the world?"

"What kind message is that? You know they are the same in Hebrew, the words for messenger and angel? It's for the teacher his responsibility to bring the good news."

"Even if it's a lie?"

The rabbi ignored him. "I'm a busy man; I got now to meet my Tantric Kabbalah group." The ladies helped him up from his chair and back on with his ritual garment, dusting him with the powder puff and whisk broom again. "I'm very gratified we had this little talk, baruch haShem and all that."

He was nearly out the door when Bernie collected himself enough to cry, "Rabbi, wait!"

Turning only halfway 'round, "What is it you want?'

"Your blessing?" said the boy.

"Sure, sure. Gezunterheyt. Knock yourself out." And he was gone.

1908.

They slept together like brothers in the same bed, which Shmerl lowered each evening from the ceiling and raised again (sometimes with Max still in it) in the late mornings when he woke. For although Max had adjusted to Shmerl's odd hours, he often continued to sleep in his borrowed longjohns through much of the day. In fact, during those first days after his rescue Max never set foot outside the automated shack, as if the ordeal of the previous months had finally caught up with him and laid him low. Even though his wound was minor and largely healed before the week was out, he remained convalescent, and Shmerl was happy to indulge him in his prostration. Having saved him, the dung carter now felt somehow responsible for securing his guest's enduring safety and health. Though Max assured him the attack in the alley was merely a chance episode not likely to happen again, Shmerl remained anxious concerning his new friend's welfare. He changed his head dressing daily, examined him for any symptoms of concussion, and continued to apply the vile medicinal compresses; he cooked him meals: mostly a gluey amalgam of kasha and eggs, though sometimes there was Jewish fish: "Is now my namesake, Karp." And Max, who had eaten all manner of treyf these many months, was appreciative, not to say amused by the crucibles and alkaline cells Shmerl employed in his culinary endeavors, the results of which were more often than not inedible. Nor did it help that the aroma of every dish partook of the stables' distinct bouquet. All the same, in a show of abiding gratitude (and in deference to Shmerl's insistence that he keep up his strength), Max would dutifully sample the fare; though in time the guest, begging his host's permission, revived Jocheved's dormant skills and took over the cooking himself.

Of course the subject of the frozen rabbi had necessarily to be broached and dispensed with before the ice (so to speak) could be broken between them. It was Shmerl, protesting all the while that he had no wish to pry, who had nonetheless initiated the conversation on that very first night.

"So how by the old chasid did you come?"

Max demurred, not inclined to lie to the hunchback but also unready to state the plain truth. "He is in my family a cherished memento," was his lame explanation.

"What he makes you to remember?"

Again Max was stymied, while Shmerl, to his relief, seemed to dismiss his waffling silence as an occasion to offer a theory of his own. "I think he is yet alive, di alter mensch," he stated, a faraway look clouding his eye; "he is only asleep and dreaming. He dreams the dream of the world that we are all of us in it, and to wake him now might make already the end of the world."

While questioning the dung carter's sanity, Max acceded at the same time to Jocheved's endorsement of a concept she regarded as rather sound.

At first Shmerl had worried that Reb Levine (who lived above the stables) might discover his guest and evict them both, but the contractor had little need to venture into the shack anymore, now that his employee had made himself so indispensable. In fact, thanks to Shmerl's vigor and ingenuity, the old livery stable proprietor was enjoying a state of semi-retirement. As a consequence, his lad-of-all-work had never had to explain the jungle of gadgetry (the Otto cycle engine that ran on feces and moon-

beams, the battery that alternated currents the way a prism divides a wave
of light into a rainbow) that had overtaken the tarpapered outbuilding.

Rivaling his passion for invention, however, was the prospect of continuing his explorations of the Golden Land with a worthy partner; and
solicitous as he was of his guest's recuperation, after a reasonable time
had elapsed, Shmerl invited Max to walk abroad with him. The invitation
triggered in Max the first pang of alarm he'd experienced since taking
advantage of Shmerl's hospitality; then it passed, and he donned the shirt,
trousers, and Kitchener vestee that the dung carter had bought him off
a secondhand rack in Orchard Street. (His own clothes, beyond bloodied, were clownishly voluminous.) It was a late afternoon at the outset of
spring, no doubt approaching Pesach, though who remembered holidays
in this heathen land? Nevertheless, Shmerl was in a holiday mood. He had
just returned from paying the livery stable's weekly extortion fee to members of the Yid Black Hand in their fumy backroom behind Grand Street.
There, he was brought up short upon recognizing a couple of characters
seated at the bottle-laden table—the caddy cap in new knickerbockers
and argyles, his sidekick stuffing burny up his beak—who thankfully
showed no signs of recognizing him. Seeing them in their natural habitat
left Shmerl with the conviction that they were merely a pair of garden variety gonifs of a type that were a common hazard in the Tenth Ward; they
were finally no more a menace than bedbugs and rising damp. So when he
arrived back at the wagonyard, Shmerl proposed to the yungerman, whom
he decided had been idle too long, that they take a stroll; though just in
case he carried along his galvanic cane.

Mild breezes nipped at the heels of a gusting wind in full retreat as the
dung carter and the dissembler browsed the East Side streets, observing
together the same sights they'd witnessed countless times on their own.
But each, though he never said so, had the peculiar sense of seeing the
neighborhood afresh, Shmerl as if peering through the eyes of his newfound friend, and vice versa. Outsiders for so long, together they felt what
neither had before: that they were young men out on the town, a couple

of rubbernecks ogling the ghetto's attractions, gauging the potential of an East Broadway shmooserie or candy store for fellowship and intrigue. With only a spotty understanding of how his companion had survived the winter, Shmerl felt he was introducing a greenhorn to the omnifarious city, and Max reinforced his attitude by perceiving the streets for once as amusement rather than likely threat. Relinquishing a little his habit of eternal vigilance, he also let go of the impulse to cloak himself in yet another disguise, so protected did he feel in the company of his bedfellow, this patent meshugener with his strange avocations whom he was nonetheless growing to admire. There even came a point in their stroll when, watching some girls in their dove-gray shifts playing potsy, chanting "Chatzkele, Chatzkele, shpil mir a kazatzkele" and using a fisheye for a marker, Max's spirits rose almost past containing. "What a jubilee!" he exclaimed, then was immediately embarrassed, feeling that such an indecorous outburst must be a joke of Jocheved's at his expense (while Jocheved, from her concealment, wondered if Max had lost his mind).

Another awkward moment for Max came when they stopped for a bowl of borscht at a dairy café, and Shmerl — digging into his knippl, the little knot of cash he'd been hoarding since he'd become a hired hand — insisted on paying the tab. Having passed a dark season as the object of charity, the beggar now wished to be benefactor, despite having no material resources to speak of.

"It is for me my pleasure," his host assured him, proud to be arm-in-arm with such a silken youth, so delicate-featured and slight of frame, attributes almost unseemly for a man. With a sigh Max had accepted the refreshment, just as later he learned to graciously accept the ticket to a Yiddish theater production of *Hamlet, der yeshivah bocher*, translated and improved for the edification of the general public, or the price of admission to a cabaret. For his part, Shmerl felt heartily beholden to his companion for allowing him to show them both a good time. How long he had waited for someone with whom to share his enthusiasm for the knockabout streets and the institutions he'd been too shy to enter alone. It was as if he finally belonged to the teeming neighborhood and had at last arrived in America.

As for Max, he still couldn't quite believe that he'd fallen into such agreeable circumstances. For one thing, despite the forced physical intimacy of their digs, it was relatively effortless to hide Jocheved's gender from his host. This was thanks in part to Shmerl's consideration of his guest's privacy, that and his discretion regarding his own modest habits. As a consequence, even the concealment of Jocheved's menstrual rags was not an issue, though the smell sometimes lingered; but Shmerl seemed to regard it as Max's distinctive scent. Given Shmerl's cavalier inattention to his own sanitary needs, and conditioned as he was by the fetor of the wagonyard, a fundamentally human essence was in no way offensive to him. In this environment Jocheved sometimes felt she might even relax a bit her tenacious secrecy; she might steal a peek on occasion from behind the mask of Max Feinshmeker, as if the world were not such a daunting place after all. This isn't to say the girl didn't sometimes have second thoughts about sharing such close quarters with a bunchbacked companion, involving as it did a moral compromise that Shmerl was not even aware of; there were nights when she lay awake on the flock-stuffed mattress acutely conscious of the fact that the creature lying next to her was male. Men, she must never forget, were the enemy, though this one, this luftmensch Shmerl, seemed of an entirely different breed; and in the end all her reservations with respect to their proximity were overruled by her host's assurances that Max's presence was a great relief from loneliness.

Still, they preserved between them a chummy formality, addressing one another as Feinshmeker and Karp, though each had been known on occasion to let slip the other's given name. Naturally their honeymoon period couldn't last indefinitely, nor did Max, now that his mental acumen was reawakening, wish to maintain much longer the purposeless status quo. Eager to repay his host's generosity, he had begun to get ideas. One evening, a few hours before the start of the nightwalking circuit, at the time when they were accustomed to making their rambles, Max—or was it Jocheved? because it was getting harder to determine whence derived his lapses of voice into a reedy soprano—asked Shmerl to explain again how he had renewed Rabbi ben Zephyr's compartment of ice.

"Zol zayn azoy!" replied Shmerl; "was a trifle." He became abruptly animated as he began to describe how he had magnified sunlight through a filched headlamp in order to melt the original ice in the casket's interior. Then the rabbi might have thawed out like a mackerel on a slab had he not refilled the casket, even as he drained it, with ground water pumped through a rubber hose. After that he'd caused the fresh water to freeze again. "Which is the part that to me it ain't clear yet," interrupted Max. But when Shmerl began his exegesis, using phrases for which there was no Yiddish equivalent—"volatile gas," "pressurized ether refrigerant," "homunculus" (since he regarded the rabbi himself as a stage in an alchemical process)—Max interrupted again to ask him, please, to demonstrate the operation once more. Then again his guest was transfixed by Shmerl's performance, which he re-created in a tinned strainer pail. Such a presentation, he thought, could captivate the crowds on the Bowery; it could command a respectable billing at the Barnum Museum farther uptown. But then Max's mind took a more expedient turn, which was possibly due to the influence of Jocheved, with whom he seemed to have entered into a period of detente.

Snapping out of his role of passive observer, he stood up from his seat on the floating bed. "Karp," he said, "do you ever think you will like to make a gesheft?"

"A beezness?" Shmerl enjoyed showing off his expanding vocabulary, though the word tasted sour on his tongue. Of course, he seldom thought beyond his dreams, which, though they were lately more earthbound, had never God forbid included any commercial ventures. But so taken was he with his new companion that he felt himself inclined to go along with any scheme he might suggest, if only to maintain their close association. Still, he wondered exactly what it was about Max that so beguiled him and inspired his loyalty. True, he was physically quite prepossessing and unquestionably intelligent, and his connection with the deep-frozen tzaddik elevated him all the more in Shmerl's eyes. There was also the possibility that his coattails might carry the inventor toward a prosperity he'd never sought, though for his friend's sake he supposed he wouldn't refuse it. But beyond all that, Max remained for the dung carter the embodiment of a nameless mystery, and Shmerl felt that he couldn't part from him until he'd discovered its origin. So while there was much to be said in favor of solitude and bare subsistence, there was more reason to hang on to the yungerman's company at any cost.

LESS THAN THREE weeks later, they were standing in the presence of the financier August Belmont II, who had risen from behind his desk as if to shoo away a pair of stray alley cats. "Get out of here!" He was wearing on his anointed head a plum fez with a tassle that looked to Shmerl like the roots of an upturned flower pot, though he was in every other respect a striking gentleman. The tall window at his back, which gave on to the verdant park across Fifth Avenue, outlined his trim figure in a corona-like glow as he pulled tight the cords at the waist of his dressing gown.

"A moment of your time, Your Excellent," pleaded Max Feinshmeker, potato-shaped in the overalls and machinist's apron he'd adopted for their artifice. Next to him, similarly clad, stood Shmerl, holding the handle of a device on wheels that resembled a dwarf pachyderm with a dangling snout. Unable to transport the ungainly thing by omnibus, they had hauled it all the way uptown in a rattling dogcart, marveling at how the city altered its character from block to block. The old-law tenements, waist factories, and warehouses gave way to the cast-iron fronts of offices and department stores, which were deposed further on by brownstone terrace houses. The brownstones ebbed at the hotel towers with their striped awnings and liveried doormen, the hotels shading into a rialto of Moorish theaters ringed by touring cars and flocked about by billboards proclaiming the virtues of Doan's Pills and Russian Caravan Tea. Then, at Fifty-ninth Street, the commercial farrago halted in deference to the grandeur along the eastern border of Central Park. For adjacent the budding foliage of a spring afternoon in full spate stood a row of châteaux, palazzi, and fortresslike mansions, the architecture ranging the spectrum from ancient Egypt to Versailles. Amid this grand parade was the showy arabesque of Temple Emanuel, where, it being Shabbos, well-to-do yekkes removed their straw boaters before passing under its Olympian arches.

Confronted by such a density of splendor, both young men had experienced a momentary failure of nerve, though neither was willing to admit to the other how entirely out of his element he felt. Nevertheless, throughout the weeks they had already wasted in attempting to gain an interview with the man of commerce, they had become resolute, Max for the sake of a mission whose upshot would secure them a foothold in the New World, Shmerl for the sake of Max.

The choice of the philanthropist and financier Belmont as their quarry was not random; he was in fact the only millionaire (other than Rothschild) whose name Max was familiar with. ("I am with him very famillionaire," he'd quipped, buoyed by his plan and an increasing aptitude in the language he and Shmerl now spoke almost exclusively.) For Belmont Jr. was that scion of an auspicious family whose name Zalman Pisgat the ice mensch had let slip in connection with the purchase of the bulk sturgeon roe, which commodity Max had spirited across an ocean. Didn't such an undertaking constitute a bond between himself and the banking magnate? Moreover, despite having been christened after his father, a practice unheard of in halakhic convention, Belmont was rumored to have been born a Jew. Thus, in an act of unexampled optimism, Max had indited a letter to the g'vir, introducing himself and alluding to the service he'd once performed for him. In this way he hoped to gain an audience for himself and his associate with the celebrated gentleman.

Made privy over time to his friend's shady past, with which he had no particular qualms (hadn't he smuggled himself out of Russia?), Shmerl helped compose the letter, taking dictation from Max, who in that way concealed his functional illiteracy, though Shmerl's own self-schooling in

English left much to be desired. Together they labored for days over the epistle, which began "Esteemed & Darling ['How do you say ongeshtopt?'] Man Made from Money, In the name of the great tradition that like the beluga fish eggs which from the sea of Riga to America I am bringing you has spawned us, I most humbly request by you an audition . . ." and continued in that vein. Satisfied that they'd struck a fine balance between dignity and groveling, Max posted the letter, but after a week had received no answer. Undaunted, however, he tried again with another even more fulsome communication. In it he and Shmerl assured the mogul that their meeting would serve the best interests of all concerned, but again they received no reply. Still Max was convinced that Belmont was their man, for the banker was known to enjoy taking risks. Besides trafficking in contraband (which a man of his means clearly did for the thrill of it), he had pioneered the first subway and kept his own lavish saloon car, and had invested a fortune in constructing a canal. Moreover, he had a reputation for being a wagering man, a tout with such a passion for the ponies that he was building a national race track in his own honor. But when the appeals had failed to get a response, the companions decided that a more straightforward approach was called for.

It was Shmerl, not ordinarily known for his diplomacy, who pointed out that reminding the rich man of his connection with illicit activities might not be the best way to gain his confidence; better they should simply make their case in person. So they spruced themselves up as well as they were able and presented themselves at the banker's princely Wall Street offices, where, having no appointment, they were promptly shown the door. Rejection, though, seemed only to fuel their shared sense of purpose. Thus, on the following Saturday, when they supposed the odds were likeliest of finding their man at home, the immigrants, posing as workmen hired to vacuum-clean the carpets, arrived at the merchants' entrance of the banker's Fifth Avenue mansion. There they were met by a broad-bottomed manservant who, complaining that he should have been informed prior to their calling, nevertheless let them in.

"You can start with the vestibule," he told them shortly, and waved them in that direction, saying he had business elsewhere and would check on them by and by.

If they'd had second thoughts on beholding the uptown houses from without, the interior of the Belmont residence—said to be the least of the family's holdings—staggered them to near paralysis. "I think," whispered Max, attempting to articulate what had occurred to them both simultaneously, "we are from the East Side as far as is the East Side from the Russian Pale." The entrance hall was a circular chamber with a stained-glass dome that loomed (said Shmerl) like God's own skullcap above a black marble fountain with a single dancing jet. A naked nymph was balanced on one arched foot atop the fountain, from which Shmerl, as if in the presence of some celestial mikveh, was unable to budge until Max shoved him forward. From the hub of the fountain the hallways appeared virtually endless, their walls hung with mirrors facing mirrors, creating transepts that stretched to infinity. Between reflections there were fantasias of antique tiles and hardwood cabinets inlaid with mother of pearl, coves thick with palm fronds, giant bell jars in which swarms of butterflies were suspended in flight. Doors opened onto the Middle Ages, the Late Empire, Byzantium. Trundling over the parqueted floors, the creaking wheels of Shmerl's wooden cart threatened to alert the domestics to their nosing about, though the sound of the cart was soon upstaged by an ear-splitting vibrato that caused the screens to tremble like typanums and bade fair to shatter the vases on their pedestals. The companions froze in their tracks, until Max, who'd done his research, remembered that the rich man had married an opera diva. The explanation did little to dispel Shmerl's impression, which he related under his breath, that they had stumbled into the hekhalot, the very corridors of heaven as described in the *Seder Gan Eyden*, though the book had failed to do the place justice.

Having inspected one whole wing of the mansion without encountering either master or servants, they were less disappointed than relieved. Still, duty-bound to press on, they reversed direction and, after another quarter-hour's exploration, found themselves in front of a door at the end of a passage framed by columns with gilded capitals. The door was slightly ajar and, peeking in, they saw bookshelves climbing the walls to a cambered ceiling, a fireplace above which hung the portrait of a mutton-chopped ancestor, and a desk as broad as a catafalque. Behind the desk, unsealing letters with an ormolu file, sat a well-kempt gentleman Max was able to identify from newspaper photos as the lord of the manor himself. Bestowing an incautious wink on his friend, Max nudged the door wide open, and the two companions stepped over the threshold dragging their camouflaged apparatus behind them. The banker rose from his chair in a show of vexed agitation, demanding "What are you?" while enfolding himself in the skirts of his moiré dressing gown. Then even as he shouted for them to be gone, Max gave Shmerl a nod, upon which the inventor removed the accordion nozzle from his contraption and, like a waiter un-veiling an entrée, snatched off the paper canopy to reveal his perpetual winter machine.

"Your Eminent," said Max, assuming the role of impresario, "if you please."

The financier fixed them with a baleful stare. "Wexelman!" he called, and the servant arrived, huffing. "Did you let these persons in?" Dabbing at the folds of his brow with a hankie, Wexelman tried to mutter an excuse— the housekeeper *had* mentioned having the carpets cleaned—but his mas-ter cut him off, directing him to notify the authorities at once.

As Wexelman withdrew, Shmerl turned a crank that sparked a flame, the flame igniting a pilot the feathery length of a dragon's tongue. Almost instantly wheels began revolving, a cylinder to rise and fall, the inven-tor explaining that his was an ethyl ammonia compression system: "The piston compresses in the vessel to a pintele from its normal volume the or-dinary air," then releases the pressure which allows the air to expand. The chilling effect of the expansion pulls the heat from the brine surrounding the vessel, which in turn draws the warmth from the water inside the receptacle. This method was opposed to the absorption system favored by his predecessors. Of course, you could also use sulfur dioxide or methyl chloride, though these were toxic compounds and might result in the ultimate death of the operator. . . .

"What's he talking about?" the irate financier demanded to know.

Over Shmerl's giddy discourse Max submitted matter-of-factly, "Making ice, Your Honor; he's talking how by this machine we can manufacture industrial ice. My colleague Mr. Karp—"

"This is not a patent office," protested Belmont, aghast at the sight of this troll-like individual fiddling with an infernal mechanism that might for all he knew explode. It might in fact be an elaborate anarchist's bomb. These ostjuden were mostly anarchists, weren't they? who targeted the wealthy with their insane ideological program. It was at this point that Wexelman returned, preceded by the medicine ball of his paunch and a pair of liverish-looking policemen whom he was shepherding with imperious gestures into the study.

"Gentlemen," said Belmont, "these men are trespassing. Apprehend them."

The cops, in mackintosh capes and cupola helmets, chin straps hooked beneath pursed lower lips, exchanged an arch glance between them. Then they at once commenced to lay hands on Max (still petitioning the millionaire's patience) and Shmerl (still explaining the dynamics of mechanical refrigeration). Seeing, however, that his friend was in the grip of an arm of the law whose opposite arm brandished a nightstick—and despite being in identical straits himself—Shmerl managed to wriggle free of his captor and fling himself upon the other officer, grabbing his upraised club. Taking advantage of that cop's distraction, Max broke free of the head-hold to make a dash as if for protection behind the financier's desk, where he was presently joined by Shmerl who now wielded the billy club. Spitting curses despite Wexelman's admonishments that they should watch their language in the presence of Mr. Belmont, the cops approached them from either side of the desk, while the banker stood as a hostage between the pair of imposters who flanked him. Meanwhile a steady chugging issued from

Shmerl's device, its hoarse combustion counterpointed by a silvery aria (from *Tosca?*) that rang throughout the mansion. It was here that August Belmont II, clapping hands to elegant temples streaked with gray like the wings on Mercury's helmet, cried out, "This is most irregular!" Then, because he knew a good thing when he saw it, he called an immediate halt to the pandemonium—because Shmerl's machine, coughing and sputtering, had begun to regurgitate transparent ingots, one of which cracked apart from an impossibly high note struck from somewhere beyond the study walls.

THE GRUMBLING OF Officers Golightly and McCool was soon assuaged by the banker's generosity in compensating them for their troubles. Then, after Shmerl had returned the billy club with all the pomp of a surrendered saber, the bank was contacted and an attorney brought in to draw up the terms of the loan. Five thousand was the figure that was proposed, but as Shmerl looked to his partner to join him in nodding agreement, he was astounded to hear Max counterrecommend a cool ten. Without missing a beat the banker altered the sum to seventy-five hundred as sufficient to cover the cost of venue, equipment, and preliminary labor, it would also provide the proprietors (insolvent at present) with an adequate salary they might draw from the surplus capital. The language of the promissory note was intimidating ("For value received, the undersigned jointly and severally promise to pay to the order of the lender the sum of ———, together with interest of twenty-five percent per annum on the unpaid balance, etc."), but the new corporation of Feinshmeker & Karp was assured that the contract was pro forma; and at least one of the partners understood that the sum was a drop in the bucket for the banker, who stood to benefit disproportionately from the transaction. While business was negotiated, the two friends, their work clothes in disarray from their recent dustup, were served brandy and offered Cuban cigars by the same retainer who had set the authorities upon them earlier. Moted sunlight poured in through the high windows, making the room and its contents—the brass cartouches and crystal decanter, the nickeled pince-nez perched on the financier's regal nose—appear as if viewed through a jar of golden honey; and it seemed to the immigrants that they had passed, in a single day, from civilization's wild outer reaches to its very core.

The attorney, there to notarize the document and issue the check, seemed unfazed by the incongruous appearance of the partners. If he perceived any impropriety in the proceedings, as he handed the friends a gold-nibbed fountain pen, he never showed it, and his ease in officiating the affair inspired the companions to sign with unreserved zeal on the dotted line. They exchanged handshakes all around, first with lender and witness, then with each other, both tacitly acknowledging that notwithstanding the glacier of ice cakes heaped in the tray of Shmerl's machine, a miracle had occurred, both supposing they would now live in a world where they would have to accustom themselves to miracles.

Invited to use Mr. Belmont's own venerable institution, the young men politely declined, preferring to deposit the cashier's check closer to home, in an account in Jarmolovsky's Immigrant Bank on Canal Street. It was to be a joint account, nor did they feel the need to formalize the pact between them; the terms were understood, that Max, a fast learner in the area of finance, would handle the fiscal end of the business while Shmerl saw to technical matters. They placed the loan document in a safe deposit box and straightaway began their search for a property they might convert into a plant for manufacturing ice. They hadn't far to look, since as it turned out the Gebirtig & Son's facility, just a few doors down the road from the bank, was for sale. Owing to an anonymous tip, the police had raided the thriving East Side business, where they'd uncovered a large cache of illegal goods. The owners were promptly arrested and charged with several counts of receiving black-market merchandise and evading tariffs, the cost of their bail and ongoing legal fees (and the bribes to underworld parties who reneged on their promises) having forced them into bankruptcy. As a result, their business was placed on the auction block and the partnership of Feinshmeker & Karp, handily outbidding the competition with their newly acquired funds, purchased the Ice Castle at a virtual steal. Then they proceeded with all due haste to hire contractors to revamp the several cavernous floors of the old warehouse into a factory for the large-scale production of ice.

Neither of the immigrants could have anticipated the speed with which things progressed. Drawing on a business sense he owed in large part to Jocheved's prior experience, Max set about purchasing equipment according to Shmerl's detailed itemizations and then turned to the more complex issue of labor. Since the modified Ice Castle would continue the cold storage operations of its previous owners, it would be possible to keep on much of the staff laid off in the wake of the police shutdown. A number of employees would naturally have to be trained to operate the ice-making machinery; they would have to acquire the skills necessary to regulate a steam generator, adjust levels of absorption and compression according to the effects of temperature on the solubility of gases, and so forth. But the workers, once educated by the journeyman Shmerl Karp, could then expect a rise in salary, and their promotion would mean the promise of upward mobility to those menials aspiring to be "apreyters" and engineers. It was a situation sure to increase the level of performance at every stage of the operation — or so Max theorized, surprising himself with his newborn interest in commercial productivity, an enthusiasm he also attributed to the Frostbissen girl. Meanwhile Shmerl made his calculations and supervised the assembly of machinery on a scale that for once nearly matched his imagination. Of course, due to practical considerations, he was forced to eliminate some of the aesthetic features of his original ice-making contrivance in favor of the more strictly functional. He had to admit that his elaborate new machine, impressive as it was, had no real value beyond the utilitarian, but as he oversaw the mounting of the turbine with its floating vertical shaft fashioned according to his own specifications, or watched the metallic bellows fill like a bullfrog's throat with gas as it expanded to rev the motor, Shmerl was as elated as if he were present at the Creation. He was, however, uncomfortable in his role as foreman, awkward at delegating authority to others, a problem he eventually confided to his friend.

Too busy to think about changing their current address, the companions still resided in Levine's rank stableyard. In his unfailing gratitude to the old man, Shmerl had continued to fulfill his nightwalking duties, giving up much needed sleep and exhausting himself in the process. Worried about his friend, Max decided it was time he was emancipated from the shit patrol and, also well disposed toward their spry old benefactor, proposed this solution: Offer Levine the foreman's position at the ice plant. Which was how Elihu Levine, after personally escorting Akivah and Bar Kochbah, his beloved bags-of-bones, to the glue factory, took up the management of New York's premier facility for the high-volume production of economical and sanitary block ice. Shmerl was amazed at how readily the veteran stableman, when presented with so speculative an opportunity, had been prepared to scrap a decades-long livelihood. But released from circumstances defined by animal waste, the old drek shlepper was fairly rejuvenated; he threw himself into his new role with a passion, assiduously adjusting prices and filing invoices, inspecting meat lockers and equipment, hiring laborers with the shrewdness of a captain interviewing a crew for a dangerous voyage. He also appointed himself shop steward of the IMU, the Ice Man's Union, a collective of his own formation for which he obtained a national charter, making him both an essential liaison between management and labor and a thorn in the side of his employers ever after.

In private moments, of which there were lately precious few, Shmerl asked himself if this was really the life he desired; was he a hypocrite for his headlong entry into the world of free trade? But such questions, he had to admit, came more from force of habit than any genuine consternation on his part, since for better or worse his total immersion in temporal affairs kept him in a state of mild intoxication. He was gratified as well by the way his partnership with Max seemed to consolidate the friendship that had preceded their business arrangement. While he remained puzzled at times by the yungerman's periodic aloofness and inordinate modesty—Max still refused, for instance, to attend the public baths despite Shmerl's example, opting instead to reduce his gaminess by the occasional sitz-bod behind a canvas tarp in the shack—these were trivial imperfections that in no way impeded the inventor's ever increasing admiration for his friend.

Their division of labor, however, left them less inseparable than they'd been before commencing their entrepreneurial relationship, which made Shmerl cherish the time they spent together all the more. Sometimes they might take a meal at a Grand Street cafeteria (they could afford it now), then repair to an East Broadway tearoom where the intelligents gathered and the companions, feeling a little like capitalist spies, kibbitzed conversations about rallies, strikes, and the impending revolution. Once in a while they took in a Yiddish play on Second Avenue, where they saw Mrs. Krantsfeld and a pop-eyed Ludwig Satz sink into deepest depravity in Zolatarevsky's *Money, Love, and Shame*, and hailed Boris Tomashevsky wearing tights that made sausage links of his legs as he strutted the boards in *Alexander, Crown Prince of Jerusalem*. Once, taking a rare holiday, they rode the New York & Sea Beach Line out to Coney Island to see the Elephant; they had their weight guessed and their fortunes read by a gypsy (who seemed diverted by Max's soft palm, troubled by something she saw in Shmerl's); they tested their strength, ate chazzerai, and threw baseballs at the head of a Negro, then strolled the boardwalk past couples spooning along the Iron Pier.

Max teased Shmerl because he was leering at the girls gamboling in the surf in their revealing costumes. "Perhaps they are numbered your bachelor days." But no sooner had he poked fun at his friend and seen his subsequent chagrin than Max flushed a deep crimson himself.

On the eve of the grand reopening of the Ice Castle, the partners celebrated over dinner at Virág's Hungarian Noodle Shop in a cellar on Forsyth Street. For all intents and purposes, their business was already under way. Ads had been placed in both Yiddish and mainstream papers, sparking a small controversy, some of the natural ice houses having complained in the press that "artificial" ice was ungodly. To counter the attacks, Max had managed a deft feat of public relations, engaging local clergy, both Jewish and gentile, to endorse their product. In the end, having focused attention on the Ice Castle's innovation, the discord proved a useful marketing ploy, and already there were orders from several breweries and meat-packing companies; in addition, the Gebirtigs' legitimate cold storage clients had renewed their contracts with the novice owners. The lockers and vaults of perishables were stocked to near capacity, making the official launching of the plant somewhat after the fact. Nevertheless, decked out in sporty new threads for the occasion (dress worsteds with pencil stripes) the two friends dined on hot shtshav and goulash and, characterizing themselves as "two corpses gone dancing," toasted each other with sweet Muscat wine.

"To the Ice Castle . . . ," proposed Max.

". . . that ice folly it don't turn out to be," said Shmerl, clinking his partner's glass.

"L'chayim."

Beneath a hat rack in the corner a fiddle and bass played an apathetic schottische as the partners discussed their joint venture, waxing nostalgic over the distance they'd traveled together in so short a time. Whatever misgivings Shmerl may have had about abandoning his autonomy were dispelled by his attachment to his capable friend; while for his part, Max, basking in the inventor's fond regard, felt at ease enough to bring up a touchy subject.

"I lied to you, Karp," he confessed, eyes inclined toward his small hands folded almost prayerfully before him on the table. "I lied that was a chance occurrence the attack in the alley." He admitted that, while he'd never felt so safe as when in his partner's company, he was in effect still a marked man, targeted for an untimely end by the agents of a party who believed Max had cheated him.

Appalled by the information, Shmerl snapped at his friend for the first time in their mutual history, "Why you didn't tell me before!" All these weeks Max had spent in harm's way could have been avoided. Shmerl knew where the culprits hung out; he would go there and challenge them to their face, he would blow them all farplotzn with a chemical cocktail, he would . . . But Max calmed him down with the assurance that he'd taken the liberty of sending a small portion of their capital to Pisgat, the offended party, as an installment on his lost money, promising the balance in due course; so it was possible that by now the ice mensch had called off his dogs. In the meantime, however, just to stay on the safe side, Max Feinshmeker would remain "by the Ice Castle a silent partner."

The inventor tilted his head in an effort to see better the logic of his friend's proposal.

But Max had not been entirely candid. He'd neglected to say that this intended arrangement had as much to do with distancing himself from Shmerl as it did with protecting his own neck and their business. For he'd come to feel that he and his associate had grown too close; they depended too much on one another. It was an attitude prompted in part by Jocheved, with whom Max no longer felt so much at odds. Both he and the girl were painfully aware of the danger of overmuch intimacy with a member of the opposite sex, even one as ultimately harmless as Shmerl Karp. But was he harmless? Because the inventor had become altogether too necessary to the yungerman, who was ever more conscious lately of being female. Lately he felt he was equal parts Max Feinshmeker and Jocheved, with Jocheved beginning to tip the balance as he deferred more and more to her native commercial flair. Moreover, Max was growing weary of always pretending. Sometimes he wanted simply to set the girl free, if only for a little while, but for that a greater privacy was needed; for that, he admitted, "I rented also an apartment uptown."

Assuming at first that the apartment was for both of them, Shmerl protested albeit mildly, "What if I don't want to leave the East Side?"

"*You* don't got to," replied Max.

"But . . ."

"It's for me the apartment."

A rush of conflicting emotions fought for dominance in Shmerl's brain: Max was tired of his company; perhaps he had met a girl; funny they never talked about girls. Shmerl could feel himself beginning to seethe with jealousy, never mind how irrational the response; he was on the verge of starting a quarrel. I'm mad on you, he had it in mind to say, but the words stuck in his craw, arrested as he was by Max's obsidian eyes, his cream-pale cheek that seemed never to require a shave, his swanlike throat minus (interestingly) an adam's apple. Then the inventor reasoned with himself that his friend's independence was his right, and in the end he merely mouthed a silent Oh. When he could find his voice, Shmerl said it was natural Max should want a place of his own, though as for himself he preferred to remain in the ghetto where he belonged.

Max settled with a pomatumed waiter, who bowed in a kind of haughty self-effacement, and rose to leave the cellar while Shmerl, still seated, said he'd meet him outside in a minute. "They got here a indoor water closet." Sodden from overmuch wine and spent emotion, Shmerl was just getting up from the table when he heard from the street a cry that pierced his ear like an awl. He looked about for his stock prod only to remember that, a technician now, he no longer carried the thing; then he bolted up the stairs from the sunken eatery, reaching the sidewalk in time to see his friend cornered between a waffle wagon and a haberdasher's stall. Surrounded by a pack of assailants with kerchiefs pulled over their faces, among whom the caddy cap and his sidekick were still recognizable, Max remained standing, though the blood coursed in a muddy torrent from his head. Then letting loose another heart-stopping shriek that alerted the whole street to his extremity, he sank out of sight in the midst of his attackers. Alarmed by the attention they'd drawn, the attackers lowered their cudgels and, exchanging quizzical looks, beat a hasty retreat in unison from the scene. No sooner had they departed, however, than a crowd of pedestrians closed ranks around the mauled victim, while in the near distance the skirl of a siren could already be heard.

Jolted out of his shock the moment that Max vanished from view, Shmerl gave forth an animal yawp of his own. He lunged into the street, leaping onto the backs of the gathered spectators as he tried to claw his way toward his friend. He was struggling frantically to part the crowd, ignoring the forceful tugging at his sleeve, until its urgency compelled him to turn toward the nuisance in anger. And there stood Max caked in blood but firmly on his feet, signaling Shmerl to hurry up already, let's skidoo. Together they made tracks through the backstreets, ducking into a doorway only when they'd distanced themselves by several blocks from the site of the attack. During that interlude, while Shmerl tried blotting his tears with a sleeve, Max licked the clotted blood from his lips.

"Red currant," he pronounced discerningly. "Geshmakh."

FROM BEHIND THE tarp in the stableyard shack where he was wiping the gory mess from his face and neck, Max explained that, despite his gesture of appeasement toward Zalman Pisgat, he'd thought it best to stay prepared for the worst. Recalling his skill in creating cosmetic effects, he'd kept about his person at all times a packet or two of the jellies used for stage blood. That way he might deceive any would-be assassins into believing they had inflicted the damage they intended. If in the confusion of an assault their victim appeared to have been mortally wounded, each assailant might assume that the other had delivered the coup de grâce. That was his plan, "which it worked!" declared Max, prompting Shmerl to snuffle skeptically through the tears he was still trying to stanch, while his heart continued to outrun itself. Having described his bluff in boastful detail, his partner then stated that, to further corroborate the demise of Max Feinshmeker, he would take immediate possession of his uptown residence on Riverside Drive. This was the legendary uptown avenue of grand apartment houses called Alrightnik's Row by the ghetto Jews, far from the Tenth Ward with its plagues of consumption and suicide. He realized, of course, that the move might be viewed as inconvenient, given the distance it put between himself and Canal Street, but now that the plant was poised to begin full operation, Max surmised that his discretionary services no longer required him to show up on site.

Then it was true that, once launched, the ice factory seemed fairly to run itself. This isn't to say there weren't daily concerns, though nothing that Shmerl, wielding a monkey wrench in place of his retired animal prod, couldn't handle. In fact, he welcomed the odd mechanical snafu as an opportunity to demonstrate to his apprentices how an oiled piston or a tightened crank pin, an increase or decrease in atmospheric pressure, could facilitate production several fold. Meanwhile Mr. Levine also had his hands full—the same horny hands he'd washed of his former medium in order to embrace a new one that was odorless and free of flies. Reinvigorated, the bandy-legged old stableman was everywhere at once, shmoozing potential clients, reviewing delivery routes, taking inventory, and dressing down machinists who failed to pay their union dues. But the plant was finally larger than the sum of its constituent parts, and once it was recognized by the public as more than a novelty, it began with breathtaking swiftness to establish its supremacy in the field of ice merchandising.

In a matter of months Karp's New Ice Castle, as it came to be known, had surpassed its competitors still yoked to the costly process of harvesting, hauling, and warehousing what they continued to insist on calling God's ice. Artificial ice (though unimpeachably real) could be produced at a fraction of the expense of paying contractors to carve blocks from frozen lakes as far away as Vermont and Maine—not to mention the loss through melting during transit and the short shelf life in the facilities where the ice was stored. Moreover, natural ice was subject to famines during mild winters; it was often contaminated by sewage and sometimes contained indescribable foreign objects. Whereas Karp's Castle could manufacture tons of crystal clear ice a day, delivering it in wagons throughout Manhattan and the borough of Brooklyn in twenty-pound blocks at the giveaway rate of five cents a pound. Its low overhead enabled the Castle, having undersold all its competitors, to reduce its storage fees as well. Naturally the plant's growing dominion inspired a belligerence on the part of the outmoded houses, and there existed a genuine threat of sabotage. But the Castle's employees constituted a small army whose liberal wages promoted a fanatical allegiance to their product, and some were even heard to engage in battles with their rivals outside the workplace. As a consequence, it was not long before the weatherboard turrets of the New Ice Castle façade became a landmark and a testament to immigrant ingenuity among the institutions of the Lower East Side.

As ordained, the rank and file of the Castle were kept in the dark about Max Feinshmeker's existence, to say nothing of his importance to the company as pecuniary brain trust. Of course it was taken for granted that such an elaborate enterprise couldn't function without its cadre of lawyers, accountants, and executive administrators; higher-ups had to be keeping books, checking balance sheets, fixing rates, and gauging budgets and expenses. But other than Shmerl only Elihu Levine knew that a single hidden hand served in all these capacities, and as contrary as he could sometimes be, the old man never questioned the arrangement. Loyalty itself, he generally approved the judgments that came down from above; indeed, having as yet no reason to dispute it, he accepted the word from its nameless source as a kind of gospel. Why shouldn't he? Since becoming the Ice Castle's foreman, his lot had improved immeasurably; he made a handsome salary and, with that and the proceeds from the sale of the livery stable, had begun life anew in his wintry years.

His migration from the stables to a hotel suite off Second Avenue, however, had uprooted his former hired hand, who was forced to dismantle the shanty and relocate his own base of operations. This Shmerl accomplished with the help of some Ice Castle workmen and a small caravan of delivery wagons, reestablishing himself and his accumulated impedimenta in the plant itself. Their newly acquired wealth could, of course, have secured him accommodations as lavish as he imagined Max's to be (he'd yet to visit), but he found it more advantageous to sleep where he worked — on a cot in a thermally insulated locker with eight-inch-thick walls, which he sometimes shared with dressed sides of beef. There, scratching on rolls of butcher paper spread over recessed shelves, he improvised calculations and drew up blueprints for improvements to the factory. Among these were plans for a chain-hoisted thaw tank, a pre-piped compressor and water-cooled condenser, and an automated conveying system with a vertical comb, a scale model of which he'd meticulously constructed. When not involved in devising newfangled refinements, he turned to more theoretical projects; for despite having disavowed it, he'd begun again to entertain the possibility of reversing the fall of man through technology.

He was also pleased that his living quarters allowed him to maintain close proximity to the frozen rabbi, who had his very own chamber in the icehouse. In fact, he was ensconced in his original lodging, the sanctum the Gebirtigs had once reserved for black-market goods, which they'd called the Castle's Keep. Only, now Rabbi Eliezer ben Zephyr had it all to himself, since Shmerl saw to it that he remained in his vault behind lock and key. But late at night, in the sheep's pelt he wore at all times due to the pervasive cold, Shmerl would unlock the Keep and sit like a mourner on a crate next to the rabbi, who had been his companion throughout his solitary months. These vigils beside the casket with its opened lid, its contents effulgent in the light of a naphtha lantern, gave the inventor a proprietary sense, as if the rebbe were a gift from Max, one he was nevertheless prepared to return on demand.

But if he were mourning anything, it was the absence of his partner, who had yet to visit the factory since its opening. Driven as he was to hard work, Shmerl sometimes wondered if all his activity was by way of distracting himself from making an occupation out of missing Max. He missed reading aloud to the yungerman the appeals for sympathy if not outright love in the "Bintel Brief" column of the *Jewish Daily Forward*; missed relating the preposterous dreams which Max, covering his ears, refused to hear, though he might sheepishly submit some incubus of his own later on. He missed—what didn't he miss?—his partner's eyes when their black opal irises reflected the sap green of a gas flame. But this was all baloney. Then Shmerl would try to isolate the features of his friend's face—the burnt rose lips, the aquiline nose, the hint of a widow's peak at the height of his calcimine brow—in an attempt to find fault with each, but they kept coalescing in their perfect symmetry. He tried to hate the rhythmic snoring and soft petards that had issued from the lithe form that had lain beside him so many nights. Because finally such feelings as he had for the yungerman were improper; men did not feel such intense affection for other men, did they? There were David and Jonathan, of course, Hillel and Shammai—he ransacked the tradition for other examples; there was Weber & Fields. But here was the thing: Shmerl was unable to disentangle his longing for his friend from his baser instincts, from fantasies concerning the ladies which had lately beset him. For it seemed he had needs that were reaching the point of obsession and might require the intervention of the Allen Street nafkehs to release the ache. The Law, which he only selectively observed, explicitly forbade consorting with professional women, but "A minhag brekht a din," as the proverb said. "A custom breaks a law." Whatever the case, Shmerl was of an age when the young men of Shpinsk were already married householders experiencing the joys of Shabbos copulation, while he had yet to know a woman in any true sense. Rocking himself on his crate in the Castle's Keep, he might turn toward the porous casket as if expecting the saint to hatch already from his block of ice and offer counsel.

Meanwhile, from his vantage on the sixth floor of a Beaux-Arts apartment house with a view of the Hudson, whose surface was flecked with the skittering of crescent sails, Max judged himself to be in some respects as good as dead. Having sent a final remittance to the ice mensch back in Lodz, labeling it a bequest, he felt he had laid Max Feinshmeker—never more than an unfinished work-in-progress—officially to rest. It was an attitude the girl Jocheved, who'd begun to express herself more openly, nevertheless thought somewhat premature. Habitually cautious, she had never reassumed women's apparel, not even in the privacy of her West Side apartment, though on the sidewalks along Upper Broadway she might pause to appreciate a stone marten muff in a furrier's window or a milliner's straw bonnet trimmed with lacquered cherries. Not that Jocheved had ever been vain of her appearance, but tentatively she began again to explore the distaff side of life. Purchasing a noodle board, she rolled the dough into circles, cut the circles into strips, and draped them over the backs of chairs like clothes wrung through a mangle and left to dry. Later she would boil the noodles in chicken broth or bake them into kugel on a gas-burning range. She acquired two sets of pots and dishes, for meat and for dairy, and, reviving a long defunct passion, bought a pewter mold and a bag of rock salt for making syrupy sherbets and frozen desserts. Despite having a bathroom that featured a clawfooted tub, she thought she might even like to visit a mikveh again. While such concerns could never comprise the whole of life, business having taken precedence over all (as witness the ledgers heaped atop the drop leaf of a mahogany desk in the parlor), she delighted in her secret dabbling in womanly pursuits, a pleasure that in no way diminished the contempt she felt for the woman she had been.

Since the partial resurrection of Jocheved tended to keep the girl largely shut in, she communicated with Shmerl (as Max) via messengers, which was unsatisfactory to them both. For Jocheved still shared Max's fellow feeling for Shmerl; and Max, who had essentially swapped places with Jocheved and was reduced now to a residual voice, missed his comrade with a fervor that made sense in no category the girl could understand. Missing him made the uptown streets, awash in fallen leaves and garment magnates with their stout, bedizened wives, seem as much exile as refuge. But Jocheved reproved Max for such thoughts. Shmerl Karp was after all tsedrayt, was he not? A screwball. That much was even more apparent from her West Side elevation. And God knew he wasn't that easy to look at. Though she'd always averted her eyes from his unclothed body, she thought that his hump had become more pronounced during the relatively short time of their acquaintance. His bandit eyes were beadier, and his ginger hair resembled the ruffled feathers of a turkey cock. Then there was his odor, the scent of the stables (despite his much trumpeted visits to the Rutgers

Square baths) having never really left him. Of course, he had his talents: There was that rogue brain of his that made him some kind of a deluded crank, perhaps even a visionary of a specialized nature, and so impetuous was his energy that he seemed never to yawn. That had always impressed Max. Also, he was fearless in his devotion to his friend and apparently without an ounce of guile, which made him vulnerable in ways that would surely be a burden to any woman who would have him; though who would have such a total shlemiel as Shmerl Karp? As for herself, for Jocheved, the whole issue of men and women was in any case moot. The stigma she'd incurred in her former life—lest she forget—was still heartsickeningly active and would expose to infamy any man who entered her purview. But for all that, she sometimes had an impulse to award Max's bosom friend with some token of her esteem, some gift of a rare significance . . . though what should it be? The rabbi was already effectively his.

With or without Max's presence, however, the business prospered; the creditors were soon paid in full. The ice men circulated throughout the city in wagons bearing the Ice Castle trademark (a castle carved out of ice—what else?). They had become a fixture in the neighborhood streets, the Castle's agents, cutting ice to order with their picks before swinging the blocks onto broad shoulders protected by hemp, carrying them up several flights to deposit in enameled ice safes. In the factory, Shmerl's crew of engineers took pride in their increasing expertise at maintaining the machinery, sometimes even anticipating their supervisor's improvements, so that the inventor was able to spend more time in his "laboratory." He enjoyed working in his locker in the heart of the industry, surrounded by the clatter of equipment and the rowdy exertions of men moving goods. Still, he never neglected his responsibilities as chief technical engineer and met regularly with Mr. Levine to ensure that things were in order. They were not always in order, nor did he and Levine always see eye to eye, but Shmerl suspected that their disagreements had more to do with the old man's enjoyment of a heated exchange than with any urgent bone of contention; and the inventor tried his best to hold up his end of the argument

It was diverting enough, his life, to counteract from time to time his inveterate yearning, and there was always the satisfaction of knowing that his efforts were making his absent friend rich.

Then a message arrived at the icehouse, relayed from the foreman to the chief engineer, requesting Shmerl's presence for dinner at a posh address on the Upper West Side. Scarcely able to contain his excitement, Shmerl instantly tried to damp it down, pretending that there was nothing unusual in the invitation. No doubt Max only wanted to talk business, as what else did they have in common these days? Perhaps, now that the Castle had acquired its own head of steam, Max would inform Shmerl that his services were no longer needed. But that wasn't right, they were partners, though Shmerl always deferred to Max as the de facto head of the Ice Castle, which nevertheless bore the name of Karp: a paradox. Then Shmerl remembered that he was essential to their enterprise and that this line of reasoning had no basis in reality—so why was it with such a mixture of dread and anticipation that he took the Elevated uptown that evening?

On the train, though, he had the quickening sensation he felt whenever he traveled beyond the neighborhood, which made him ask himself why he didn't do it more often. Because Max wasn't around to accompany him, that was why. Unlike the flat grid of the ghetto, Riverside Drive rolled uphill and down, a complement of elegant cliff-hanging apartments facing the sandstone palisades on the river's New Jersey shore. It was, incidentally, the week of the festival of Sukkot, and a number of balconies sported pergolaed bowers, poles apart from the squatters' sheds sprouting lulavs like donkeys' ears on fire escapes all over the Lower East Side. Beneath the marquee outside Max's building stood a massive doorman in an epauletted greatcoat, between whose legs Shmerl was prepared to scramble if the man tried to block his path. But once he'd announced himself, the man actually touched a finger to his visor and led him through the lobby into a hand-powered lift, which he proceeded to operate by hauling on a steel cable. A little breathless from their swift ascent and the pavonian wallpaper in the sixth-floor hallway, Shmerl was convinced that Max must

have graduated to a whole new order of existence; he was only slightly
heartened at the sight of a tin mezuzah on the jamb outside his friend's
door. Knocking, he half-expected to be greeted by a servant, and was
further relieved when Max himself, dressed informally in an unbuttoned
waistcoat and pin-striped shirtsleeves, opened the door.

"Gut yontev," he greeted, then: "Forgive me, I'm a bit ongepatshket
from toiling over the stove." This vaguely disconcerted Shmerl, who wondered since when were apologies necessary between them, but in truth
something about Max did look different, and as they shook hands, Shmerl
was unable to meet his friend's eye. Instead, as the yungerman showed
him around the apartment, the inventor kept stealing peeks at his friend
to determine exactly how he had changed. For one thing, his sable curls
were a little longer, hanging over his forehead and ears in a manner as winsome as it was careless, and his features seemed to have softened a touch
at the edges, as befitted his new affluence. He was still compact of figure,
though he might have put on a pound or two, but otherwise there was
nothing dramatically altered in his appearance. So why did Shmerl have
the unsettled impression that this person was doing no more than a fair
impersonation of his partner, Max Feinshmeker?

He tried his best to shrug off his nervousness and revive the ease he
and his comrade had formerly shared. Nodding his approval of the roomy
apartment, he remarked upon its modern amenities: the steam heat, indoor
plumbing, the ornate gas girandoles; it was spacious without being preten-
tious (he actually said this), all "tishelekh un lompelekh," little tables and
lamps, and in the bedroom an iron bedstead with a cotton-batting mattress and flat springs. There were other homey touches: a mizrakh plaque
on the eastern wall, a silver menorah and a sewing kit containing a color
wheel of spools on the sideboard—all made the more haimish by the
savory aromas wafting in through the kitchen door. Having no domestic
sense of his own, Shmerl was impressed that Max had developed his to
such a degree. Though he was content with his compartment in the ice
house, its windowless walls so conducive to dreaming, the inventor was

not indifferent to his friend's feathered nest, admiring its creature comforts in their warm contrast to the crisp autumn evening outside. Once again he was struck with what a long way they'd come in so short a time; it was truly the kind of rags-to-riches story so often hymned in the popular press. If ever his own family emigrated—and he'd begun a correspondence with his still breathing papa toward that end—he would see them housed in similar accommodations. For himself, though, Shmerl had no immediate plans for relocating, nor had his improved financial straits brought him any sense of personal triumph. The fact was, he could have wished that the two of them, he and Max, were back in the stableyard where he'd never been happier.

His host invited him into the parlor with its oaken dining table set in a bay, spread with an embroidered cloth and hand-painted china, its centerpiece a seasonal bouquet of marigolds. "I was your guest," said Max with a formal bow, "and now you are mine," which statement had a certain spider-to-fly ring in Shmerl's ears. Again he expected a cook or a maid-servant, but excusing himself, Max disappeared into the kitchen, returning momentarily with bowls of creamy mushroom and barley soup. When they'd finished the soup course, there was baked fish with horseradish, knaidlech, and spicy brisket; a meal, commented Shmerl inanely, like a regular Belshazzar's feast. Other attempts at conversation were just as forced, such as when Shmerl tried in vain to alleviate the tension with a jest—"Feinshmeker, you will make for someone a fine wife"—and heard how blustering and unnatural was Max's surname on his lips. After that gambit, though food was never for him a priority, Shmerl limited his observations to the tastiness of the meat and roast bulbes. For dessert there was homemade lemon sherbet with macaroons followed by bronfen, the rye whiskey usually reserved for kiddish ceremonies, one sip of which went straight to the inventor's head.

In the end it was Max who punctured the strained atmosphere, rubbing his palms together expressively as he asked the inventor how he'd enjoyed the sherbet. For just as Shmerl had assumed, his partner wanted to talk about business; he had ideas, born in good part from Jocheved's nostalgia, for the diversification of the plant: "How about, along with ice, we should manufacture different kinds ice cream?" It was already a popular item throughout the city, the hokey-pokey vans ubiquitous in the ghetto streets during summer. "So why we shouldn't hop on the band wagon?" He began to discourse excitedly about the molds, caves, and various implements involved in the ice cream–making process, the palette of available flavors from vanilla and pistachio to bergamot orange. Shmerl was himself briefly caught up in the idea, picturing giant mechanized churns containing Ararats of frozen custard—which no sooner materialized than melted in his mind, so abbreviated was his span of attention due to strong drink. He was also a little stunned by the breadth of his friend's ambition, and had actually to remind himself that whatever made Max happy made him happy as well. But even his less than wholehearted response seemed enough to encourage Max further, who had changed the subject again. He was recalling his recent reading of socialist tracts by the East Side's own Morris Hillquit, who recommended progressive strategies for success in business: The reconciliation of capital and labor, he contended, could be achieved through profit-sharing alliances that would revolutionize the workplace of the future. What did Shmerl think?—not that Max gave him an opportunity to respond.

With no head for the various isms so dear to the hearts of the citizens of the Lower East Side, Shmerl gave in to a general sinking feeling; he ceased listening and satisfied himself with simply observing his animated friend, his treasured companion whom God help him he wanted desperately to kiss. That's when the inventor, his cheeks burning, realized he was well on the way to being shikkered. To try and distract himself, he picked up an apple from a bowl on the table and began to peel it with the bone-handled paring knife. The peel, still attached to the naked apple, assumed the shape of a corkscrewing tail like the trajectory of a small planet spinning out of its orbit. Contemplating it until his eyes crossed, Shmerl was aware that Max was also focused on the apple, and had slowed his galloping monologue almost to a standstill—at which point, seized by a spasm of pot-valor, Shmerl interrupted his host to ask with sham devil-may-care: "So, Feinshmeker, do you think you will ever get married?" Replacing the uneaten fruit still trailing its spiral skin, he helped himself to another shot of the ritual whiskey, his throat having gone suddenly dry.

Max, still fixated on the apple, snapped out of his trance to reply, "I like my freedom."

Shmerl nodded in emphatic agreement; they were on the same page. But in the awkward silence that followed, prey to the creeping mischief the alcohol inspired, the inventor was moved to pose another question. "Was you ever in love?"

The yungerman looked abashed. "Was you?"

"I'm asking first."

Max's sloe-black eyes narrowed nearly to reptilian slits. "What kind question is this!" he protested.

Taking his friend's show of temper for a negative, Shmerl assured him, "Me too never," giving his head a sharp shake, which set his brain throbbing, his ears aflame, his entire anatomy in revolt against the lie. "That is," he began again, "I mean…" But what did he mean? That he loved Max Feinshmeker, a man? Of course he loved him, but in a way that had nothing to do with the kind of love they were talking about. That kind was impossible between men in the world as he understood it, an abomination, in fact. But why? He realized it was only his intake of spirits that even allowed him to entertain such a question . . . despite which he took another drink. As if not to be outdone, Max followed suit. Then Shmerl felt the words rising like some kind of volcanic rudeness from deep in his gut, an utterance he could no longer withhold. "I—," he pronounced, while at the same time Max fell victim to a sneeze.

"Gezuntlikheit," said Shmerl, grateful for the reprieve. Then realizing his slip of the tongue—he'd wed the blessing with the word for a cozy congeniality—began helplessly to giggle, making an effort to bite off the laughter when he saw that Max remained unamused. "They say," he tried again, apropos what?, "is not so important between men and women the division as it is the multiplication," which only triggered another fit of giggling.

His host had shut his eyes as if against a sudden cloudburst, and Shmerl endeavored once more to get hold of himself. Clearing his throat, he attempted yet another conversational sally, this time trying hard to preserve a neutrality of tone. "Do you know perhaps from the false messiah Shabtai Zvi?"

This at least elicited a sardonic, "Not personally." Max's eyes opened one at a time.

"The Jews in olden times, that they believed by him they would ascend to Gan Eydn until he converted to the cult of Ishmael. He was famous for the saying, 'Praise God who permits the forbidden.'"

Max squirmed in his chair, took another drink. "Apostates and epicurians we may be," he offered, "but leastwise we ain't in his camp, eh, Karp?"

"God forbid," said Shmerl, though with faint conviction, after which, feeling sufficiently chastised, he fell silent. He was surprised when a mirthless tear escaped his eye, and as he dragged it with the palm of his hand to his tongue, he clenched his stomach as if to close his ribcage like floodgates around his heart. So harsh was his judgment of himself at that moment that he thought he must have absorbed his friend's censure as well—because Max had clearly let go of his disapproval. His expression had softened as he gazed at his friend with a sympathy that Shmerl had not invited and did not want. The inventor was on the verge of asking the alrightnik what he was looking at, but Max spoke first, the edge gone from a voice pitched perhaps an octave higher than its normal tone. "Shmerl," he said, using the familiar form of address, "you can't love me, you know." And there it was.

"I know," Shmerl was quick to respond, though he didn't know; he knew nothing then but that they seemed, the two of them, to have entered a zone wherein all bets were off. The universe was again formless and void, there were no laws or even names of things, and if the righteous so willed it, they could make a world—that was in Talmud. But who here was righteous?

"No you don't," insisted his friend, his speech melodious if a little slurred. "You don't know."

"I don't?" Shmerl tried to remember exactly what it was he didn't know.

"You think you can't love me because I'm a man."

Shmerl could see no contradiction.

"But I'm not a man."

"You're not?"

Max shook his head.

Thoroughly befuddled, Shmerl asked, "Then what are you?"

His host took an instant to deliberate, then submitted evenly, "A who-er."

Shmerl wasn't sure he had heard him correctly. "Vos du zogst?"

Max was on his feet, repeating hotly, "I'm a who-er!" Whereupon he removed his waistcoat, shrugged off his suspenders, and tore open his collarless shirt, spraying a volley of studs that forced the inventor to duck. He lifted his head in time to see the yungerman haul the undervest over his head, upon which Shmerl had to shield his eyes again—because he was gazing at a pair of breasts so orient and ripe, their nipples like the stems of marzipan pears, that they stirred what he felt was a life-threatening ache in his vitals. It was an ache Shmerl thought he might be glad to die of.

"You still don't understand?" inquired his friend, disappointed that the revelation had apparently not had its anticipated effect; since instead of being revolted by a body deformed by abnormal appurtenances, the inventor appeared to be merely struck with awe. Furious now, tears starting in freshets down his cheeks, Max pulled apart the flies of his pants, launching another salvo of buttons as he shoved the pants to his ankles along with a pair of frilly drawers. Then the spare ivory legs stood exposed to their fur-brushed juncture and the bald nub nestled like a cleft fig therein.

"If it don't disgust you what I got," she challenged, "then maybe makes you sick what I don't got, fallen creature that I am."

But Shmerl was of another turn of mind. Rising from the table, dragging with him the tablecloth as the flowers and leftover dishes slid clattering to the floor, he came around to enfold the girl's bare shoulders in the damask material. It was a gesture whose unconditional tenderness inverted Jocheved's topsy-turvy logic and robbed her of her capacity for shame. Then both of them were sobbing feverishly, the girl for her joyful reunion with the lost daughter of Salo Frostbissen, the youth for the gift of a transformation that he alone, wizard that he was, had effected: for he had caused by simply wishing it the metamorphosis of his beloved companion into the woman of his dreams.

2001.

That night, from his coign of vantage somewhere in the empyrean, Bernie Karp viewed his body convulsed on a pastel toilet seat from the bout of diarrhea that had beset him after his encounter with the rebbe. Something about their meeting had apparently not agreed with him. Floating free, the boy felt what he'd felt so often before: a deep compassion for his own suffering self, the pity extending from his specific case to a general homesick concern for the wretched of the earth. It was a pity that compelled him, in the spirit of solidarity with his species, to want to reinhabit the poor kid doubled over with abdominal cramps, his pajama pants gathered around his ankles. In that way he would assume his share of the pain that was an inescapable part of the human experience. Previously, however, his embrace of mortal pain had resulted in the corresponding desire to escape the human condition altogether, thus perpetuating the ongoing tug-of-war between Bernie and the cosmos. Settled into his skin again, he would instantly conceive an impulse to shed his physicality and reinvite the shefa, the inpouring of divine emanation that displaced his consciousness, which was then free to wander in time and space; though the exile would in turn leave him lonely and pining for the human vessel he'd left behind. But tonight, while his parents slept a wall away, dreaming the dreams with which their "interface" with Rabbi ben Zephyr had filled their heads, Bernie discovered that, knotted intestines aside, he wanted achingly to hang on to his earthbound self and, by extension, the world.

It was then that Bernie thought he understood what the resurrected rebbe was up to: He was practicing the discipline known as aliyah tzrichah yeridah, descent for the sake of ascent, an extreme corrective measure the boy had first heard mentioned in the writings of the eighteenth-century teacher Yakov Yosef of Polnoy. The Polnoy Zayde, as he was fondly called, had descended from his lofty rung of holiness to raise the fallen souls of his abject community to the source of light. "Sometimes, for the sake of the evildoer, the adept must fall from his height." Familiar with the odious concept of redemption through sin as espoused by those guilty of the Sabbatean heresy, Bernie realized that this could be a dangerous undertaking. He knew the perils: "Descent is certain while ascent is not." And furthermore: "The tzaddik must take special care how he will again ascend, and not, God forbid, remain below. For I heard from my teacher [said the wise Polnoy Zayde] there are many who did remain." On the other hand, "Only he who is himself guilty can help remove the guilt of others." It was time, thought Bernie, that he got himself truly defiled.

Surrendering to what was at first a nebulous desire to coalesce with his own kind, he soon narrowed his focus to a single object manifest in the squirrely person of Lou Ella Tuohy. Her milky flesh, it suddenly seemed to him, was a necessary prerequisite for his own redemption, if not the redemption of the race at large. By the same token, the stay-at-home handmaiden who had so often blessed his solo flights to glory would also (Bernie flattered himself) be carried away. This was why, the next evening when they'd parked her mother's Malibu in a long-abandoned drive-in theater, Bernie was resolved that their bundling should be more than just another mechanical prelude to his own transcendence. They had visited that petrified ruin on the southern edge of town before, a spot still anchored to the 1950s, with owls perched on posts that once sported metal speakers and skunk cabbage overrunning the wavy asphalt like a Sargasso Sea. Lou

Ella liked to sit on the hood of the coupe of a starry evening, imagining black-and-white movies projected onto the kudzu-choked screen, its torn fabric illumined to saffron by the car's high beams. Tonight she envisioned another monster movie of the type she'd seen on late-night TV.

"There's this kid gets a chameleon at the circus, the kind you fasten to your collar and it turns the color of your shirt. He visits his mama in the hospital where she's getting radiation treatments and the chameleon is exposed and by morning it's grown to the size of the Rock of Gibraltar."

"Is it still attached to his collar?" asked Bernie.

"No, fool. It wadn't but a dinky plastic chain. But there's still like a bond that connects the boy to the monster. Anyway, the monster devours whole cities but the army can't find it 'cause it blends into whatever land-scape it's in. So—"

"Lemme guess. The army enlists the kid, who's the only one that can see the monster, and he feeds it an A-bomb concealed in a giant meatball."

"You saw it too."

"So what becomes of his mama?" He knew she was fond of sentimental endings.

"Oh, her and every other cancer patient on earth is cured by the green cloud that surrounds the planet after the monster explodes." She made to dry her eyes with her sleeve. "Your turn."

Bernie had to think, though not for long. "There's this kid"—there was always *this kid*—"who wakes up on a day that's like an extra calendar day, a day that contains all other days."

Lou yawned demonstratively. "Here it comes," she said, because Bernie's tales always involved some occult concept with no discernible plotline.

"Everything that's ever happened is happening all at once, and the kid—he's past puberty—meets a woman who's Bathsheba but also Queen Esther and Bess Myerson and Penelope Cruz . . ."

"Another chameleon," remarked Lou, who despite her feigned boredom had a weakness for Bernie's peculiar line of guff.

"And she invites him into her tent or boudoir," he continued, and here began to describe the seduction in graphic terms: "She asks him to suck her nipples like they're jujubes, and part her thighs—"

"Like the handles on a posthole digger. You didn't tell me this was a porno."

It was then that Bernie believed he could see on the tattered screen all the mythical ladies melding into the single image of the girl beside him, the soft whorls of whose ear he had begun to trace with his tongue. She let him, allowing their canoodling to reach an intensity that her companion, despite some lingering frailty from the previous night's intestinal purge, was single-mindedly advancing. He had initiated, to his way of thinking, actual foreplay leading toward an inevitable consummation. Over time Lou Ella had come to regard their groping as merely a means of launching her "friend" into astral realms; it was more like an exploratory intimacy between schoolkids than lovers. But although she was dressed provocatively as usual, a paste ruby stuck in her navel, the low-riding jeans grazing her pubic bone, she was nonetheless alarmed by Bernie's ardor.

"Cool your jets, dude," she cautioned him, having had enough of false hopes. "Put a lid on your id," shoving him away to arm's length.

But when Bernie persisted blindly she detected that some new dispensation was afoot.

"What is it you want?"

"Oo," mumbled into her neck.

"Me or my bones?"

"Phame differumph," he panted while gnawing her shoulder.

She cocked her head quizzically. "That's a mouthful coming from alias Mr. Incorporeal."

Still she asked him to hang on a minute while she transferred the car seat that Sue Lily was quickly outgrowing from the backseat to the front. Having traded places with the lackluster infant, they proceeded to tear at each other's clothes. In the throes of a carnality that had clearly infected the girl as well, Bernie felt her fingers beginning to invade his fly, taking him in hand with a hopefulness that, for her part, she hardly dared to indulge. But while her touch did not elicit the combustion that routinely catapulted him into Elysian precincts (leaving behind a body in which passion was no more memorable than an aborted sneeze), neither did it result in their long-deferred union. Instead, her touch caused the seed to spill forlornly from his drooping organ. When he recovered from the paroxysm that had blasted his thoughts and defibrillated his racing heart, Bernie observed that the girl was holding in the palm of her hand what appeared to be glowworms lit by golden filaments.

"Next time," advised Lou, "as a precaution against your hair trigger, when I touch it, try to think of something gross."

1912 – 1929.

My mama was a sensible lady, my papa a dreamer," Bernie read to Lou Ella Tuohy from the dogeared journal of Ruben (called Ruby) Karp, "and from them I inherited exactly nothing. Sometimes I even thought I wasn't their son; I'd been dumped in the cradle in place of their real child by demons, the ones my father said the immigrants had left behind in the Old Country when they came to the New World."

BETWEEN THE TWO of them my parents had a corner on most of the virtues on earth, so there was nothing left for me but to become a black sheep. My papa for all I knew was a tall man, though his crimped spine caused him to stoop as from a heavy load, but I was short like (okay) my mama; I was pint-sized but wiry and handy with my fists, with a temper that could take me to the brink of delirium and beyond. In a fight I was blind, while my body, compact and fierce, followed instincts of its own, and when my vision cleared, I would find my opponent (or opponents, since I never backed down from the odds) unconscious or fled. Growing up, I was oppressed by the prevailing tranquility of our household, so that once I was old enough to seek it out, I put myself in the way of brute behavior. I attended prizefights, dogfights, instigated back-alley brawls; wherever a shemozzle was likely to break out, there you'd find me, rubbing elbows with the disreputables that frequented such places. At first they challenged me, my lowlife cronies, then they initiated me, and afterwards I was a member in good standing of their tribe. Of course the old guard hoodlums, the Yid Mustache Petes like Monk Eastman and Dopey Benny, were all dead or gone straight by then; the climate had changed since the days when the shtarkers were content to poison horses and set fires, and labor-racketeering was in the toilet since the rise of the unions. This is not to say that old-fashioned mayhem was obsolete. The gangs still kept their hand in the traditional rackets, but the real action since the passage of the Eighteenth Amendment was in illegal whiskey. The whole ghetto had been colonized by homemade cookers and bootleg stills, speakeasies having cropped up in every cellar and barber's closet, so there was no end of trouble available to the resourceful young man.

Naturally my family saw to it that I remained unacquainted with the city's seamier quarters during my childhood, which must have looked from the outside to be more or less idyllic. My world then was mostly restricted to the Upper West Side, its tidy streets populated with Jews-made-good, but every least excursion whetted my appetite to stray farther afield. They dressed me in middy suits and Buster Brown caps and took me for strolls along the river or boating in the Central Park basin, where I might try to rock the dinghy till it was swamped. I was equally bored by our family outings to the Yiddish Art Theater on Second Avenue, where Muni Weisenfreund would age half a century while waiting on stage for a messiah that never came. Nor did I have much patience for the flickers we viewed from the jewel-box balconies of picture palaces; all those blood and thunder romances featuring foppish John Gilberts and Valentinos gave me a pain — though I'll confess to a weakness for the Raoul Walsh three-reelers in which Bowery toughs battled the cops over downtown turf. I was a witness to some of the premier attractions of the day: Shipwreck Kelly swaying atop a flagpole above the Hippodrome, Harry Houdini escaping

a straitjacket while dangling from his heels twenty floors above Times
Square — all of which made me the more anxious to commence some
exploit of my own here on earth.

On high holidays my mama and papa would take me to the Greek
Revival synagogue on West End Avenue, where a rabbi in ecclesiastical
robes and top hat preached pap to the choir. I would grind my teeth while
Papa, to calm me, whispered that I shouldn't be fooled by the tiresome
ritual: there were creatures, golems and kapulyushniklim, hidden away
in the attic.

"I thought you said the Jews left all that stuff back in Europe," I protested, but he explained that this was "some of the *stuff* that in the hold of
the Hamburg-Amerika Line they stowed themselves away."

Only once do I recall having been to the old immigrant district in my
early years. That was when my father took me for a ride on the top of a
bus to visit his Canal Street ice plant, where he showed me around the
workings of the whole operation. He also introduced me to an otherwise
vacant locker in which a cedar casket propped on trestles contained an old
man in a block of ice. Both the business and the boisterous neighborhood
captured my interest, but the old man made so little impression that over
time I came to confuse him with a dream.

They were an odd couple, my parents: my mama with her Dresden
china complexion and cascade of blue-black hair, which from vanity or indifference she refrained from bobbing in the fashion of the day; Papa with
his rooster comb and camel hump, his bughouse ideas and the curdled
Old Country accent he never lost. Sometimes I think I hated him for
being a cripple, or rather for not realizing he was a cripple and behaving
accordingly. I never understood how my mama could be so adoring of
a character that should have embarrassed her by his very presence — or
did she think he was a complement to her beauty? Not that Mama ever
seemed to notice the way she turned heads. They doted on me, the pair
of them, so much that from the first I felt I might suffocate; their brand
of devotion could shrivel your petsel like a salted slug. Meanwhile their

affection for each other was such an exclusive affair that it kept me confined to the circle of their intimacy. "Don't love me so much," I pleaded from as far back as I can remember, and when they persisted I set about proving I didn't deserve it.

Our apartment, which had seemed so ample in my infancy, shrank as I grew, crammed as it was with heavy furniture—the vaultlike wardrobes and diamond-tufted divans, with Mama's library of ledgers, Papa's journals and mystical books, the newspapers in a Yiddish I could barely read; though I soon enough absorbed the headlines of their American counterparts: RITES OF FLAMING YOUTH EXPOSED, SACCO AND VANZETTI FRY—items suggesting that the world was full of a number of things unaccounted for in Mama's budgetary meditations or the harebrain researches that kept my father away from home so much. Occasionally the perfect harmony was disturbed by an invasion of my papa's family (my mother had brothers but nobody knew where they were), or anyway those members of it that had not been seduced by the Bolsheviks or scattered upon reaching the shores of America. They consisted of Grandpa Todrus and his wife Chana Bindl, both apparently shellshocked from their encounter with the New World, and their daughter, Shinde Esther, youngest of an otherwise exclusively male brood. Papa had brought them over from Russia, settled them comfortably in a nearby residence, and had them outfitted in factory-fresh ready-mades. But the young men, emancipated after their long confinement to shtetl and steerage, set off (as who could blame them?) in their several directions to seek their fortunes. Only the plain Shinde Esther, whom my mama took under her wing like a little sister, stayed at home to care for her infirm parents. But distraught as they were—Todrus complained of a lingering seasickness, Chana Bindl of harassment by the ghost of her mother-in-law—even their visits stirred my restlessness, if only for the fishy odor that clung to their clothing bespeaking a voyage from distant lands.

I was sent to a local school, an academy, along with the sons of garment manufacturers and department-store magnates. They were a toffee-nosed,

knock-kneed lot in their tub suits and riding breeches, predestined by
their families for high-toned professions, and I disliked them from the
start. You wouldn't have called me a bully, exactly, since the kids I picked
on were usually bigger than me, but I quickly established a reputation for
being incorrigible. Often I was sent home with notes to my parents that
I made certain they never received, and frequently punished for what my
teachers called poor deportment. They were feeble punishments, cloak-
room detention and half-hearted paddlings, that only made me the more
defiant. When my teachers, nervous women despite formidable busts and
behinds, complained that my behavior was a waste of a good mind, I
got even with them by refusing to learn anything at all. There were also
girls in my school, some of them pink and comely, but for reasons I never
examined I begrudged them their prettiness, as if they'd cultivated their
attractions only to taunt me with. Often I was truant, trolling the uptown
streets in search of an unpredictability that always eluded me in my own
neighborhood. Then sometime during the summer of my sixteenth year,
my papa, ostensibly to keep me out of trouble, invited me to come work
in his ice house on Canal.

As the first facility in the city to manufacture industrial ice, Karp's Ice
Castle (no longer New) had once been the pride of the ghetto. But compet-
ing houses had since sprung up like mushrooms all over town, while the
advent of the refrigerator (five dollars down and ten a month) had diminished their need to exist at all. For a while Karp's had tried supplementing
the sale of ice with a sideline of frozen custards, the proprietor himself having custom-built for that purpose a servo-motorized ice cream–making
machine. But Karp's Frozen Delight, sold in swirls to look like the Statue
of Liberty's torch, could never compete with the near monopoly of Good
Humor wagons circulating throughout the city. Still, many families remained dependent on their outdated ice boxes, and though the fleet had
been reduced in favor of expanding the storage capacity of the warehouse,
Karp's delivery vans endured as a staple of the East Side's congested streets.
Thus, while Papa's business had to struggle to maintain its standing in

the industry, it remained a going concern that continued to keep the wolf from the door. Not that it concerned me a whit whether the business succeeded or failed, nor was I especially eager to enter my papa's employ, but I leapt at the chance to smirch myself with something akin to real life.

The old Tenth Ward, as I came to understand, had changed since my parents' greenhorn days. For one thing, the rag trade, grown ever more prosperous, had moved steadily uptown so that the sweatshops were no longer as prevalent in the area. Many of the original immigrants, having unshackled themselves from pushcarts and sewing machines, became shop clerks, office hacks, bookkeepers, and the like, while those who stayed in the factories also saw improved conditions owing to the ascendency of the trade unions. Their children were moving out of the ghetto altogether—across the river to Williamsburg, uptown to Harlem and the Bronx—and since the government had had its fill of foreigners and put the kibosh on immigration, the old neighborhood enjoyed a bit more breathing room. I don't mean to suggest that the Lower East Side had become a hospitable place; there was still plenty of squalor and disease to go around, and Prohibition had incited everyone, Jews included, to get drunk. But until Naf the Sport's lieutenants waltzed into the icehouse to lean on my father, I had supposed that the underworld existed only in films, and it cheered me to discover that Jews could be ruthless as well.

Since the Castle's inception Papa's foremen had all been steadfast union men, beginning with old Elihu Levine (deceased) who'd inaugurated the tradition of resisting the arm-twisting of the local syndicate. This was a dicey position to take. But the heyday of the ice plant had coincided with a time when Yoshke Nigger, the ghetto's chief goon, had withdrawn his energies from the standard extortion rackets to place them squarely in the service of Tammany Hall. Then along came the Volstead Act and Tammany be damned: Peddling hooch was now the order of the day. Yoshke's successor, Naf the Sport, né Naftali Kupferman, however, was a more ambitious breed of felon with a penchant for diversifying. After his mentor's unnatural death (via cement galoshes), he decided to reactivate

old accounts, sending his gorillas to collect tributes from the businesses
that Yoshke had exploited in the past. Meanwhile Karp's Ice Castle still
refused to cave in to mob intimidation, while Karp himself, absorbed in
his latest pipe dream, paid no attention whatever to the renewed demands
for protection gelt.

My papa. Though he had an office adjoining his foreman's on the Ice
Castle's upper tier, complete with a monkey puzzle of pneumatic tubes
for sending messages, he was seldom in it, keeping mostly to the so-called
laboratory where he conducted his "experiments." It's true that he was
credited with certain technical innovations, the fruits of which outfitted
the ground floor of his gesheft, but any contributions of his to the material world were in large part accidental: The material world was a place he
visited for his family's sake. His employees, if they regarded him at all,
treated their titular boss with the deference you'd pay to a holy lunatic.
Only once during my tenure at the Castle, where he often passed me with
no hint of recognition, did Papa (think of Lon Chaney in *The Forbidden
Room*) drag me into his airless locker to describe the current project. The
place was dense with conflicting odors: brimstone and ozone and human
sweat; there were shelves of what appeared to be objects out of the Middle
Ages sitting cheek-by-jowl beside cutting-edge technological devices: a
glass furnace containing a luminous residue next to a crackling electrical transformer, cathodes and diodes nestled among jars of quicklime,
asafetida, and dragon's blood. There were Hebrew texts by authors with
names like Abraham the Python lying open across articles on polyphase-
induction engines; there was the cot where Papa catnapped and sometimes
spent the night.

The project he was presently at work on, with its pulleys and zinc alloy
gears, had the look of an amusement park ride.

"When complete, will simulate, my machine, the bang at the birth of
the world," he declared, eyes aswim behind the horn-rimmed spectacles
he'd recently affected. He further explained that the explosion he referred
to had resulted from the volatility of the divine light stored in the vessels

that contained the original Creation. Why he wanted to perform this particular imitation of God, he never made clear, but where his previous inventions had had (often despite his intent) some practical application, he was determined this one would defy all usefulness. Of course he was nuts, my papa, and although he was the acknowledged executive head of the business, I knew it was really Mama, consulting account books and telling the beads of her abacus, who actually ran the Ice Castle from our West Side apartment.

Papa's mishegoss aside, I don't mean to imply that I didn't like working at the icehouse. Physical labor had a certain appeal for me, and slinging lettuce crates or lugging giant sea bass across sawdusted floors, I felt my body becoming toughened and strong. Sometimes I would ride the ice, sliding toboggan-style down aluminum flumes straight into an insulated van in which I would later ride shotgun, swapping indecencies with the drivers as we navigated the city streets. I liked swinging the iron tongs to hoist the cakes onto my shoulder and the sense of my own surefootedness as I carried the dripping burden up steep flights of stairs. In garlicky kitchens I drew the pick from its scabbard to split apart the ice cake, spraying shards while the daughter of the house admired the knotted muscles of my arms. Once or twice I even imagined taking over the Castle from Papa and expanding it into a veritable empire of ice. But when Naf the Sport's ambassadors strolled onto the premises declaring that Karp's owed their agency a fortune in back subscriptions, I was as impressed with their brass as I was outraged by their demands.

Schultz, Papa's horse-faced foreman, shoving hands deep in his overall pockets, said he would have to discuss the issue with the proprietor, that the gorillas should come back later—which, I could tell from the smirks they exchanged, the gorillas had been told before.

"Sure, sure, take your time," replied the spokesman of the pair, his novelty jacket pasted to his broad back with perspiration. "Take all the time you need. We'll be back tomorrow for the cash."

Observing all this from under the eel I was wrestling onto a meathook,

I was so struck by their effrontery that I straightaway hung up my apron and followed them out into the muggy afternoon. They seemed to be in no hurry, pausing at here a candy butcher's, there a newsstand to threaten the merchant, fanning themselves with their skimmers as they ambled leisurely over to Forsyth and Grand. There they mounted dusty stairs and entered the door of an office on the second-floor landing, gilt letters across its pebble-glass pane reading Acme Insurance Group. Hesitating only long enough to give my cap a cunning tilt, I opened the door into an anteroom that was bare but for a desk, a telephone, and a young woman applying makeup to a theatrical degree. Under the desk I could see the sheen of her crossed legs in their rolled-down stockings; I could hear a radio playing "Ukelele Lady" from beyond the inner office door.

Several moments elapsed before the young woman deigned to acknowledge my presence. When finally she did, she ran her eyes over the length of me and seemed not displeased with what she saw, though she said in a tone of bedrock boredom, "What do you want?" closing her compact with a gesture like snapping teeth.

Remembering the sign on the door, I submitted: "I wanna take out a life insurance policy."

The feather aigrette in her sulfur-yellow hair shimmied beneath the ceiling fan. "We only deal in property insurance," she announced in a listless impression of an actual receptionist.

"Then I wanna life insurance policy on my property."

She smiled with her tight mouth only, apparently used to wiseguys. "You look like a nice boy," dropping the charade. "Better get outta here if you know what's good for you."

Removing my cap which I used to wipe the sweat from my brow, I decided to try a different tack. "Is Mister, um . . . ," I began, but "Mr. the Sport" somehow didn't seem right. "Is Mr. Kupferman in?"

"Who wants to know?"

I considered. "Tell him Ruby Kid Karp."

She said with her kohl-ringed eyes that I had to be kidding. At that point the door to the inner office opened a crack, the radio blared, and one of the characters I'd tailed from the ice plant, the spokesman, in fact, poked his eagle beak into the anteroom. The height of his head suggested that he was seated, his chairback probably propped against the wall as he twisted his neck to peek beyond the door. "Hey, Birdie," he said in a voice like an emery board, "how bout a shtikl your sweet pierogie later on?" Then he noticed me. "What's this?"

She raised her plucked brows. "This," she announced with a sigh, "is Kid Karp. Kid, meet Shtrudel Louie Shein."

"Howdja do," said the tough guy, whose reputation (like his boss's) had preceded him in the lore of the neighborhood. "Now get lost."

That's when the righteous anger came over me again. "My papa don't need your protection," I practically spat at him, thrilled by my own impertinence.

Shtrudel Louie frowned, his head disappearing from view as the door shut again. I heard a muffled mumbling under the voice on the radio cautioning the audience to stay tuned; an orchestral arrangement of "Runnin' Wild" was next on the program after a message from "Quick, Henry, the Flit!" Then the door opened again and out stepped Shtrudel Louie with his shnozzle and monobrow, his crooked bowtie, from a room I now saw was as barren as the one I stood in: a few items of furniture paying homage to the radio receiving outfit with its tuba-size speaker that served as centerpiece. Shtrudel was followed by his shorter, stockier companion from the icehouse, who was tugging his waistcoat like a corset over his tumid belly. They took up their stations on either side of me like groomsmen, as a third man emerged from the office to confront me, his expression—as he gave me the once-over—seeming to infer that this was going to be fun.

"Who comes at the Cliquot Club Eskimo Hour to disturb us?" he asked, like *fee fi fo fum*.

A sensible person might have beshat himself then and there, but fear didn't yet figure in my frame of reference. "Ruby," I told him, "Ruby Kid Karp," exulting in the sense that now there was no turning back. "Who are you?" Of course, his patterned golf hose and knickers, along with his patent leather shoes and center-parted patent leather hair, had already identified him as Naf the Sport himself.

Ignoring my question, he continued his own line of inquiry, a heavy lid drooping over his lazy eye. "And your papa, kid? What did you say his name was?" Hearing the "kid," I wondered was he patronizing me or earnestly employing my freshly coined nom de guerre? In either event, I saw no reason to prevaricate.

"Shmerl Karp of Karp's Ice Castle," I pronounced as if I were proud of it.

"Am I to understand he sent you here, your papa, to reject the generous offer of our health protection package? What other plan, I ask you, is so excellent as to give compensation for your gouged-out eye and broken skull?"

"Nobody sent me," I assured him. "I come here on my own."

Naf the Sport tugged at his suspenders, rocked on his heels. "Why, that demonstrates real initiative, son," he said with questionable sincerity.

My impulse was to tell him "I'm not your son," while on the other hand I thought that one could do worse.

"Problem is," he continued, "our records show your papa is already on our books. Mr. Shein, Mr. Turtletaub," he shifted his eyes, one lazy and one lynx, toward either of his colleagues, "what is our policy toward clients that get a little behind in their payments?"

Said the chinless Mr. Turtletaub, whose age I reckoned as somewhere between twenty-five and sixty, "We nail their putz to the doorpost and eat their family."

Naf the Sport made a face. "I don't think we need to resort to such extreme measures in this case. In fact, I think the kid here is mistaken about his own mission. Didn't your papa send you over as a gesture of good faith? You're like collateral, what they call surety, ain't that right? Until he gets his finances in order, you are your papa's marker, so to speak."

"My papa is giving you bupkes," I stated categorically, and felt ticklish all over.

Naf the Sport fastened a look on me with his good eye, then shrugged regretfully. "In that case," he said, "the marker's no good to us, is it gentlemen?" which meant he'd abandoned the hostage idea. Then he gave the nod to his yeggs, who abruptly grabbed me about the chest and ankles. Before I could wriggle free I was lifted horizontally, carried kicking across the room, and tossed through the window that Naftali Kupferman had opened onto Forsyth Street. There were some seconds when I was pleasantly airborne: laundry flapped, pigeons cooed; then I plummetted ass over elbows into the awning above a grocer's cart. The soggy canvas tore apart from my weight, dumping me into the produce bin underneath, which itself collapsed in an avalanche of ripe tomatoes. I tumbled along with the fruit onto the pavement and scrambled instantly to my feet, saturated head to toe in pulpy juice. The shag-bearded grocer cursed me, the market wives mistaking the juice for gore screeched like magpies, but I was too incensed to even pause and inspect myself for broken bones. Setting my jaw, I charged back into the building, taking the steps three at a time; I reached the landing and flung myself into the office, where all three men and the peroxide receptionist were still gathered at the open window, looking out. The advantage of surprise in my favor, I leaped onto Shtrudel Louie's back, somehow managing, even as I tightened my hold on Shtrudel's throat, to deliver a battery of swift kicks to Turtletaub's breadbasket. In the ensuing knock-down-drag-out I must have inflicted some damage and damage must have been inflicted on me, but I was unaware of anything but the euphoria of battle. At some point their dandified ringleader, looking on from his vantage by the window (the receptionist having crawled under her desk) shouted, "Cease already and desist!" His colleagues backed off without argument, leaving me to continue throwing haymakers at the stuffy air. Eventually I became conscious that my adversaries, their disordered garments stained with blood or tomato juice, their bruised heads glazed in sweat, were staring at me with something like wonder.

"So, Kid," said Naftali, "is shlepping ice your chosen profession, or are you looking for something with more opportunity for advancement?"

It was the invitation I'd been angling for all along.

I left Karp's Ice Castle without a backward glance, nor do I think that Karp even missed me, while my worried mama took every occasion to quiz me about where I spent my days, never mind the nights. I made sure, however, that those occasions became less frequent, and in the end Shmerl Karp and his sightly wife had to accept the fact that their son had grown beyond their control. If they were at all aware of my associations, I gave them no chance to object — though I might have pointed out that my connection with Naf the Sport was in essence a mitzvah, since my membership in his organization prompted the gangleader to give my father's business a pass. Meanwhile, though the school term had begun again, my former alma mater saw me no more; the Acme Insurance Group and all it fronted for became my academy, and I was its true-blue cadet. From then on I was a stranger to the Upper West Side, returning to the apartment only to sleep; then I practically stopped sleeping altogether, spending my nights in the speaks operated by Naf and his affiliates, sacking out in the rooms upstairs, where I was sometimes not alone. For the receptionist Birdie Pomerantz, who moonlighted in an older profession, had taken it as her duty to introduce me to what she called, in deference to my age, "playing doctor." Afterwards she flattered me by saying, "You've done this before," a statement I heard repeated by other ladies with whom I continued to feign inexperience, a strategy that earned me many a free ride.

I was often impatient with the gang's endless capacity for idleness. They could kill an afternoon in the Acme office speculating on the tabloid headlines of the day. They boozed, played pinochle, shot pool, ate rolled brisket slathered in schmaltz in Naf's subsidiary interests on Ludlow or Allen Street, and I joined them, telling myself that at last I'd found my true family. But when it came time to go to work for the good of the syndicate, I was the first to volunteer. In the beginning the commissions we received kept me close to our home base south of Houston and east of the Bowery. During that time I was still a foot soldier, traveling in the ranks populated by the likes of Twinkl Saltzman, Morris "the Worm" Baumzweig,

Pretty Pinski with his parboiled face, the ex-welterweight Little Lhulki, and others. In their company I was sent into the East Side's steamy streets to grease the wheels of commerce. The gambling and prostitution rackets over which Naf presided required an experienced staff, but the extortion and loan-sharking operations wanted oversight of a less specialized kind, which was where we plug-uglies came in. Usually things went smoothly enough to qualify as routine: the delinquent debtor, having pissed himself, would hand over the vigorish without debate; though occasionally some young hothead or old duffer who thought he had nothing to lose would require a little persuasion.

My comrades were all ghetto-bred, mostly Jews, though a few stray Italians from Mulberry Street and Irishers from the East River docks had found their way into the mix. All were alumni of the state reformatories and had done time in the city jails, some despite their relative youth in federal pens. Coming as I did from what they considered a pampered background, and because of my green age, I had constantly to prove myself worthy of their fraternity. I cherished those opportunities, and while I don't think any of my victims actually expired from their wounds, I was sometimes a little overzealous in demonstrating my allegiance to the gang.

For all his irons in the fire (and despite his graduation from turned-around golf cap to silk Borsalino), Naftali Kupferman remained a small-time bootlegger. This was not for want of aspirations. But despite the racketeering enterprises that had made him a known and feared quantity throughout the Tenth Ward, he lacked both the financial and influential capital required to bankroll a major rum-running operation. For that you needed alliances in the higher strata of gangland; you needed the judges and politicians in your pockets, the cash to float the boats, rent the warehouses, provide the trucks, the bribes, the gunsels to guard against hijackers, and of course the alcohol itself. Still and all, Naf made quite a comfortable living by the standards of the day, though the big money always seemed to elude his grasp. He had to content himself with funding a number of basement stills and owning a piece of a brewery across the Hudson. The Hoboken Cereal Beverage Company, officially licensed to make "near beer," turned much of its product into the headier illegal stuff, this via a system of underground pipes that led to another building several blocks away. From there the beer was barreled, bottled, and loaded onto trucks under cover of night. It was during these after-hours activities that our orbit intersected those of the more notorious underworld echelons. While they waited for delayed overseas shipments, the bigshots, through a network of hole-and-corner alliances, might approach Naf for an interim replenishment of their depleted stock — requests generally accompanied with derision for the inferior quality of the Hoboken hooch. Then, at an appointed dropoff in the meatpacking district, we would make the exchange of goods for cash. It was at these times that the envoys of Waxey Gordon, who answered only to Arnold Rothstein, prince of schemers, might feel moved to remind us of our lowly rung on the ladder of crime. This didn't sit well with me. Though I wasn't much concerned with the big scores they boasted, neither did I like having my face rubbed in the fact of our second-class citizenship.

One of those especially vocal in calling attention to our small potatoes status was Dago Cohen, the razor-suited captain of the bunch that worked for Waxey and his partner, Maxey Greenberg, who'd made a killing from imported rum. When I decided to give him and his stooges a lesson in manners in the gravel lot a stone's throw from the Cunard pier, I was noticed for my pugilistic gifts. How could I not be when the odds were four to one, two of whom I sent to hospital with extra joints in their busted limbs? — this while my own cohort, including the palooka Lhulki, looked on and placed indolent bets. The incident led to my being "borrowed" by Waxey's boys to help with certain of their more hazardous undertakings. It was a needless arrangement of course; there was no shortage of goons to fill the bill. But it was clear that Dago and company respected me for the drubbing I'd given them, and my enlistment amounted to an induction into a more exalted criminal sphere.

My loyalties, however, remained with Naf and his crew for having rescued me from ordinary life; nor did I have any ambition to climb a ladder that only led back to a burlesque of the ordinary. I liked our penny-ante situation in the underworld proper. Maxey's crowd could have their Hotsy-Totsy Club, their Dempsey versus Firpo at the Garden; we had Battling Levinsky at the Roumanian Opera House, who took his legendary dive in the first seconds of Round One. They had Aqueduct and the Belmont Stakes, but we had the casinos at Hesper's on Second Avenue and the Sans Souci on Broome, which could turn into knitting parties at the hint of a raid. We had dope sheets on the walls of every poolroom, stuss parlors where you had only to mention the Sport and your credit was good; we had the disorderly houses run by Madams Mildred the Mattress and Sadie the Chink.

Still I'd be lying if I didn't admit that I enjoyed the opportunities Dago Cohen and his bunch gave me to see the world above Houston Street. Thanks to them I traveled as far upstate as Saratoga, an important way station along the booze route's northeastern corridor and a wide-open town totally given over to vice. I rode shotgun (for real) in the convoys coming down from Canada carrying cargos of schnapps brought from the islands off the Maritime, where the ships from England and France had dumped them. Along the way we distributed the hush money, first to the Coast Guard and then to the cops from Suffolk County on down to the City. Usually we were flagged past the checkpoints at county lines with immunity, but once we came upon some stainless state troopers that couldn't be bought. During the chase that followed I fired a tommy gun from the running board, hanging on to a rearview mirror with my free hand to keep from being bounced into a ditch by the jackhammer report. I rode with Dago and his operatives in the speedboats that kicked up a spray like sailfish fins out to Rum Row, where the ships were anchored past the three-mile limit off Montauk Point. From the boats we transferred the freight to a fleet of trucks that transported it in turn to a warehouse in Astoria, from which the booze was dispersed among restaurants, clubs, and two-bit

bootleggers who sold it on the Manhattan streets. Naftali Kupferman, by
Waxey's lights, was one of those petty beneficiaries, though I saw to it he
received the goods at a discount. (A price he then inflated by doctoring the
pure spirits for resale with everything from radiator coolant to creosote.)
As a go-between I was able to keep Naf abreast of the ebb and flow of the
whiskey traffic; I alerted him as to which districts were flush and which
wanting, so he could get a jump on the competition. In exchange for such
information I was admitted into Naf's inner circle and deemed, albeit
reluctantly by his ambassadors-at-large (for Shtrudel and Turtletaub had
never gotten over their shellacking), as indispensable.

I had become a person to be reckoned with on the East Side while at
the same time enjoying carte blanche in the uptown haunts of the sultans
of capital crime. Some of these establishments you entered through cellar
doors with spyholes or a meat locker in the rear of a butcher shop; others
operated brazenly under the averted eye of the law. Among the latter was
Dutch Schultz's Embassy Club, where I once saw the Dutchman himself drag Francis X. Bushman out from under Vilma Banky's table, while
Helen Morgan swayed on the bandstand in a lavender spot. I suppose it
turned my head a bit, the rubbing elbows with celebrity. After all, Waxey
and his boys had the trappings of an organization that was here to stay;
they were professionals, whereas Naf the Sport's outfit was a fly-by-night
sideshow by comparison, and the Lower East Side was Broadway's dirty
backyard.

What's more, despite the advantages I had personally put in his way,
Naftali Kupferman's fortunes were in decline. He was mortgaged to the
eyeballs from trying to maintain his stake in the great vertical combine
that was bootlegging. His payoffs to the Tammany satraps, the municipal judges and district attorneys, were eating up the revenue from his
other rackets, and his trespassing into territories outside his control had
prompted rumblings throughout the fragile alliances of the underworld.
As a consequence, beyond bankruptcy he was worried about becoming the
target of a gang war he couldn't hope to survive. From the vantage of my

own mobility I sort of enjoyed watching him squirm, but I never forgot what I owed his largess. Still, with a personality that fluctuated between peacock posturing and hand-wringing despair, Naftali was never easy to warm to. The nine-iron he wielded sometimes like a scepter, sometimes a popgun, he now leaned on like an invalid's walking stick, and there were rumors that his syphilis was entering a dangerous stage.

While his moodiness was not apt to inspire sympathy, even less endearing were the remarks he and his lieutenants made to the effect that Kid Karp had outgrown their humble company: "The Kid has bigger latkes to fry," and so on. I made an effort to reassure them that I was still their boy, though they were right, of course; the old ghetto had become as constricting to me as Alrightniks Row. Then Naf let it be known that he'd recently raised his protection rates, and the businesses that he'd once let slide he now felt compelled to dun for welshed payments. This included Karp's Ice Castle, which particular concern was still being difficult and needed to be taught a lesson.

"You understand this is nothing personal, Kid," he assured me, his sleepy eye weeping a nacreous matter, and while I was perfectly aware I was being tested, I told him I understood. Then he said he wouldn't think of letting anyone else do the job.

For maybe the first time in my life I asked myself if I had a conscience; I concluded that I apparently did not. Naturally I vacillated, but this was mostly due to my resentment at having my loyalty called into question. With Dago's guarantee that there was always a place for me in Waxey's bunch, I had a good mind to switch allegiances on the spot. But something in me didn't like to burn bridges; Naftali was my original benefactor, and what would it cost me to win back his respect? I confess I'd thought that arson as a means of persuasion had gone out with thumbscrews and iron maidens; the businesses themselves were anyway more likely to anticipate the gangs in torching their property, "Jewish lightning" having been epidemic in the neighborhood for generations. My father had insurance in any case; he wouldn't be ruined, and wasn't the cankered old wooden Castle an accident waiting to happen? I'd be doing him a favor, after which he could reconstruct the place according to modern specifications. Moreover, Naf was right: He did need to be taught a lesson; and besides, I'd never lit a really big fire before.

NAFTALI ASSIGNED PRETTY PINSKY, the gang's resident arson mechanic (his scalded face his best credential), and Morris Baumzweig to accompany me. Since the Ice Castle's personnel worked late and started early, we had only a brief interval in which to do our business with impunity. Pretty and Morris the Worm, his nickname derived from his rumored ability to crawl through keyholes, carried seltzer bottles filled with gasoline and tar (the better to stick to burning surfaces) and stoppered with oil-soaked rags, while I humped on my shoulder a five-gallon jug of wood turpentine. Anyone who'd spotted us would have known exactly what we were about, but we were reasonably cautious, wearing dark rain slickers and balaclavas and keeping to the back alleys. As the Ice Castle was a virtually windowless structure, I assumed that the Worm would demonstrate his expertise by picking a lock on one of the side doors. Instead, having surveyed the Castle's façade, he stepped over the road and addressed the barn-size portals facing Canal Street, its cobbles deserted in the hour or so before sunrise. His rationale was that opening those massive doors would draw the watchman, whom we would then take out of commission. So, in the predawn frost of that late-March morning, Morris spread the wings of his oilskin to reveal an array of tools hung in its lining. He invited Pretty to do the honors, but when the firebug wavered as if selecting an item from a tray of hors d'oeuvres, Morris barked at him impatiently, "The crowbar, codface!" Pretty removed the iron bar from its hook and thrust it unceremoniously at Morris, upon which the cracksman shoved the bar through the narrow space between the doors. He gave it a twist and, satisfied that the gooseneck had snagged its objective, raised it, releasing the latch beam that barred the entrance from the other side. In their heaviness the doors swung toward us so that we stepped back out of the way, surprised (at least in my case) that breaking and entering promised to be so free of obstacles.

But where was the watchman we'd expected to flush out? We made a deliberately unstealthy entrance into the icehouse, clunking up the incline and pulling the doors to, shivering from an arctic chill that took our breath. Still nobody came to greet us. In the stone-cold gloom Morris opened his coat again and removed from it a small bull's-eye lantern, which Pretty lit with a storm match he struck on his stubbled jaw. Morris swung the lantern here and there like a signalman shedding light a few yards ahead of us along the locker-lined corridor. The little that was visible, however, made me all the more aware of what was obscured: the parapets of ice buttressed by produce crates in the lofts and galleries, the trusses and creaking collar-beams that propped up the sagging roof. But as familiar as I'd once been with every corner of the Castle, tonight the place seemed alien. There was nothing about it of the commercial or industrial facility; rather, it had a kind of austerity, like a magazine where winter itself is stored. If they shared any of my reverence for the atmosphere, my companions never showed it — Pretty peering with his pinball eyes from a face the texture of stucco, the Worm discoursing like the blowhard he was: "I read somewhere that potassium chloride don't even need to be lit to start a fire . . . ," while Pretty, a traditionalist, disparaged the technology. I wondered what I was doing with this pair of trombeniks; why did I feel the need to prove myself to such as they? Morris continued waving the lamp about until I told him, "Stop it already, you're making me nauseous." "Who made you the boss?" he wanted to know. I sighed and said we should make a pass through the plant to confirm there were no civilians at large; not that we were especially worried about incinerating the innocent, but it wouldn't do to have witnesses. And where, incidentally, was the watchman?

Making professional noises, Morris suggested we split up and reconnoiter, but I warned him that the icehouse was full of angles and blind passages; "I don't want to lose you two," I said, a touch disingenuously, and though they sniffed at my caution, we nevertheless set off down the central arcade together. Along the way I shifted the turpentine bottle to my hip, allowing a trickle to spill behind us like a thread we could follow back to where we'd begun. The lantern light darted like foxfire over the loins and flanks dangling in their lockers, the racks of bear and curly dog hides. In the middle of the factory the ice was stacked in blocks graduated in size from fifty to four hundred pounds, their seams outlined by whiskery bits of straw. A low hatch in the wall of that stronghold led to a maze of sleeping machinery, a roller-coaster configuration of belts, sprockets, motors, and gears.

"That's your chain hoist there above the water-cooled condensing unit," I indicated somewhat pedagogically, "and your galvanized steel stacking bin with the pallet lift. . . ." I don't know what had come over me that I suddenly felt compelled to introduce my companions to the apparatus of my father's design. I had little interest in the machines myself, nor could I have explained their operation in any coherent fashion, but I was seized by an impulse to pay some last-ditch homage to Shmerl Karp's ingenuity. The Worm interrupted me to complain about the onset of frostbite, while Pretty asserted through chattering teeth that it was time we warmed the place up a bit. Assured that nobody else was abroad, we cut short our tour of the premises and returned to the broad aisle we'd set out from.

Then I wondered what we were waiting for, until Morris spoke up: "You give the signal," adding with caustic emphasis, "*Boss.*" I guessed that Naftali had charged them to see to it I took the initiative. So I nodded, that was all, just a slight tilt of the chin, which was sufficient to prompt my accomplices to light the rag wicks and lob their incendiary bombs. One struck a rafter nearly at the height of the cockloft, the other a six-inch locker door, both exploding with a muffled sound like the flap of a tablecloth being spread, and instantly blossomed into flame. The original bursts spawned others until a hanging garden of fire grew along either side of the arcade, its petals waving like serrated hankies. Flames climbed the walls as the garden ran riot, taking over every available surface of that tinderbox structure. Then it was my turn and, borrowing a match from Pinsky, I struck it on my heel and dropped it into the spilled turpentine. We watched the flame travel as if along a serpent's spine, the snake undulating as it stretched to the opposite end of the building, where it disappeared around a corner and, having made its loop of the warehouse interior, returned to swallow its tail at our feet.

We beat it out the front doors and across the trolley tracks, ducking into the alley beside the Metzker landsmanschaft on the other side of Canal. We were headed back to the sanctuary of Simmie Tischler's gin mill on Grand Street, where we would report the success of our mission and drink a health among fellow conspirators with Naf's watery brew. But after the first block or so I slackened my pace before coming to an eventual halt. Turning around to see what had happened to me, Pretty and Morris also drew up short, Morris inquiring, "What's your problem?" Unable to answer, I rested my hands on my knees as if trying to catch my breath. What I couldn't tell them was that a memory, lost until now in unreality, had chosen this moment to reassert itself. During my time at Karp's I had studiously avoided the compartment toward the rear of the plant that Papa liked to call the Castle's Keep, having no desire to revisit what I regarded as a bad dream. Now I decided that, even if the thing did exist, my father was still out to lunch and the Castle better off going up in flames — which you could already see billowing above the rooftops from where we stood.

"I must've dropped my pocketwatch back at the icehouse," I lied, slap-frisking myself as I spoke.

Pretty Pinsky squinted at me with a searching malevolence, while Morris shrugged and began tugging his crony forward by the lapel. "See you 'round campus," he called over his shoulder without a tinge of conviction, as if they'd anticipated my defection all along.

By the time I arrived back at Canal Street the icehouse was a furnace, flames groping through the open doors and curling from under the eaves, a pall of smoke and grease having overspread the vacant street. Soon the neighborhood would wake up, choking; alarms would sound, crowds

gather, sirens lacerate the air. But, for now, the place seemed almost qui-
escent, as if a burning building on an arc-lit ghetto street were a natural
feature of the early-morning cityscape. Even from the opposite sidewalk I
could feel my cheeks flush from the blaze. Then what I was contemplating
made me question if I was nuts, if in the last analysis I was my father's son,
a notion I rejected with all my heart; and satisfied that I'd made a clean
escape from a happy family, I lurched across the cobbles and plunged into
the conflagration.

Gagging from the heat and smoke, I pulled a bandanna from my pocket
and wiped my watering eyes before tying it over my face; then hearing
what I took to be gunshots, I dropped to all fours before realizing it was
only the pop-pop of bursting bottles. While the fire raged in the galleries,
the thick walls of the ground-floor lockers still provided a degree of insulation, though maverick flames had penetrated far enough to flick the odd
slab of meat—which caused the fat to drip from the roasting chuck or
tenderloin, further feeding the blaze. The herring barrels had their crowns,
the hanging game their ruffs and skirts of flame, and in one locker I saw
a ten-point stag with its antlers on fire. A ladder on the mezzanine was
limned in incandescence before disintegrating into ash; a freight elevator
dropped its open cab into coruscating cinders. The ice ramparts were melting in a niagara that flooded the well of machinery, thereby cheating the
flammable gases of their chance to detonate—not that there was any want
of combustion. All around me the fire waved in sheets, whirled in flutes
and funnels like classical flourishes.

Against a stack of smoldering bushel baskets I spied a lone hand truck
and made to grab it, but the steel frame was too hot to touch; so I removed
my slicker and wrapped it around the handle. Then I began pushing the
two-wheeler ahead of me like a battering ram, dodging sparks and falling
debris in a furious slalom through the burning plant. At the far end I ca-
reened toward the sanctum, ordinarily distinguished from the other refrigerated chambers by its coffer-size padlock, though tonight the lock hung
loose and the door was wide open. Skidding to a stop at the threshold,

I beheld a scene I had to rub my smarting eyes to make come clear: for there stood my humpbacked papa in his collarless shirtsleeves, his shed sheep's pelt on the floor at his feet, gibbering to himself as he tugged at a rope like Quasimodo hauling on his bellpull. The rope described a taut triangle running up through an overhead pulley, then down to the ancient casket mounted on trestles, whose girth it encircled. The weathered planks were lacy from the perforations of termites, the casket's contents leaking (despite the visible zinc lining) through its many holes. How my father planned to remove the box once he'd lifted it from its horizontal repose, an impossible task from the look of it, was anyone's guess—unless he was expecting someone to arrive with a vehicle to cart the thing away.

Leaving the two-wheeler in the doorway I stepped inside the Keep, where the air was scarcely cooler than in the warehouse proper, and grabbed hold of the rope alongside my papa. Turning his head to look at me, his eyes salmon pink in the absence of his spectacles, he seemed to see a stranger; then he turned away only to look back momentarily, taking advantage of my occupied hands to pull down my mask—whereupon he gave my torrid cheek a pinch and grinned a foolish grin. Again taking hold of the rope, he resumed muttering what sounded like a mix of devotions and numerical formulae. Together we did make some progress, managing to elevate the coffin a few inches from its bier, but a plume of smoke with a flaming pistil had invaded the locker, promising to turn the place in a matter of minutes into a crematorium. At the same time flames from the ceiling were sliding down the rope, which sizzled as it snapped in two, dumping the casket back onto the sawhorses, which, themselves on fire, crashed to the floor in a dazzle of embers. Stymied for no more than a heartbeat, my papa attacked the casket as if he thought he might wrestle it upright with his bare hands. Judging his effort useless, I took hold of his shoulders to pull him away from his unavailing labor, but he twisted out of my grasp with a violence that made me shudder, so much did his rage remind me of my own. I realized I would have to knock him senseless in order to haul him out of there, but before I could move forward with my intention, a beam dislodged from above swung down in a shower of sparks to pin my father beneath it. I bent to try and remove the impediment, searing my fingers on its charcoal surface while Papa lay groaning face-down under the weight of the spar. Unable to get a grip on his torso or the torch of his ginger hair, I tried pulling him by the ankles but succeeded only in dragging the beam along with him. It was then that a second rafter toppled, splintering into cinders that left my father nearly buried beneath a mound aglow with salamanders of ash. I stumbled about, looking for a tool with which to dig him out, vaguely aware of having been injured myself, my fingers blistered, head gashed, lungs gasping beyond their capacity to breathe more smoke. Then all at once the room began to recede and I was somewhere else, in a place where if you fell you were raised up again, higher perhaps than you had ever known.

I was riding someone's broad back through the inferno, gliding out of the Castle and into the street, where I half expected my conveyance to take to the sky. Instead, I was gently set down coughing and sputtering onto the curb, where I proceeded to swallow great gulps of air in an effort to displace the smoke in my lungs. Wiping my eyes with my fists, I turned in time to glimpse my rescuer—shoulders stretching the seams of a peas-ant shirt, a neck as thick as his shaven head—disappearing again into the Gehenna of the icehouse. After some minutes of throbbing anticipation I watched him reemerge, having apparently duplicated himself; for he was accompanied by his identical twin, the two of them straining under the burden of the scorched and dripping cedar casket. They set it down with a weighty thud on the pavement beside me, as from my slump I pointed with a cauterized finger toward the burning building.

"My papa," I mouthed, and the stocky pair exchanged puzzled glances. Then they turned back toward the Castle just as a tremendous explosion rippled the surface of Canal Street like a beaten rug. A black cloud the shape of a giant cauliflower with a fiery stalk rose from the wreckage of the icehouse and merged with the sunrise over the river to the east. I leaned against the casket, pressing my cheek to its dampness, inhaling its mildewy odor as I sheltered from the hail of rubble. In the distance the sirens, whistles, and bells drew closer, sounding like a parade that heralds the end of the world . . .

2001.

. . . read Bernie to Lou Ella, as they sat in the crotch of a live oak
in the botanical gardens or over a bowl of cobbler in a booth at the Dixie
Café—while she assured him that, notwithstanding the cannibals, Ku
Kluxers, and motherfuckers among her own relations, his family had a
lot to answer for. Bernie, for whom his great-grandfather's burning alive
was also news, was inclined to agree; and the closer they came to the end
of Ruby's journal, the more he felt that answer should come from him.
But not yet, not yet; there was more of the story left to read, and Lou Ella
urged him to continue. She clearly cherished the time they spent tracing
the history of the Family Karp's peregrinations while she and Bernie themselves peregrinated about the city of Memphis seeking out the scruffier
corners—abandoned recording studios and heartbreak hotels—where a
sanitized present had yet to laminate the past. Both he and the girl were
conscious of enjoying an interlude. It was a period during which Bernie
Karp, energized by his affection for Lou, his almost lover, and by extension for everything else on earth, was changing in discernible ways. For
one thing, he was no longer satisfied with the visionary journeys that now
seemed to him so selfish and self-absorbed. Sure, it was nice to become
one with the Godhead and all that, but in the end, as the sages said, "Life

is with people," and if you couldn't take anyone with you, what was the good of leaving your body at all? That said, Bernie had no clear idea of what was next in store for him, though whatever it was he knew it would involve taking as Lou said "the bull by the pizzle." Still, while Lou Ella had been instrumental in persuading him that he shouldn't miss out on the experience of dwelling on earth, herself a prey to forebodings, she now campaigned actively to postpone whatever was coming.

In the meantime the world around them had begun to catch up with Lou Ella's bleak assessments of its status. While Bernie might command in his flights an aerial view of history, Lou had her own brand of second sight and seemed not at all surprised when the world began to show signs of being in its final days. It was an attitude in keeping with her Pentecostal background, though she judged the rabid voices from that quarter as themselves material signs that the end was at hand. She was a complicated girl, at odds with her own fatalism, who seemed to take for granted the toppling of the towers by terrorists in New York City and the nation's berserk response; she anticipated the thirst for vengeance that would fan the flames of an already smoldering planet, presaging a universal conflagration. In the name of protecting the homefront, faceless bureaucracies had overnight rolled back liberties to a degree that constituted a shadow police state, and the subsequent paranoid atmosphere left citizens unable to distinguish between real and imagined threats. There was also a crackdown on illegal aliens which, if anyone bothered to notice, the formerly frozen rabbi happened to be. Not that the current climate had put a damper on his enterprise; on the contrary, as fear gave a healthy fillip to the quest for spiritual solace, the times proved especially favorable for Rabbi ben Zephyr's project. Citizens of the Mid-South flocked to the New House of Enlightenment in unprecedented numbers, and announcements in the papers, always interested in the rabbi's proceedings, trumpeted his plans to franchise his ministry worldwide. Naturally, the more publicity he received, the more voices were raised in dissent of his methods. Aside from

the cautionary bromides of the clergy and the usual canards regarding the
Elders of Zion, there were those who attributed cultish tactics to Rabbi
ben Zephyr's community of disciples; there were charges by professed
"escapees" from his center that the rabbi and his followers were guilty
of coercion, brainwashing, and gross sexual misconduct. Nor did it help
matters that the Boibiczer Prodigy had recently been heard making extravagant claims from his pulpit, including the not-so-veiled suggestion
that he was, if not the Messiah himself, then at least a harbinger of same.
All of which made its way into the local papers, invested as they were in
keeping his controversy alive. Still, his defenders remained in the majority,
always more ardent in singing their rebbe's praises than his detractors were
in citing his imperfections.

They quoted from the official tracts and testimonials disseminated by
the House of Enlightenment, ghostwritten by Bernie's father's accountant-
turned-publicist, the versatile Mr. Grusom. Then there was the rabbi's own
memoir, which you could now find on sale in chain stores and airport
newsstands and which stood to become a classic of inspirational literature
in the vein of *The Prophet* or *Autobiography of a Yogi*. Bernie had dutifully dipped into the slickly packaged *Ice Sage* as a companion piece to
Grandpa Ruby's journal, then passed it along without comment to Lou
Ella, who had a peculiar tolerance for such narratives. She appreciated the
gloss this one provided on the more prosaic chronicle outlined in Bernie's
grandfather's ledger. Ostensibly *The Ice Sage* (also ghosted by Grusom, who
convinced the rabbi that his original title, *The Erotic Tzaddik*, was undig-
nified) was Rabbi ben Zephyr's own version of his spiritual adventures during the time his body was immersed in the ice of a horse pond on Baron
Jagiello's estate. There, while his head was wreathed in a nimbus of static
tadpoles and minnows, his spirit attained the highest rungs of the world
to come. He'd sat in the celestial academies, participating in roundtable
discussions with prophets and patriarchs parsing the thornier points of the
ancient mysteries. Meanwhile his body had been carved from the ice and

carted halfway round the globe. The family responsible for shlepping him about for the better part of a century was given short shrift in the rabbi's recounting; they were merely a means to an end, and if he acknowledged their efforts at all, it was only by way of explaining his geographic mobility. Also, though the book was subtitled "Rabbi ben Zephyr's Adventures with God," God Himself was seldom mentioned. The text focused instead on techniques for overcoming phobias, realizing desires, and taking control of your life by exploiting the power of something called the Light of Creation. The hallowed mystical tradition was de-Judaized, its esoteric elements soft-pedaled in an effort to pander to a popular audience. Having perused as much of the memoir as he could stomach, Bernie couldn't help feeling saddened by how the Prodigy had among other things co-opted his family's history for his own purposes. But then it was the rabbi's history as well, wasn't it? — to bend, fold, and swindle as he saw fit. Still, the book seemed a betrayal of the days they'd spent together in the guesthouse and the basement rumpus room, that distant time when the hidden rebbe had condescended to instruct the boy in the ways of the inexpressible and to help him in his first limping efforts to translate his grandfather's journal.

For all that, Bernie was worried about old Eliezer, just as he worried about a world that had lately claimed his attention. It seemed to him that each time he looked up from reading to the girl, yet another international atrocity had occurred. Lou Ella would plead with him to keep his head down, don't stop reading, and when he wavered, she pumped him with questions about the handwritten script: Why, for instance, had Ruby, whose native language was English, chosen to pen his confessions in a spiky Yiddish? She was convinced they would discover the reason if only they forged ahead; the tale was especially suspenseful now that Ruby and the frozen rabbi were headed their way — that is, coming to Memphis.

"How do you know?" asked Bernie, who translated haltingly as he went along and knew no more of his grandfather's fate than did the girl.

" 'Cause I'm psychic," she replied, one hand on the steering wheel, the other reaching into the backseat to shove a pacifier in her baby sister's open mouth. "And besides, they have to get to Memphis so your daddy who ain't been born yet can meet your mama and have you."

At that Bernie became thoughtful. "Do you know," he mused, "I'm about the same age as Grandpa Ruby was when he killed his father?"

"It wasn't exactly murder," qualified Lou, though Bernie remained unconsoled. He gazed through the windshield at the passing rat-hole projects, where stray bullets from drive-by shootings nightly claimed the lives of children asleep in their beds, and somehow felt implicated in his grandfather's crime. The guilt was perhaps an indulgence that helped correct the imbalance in his system, because lately he felt altogether too much at home in his own skin. It wasn't right to feel so at home on a planet going to hell in a handbag. How could you reconcile, for instance, the precarious footing of current events with the scent of lilac that penetrated the brain like some metaphysical spice? Everything he observed had its extra dimension: a throng of starlings was a tattered flag whipped by the wind; the holes in a matzoh were a mysterious Braille. If he farted he recalled Isaiah: "Whereof my bowels shall sound like a lyre"; when Lou wiped egg from Sue Lily's lips clouds passed from the face of the moon. The backwater of Memphis was a safe harbor on the coast of eternity where he lingered with the girl, his lust subdued now to an enduring affection. On the other hand, Bernie had a gift, and it seemed to him it was high time he used it for the greater good.

"Awesome," said the girl, unimpressed. "So why don't you get a job?"

Bernie agreed that that was probably a good idea. His attendance at school during what should have been his junior year was intermittent at best, and eventually his self-involved parents would return the phone calls from his teachers and his scofflaw existence would be exposed. When that happened he should be prepared to secure his own independence. Wasn't it anyway shameful that he still occupied a room in his family's house, where he spent his days riffling the books he'd "borrowed" from the genizah at the Anshei Mishneh shul? — texts for apprentice holy men whose pages were marked with hairs from his first growth of beard, their Hebrew characters becoming entwined with his DNA. At the same time, though she assured him it wasn't a problem, Bernie was also ashamed that it fell to Lou to foot the bill for their junkets. She bought the gas for her mother's Malibu and paid the checks at the Arcade Diner across from the train depot with funds from clerking at a video store after school. That meant their time together had become more compromised, limited as it was to the evening hours after Lou Ella, who'd finally acquired a license despite years of driving without one, had dropped her mother off at work. It also meant that Sue Lily was always with them, though Bernie had come to accept the toddler as a docile appendage of his darling Lou.

His attempts at gainful employment were disastrous. The first was at the Shelby County Fair, where a seasoned carny gave him a trial run at operating a game of chance. It was a classic sideshow hustle where the patrons hurled baseballs at pyramids of milk bottles filled with lead. With only three throws allotted to knock down three sturdy pyramids, no one ever won the stuffed animals displayed above the concession, but that was before Bernie's term as concessionaire. Open to persuasion, he allowed the patrons to negotiate extra opportunities to knock down the bottles, and ended by giving away a number of grand prizes. He was in the process of handing over a giant panda to the son of a man who'd talked him into extra throws when the manager of the joint appeared, demanding to know what was going on. Bernie's explanation resulted in the manager's wresting the panda from the arms of the shrieking child, as the father threatened legal action and the employee was dismissed in opprobrium. His second job was as a day laborer at a midtown construction site. There he was asked to carry sheets of plywood to a carpenter's station via a ramp extending over freshly poured concrete. On his initial trip, a sudden gust caught the plywood, lifting Bernie from the boards and casting him down into the wet foundation. When he presented himself thus encrusted to Lou Ella in the parking lot of her video outlet, she remarked that he looked like the statue from *Don Giovanni* and proceeded to worry grievously about the boy.

Whereas the boy, otherwise exuberant, continued to feel anxious about the rabbi, with whom he had yet to rule out the possibility of joining forces. He was aware of course of Maimonides' criterion for humbug as stated in *The Guide for the Perplexed*: how if the claimant by his life or teachings subverts established moral norms, then you have evidence of deception. But Bernie still believed in the Boibiczer Prodigy even as he wanted to save the old man from himself. Meanwhile besides the clergymen and journalists, a number of local politicians, albeit leery of running afoul of their constituents, had joined the chorus of challengers to the rabbi's legitimacy. It was only a matter of time before malevolent forces would conspire to bring down the House of Enlightenment, and Bernie might be called upon to rescue the rebbe from the brink of his own self-destruction.

"Cool," said the girl, wondering who was more in need of rescuing. Because now that his appetite for the terrestrial had supplanted his desire for transcendence, while those opposing desires were challenged by his passion for Lou Ella herself, she fretted over Bernie's vulnerability. Feeling in good part responsible, she no longer urged him to declare his powers openly; she abdicated her role as his conscience and pressed him to please just get on with reading aloud the tale of the patricide. Since their mutual absorption in Grandpa Ruby's journal had increased, the absence of a physical component to their intimacy seemed almost irrelevant, and it was sometimes possible to think of their relationship as ordinary. Lou was surprised to find that she wished her friend to be ordinary, just as she wished (as did Bernie himself on occasion) that the old man had never been released from the ice.

"Cool, Uberboy, save the rabbi," she said, "save the whole fucking world for all I care, but first finish reading me the story."

1929.

After his head was stitched and bandaged, his burnt hands wrapped in gauze mittens, Ruby was commended by one and all for his good intentions. He'd been heroic, really, a fact that even his stricken mother seemed to register, the failure to rescue his father notwithstanding. His withdrawn silence at the funeral—a redundant affair, given the inventor's prior cremation along with his factory—was interpreted as inconsolable grief. It was a surprisingly large funeral for a man with no close friends. The burial itself took place in the Mount Zion Cemetery, a sprawling necropolis located in the borough of Queens, on a hill with a view of the Manhattan skyline rising in the distance like spikes on a dragon's tail. The entire dispossessed staff of Karp's Castle, come to pay their respects, filed past the unvarnished pine casket after the rabbi's graveside eulogy. Each man released a handful of earth in passing, which thudded hollowly atop the sealed casket containing the only identifiable remains of their putative boss: the charred violin scroll of a vertebra, an eggshell chip from his skull. The relict Mrs. Karp, whose natural pallor had retreated to a near transparency, was supported on the arm of her sister-in-law, Shinde Esther, both of whose parents had passed away the previous year and were buried in an adjacent plot. Flanking Jocheved and Esther were Jocheved's twin brothers, who had arrived from Palestine in time for the wholesale incineration of their sister's life. Ruben Karp, his vacant expression at variance with his rakish head dressing and natty suit, stood apart from the others in the shadow of a stranger's stone.

Jocheved's brothers had come to America to help raise funds for the settlement movement in Palestine, which advertised itself as the advance guard in the establishment of a Jewish national homeland. Longtime veterans of the struggle to colonize Eretz Israel, Yachneh and Yoyneh, since become Yehezkel and Yigdal, had been elected to accompany the Zionist spokesman Zerubavel ben Blish on his tour of the Eastern states. Soldiers as well as pioneers, the twins served in a dual capacity, functioning as bodyguards if needed while applying, by virtue of their brawn, a little pressure toward encouraging contributions to the Yishuv. As it happened, the very first speaking engagement on Comrade ben Blish's calendar was at the Baron de Hirsch Synagogue on the Upper West Side of New York, where Mrs. Shmerl Karp, deserted that Shabbos eve by her nocturnal husband, was also in attendance. A young man with the formal manner of an elder statesman, the bespectacled Comrade ben Blish took the stage after the service and the rabbi's brief introduction, while posted on either side of him, like a pair of mamelukes with their folded arms and buffed heads, stood the imposing Frostbissen brothers.

As Comrade ben Blish launched into his standard recital of miracles performed in the desert, cataloguing fruits that had not been grown there since the time of the prophets, Yigdal and Yehezkel surveyed the congregation. It was their habit even in the friendliest environments to stay alert to the possibility of trouble; to the enemies of Zion no place was sacred. They scanned the faces of the prosperous men in their velvet skull caps and their caparisoned wives in the gallery, focusing on one whose disturbing beauty struck a chord. They turned briefly to each other as the chord thrummed musically in their barrel chests, increasing in volume; then, though it was unseemly to leer for any length at the weaker sex, they turned back toward the handsome woman. Jocheved, from her own angle of vision, felt a similar tug of attraction, the tremor building to a quake that opened a fissure

between the moment and a long-buried past. As the speaker began to wind
down his talk, he looked ceremonially left and right, which was the signal
for his assistants to step from the altar and begin circulating the blue tin
collection pushkes. But the twins had already fled the altar, having made
a beeline for the stairs to the women's gallery, where the ladies were astir
over the impetuous exit of the decorative Mrs. Karp from their midst.
From the staircase beyond the high-domed sanctuary the assembled could
overhear peals of laughter signifying a joyful reunion.

She invited them back to the apartment to meet her absentee family, apologizing that her son Ruben was seldom around and her husband
Shmerl often worked late on projects at his plant. She tried phoning him
but as usual got no answer, since it was after hours and, on nights when
he planned to stay over, the inventor would send the watchman home.
She busied herself with serving tea and homemade schnecken; there was
also—as despite Prohibition Jews were allowed a portion of wine for ritual
purposes—some sugary muscatel. She wouldn't cease her bustling about
until the brothers forcibly sat her down in a wing chair, urging her not
to be nervous, it had after all been no more than twenty-two years since
they'd said good-bye. "Look on you," exclaimed Jocheved when she'd collected herself enough to take in their brute demeanors, "like overgrown
Boy Scouts." The twins grinned with damp eyes as if to acknowledge that
their rubashka shirts and bandannas, khaki shorts and chukka boots, did
perhaps resemble the uniform of some children's brigade. For their part
Yehezkel and Yigdal, between whom Jocheved made no attempt to distinguish, assured her that the pretty sprig they remembered had blossomed
into exquisite fruition in her married estate. She touched her thick curls,
blushed in an excess of pride in her truant boys, despite the fact that one
was given over to wickedness and the other a hostage to his own loopy
imagination. Reunited with her brothers, it seemed to Jocheved, at least
tonight, that her life had progressed in a triumphal arc from the pestilent
ghetto in Lodz to the Upper West Side of New York City.

They filled each other in on the histories they'd missed the way you'd pitch stepping stones from either bank of a stream. Each item of information—Jocheved's silent partnership with her husband, Yehezkel and Yigdal's labors on a collective farm in the Galilee—constituted another stone that brought them a little closer to connecting their respective pasts. They chose, however, only the steadiest and least slippery stones, letting lie the more misshapen and bruising to the touch, for both parties had memories that might not advance their proximity. In this way the ordinarily taciturn brothers and the sister intent on drawing them out passed several charmed hours together; they ate the rolls, drank the cloying wine, and determined that all concerned could not be more content with their lot. The twins had remained unmarried, though in the communes the men and women felt little need for official sanctification of their unions; but they were without wives or issue, having dedicated themselves with the zealotry of the Essenes of old to the creation of a Jewish state. Jocheved listened with a slightly affected awe to their tales, since her time as a man among men had made her no stranger to the anomalies of human behavior that her brothers described. In the small hours when their sister despaired of her husband's returning home that night, Yigdal and Yehezkel, enlivened by the happy occasion, declared they would go downtown to fetch him. Jocheved protested: No subways or buses would be running at that late hour and taxis would be scarce; they should sleep awhile and wait until morning. But the brothers were restless, insisting that they would walk if they couldn't find transport; they could in any case use some air, and besides, sleep was something they had learned to do without in the Holy Land.

THE FIRE AND its attendant explosion, about which a number of unresolved theories had evolved, took three hook-and-ladder brigades and a corps of volunteers to put out. Since the Ice Castle occupied the entire block, the devastation had been largely contained; the neighboring structures suffered only minor damage, and though several firefighters collapsed from inhalation, only one life was lost. But the ash pit which was all that was left in place of the Castle smoldered for days, as if some volcanic landscape complete with smoking fumaroles had erupted in the midst of the ghetto. In the dreary aftermath of the event the twins found themselves unable to abandon their newfound (and newly desolated) sister. Her son, whom they'd discovered in his reckless effort to extract his father from the catastrophe, remained in apparent shock, and was therefore incapable of tending to his mother in any useful way. Informed of the misfortune, their compatriot and charge, Zerubavel ben Blish, was sympathetic. He downplayed the inconvenience, assuring the twins he could manage on his own, though he nevertheless delayed the continuation of his tour and accepted more invitations to speak at Jewish venues around the city.

In the meantime it seemed to the brothers that they had become reacquainted with their beautiful sister only to see her fade into a black bombazine specter before their eyes. They'd encountered her luster just in time to see it cruelly snuffed out. Overnight her native composure had folded into a grim passivity, her sable hair uncoiling into gunmetal gray. If she said anything, it was only to utter some self-indictment, such as, "This is my fault for the obscenity I was," while the untidy attitudes she assumed in the chair she never vacated during the week-long shivah period were oddly genderless. Only on the subject of money did she recover any of her former energy. Due to receive a generous settlement for the factory, whose destruction the twins urged the insurance company to declare an act of God, she said flatly that she didn't want it; and though her brothers respectfully argued that she was being unreasonable, she refused to accept any benefits from her husband's death. Needless to say, she had no heart for rebuilding the business; she had scarcely the impetus to feed or clothe herself, and were it not for the efforts of the spinster Shinde Esther, who coaxed her to take a little nourishment, she might ultimately have followed her Shmerl to an early grave.

As it happened, the inventor's premature passing had come on the eve of a trip that Esther had been planning for some time. Ever since the loss of her parents over a year ago (one from a terminal mal de mer, the other frightened to death by her husband's ghost), she'd decided to accept an invitation to visit the only surviving brother save Shmerl that she was still in touch with. The others had been swallowed up by the mammoth American interior, and only Melchior, now Marvin and residing in the exotic fastness of Tennessee, had continued to write. But the trip had been repeatedly postponed due to Esther's cold feet. It wasn't until the family-minded Marvin had proposed her outright relocation, offering her a position in his retail emporium — and adding somewhat illogically that her marital prospects might be more promising in a warmer clime — that the top-heavy little woman made up her mind to go. Her parents' caretaker and crackpot brother's dependant for far too long, she craved her autonomy. Then came the fire and once again the trip had to be deferred for the sake of looking after the sister-in-law to whom she'd grown attached.

But sometime during the stagnant days that followed the week of mourning, Esther had a radical idea: Why not make the journey with the widow? After all, what did Jocheved have to look forward to in New York other than sitting alone in an apartment appointed in obsolete account books and revenant memories? At the very least the trip might distract her, at best jar her into a renewed interest in life. It might even turn out that the town of Memphis, devoid of unpleasant associations, was a desirable place in which to make a new home. Esther talked over her plan with Yehezkel and Yigdal, who agreed it was worth a try and even volunteered to escort the women as far as their destination. They discussed their intentions with Comrade ben Blish, who suggested that, since his itinerary might be altered to include a swing through the southern states, they make the trip together in easy stages. For despite his self-possession on the podium, Zerubavel was a timid man, insecure in the face of traveling alone into the remoter regions of this goyish nation.

When it came time to present the proposition to the widow, all were braced against her expected resistance. But once her wishes had been honored with respect to the insurance benefits — the attorneys were instructed

to distribute them as severance packages among the unemployed staff of
Karp's Castle—the emotionally destitute Jocheved became almost lamb-
like in her docility. She accepted the judgment of her fellow mourners
that the trip would be good for her with the resignation of a prisoner
receiving a sentence that could not be appealed, a sentence she felt she
deserved. Of course, arrangements had to be made: The apartment must
be sublet, Shmerl and Jocheved's joint account liquidated, the Canal Street
property placed in the hands of brokers licensed to sell it at auction, its
profits allocated as a sop to the Ice Castle's investors. Finally it was almost
exhilarating how quickly the life the widow had shared with her chime-
rical husband had been revoked, and with it the able woman she once
was. More than merely neglectful of her appearance, she seemed to have
reverted to the ambiguous being she had been before her marriage: She'd
either hacked off or shed her luxuriant hair until it resembled the bristles
of a seven-cent brush, and exchanged her mourning dress for a pair of her
dead husband's trousers; she had also acquired a stoop from the dowager's
hump that had recently risen between her shoulder blades. She was judged
now to be frankly unhinged, but at least she was pliant, a small blessing
for which all gave thanks.

There was meanwhile one last detail the brothers had yet to see to, one
that when it was mentioned to the widow caused her to stuff her fingers
into her ears and cry "Yemakh shmoy!" May his name be blotted out. For
hadn't both her father and her husband made a sentimental fetish of the
ghastly thing in its ice-bound hibernation?—and just look at the untimely
ends they had met. Jocheved flared up at the rabbi's mention and let it be
known she would be content to leave him atop some rubbish heap where
he could melt and decompose as food for the crows. So it was up to her
brothers, in deference to the memory of their father and a dead man they
had never met, to take care of him. They arranged for his temporary storage in a basement locker at Duckstein's Funeral Salon on Henry Street,
where they supervised the recaulking of his wooden container; they had
the zinc lining refilled with water, thus reconstituting via an ammonia

absorption agent the frozen mass that had been diminished in the fire. Then once the holy man's protruding toes and furry ears were again sealed for safekeeping in ice, the twins agreed that the continued maintenance of this reverend family tradition should fall to young Ruben Karp, who needed something to do.

He had been lurking about the margins of the apartment, an unkempt, brooding figure to whom everyone gave a wide berth. Since the fire he had refrained from washing his face, thinking perhaps that the ashes that smudged his forehead belonged to his father. The neglect was due not so much to reverence as the wish to be marked like Cain for his deed on that fateful night. He kept aloof from participation in the mourners' minyans that took place whenever there were sufficient visitors to say Kaddish; though from time to time he was compelled by some vague instinct to plant himself beside the chair of his mother, who despite her general inattention might consent to acknowledge his presence with a touch. This he would suffer with a stoic shiver, mildly amazed at the disdain he felt for the woman his actions had so effectively undone. On occasion he had the urge to add insult to injury by confessing his crime. It was certainly no secret, notwithstanding the insurance company's pressured decision, that the fire had been the result of arson; so intimate were the cops with the trademark methods of the local arson mechanics that they doubtless could have fingered the culprits off the bat. But Naf the Sport had always been punctual in distributing his sweeteners among the local authorities, so the heat from the icehouse fire never touched his tribe. For this Ruby was almost sorry, as a lifetime of penal servitude would have suited his mood.

Already crushed, his mother would most likely be shattered beyond a hope of retrieval by his confession, but wasn't that how restitution was made? He knew from the Yom Kippur services of yore that guilt was something you expiated through atonement, and knew also that for what he had done he could never atone. But surely, as action had always been his medium, there was some course of action he ought now to take. It occurred to him that, having destroyed his own father, the next obvious

step should be to destroy himself. Then it struck him that this was his conscience speaking—had he suddenly developed a conscience? But the logic
it asserted was as foreign to him as a conversation overheard by chance,
and if he tried to listen a little harder his brain would cramp up, as if
squeezed like a sponge leaking toxins that rankled in the gut. This Ruby
supposed was remorse. It was the single identifiable emotion left in his
depleted arsenal, while on the other hand it didn't seem to belong to him
at all. He was in any case paralyzed by his present circumstances . . . until
his mother's brothers lumbered toward him with a proposal.

He glowered at them from the kitchen table, as who were they, this
meddlesome Tweedledum and Tweedledee? True, they had saved his life
(thanks for nothing), which he grudgingly supposed gave them the right
to an audience. Since the brothers had virtually no English and the Hebrew they'd been speaking for two decades had left them impoverished
of their mameloshen, they anticipated some difficulty in communicating
with Ruby—who had little enough Yiddish himself, never mind his dis-
inclination to speak to anyone at all. So they engaged his aunt Esther as an
intermediary, since, once she'd determined he wouldn't bite, she had been
almost as attentive to the son as to the mother during the past few weeks.
Tolerating her ministrations with disregard, Ruby had allowed her to
change the dressings on his hands and head, applying salves and ointments
as a result of which his wounds were practically healed. But now Esther
appeared a little puffed with importance in her office as mouthpiece, and
Ruby was almost amused to see how her baked-apple face puckered in the
effort to translate the twins' Hebraized Yiddish into American.

"As you know, must not be abandoned, our family treasure," she submitted, turning to ask the twins: "Vos iz der taytsh 'treasure'?" The twins
advised her to please just repeat after them, which she did tugging at her
corset in a show of displeasure at having been left out of the loop: " 'We
offer to you the privilege exceptionalary that you should escort it, the
legacy—' What legacy?"

At that point Ruby, having already heard enough, pronounced one of the few Yiddish expressions he knew, "A klug tse eykh alemens (Screw you all)," after which the brothers made it clear to him through an esperanto of persuasive gestures that *no* was not an option.

The plan was for Ruby to watch over the casket, much as he'd once guarded truckloads of contraband hooch, on the trip down to Tennessee. He would travel with the rabbi by freight train to Memphis, while his recently extended family took a more leisurely route via Philadelphia, Baltimore, Cincinnati, and St. Louis, with Zerubavel ben Blish promoting the Zionist dream along the way. Once Ruby had grunted his tepid assent, things happened swiftly: He left the apartment for the first time in weeks with his strongarm escort. They took a subway to Hell's Kitchen, where it was Ruby's turn to play translator, a function he performed with brusque economy on the loading dock of the Armour Star meathouse adjoining the Hudson railyard. Having assumed that the company men in the freight office would either balk or up the ante, Ruby decided to bypass them in favor of going straight to the dockhands, with whom he and his uncles soon struck a deal.

A few days later on a misty morning in early April, a freshly waxed Phaeton hearse from Duckstein's Funerals drove into the gravel yard. From the rear of the hearse the rabbi in his moldering sarcophagus was transferred by an overhead conveyor directly into a Union Pacific reefer car filled with hanging hams. "You can't put him instead with flanken?" the twins had inquired, disturbed by the indignity, but Ruby scoffed at their concern. Throughout the operation the railroad laborers, whose palms had been previously oiled, looked the other way. In the meantime, so active was the yard with its switching and shunting, with the clamor of coupling and the hiss of hydraulics, the thud of truncheons cracking hoboes' heads, that the loading of an old coffin onto a boxcar went virtually unnoticed. Ruby had already swung his duffel along with his father's salvaged sheep's pelt onto the refrigerated car. He was in the process of stowing Aunt Esther's hamper containing a three-day supply of knishes and a thermos of tea, and was about to climb on board himself, when a flashily dressed

contingent stepped onto the platform through a billow of steam: a delegatz
as it turned out from the mob captain Naftali Kupferman. Ruby wondered
what had taken them so long.

They were led by Naf's chief stooges Shtrudel Louie and Turtletaub,
both wearing belted topcoats over their tropical suits. The moron Little
Lhulki was also in tow, along with a couple of rookies in Oxford bags that
Ruby didn't recognize. The lot of them appeared to him now as figures of
make-believe, caricature gangsters with cute nicknames stepped from the
columns of Damon Runyon, the newspaper scribe.

Shtrudel Louie gave Ruby a neutral salute with a finger to the brim of
his Stetson: "Naftali says sorry for your loss but it's not nice to leave town
without you should say good-bye." Mr. Turtletaub seconded the sentiment, adding that the boss's feelings were deeply hurt, while Shtrudel narrowed his eyes to assess the duplicate brutes that stood in their short pants
beside Kid Karp.

Indifferent to the menace in their voices, Ruby said only, "I'm touched."
He had supposed they were keeping tabs on him, had even expected they
might try interdicting him if he left the apartment, though he hadn't
thought they would wait till the last minute. Still he knew better than
to believe he could simply waltz out of Naftali's orbit scot-free. Nobody
just walked away. For one thing, he knew too much about Naf the Sport's
organization to be allowed such an uncurbed liberty. Though assured as he
was that one could never turn his back on the rackets, turn his back was
precisely what Ruby did, as he began again to board the train. That was
the cue for Naf's senior cat's-paws to haul out their heaters from the hol-
stered concealment of their armpits. Almost simultaneously Yehezkel and
Yigdal dredged their pockets to produce weapons of their own, waving
Mausers that held the Browning semiautomatics in a stalemate of silent respect. In the ensuing standoff Ruby felt a twinge of fellowship, even gratitude toward his uncles for backing him up, a feeling that just as quickly
dissipated. Then, allowing his cardigan to slip from his shoulders onto
the concrete dock, Kid Karp was once again prey to eruptive reflexes.

Seeing his nostrils flare and the vein throb at his temple, Shtrudel Louie
and Turtletaub, who recognized the symptoms, lowered their pistols and
took a step backward, then seeking the better part of valor turned about
and reluctantly quit the field. Left to their own bewildered devices, Little
Lhulki and the fledgling goons also fumbled for their sidearms, but Ruby
was on them before they had a chance to draw. In his rage he began to feel
a familiar rapture that was as short-lived as his gratitude had been; there
was finally no pleasure in throttling his enemies, no pleasure to be had by
any means, a realization that slowed his battling limbs not at all.

As they watched their nephew's one-man juggernaut, the twins exchanged sidelong glances, Yigdal raising his left eyebrow in an approving
gesture complemented by the raised right brow of his brother.

THE TRAIN WAS already in motion, the station bulls blowing their
whistles as they charged down the platform toward the scuffle, and Ruby,
disengaging himself from his flagging opponents, dove into the reefer car.
He peeked out to see the hoodlums dispersing at a stumble in their several
directions (the twins had already vanished), then slid closed the heavy boxcar door. If he'd been listening, as the train nosed under the Hudson and
resurfaced in the industrial wasteland on the other side, Ruby might have
heard what sounded like the belated echo of that slamming door — but
was in fact the crash of the New York Stock Exchange. Not that the noise
would have meant much to Kid Karp, for whom the party was already
over. Without checking to see if the door would open again from the
inside, he had pulled on his dead papa's sheep's pelt and hunkered down
with his back against the rotting casket. The dense air machines moaned
as they circulated a polar draft tinged with the stink of ethyl chloride from
the bunkers at either end of the car, while Ruby huddled in the pitch dark,
shivering on the wood-sheathed floor. Already a numbness had begun to
infect his extremities, a corollary to the numbness that gripped his brain.
Never once during the journey was he tempted to get up and inspect the
cargo the casket contained; neither did he relieve himself in the bucket his

uncles had provided for that purpose behind a rack of cold pork shoulders and butts, so bound up were his insides with frost. His limbs became rigid, eyelids stuck at half-mast, ice riming the sparse stubble of his beard, and his lips were aniline blue. Transporting the rumor of a man trapped in a block of ice, he was himself becoming solid ice in the shape of a man.

The rhythm of the rails with its half-absorbed incantation — *meshuguneh meshuguneh a shreklekeh zach* — worked to seal Ruby's trance, leaving him a passive witness to memories of the bones he'd broken, ladies degraded, gents humiliated on a whim in the backstreets and cellar clubs. He reviewed them like a succession of shades left over from another incarnation, one that had no bearing on the present rattling mortification of this life after life. He had no sense of the passage of time, of whether he was awake or dreaming; if he froze to death it would be an anticlimax, and insofar as he could think at all, Ruby thought he might remove his papa's parka to help facilitate that end. But that would be letting himself off too easily, and besides he wasn't sure he could lift his arms.

Lynchburg, Virginia, was the train's terminus. When the roustabouts opened his boxcar to unload it, what they saw held them as stockstill as the apparition within. Eventually someone sent for the plug-chewing foreman, who had Ruby carried into the station office to determine his degree of vitality. There they perched him on a potbellied stove and began to unfold his stiff limbs as if coaxing parts of a rusted machine into operation. They cranked his jaw like a pump until words spilled out, a mumbling that promised them compensation for assisting in the transfer of his lading to a westbound freight. But along with the thawing of his joints came the helpless release of his bladder and bowels. "Boy done messed his britches," declared the foreman, as the yard hands fled the office in disgust, though some returned to accept their gratuities from the hands of the sullied passenger. Then they fetched Ruby's duffel and, while he cleaned himself up, conveyed the rabbi on a handcar via an intricate spaghetti junction from the Union Pacific to the Sequatchie Valley Line. A day later at the freight-yard in Knoxville the procedure was more or less repeated, the casket transferred this time to a brine-tank reefer of the Tennessee Railroad, bound for Memphis in the far southwestern corner of the state.

It was early evening when the train pulled into the yard on the edge of the river bluff. Still poker stiff in his movements, Ruby nevertheless oversaw the removal of the tzaddik's box from the railcar to a nearby baggage wagon. It was a balmy, overcast twilight, and branched lightning above the depot and the river below it made the dome of the sky look as if he were viewing it from the inside of a hatching egg. In the prestorm atmosphere the air tasted of mercury, and the fragrance of honeysuckle overwhelmed the odor of cinders and engine grease, further narcotizing Ruby's muddy brain. As a consequence he was only half aware of a passing porter, the man leaning at an impossible angle into a hand trolley laden with lumber stacked higher than his head. Blind to the path in front of him, the porter nudged the wagon with his overloaded trolley, dislodging the wooden chock wedged beneath a rear wheel. Unhobbled, the wagon began to roll slowly backward over the gravel embankment and onto the cobbled levee, its burden bouncing about the boards of the flat bed as the vehicle started to pick up speed. Ruby watched with only moderate interest as the runaway wagon careered toward the bottom of the slope, splashing into the river in a geyser that promptly subsided along with the vehicle's forward momentum. The casket, however, was further propelled into the water, where its decayed cedar planks splintered on impact. The zinc lining floated free a few seconds like a wallowing washtub, then abruptly capsized and sank, but after the length of an inheld breath its frozen contents bobbed to the surface and continued to drift out upon the turbid Mississippi.

At that point Ruby was shaken from his stupor. His limbs were still so rigid that he felt as if he were confined to a suit of armor, but as he lurched down the hill the gauntlets and greaves began to fall from his body. By the time he'd descended half the incline he was sprinting with the alacrity he'd always relied on. At the foot of the bluff he leaped into the mile-wide river, invigorated by the shock of cold water, and began splashing toward

the escaping hunk of ice. Here it dawned on him that he didn't know how
to swim, despite which he managed to stay provisionally afloat, thrashing
and sputtering after the ice that the braided current carried farther beyond
his grasp. Coughing up a throatful of water, he churned his arms and feet
in another desperate effort to reach his frozen consignment. This time he
was able to get a tenuous grip on the slick-sided berg, only to have it slip
away again, leaving him to sink below the surface of the river. He felt the
weight of his clothes dragging him down, the tar-black water closing over
him, but just as he'd resigned himself to drowning, the current buoyed
him back up from the depths, bearing him into a whirlpool where the
stalled block of ice had begun to spin like a compass dial. There Ruby
made to grab hold of it once again, wrestling the slippery mass as it rolled
and turned turtle, clutching it in a bear hug as it spun out of the mael-
strom and continued to sail downstream. A flash of lightning illuminated
the bridge, the retired paddlewheelers moored to the Arkansas shore, and
the supine old man in his crystal coffin whom Ruby had never quite believed in till now. There was a rending sound as if the Almighty had split
his pants, another flash that sewed the water with silver, and Ruby saw
that he and the rabbi were not alone in the stream. They were escorted by
an armada of ice rafts released from the tail end of winter in the northern
states on their way to dissolve in the Gulf of Mexico. Then a thunderclap
and the sky cracked open, the deluge began, and both the youth and the
old man he was riding were captured in a casting net tossed from a dinghy
by a pair of colored kids.

2001.

ecause the video rental store where Lou Ella worked featured only films adapted from Broadway musicals (the owner was an eccentric with a private income), there was a very limited clientele. As a result, Lou had a lot of time for reading. Lately, despite the dismay the book had caused Bernie, she kept returning to the less didactic chapters of Rabbi Eliezer ben Zephyr's autobiography, *The Ice Sage.* She especially enjoyed the sections describing the rebbe's serial adventures before he was born as himself. For the infant Eliezer, a prodigy in the womb, had managed to elude the Angel of Forgetfulness, the one responsible for tweaking you under the nose at birth. This is the touch that causes an infant to forget its past lives and any interim time spent in Paradise. By curling his upper lip monkey-fashion over his philtrum as he was yanked from between his mother's legs, the newborn was able to deflect the angel's retrograde flick, thereby leaving him with a taste of heaven on his lips all his days. Consequently he remembered the entire genealogy of his previous soul migrations, his gilgulim. He recalled his humble beginnings as a locust that had participated in the ten plagues of Egypt, as a flea in the ear of the Prophet Habakkuk, a bat in the cave wherein Simeon bar Yohai spent thirteen years translating the natural world into holy writ. In his most ignominious embodiment Eliezer was a cat a Cossack hetman had sewn into the belly of a pregnant Jewess whose fetus had been excised. Thanks to an amulet blessed by a lamed vovnik, however, the woman survived and the cat was born as a human child, a pious daughter who eventually married and bore a litter of seven children, all given to burying their feces in sand. There were other human incarnations the rabbi recounted on the way to narrating his own, such as his birth to a poor Jew and his wife in the Transylvanian Alps. The baby was snatched from his cradle by an eagle and dropped over an Arabian desert where he landed in the common kettle of a Bedouin tribe who raised him as their own. But a nameless itch spurred him to wander through several countries, faiths, and lives until his soul was born again into the family of Zephyr Threefoot, a charcoal burner in the Polish village of Boibicz. There the eloi, the prodigy, was from childhood a prey to spontaneous ecstasies. He had always to check clocks to keep himself anchored in time, to wear spectacles in order to see individual persons and objects, since without them he saw everything in its cosmic unity. As a toddler he had on his own initiative slathered pages of Torah with honey and gobbled them up, so that by the time he was old enough for cheder he could regurgitate the entire Pentateuch.

"In those days you could say that me and God were thick as thieves," the rebbe had written (via the medium of Sanford Grusom's no-nonsense prose). "Together we performed your standard miracles and exorcisms; we healed lepers, vanquished werewolves, shooed away demons from circumcisions, staged mixers to introduce souls without bodies to bodies without souls — that sort of thing. And always I remained, as they say, a hand's breadth above the earth. . . ." Then after a long and auspicious career that had drawn to him a circle of devoted followers, Rabbi ben Zephyr was at his prayers in his customary spot beside Baron Jagiello's horse pond when a sudden storm came up.

The rebbe made it clear in his memoirs that he had little patience with the yokels who'd carted him about in a casket like a vampire for over a hundred years — since all they'd had to do was melt the ice (and maybe rattle a grager in his ear) to bring him out of his trance. Still, he allowed that his lengthy dormition had been a kind of blessing because he'd re-awakened to the world with renewed fervor. In his second coming he felt he had a mandate not so much to lift up lost souls as to restore them to their rightful place on earth. Of course he offered the conventional tran-scendence to seekers, but only as a preliminary relief, after which they would be better equipped to take advantage of the material world. This was the point where the argument became a bit fuzzy for Lou, twirling a coil of viridian hair around a thrice-pierced ear. She was unsure how the rebbe's ministry had swerved from the traditional theme of redemption through spiritual discipline to a passionate embrace of the free-market economy — never mind a strain of self-interest the girl had not encoun-tered since she'd first read Ayn Rand. Nevertheless she was a pushover for a good hagiography, especially one written about himself by a living saint.

Which isn't to suggest that Lou had any inclination to visit his House of Enlightenment. Having a boyfriend with his own saintly proclivities was handful enough for her, thank you very much. Moreover, she was greatly concerned about Bernie these days and felt in large part to blame for his current condition. True, she'd been frustrated at his inability to take her beyond herself, but having used what charms she had at her disposal to reel him back to earth, she now wondered if her efforts might have backfired. Lately he seemed to dwell in a kind of perpetual ekstasis-interruptus — a phrase of her own pleased coinage. Tiresomely he expressed his gratitude for what he regarded as her well-intentioned efforts at seduction, insisting that, had she not drawn him back, he might have crossed over for good. Such a woman was worth more than rubies, he assured her, prompting a dry response from Lou Ella to "that old saw."

"I guess," she chided him, not without malice, one evening beneath the Harahan Bridge as they sat watching a late-summer sunset, "I guess you got to be an inept before you can be an adept." Then she was rendered speechless when Bernie suddenly thrust aside his grandfather's journal and shouted, "Marry me!" The plea was accompanied by the ticktock of the wipers that he'd accidentally switched on in his attempt to fall to his knees on the floorboard. Wedged awkwardly between the dash and Sue Lily, whom Lou had been bouncing on her lap, he further promised that if she wasn't ready he would remain in a state of self-imposed groundedness until she was.

Lou closed the jaw of the mouth-breathing baby sister, who seemed not to be growing any older, and returned her to the backseat. "And that's what passes for being faithful in your pea-brain?" she replied, having finally found her tongue. "Ooie gevalt, I'm faithful by default," she mocked him, never able to resist a dig at the subject of his chastity. But while she was realist enough to know that a wedding was not in the cards, she nevertheless allowed herself to picture it: the gaunt groom in a tophat like Mottl the Tailor from *Fiddler on the Roof* (she'd become well acquainted with the video store's musical archive), the bride in what? — maybe Sally Bowles's merry widow, fishnet stockings enmeshing the dolphin tattoo on her thigh. The two of them standing beneath an ocelot chupeh with their feet "a hand's breadth above the earth." Impatient with herself for succumbing to fantasy, she snarled, "Get up, dude," and when he had she added almost tenderly, "Bernie Karp, you're a visitor from outer space, and some day . . ." She failed to finish the thought.

While she liked to think of herself as a girl of broad experience, Lou sometimes felt that with this strange boy she was in over her head. "I s'pose you think your mad affection for me is flattering," she said. "It makes me feel like some temptress and all, like I'm Sa-*lou*-mé." Lingering accusatorily over the middle syllable.

"Doesn't it?" Bernie asked artlessly.

She gazed at the mare's nest of his hair, his increasingly cadaverous body, which he inhabited with ever more authority. "Well, . . . yeah," admitted Lou, touching his hollow cheek before giving it a peremptory slap.

Having summoned him as a witness to the quotidian, she fretted over what she had done. Because the more closely he examined life on earth,

the more besotted he seemed to become with it, while the more urgently
in need of redemption he found it to be—in light of which his newly
hatched desire to save some corner of creation seemed all the more futile
and picayune. Thus were his emotions dangerously mixed. Meanwhile in
the present climate of global mayhem, what with the blood of foreign wars
lapping at the nation's doorstep, it was practically a crime to be in love.
Children informed on their parents, parents feared their children, and
antichrists were detected in all walks of life. Bernie's own rebbe, risen like
gangbusters from his protracted slumber, was himself in peril of being apprehended for a felon. Recent newspaper editorials tried to link the Prodigy and his followers to subversive activities, even insinuating that the
House of Enlightenment was a terrorist cell. This despite a philosophy that
seemed to the girl to have less in common with Osama bin Laden than
with Norman Vincent Peale. But it troubled her to see Bernie so obviously
distraught: Whether or not he had the makings of a saint remained in
question, but she didn't think he was hero material, and heroic measures
were what she figured it would take to save Rabbi ben Zephyr. Her only
solace was that they still had some chapters ahead of them before finishing Grandpa Ruby's journal, and she thought she could keep the boy from
doing anything stupid until they got to the end. Lou wanted never to get
to the end.

1929 – 1947.

Imust have contracted some kind of Yid virus from wrestling with the rabbi in the river," Bernie read to Lou Ella in her bedroom, where Lou sometimes referred to herself acidly as the unmade girl on the bed. "It was a virus with a long incubation, because many years passed before the fever woke up in me."

WHEN HIS FAMILY arrived several weeks later, they found Ruby bivouacked beside a packing crate containing the frozen holy man in a "frigidarium" at Blochman's Cold Storage just off North Main Street. Blochman's was an all-purpose facility housing wine, furs, antiques, and pharmaceuticals as well as meat and produce, located around the corner from Karp's General Merchandise, the concern owned and operated by Ruby's Uncle Marvin. A paunchy, balding, ordinarily generous man, Marvin had initially offered his young nephew accommodations in his Mediterranean-style house out on the Parkway but had been visibly relieved when the uncommunicative kid declined his invitation. For despite having been notified of what was coming, Esther's brother, who'd arranged for the stowage of Ruby's freight, found the deadpan nephew and his charge a bit more than he'd bargained for. On his side Ruby had reached the end of his tolerance for newly acquired relations and preferred to stay behind the cam-locked door of the warehouse cold room, where he could continue to keep an eye on the rabbi.

Both Blochman's and Karp's establishments were situated in a downtown district called the Pinch, a neighborhood of mom 'n' pop businesses run by Russian-Jewish immigrants who lived in the rackety apartments above their shops. They were the dross of a vestigial community who, unlike the enterprising Marvin Karp (who'd voluntarily dropped the *inski* from the end of his name), had not prospered enough to move out of their ghetto and clung to it as to an island in uncharted seas. It was an island bounded on the west by the river, clogged with barge and packet-boat traffic, and surrounded by a city that often hosted spectacles that tried the nerves of the Jews. There were the parades down Front Street of the syklops and kleagles of the Ku Klux Klan marching in their cotton sheets, some of which had been purchased at Karp's General Merchandise. There was the tabernacle erected on the river bluff from which the voice of an itinerant Billy Sunday challenging the devil to seven weeks' combat could be heard all the way to North Main. Sometimes the sovereignty of the Pinch itself was violated, such as when the city fathers shut down the Suzore Theater for showing a film featuring Theda Bara (neé Theodosia Goodman), a film star of questionable morals; or when a representative from the board of health came to the Neighborhood House on Market Square to declare that dancing the Charleston (since when did Jews dance the Charleston?) could lead to death through inflammation of the peritoneum. There were the creepers and poison lianas that overtook the tenements in spring, and the sickly scent that lingered for days over the Pinch after the auto-da-fé of a Negro a few blocks north at Catfish Bay. So the Jews had enough already to rattle their composure without the additional bogey of a sinister young stranger rumored to be the guardian of an old man in a lump of ice.

For rumor was mostly what Ruby was, since he seldom appeared in the street, venturing out only to purchase an occasional plate of kishka from the sidewalk window at Rosen's lunch counter. Unwashed and unshorn, his blue flesh mottled with chilblains, the sheep's pelt steaming in the sun, he was an eyesore the citizens of North Main Street could frankly have done without. There was about him the unhappy air of the penitent, and what with the daily penance of making a living with which the Jews had been cursed since their expulsion from Eden, who needed more emphatic reminders of their fate? Though in truth Ruby had no formal program for scourging himself, having advanced to a state of dispassion far beyond self-loathing. It was just that, since rescuing the rabbi from watery ruin, he'd concluded that his place was now to look after the old antediluvian, an attitude as near to purpose as he could come. Also, there was the habit of numbness he'd acquired during his refrigerated transit that made the temperature in the cold storage locker seem almost favorable.

But the twins had other plans for their nephew. Certain matters had been neatly resolved, if not during the train ride down to Memphis then shortly thereafter. For one thing, Zerubavel ben Blish and Shinde Esther, both daunted by the size and disharmony of the American continent, had tended to cling to one another out of a mutual solicitude. More adaptable, Esther had summoned untapped reserves of pluck for the sake of soothing Zerubavel, who by journey's end had come to esteem her just this side of idolatry. In the meantime Esther had been thoroughly indoctrinated by Comrade ben Blish's Zionist propaganda, so that by the time they reached Tennessee her thoughts (when not of him) were almost exclusively of the Jewish National Home. In this way the spinster decided that, once she'd seen Jocheved comfortably settled in Memphis (there was no talk of her returning to New York), she would follow her destined one back to Eretz Israel where they would be wed. Meanwhile, though the widow, stooped and wearing items of her late husband's apparel, no longer resembled her former self, her new persona had lost some of its fog of melancholy. This was perhaps owing in part to the city of Memphis itself, with the aromatic musk of its sultry spring, which may have worked as effectively to reduce Jocheved's paralysis as refrigeration had to consolidate her son's. Despite her unseasonable aging and a countenance euphemistically referred to as "bo-hemian," Jocheved exhibited an animation that manifested itself, upon her arrival in the mid-South, in a furor of concocting glacés and ice cream.

Marvin and his good wife, Ida, whose pinched face belied a sanguine disposition, were understandably overwhelmed by such an infestation of family, most of whom they had never met. They were intimidated by the bullet heads and oxlike brawn of the twin brothers, nonplussed by Esther's announcement of her wedding plans and by the widow's idiosyncrasies. Nevertheless they provided lodging for one and all, both in their rambling house with its green-tiled roof and in a guest cottage entered through a wisteria arbor in the garden out back. It was in that little mother-in-law annex that Jocheved began to set up a kind of laboratory—assembling there the pails, spaddles, and confectionery ingredients commandeered with Ida's consent from her well-equipped kitchen—that she would need for the manufacture of her frozen treats. In light of her own bliss the affi-anced Esther was now anxious to get Jocheved off her hands, and toward that end she had early on consulted with her brother. Since the guesthouse stood empty most of the year, why not reap some bonus income from rent-ing it out to the widow? On that score Marvin had needed no cajoling: "I thought already the same thing myself." A childless couple who compen-sated for their barren union with cats, Marvin and Ida had already begun to look fondly on the widow, as if in her hoydenish habits she were yet an-other stray. Then there were the sorbets, tutti fruttis, and frozen custards that Jocheved served at their communal dinners, which had given Marvin a bright idea. Pixilated though she was, Jocheved was at the same time a fully functioning agent: He would set her up under an awning in front of his store "where she will reign supreme as the empress of ice cream." He grinned his pleasure at the impromptu jingle. Always in great demand in the scorching southern summers, ice cream would draw more customers to Karp's than his squad of schwartze pullers-in ever had.

For a while Marvin and Ida, whose affluence had estranged them from their old neighbors in the Pinch, began to warm to the windfall of their sudden family, and though they'd run out of reasons to prolong their visit, the guests found it difficult to give up such hospitality. The twins, schooled for decades in collective habitation, performed the household chores unsolicited and with jugglerlike sleight-of-hand; Zerubavel, who wore his high collar and silk four-in-hand to dinner, recited the Hebrew verse of Bialik and Tchernichowsky after meals, and Jocheved plied the table with tasty desserts. The only note of discord—the one that finally spoiled everyone's good time—originated with Esther, who under the influence of her betrothed had become something of an ideologue. For all the gladness she'd expressed at their reunion, she soon after began to try her brother's patience with her criticisms of his bourgeois lifestyle, even taking issue with his choice of residence in such a backward jerkwater town.

"What are they anyway doing in Memphis, the Jews?" she'd asked one night as the twins, mindful bulls in a china shop, were clearing away dishes from the dining-room table.

To which Marvin, a booster for whom the Bluff City had always spelled opportunity, replied testily, "What are they doing in Palestine?"

Things degenerated from there into name-calling, the host and his sister addressing each other coolly thereafter as Red Esther and the Baron. Within a week Zerubavel and his intended had departed in a huff for New York, where they would take passage on a steamship of the Compagnie Générale Transatlantique bound for Marseilles, and from there ferry on to Haifa. But before they left, Esther had accompanied Yehezkel and Yigdal—satisfied now that their sister was in good hands—to Blochman's Cold Storage, where they informed Jocheved's son through the medium of his aunt that he would be sailing with them to Eretz Israel. Having observed him in action, his uncles had determined that the lad, despite his near hypothermia, could be of signal use in the development of the Yishuv; and since he was only marking time in America, why shouldn't he be given the chance to apply his talents to a cause greater than himself? It never occurred to them, so habituated were they to self-sacrifice, that he might have plans of his own.

Though, beyond keeping company with the rabbi beside the reliquary of his packing crate, Ruby had none. But what was Palestine? He had only the vaguest notion: something about a country without a people for a people without a country: He'd heard the slogans. But to his hibernal mind it sounded as if each side of the equation might exclude the other, and then the Jews would be nowhere at all. Of course, reasoned Ruby, if he belonged anywhere it was nowhere. He knew also that Avner Blochman, proprietor of the facility wherein he was quartered, was fed up with his unwanted tenant, and had finally screwed up the courage to evict Ruby along with his frozen charge. "This ain't no spookhouse," the hangdog Avner advised, for such had been the reaction of his clients, whom reports of the rabbi and his custodian were driving away. Out on the tree-shaded Parkway, having gotten wind of Ruby's dilemma, Marvin Karp's guests elicited the last ounce of their host's goodwill, prevailing on him to make room for his brother Shmerl's bequest. Ultimately Marvin did agree to store the ghoulish memento in an old laundry tub in his wine cellar, but with the understanding that his benevolence would end upon the repeal of Prohibition, when the memento could be replaced by a case of sauvignon blanc. He also made it clear that his charity did not extend to the rebbe's grim-visaged guardian.

Ruby received the news of his imminent eviction with a shrug. Separation from the rabbi would deprive him of his last excuse for staying put, a prospect that alternately calmed and discomfited him. The cold had in any case permeated his insides to a degree that suggested he now carried the essence of Ezekiel ben Zephyr in his bones. As for his mother, Ruby had visited her once or twice in her bower, only to discover that he had no filial feeling left for her at all. With her lick of cinereous hair and her klunky, unfeminine movements drained of the grace that once informed them, he hardly recognized her. Absently pinching his cheek or brushing the frost from his scalp before returning to her ice-making apparatus, she resembled (a chilling notion) her dead husband more than herself. In the end he concluded that, as befitted a son who'd destroyed his entire family, he was no more to her now than the cats that padded in and out of her apartment. He was cast out from everything that in theory he ought to hold dear, a situation he appreciated as heartbreaking, even tragic, the way he might have viewed some schmaltzy photoplay. Moreover, there was a fitting justice in Ruby's being dragged by his broad-backed uncles to some godforsaken desert environment, where his anaesthetized sensibilities risked thawing in the heat of the sun.

"I'll think it over," he told the twins, who told him he could think it over during the voyage to the Holy Land. For having dipped into the donations they'd collected for the National Fund, the brothers had already booked passage on a cattle boat sailing from the port of New Orleans, and had taken the liberty of purchasing a ticket for Ruby as well.

THAT WAS HOW he came to find himself, some ten years later, standing on a watchtower beside an amber searchlight in an oasis reclaimed from a swamp called Tel Elohim. It was the same communal settlement folded among the foothills of the Upper Galilee to which Ruby and his uncles had retreated after the the Arab uprising of 1929. This was the slaughter that had greeted them at the moment when Ruby first set foot upon the Land; so that it was clear to the newcomer from the outset that the country without a people was already populated, and its population not eager to share its beggarly streets, moon-dusted dunes, camel tracks, and waterless wells with the people without a country. Nevertheless Ruby did what he was told by the twin brothers, who seemed to belong both everywhere and nowhere. Since categories of right and wrong existed only for those parties with something at stake, the finer points of the situation were of no concern to the recent immigrant. Just off the boat, he was interested in little more than putting himself in the way of bodily harm (the only outlook that could stimulate his sluggish brain), and Palestine looked as if it would afford him ample opportunities to do just that. Confronted with death, however, he repeatedly cheated it. This was not so much because he wanted to live as that he thought he deserved to prolong his pain — though who was he fooling? There was no pain, nor fear, or thrill of engagement, only action and the boredom between actions that was the real dread; because, while most of his senses were unresponsive, Ruby's memory persisted, and it haunted him with unkind reminders. In the event, he'd waived his independence, placing his fate in the hands of the veteran campaigners Yig and Yez, as he called them. They saw to his formal training in arms and explosives, areas in which he already had a head start, and in stealth, which he came by naturally. They coached him in husbanding the anger that he was still able to call upon at will, although it was now entirely impersonal, which made Ruby an even more perfectly tuned instrument for redressing the offenses to the Yishuv.

Not once during the succeeding years did he relax from participating in the relentless cycles of bloodletting. Despite the end of the so-called Arab Revolt and the monotony of terror and counterterror that intervened before the beginning of the next so-called Arab revolt, Ruby never gave up his part in the general effort to turn the Promised Land into a slaughterhouse. Of course there were interludes along the way, during which Ruby's edgy impatience caused others to keep their distance. As he and the twins moved from safehouse to smallholder farm among the ranks of the maverick irregulars, the immigrant earned not only the fear and respect of his fellows but a reputation as a solitary of forbidding countenance. The Baal Shatikah, his comrades called him (though never to his face), the Master of Silence: "Silence, too, is sometimes a midrash."

Over time he picked up enough of the language to follow orders and conversations, though never enough to respond to questions with any exactitude. He figured that the lashon hakodesh, the holy language, albeit secularized, might sear his tongue if he spoke it, and his failure to master even the rudiments of Hebrew often left strangers to conclude he was mute. All of which contributed along with his monkish aloofness to the legend he was unintentionally cultivating as a man apart. He was perceived by the superstitious (and there were many among the settlers fresh from the rustic culture of Eastern Europe) as quite possibly inhuman, a creature fashioned

from clay to avenge all affronts to Israel; it was a notion that caused his
uncles to worry that they had perhaps created a golem, though who could
argue with success? And over the years, as the tit-for-tactics of terror and
reprisal became almost routine, Ruby's notoriety grew, his sketchy identity
further subsumed by the numerous masquerades he was forced to adopt. In
the end, fabled among the Jews, to himself he was no one at all: the Master
of Silence had become a symbol referred to in secret circles as Ruben ben
None, and his heartlessness among a people attempting to shed millennia
of acute sensitivity and guilt was universally extolled.

Ruby's unvarying silence, so conspicuous in places where talk was a
mania, was sometimes construed as endorsement, sometimes disapproval,
according to the attitude of the beholder. But the truth was he neither
approved nor condemned, but was finally indifferent, just as he was indifferent to the life of the k'vutzah itself—which, with its religion of labor,
was identical to the dozens of others that proliferated all over the Yishuv.
Nevertheless, since not even the guardians were exempt from the work
of the collective, Ruby became mechanically proficient at the chores he
was assigned. Though he would ultimately settle into the loner's occupation of tending sheep, he also milked goats, dug trenches, drained septic
tanks, and erected stockades; he repaired roof girders and laths and even
demonstrated some ingenuity in doctoring the commune's capricious
three-phase dynamo, called ironically Ner Tamid, the Everlasting Light.
His uncles, though they praised his industry, compared the facile work of
the current settlement to the herculean hardships of its primitive beginnings during the time called the Second Aliyah. Ruby had arrived during
the Fourth, a piece of history for which he gave not a fig. Uninspired by
the labors he conducted with due diligence, neither was Ruby aroused
by the festivals that were the rigorous calendar's only breathing spells.
Shabbat, when the settlers allowed themselves a thimbleful of sweet Carmel wine, was as unremarkable as Purim, when they donned costumes
and flogged an effigy of Haman. They sang patriotic anthems ("Yesh
Li Kinneret" and "God Will Rebuild Galilee") and danced the hora in

concentric circles, the outer circle whirling as in a game of crack the whip. Then even Yehezkel and Yigdal, still agile for all their bulk, would join in, and girls with strong thighs—wearing the shorts that caused the Mussulmen to call them whores—might approach Ruby where he sat with his back against a eucalyptus tree. These were strapping girls bred to flirting with danger and tempting fate, but when they tried to draw him into the dance, Ruby only eyed them dispassionately and waved them away as he waited for the next summons to action.

He never had to wait long. Marching orders were received from the heroes of the Resistance, who were all reputed to be half-mad: such as Orde Wingate, the philo-Semitic British colonel who'd become a sort of Lawrence of Palestine and liked to repeat with his unorthodox night squads the battle strategies of King Saul. Later came the storied leaders of the Underground like Gideon, Raziel, and the redoubtable Yair, figures whom the Yishuv simultaneously despised for their brutality and lionized for their courage. Like his uncles who reserved their independent right to attach themselves to any movement that took their fancy, Ruby swore allegiance to no special group. But he seldom missed an opportunity to participate in the lightning raids on Arab villages, where the men were pulled from their houses and selected for execution according to height or length of beard, and the women, to prove they weren't concealing small arms, were made to bare their breasts. He tossed grenades into market stalls where the resulting carnage was indistinguishable from smashed pottery and the pulp of burst melons. Whenever there were mass attacks there was mass retaliation, but when individuals were hit a more personal response was called for, and here Ruby's peculiar talents came into play. Always swift, he was groomed as well in furtiveness and in handling the Sten guns and pipe bombs he was familiar with from another life. He could be a sniper, a sapper, a strangler, an artist with the shiv or the ice pick (his stealth weapon of choice), and he preferred what his commanders also favored: that he work alone.

About hatsorer, the enemy, he had no detailed knowledge beyond what his fellows professed concerning Arabian culture at their fireside counsels:

that they prayed on their knees with their butts in the air, inviting bullets; that to the Ishmaelite the yahudy were all *wallah al mitha*, the children of death. For all Ruby knew some of his victims might even have been guilty of the crimes for which they were punished, though that was not the point. What was the point? To fill the world with terror, the way a deaf composer makes music, and for this Ruben ben None had a kind of genius. Professional that he was, he left calling cards inscribed in Arabic by the partisans' propaganda minister, notes he stuffed into some newly carved orifice, reading AKHAZA ASSAR W'NAFA ELLAR (Revenge has been taken and the shame done away with). This, he was told, was a message the enemy would comprehend. Though he took no pride in his deeds, neither did he feel any shame. He was aware that there was an end to which the Baal Shatikah was a means, but though he cared not a whit whether the nation of Israel ever came into being, he did what was expected of him to further that cause.

One night in thirty-six or -seven during the latest Arab rebellion, Ruby was dispatched with three other militia members to ambush a busload of Muslim pilgrims on their way to visit a shrine near Ein Musmus. Some-where along the Afula Road, however, they were intercepted by a British patrol that had barricaded the highway. The patrol had been alerted by one of the informers, who abounded in those days when so many Zionists were horrified by the sanguinary tactics of the Underground. Just as the bus, with the pilgrims clinging to the luggage on its roof, disappeared over the brow of a hill, an armed blockade was erected ahead of the commandos, who swerved about only to face another obstruction behind. A shootout resulted during which three of the four passengers in the bullet-pocked landau were injured; the fourth, in the rumble seat next to Ruby, died on the spot, shards of his skull embedded in Ruby's throat. The survivors were taken to the Jerusalem Central Prison, a massive stone citadel converted from an old Russian hostel, where after a brief stay in the infirmary they were confined to the zinzana cells on the jail's lower level. When they were well enough, they were taken one by one from their isolation into the harsh light of the interrogation chamber, where they were tortured. The battery of questions was as relentless as the physical battery to the soles of their feet, which were whipped with leather falakot, a persecution made the more senseless due to the gag that prohibited them from answering inquiries. Cigarettes were stubbed out in their ears, fingernails and toenails extracted with plyers, their beards uprooted by the fistful. An officer donned rubber gloves with a physician's fastidiousness to pinch their testicles; their noses were clothespinned and pitchers of water poured down their gullets in such volume that it seeped from their ears. Then they were taken back to their confinement to recuperate for the next round of abuse.

When his gag was removed, Ruby, tight-lipped as ever, refused even to divulge his name—what, after all, *was* his name? Then he heard one of his interrogators remark in an aside to his senior officer that the previous chap had offered as his sobriquet the very original, "My name is Death." Which gave the Baal Shatikah a competitive pang. "*My* name is Death!" he asserted, and though his voice rasped from his injuries, so loudly did he make his claim that others along the corridor, upon hearing him, echoed the same declaration from their cells. It was the closest Ruby had come to laughing out loud in an age, and as for the torture, it was a blessing, really, as the exquisite pain revived the anger he could no longer generate on his own.

Then one day the torture stopped and the prisoners were marched into an open-air courtyard where an ad hoc affiliation of a military and civic tribunal summarily condemned them to be hanged. They were issued the red sackcloth uniforms reserved for the doomed and transferred to aboveground cells to await execution. Ruby's companions were permitted to share a common cell, but the Baal Shatikah (whom the Brits never learned they had in their custody) was housed alone in deference to his own request. There in a tomb-size compartment with its bucket and lice-ridden bourge, Ruby set about determining his options for escape. This was not so much from any ardent desire to avoid the gallows as from an internal engine fueled by the years of barbarous application. He was further vitalized by the discovery, in a floor crevice where an earlier prisoner had secreted it, of a rusty razor blade. But before he had decided whether to use the blade to begin a tunnel or simply to slit a guard's throat, the question became moot; for the wall of the adjoining cell was blown away, taking with it the cinderblock partition separating that cubicle from Ruby's own.

It happened that his partners in crime, Aryeh and Asher, had taken it upon themselves to deprive the British command of their vengeance. Drunk on the idealism of Jewish revolution, Ruby's neighbors called themselves Hasmoneans and were frequently heard singing the Revisionist anthem: "Soldiers without names are we." In their ecstatic anticipation of dying for the Homeland, they had a fragmentation grenade smuggled into the jail inside a pineapple. What they had in mind was to detonate the grenade on the gallows, thereby going out like Samson taking the Philistines with him. But when they learned that the other prisoners were to witness the execution, they opted instead for a kiddish hashem, a private martyrdom. Singing "Hatikvah," they hugged each other with the grenade wedged between their chests like a shared heart and together pulled the pin. The building was rocked to its foundation, and through the film of dust from the rubble and the mist of blood from the fallen, Ruby walked out onto the stone flags of the prison compound. While the guards were still stunned, he scaled the wall, rolling over the barbed wire on top, which claimed his uniform and bit his flesh, then dropped to the Jaffa Road on the other side. There he prevailed upon the first beggar he found to render up his rags.

He hid in attic rooms open to the weather, in flooded cellars; grew his beard and cut it again, cut his hair and grew it back out; wore cartwheel hats, tarbooshes, and sometimes the hijab burnoose and veil of the devout Muslim woman, his eyes rimmed in antimony. At some point Ruby got word to Yig and Yez that it was too dangerous for him to return to Tel Elohim. They tracked him to a fleabag safehouse in Nahariya and teased him that the mug shot that hung now in every post office in Palestine failed to do him justice, though at least the price on his head was handsome. Then they grew solemn as they informed him that his Aunt Esther and her husband Zerubavel, secretary of the Committee for National Liberation, had been identified among the martyrs at Kibbutz Szold, and Ruby had to think for a moment to remember who they were. Later on he received the news that his uncles themselves had been captured by a British squadron lying in wait for them as they set out to mine the railroad works at Emek Zvulun—for the targets of the Irgunists had shifted from Arab to Occupation holdings. They were hanged on the ramparts of the Acre fortress, whose scaffold (it was said) afforded a view over the delft blue Mediterranean as far as Europe, which like the Holy Land was becoming a charnel house.

RUBY STOOD ATOP the watchtower in the hot khamsin wind and swiveled the mercury-vapor beam. He aimed it in the direction of the Arab village in the valley, where a dog barked, a muezzin sang, and the strings of an oud were being tuned. Beyond the village were the slopes of the Galilee, the massif of Mount Carmel, and the coast above Haifa scalloped with coves wherein lay the tramp vessels of the Beth Aliyah. These were the ships teeming with refugees fleeing a continent whose crimes were so incomprehensible that even its victims could not pronounce them. When they weren't too busy blowing up British installations, the boys of the Resistance worked in concert with the Hagganah to spirit these illegal immigrants secretly ashore from their coffin ships. Once on dry land the refugees were dispersed to the outposts of Kfar Saba, Gan Hasharon, Kiryat Anavim, and Beit Haarava, which absorbed them. Sometimes Ruby joined the rescuers, if only to distract himself from the endless rounds of bombing post offices, bridges, barracks, and trains. As effective an assassin as ever, he found himself increasingly disengaged from such operations; his famous battle frenzy seemed to be lately in mothballs, and he'd begun to eye the survivors dredged from the sea as if they might embody something he'd lost. He was invariably disappointed, ready to toss the lot of them back overboard again; Master of Silence that he was, he couldn't seem to forgive them for having no language with which to express what they'd seen.

Slated for tonight's catch was a crowd of refugees aboard a fishing trawler operated by a Greek ally of the Jews called the Goose. To retrieve them, once he was relieved from sentinel duty, Ruby descended the watchtower and pulled the knit cap with its elliptical eye slits over his head; he climbed into the tin-can Minerva alongside the others and was driven to the coast, where he boarded a launch and rowed out to net the survivors. They were the usual collection of phantoms and wraiths, none of whom would ever entirely occupy their own lives again, but there was among them a girl with a shorn head like a gosling's who for some reason caught Ruby's eye. She was wearing a long skirt of drapery-thick flannel beneath which her legs were carelessly parted; she carried slung peddler-wise over her shoulder a pillowslip containing what appeared to be books. There was nothing especially prepossessing about her, no distinguishing feature beyond the dreamy cast of her eyes—so why should his first sight of her prompt such a prickling in Ruby's brain? Then a word from the Baal Shatikah (words from that quarter being in such short supply) and the girl was dispatched to Tel Elohim, where Ruby might continue to follow her progress.

He was hard-pressed to explain the feelings she awoke in him, feelings he neither welcomed nor rejected but only suffered like an infirmity. What was it about this particular chit of a girl that intrigued him? You certainly wouldn't have called her beautiful. Her pale complexion was sprinkled with freckles that appeared to be in the process of peeling like dried mud, her hooked nose was as narrow as a rudder, and the remnant of her auburn hair resembled sagebrush. But for the patched lilac skirt she chose to wear despite the heat, and the slight swell of her breast, there was little about her to indicate that she wasn't a stripling boy. Her emerald eyes, however, unlike the inwardly focused orbs of her fellow "illegals," were wide open, their pupils (when not peering into a book) fixed intensely on a place whose center, Ruby decided, was everywhere. Among the vague emotions she provoked in him was a curiosity to see precisely what it was she was looking at.

Her name was Shprintze, which Ruby learned the way he learned everything else about her, by spying—and she remained Shprintze even as the other girls were trying on Tamara, Tirzeh, and Gabi, in the hope that a new name might erase the stain of the old. Like the other newcomers she performed the tasks the commune assigned her with a ready obedience, looking in her draggled skirt and head rag every inch the rustic peasant maid. The problem was she was playing the wrong part. Unlike the others she'd refrained from burning her old clothes and drawing new ones from the common pool, the khaki shorts, olive drab shirts, and lace-up boots that were the uniform among Zionist homesteaders. She was a milkmaid, a laundress, a bird nester; wielding her pruning shears like talons she chased sparrows from the grape arbor; she harvested olives from the grove behind the children's house, pressed the pulp between millstones, and cranked the centrifuge that separated water from oil with the motion of a schoolgirl swinging a rope. But to Ruby's practiced eye, as he watched her toting pails or cradling a peck of oranges in her apron, she seemed only to be making believe. While the others began in time to be assimilated into the life of the colony, Shprintze—not unlike the Baal Shatikah himself, who'd built a hut beyond the settlement's barbed-wire perimeter—remained aloof. She did not contribute to the impromptu truth-telling sessions conducted after meals in the dining hall, when the survivors broke down in their confessions and submitted to the consolations of the commune. (The kibbutzniks had become seasoned hands at ministering to hysteria.) Nor did she ever, at least in Ruby's hearing, attempt to use the sacred tongue.

He could only speculate as to why she chose to remain an outsider, though the answer may have been merely that she preferred the company of her books. Because when she wasn't performing her impersonations of goose girl or serving wench, she was poring over one of the vermin-nibbled volumes that were the only baggage she'd salvaged from her past. That was the posture in which Ruby was most likely to observe her—sprawled among the flowers called blood of the Maccabees that stippled the meadow just beyond the compound—as he grazed the sheep he'd appointed himself to watch.

He was as inept a shepherd as he was skilled at the trades of cutthroat and bloodletter. Wanting only the excuse of a task that lent itself to solitude, he had no interest in the science of animal husbandry. He could barely distinguish a lamb from a ewe, and regarded the randy old ram with its shit-stained crupper as merely a shofar-on-the-hoof. He was deaf to advice concerning the best spots to graze them, often leading the herd instead of to grass or stubble into unharvested fields of wheat and flax, which they devastated. He developed some aptitude in the use of the lasso but seldom had occasion to use it, since the kibbutz had voted that branding livestock was too charged a means of identification; and he failed to renew the salt licks that lay about the wadis like a sculpture garden. With the herd dog Abimelech, who belonged to everyone and no one, Ruby had never established any rapport. An odd hybrid of border collie and dachshund, the animal was more effective at terrorizing the flock than at corralling them into their fold. Nevertheless, despite his laxity Ruby had grown rather fond of the sheep. This is not to say he was moved to protect them from predators, diseases, or the poison grasses that caused them to inflate like fleece dirigibles. What he did protect them from, however, was being slaughtered or even sheared, which meant that the herd were in essence pets and a useless burden to the cooperative. Recently the secretariat had issued an ultimatum to Ruben ben None that he should render up the sheep for wool and mutton or relinquish his position to another.

"When the Third Temple is built," he broke his usual silence to reply, "you can use them for a blood offering." Which statement actually satisfied some of the more canonical among the delegates.

There came an afternoon like any afternoon when he was sheltering from the five o'clock sun beneath a red clay overhang while tending his flock. The agitation that was his companion since the arrival of the girl was accompanied at that hour by the jangling of the bellwether, the bleating of the ewes, and the yapping of the idiot dog Abimelech—all of which Ruby endured like noises plucked upon his tightly strung nerves. Suddenly he was aware of someone's sandal-shod approach from down the tussocky slope to his left, and the girl Shprintze padded into view carrying a book. Having attained the privacy of a spot beyond the settlement's boundaries and further obscured by a herd of sheep, she hoisted the flannel skirt to her haunches and squatted to pee. At that moment, no longer silenced by curiosity, Abimelech commenced yelping again.

The girl looked up but did not start and, catching sight of the dog's presumed master crouched in his cleft, inquired in a tone of perfect ingenuousness even as she continued watering the earth, "Bistu a shed?" Are you a demon?

Confounded on several counts, Ruby felt cornered and slid farther into the hollow until his back bumped against the dirt wall. For one thing, he was surprised that he had understood the question, so slight was his knowledge of Yiddish, though the language had been in the air again due to the influx of illegals who spoke it. (They never spoke it for long, since mameloshen was regarded as the language of victims and for that reason practically outlawed in HaEretz.) Then there was the nature of the question itself, asked so earnestly that it gave Ruby pause to consider. He'd been a number of things during his years in the Land, few of which had much in common with the lives of regular citizens. In the end, showing his palms in a gesture of surrender, he could only answer, "Ich kayn vays." I don't know.

Dropping the skirt, underneath which she apparently wore nothing at all, the girl rose to her feet and stepped a few paces toward him.

"Ich bin a shed," she confided in her flutey voice, and again he was taken aback by her candor. "Ich bin a shlecht yiddisher tochter." A bad Jewish daughter.

Ruby had no idea what he should do with this information, but it fascinated him that she'd divulged it without an apology or trace of apprehension. Who wasn't afraid of the Baal Shatikah? But Shprintze, so remote among the settlers, stood before him now as if she recognized him as belonging to the same species as herself. Flushed out, Ruby crawled from beneath the overhang and straightened himself to confront her, his heart galloping. Countless encounters with violent death had not caused his heart to gallop so precipitously. Nor did the girl make any movement toward withdrawing, and Ruby wondered exactly what it was she expected of him. Unable to suffer her gimlet gaze any longer, he dropped his eyes, which fixed on the book she held in her hand.

"Vos leyenstu?" he muttered experimentally, his voice still raw from old wounds.

She showed him the book, a volume of tales in a weather-warped binding by the Yiddish author I. L. Peretz, revealing in the process the garter blue numbers tattooed on her arm. When he took the book from her, she inhaled deeply as if she might not be able to breathe again until he returned it. He understood that the gesture had for her some grave ritual significance, and when he opened the book on a language he'd rejected as a child, a strange thing happened: The barbed Hebrew characters seemed to spill into his head as from a barrel of tacks, filling his brain with a thousand starbursts of pain. But with the pain also came a measure of enlightenment, because some of the printed words arranged themselves into units of sense. "Un Bontshe holt altz geshvign," he read: "And still Bontshe remained silent." It made his head ache terribly.

He gave her back the book in a rueful transaction that reminded him of something he couldn't quite place; then it came to him, the memory of a partisan attempting to replace a fallen comrade's spilled intestines. He clenched his eyes shut till the image passed, and when he opened them again, there she was in her florid expectancy; her tapered nose twitched from a brush with a butterfly as she asked him, "Shtel mit mir a chupeh?" Will you marry me?

He stared at her, searching for some taint of sarcasm, and found none. Then the laughter started deep in his bowels, erupting in spasms in his chest and escaping his mouth in a volley of loud guffaws. Doubled over, he delivered himself of a hilarity that contained as much heartache as mirth and shook him till he could barely stand. The tears that scalded his cheeks mingled with the sweat bathing his skin, as if his flesh itself were weeping after so many arid years. When the seizure began to abate and he was able to pull himself together again, she remained as before, having stoically weathered the storm. Her crested head was cocked to one side as she studied him with interest. Was she crazy, he wondered, or merely stupid? The categories did not seem to pertain.

Mustering an uncharacteristic frankness along with his makeshift proficiency, he told her, "Nem mir in acht farknasn." Consider us betrothed.

At first she visited him only at erratic intervals, usually appearing in the early evening after she'd completed her chores and before the dinner bell rang. She would sit beside him on a lava promontory or in a papyrus stand from which he watched his puny flock cropping mud and read one of her storybooks. In anticipation of her coming Ruby had begun to groom himself; he trimmed his arboreal beard and scrubbed his body in the shower bath of his own construction, a process involving half an hour's pumping of water from a receptacle tank to the barrel above. Still he deemed the operation worthwhile since his cleanliness (plus the broadcloth shirt and duck trousers) helped, he believed, to conceal the turmoil within. Shprintze, however, showed no appreciation for his efforts, and seemed at first not even to recognize him, until he reassured her he was the same hermit troll to whom she was engaged. Neither was she as fastidious in preparing to meet him, though Ruby was a little intoxicated by the civet scent she exuded.

It wasn't long before he learned her disturbing secret: that she only pretended to read the books whose open pages she never turned. He asked if she were illiterate, then immediately regretted the question, though she took no offense; she merely shook her head, and later, when he ventured to read aloud to her—still amazed at how the language reprised itself with near lucidity—she might anticipate sentences whenever he faltered, sometimes reciting them from memory with eyes closed. But mostly she was content to remain his passive audience.

It seemed to Ruby that Shprintze borrowed identities from the characters in those stories like costumes from a wardrobe rack in order to sustain her throughout any given day. But those temporary identities would wear thin by dusk and need replenishing from her bag of stories. When her assumed personae had run their course she came to him, and she appeared at those times practically a feral creature. It wasn't that she was spooked or panicked but merely uncivilized and at sea until the reading domesticated her all over again. Then she could face the collective once more with the forbearance of a Sheyndele from Dovid Pinski's "The Woodcutter's Wife" or the vivacity of one of Tevye's daughters, which would see her through another working day. Watching her Ruby remembered the multiple identities he'd adopted during his term as a fugitive; but since his post office photos had yellowed and been papered over by a new generation of Jewish desperados, he'd done with disguises. Now, but for his bare feet and checkered kefiyeh, he could have been mistaken for just another sunburnt halutz.

The girl's bag of books contained a volume of Peretz Hirschbein's stories and another collection of S. Ansky's; there was *Midrash Itzik* by Itzik Manger, which included his Hershel Ostropolier tales, the moral fantasies of Glückel of Hameln, and I. L. Peretz's fables and plays. It was a sweet and sour literature, full of worriers rather than warriors, that superseded in Ruby's mind the news of Secretary Bevin's Machiavellian policies and the assassination of Lord Coyne, the decimation by liquid nitro of the King David Hotel. But what of Shprintze's own history? Was it, like the words in her books, worn so smooth by memory that her brain could find no traction there? This was Ruby's theory, but every so often, though long out of practice in cajolery, he tried to tease her into disclosing some detail of her past. "A mol iz geven," he might begin, chunking a shard from an ancient cenotaph at Abimelech harrassing a ewe munching nettles. "Once upon a time, Shprintzele was born . . . ," making a gesture indicating that she should continue the tale. And when she refused to take the bait, he would wait a day or two and try again. It was a little like trying to kick-start the commune's old Flying Merkel motorbike, or so he told her, eliciting a flutter he took for the precursor of a smile; he had coaxed a smile. Still he was unprepared when the girl finally took up the narrative on her own.

"My papa was Reb Eliakum Feygenboim, a mokher seforim, a bookseller;

my mama who I don't remember died young. We lived on the Tsvarda Gass in Vilna, in three crowded rooms over the shop that was everywhere books, downstairs and up. As a business, the shop was nit gornisht, a failure, since my papa—if he sold shrouds nobody would die—gave away to his favored customers the prizes and discouraged who he deemed unworthy from buying the rest. It was only when he would leave the city on peddling trips to the villages that he would make from the Litvaks a few groschen. They wouldn't let girls go in cheder so I never learned to read Toyreh, but I could read from the *Tseyna Reyna* and the *Maaseh Bukh* and I gobbled up like shnecken everything in the shop from Shaikevitch to Aksenfeld. . . ." She was speaking, Ruby understood, as the heroine of a story, "Shprintze the Bookpeddler's Daughter," who lived in her papa's library and was every girl in every story she read.

"Then came in an evil hour the shretelekh, the devils in their helmets and boots that they piss green worms, and dragged me out of my books into Sitra Achra, the Underworld, where even God don't go. There they put on me their mark so that always I would belong to them. . . ."

Before she'd been abducted, however, Shprintze had hidden a bag of treasured titles in a space under the floorboards in the shop. Her father, who lacked his daughter's presence of mind, was still selecting books for the journey when the Germans burst in, and as he lingered too long in choosing, they stove in his satin-capped skull with their rifle butts. Broken heart notwithstanding, Shprintze was shrewd enough to swallow the shop key before being marched to the depot, and in the boxcar that transported them to perdition she voided her bowels and dug the key from her own filth. After the liberation, she made her way back to Vilna, whose desolation proclaimed the news that the Underworld now held dominion everywhere. She returned to the shop late at night, used the key that still miraculously opened the lock, and crept inside. Bereft of books, the place was an apothecary's, its shelves boasting potions that for all she knew gave to the devils the saberlike erections upon which they spitted young girls. In haste she pried up the floorboards fearing a vacancy, fearing the discovery of her father's bones, and reclaimed her bag of books from their cache. She hurried back into the street, where she stopped beneath the first lamppost and opened a volume at random, hoping to plunge without prelude into that element from which she'd been cast out. But the words lay on the page like flyspecks, refusing to give up their meaning, so that it seemed her exile was to be everlasting.

Transferred from one DP camp to another, she wound up on Cyprus, whence she was swept along on the current that ultimately washed ashore in the Promised Land. But the Bible was never her book, and by the same token the Jews from that epic—the kings, seers, and harlots that haunted the born-again landscape—were not her people. Then she surprised Ruby by appending to the end of her confession, "Now you." And when he hesitated, "A mol iz geven . . ."

"Once upon a time," he offered at length, feeling obliged to tender his own demonic credentials, "Ruben ben None burned down his papa's parnosseh, his livelihood, with his papa inside." But saying it didn't make it a story; it would never be a story. "Since then" he added, "murder is all he knows."

But the truth was that he wasn't murdering anybody these days, and the anger he'd once been able to conjure for the task was no longer available to him. Now he was wholly occupied by his concern for Shprintze, who inspired sensations he couldn't even name; though one of them was accompanied by physical symptoms—chronic bellyache, full-throttle heart—that might be ascribed to fear. Never before afraid on his own account, Ruby feared for the girl's fragility, for the welfare of her blistered fingers, the pulse that stirred the numbers on her wrist, the russet hair which, grown out of its featheriness, was whipped into a brushfire by the desert simoom.

In the meantime Shprintze and her association with the counterfeit shepherd were the subject of much gossip among the population of Tel Elohim. Leery of the Baal Shatikah, they speculated on his pernicious influence over the girl, who was becoming if possible ever more remote

herself. They observed with disapproval the way the ill-matched pair conspired over books in the company of a defective dog and a dingy flock,
their hind legs matted from the runs. But nobody dared to interfere with
them, as they sprawled amid spear grass or sat beneath the canvas cover of
a mired truck regarding a sunset, which looked to Ruby like a hemorrhage
behind a gauze dressing, to Shprintze a bedsheet after a wedding night.
Then the girl would go back to her walking part among the settlers and
the shepherd would return his sheep to their wattle. He would retire to his
tin-roofed hut on the chalk ridge overlooking the settlement, a habitation
so overgrown with ranunculus that it might have been a natural outcrop,
and prepare his meager supper.

It had been a long while since he'd dined with the community, though
for a time women enamored of his legend had left covered dishes at his
door: savory beef and egg noodles, pita bread and sesame paste, stewed
prunes. But since his withdrawal from the life of the commune and the
plugatsim, the terror squads, the food had ceased to appear, and Ruby
sustained himself on whatever came to hand. It might be a raw potato, a
fistful of unripe carobs, oranges bruised with blue mold. It was penitent's
fare, which he ate more out of the habit of staying alive than from any real
appetite. Despite his forager's diet, though, Ruby supposed his health was
sound enough, but while his muscles remained taut his body had grown
alarmingly thin. He had no mirror (shaved by instinct like the blind) but
could trace in his sunken cheeks the creases wrought by constant worry.
He could feel the years and the toll his rearoused sensibilities had taken,
and though he longed to articulate his feelings for Shprintze, he was afraid
that if he expressed them they might ravage her the way they had him.

For the same reason, he had yet to touch her. He was fearful that her
mostly imaginary world might not withstand the blunt impact. It was
difficult to know, given all she'd been through, what did and did not
constitute defilement; and while he might suffer the urge to stroke, say,
the tendon at the downy nape of her neck, he knew better than to risk the
intimacy. Better to ache with unrealized desires, inviting a pain that was

no less than he deserved. What he didn't deserve, however, was that the pain, though nearly unbearable, should also be unbearably sweet. Then on an evening in the month of Elul when they sat reading at the lip of a well, the chill air emanating from its stony darkness as from an ice cave, Ruby inadvertently placed a hand in Shprintze's hair. It was not deliberate, but in some corner of his mind he registered the gesture, imagining she might incline her gamin's head and allow herself the ghost of a grin — and that would be that. Instead, she turned toward him with a mouth that looked to have been gashed open, its stifled howl more shrill than any sound she might have uttered, and springing catlike to her feet, she ran away down the hill through the cyclone gates of Tel Elohim.

But later that night, as he lay twisting on the rack of his folding cot, castigating himself for his blunder, the door opened to starlight silhouetting her spare contours through a flimsy nainsook shift. "Murder me, my wicked one," she importuned him in a perfect imitation of coyness — and a few months after, she began to show the swelling that indicated she was quick with child.

RUBY HAD A FRIEND of sorts, a young Arab shepherd he'd run across years before while grazing his flock in the dried-out washes west of the settlement. The boy, perhaps mistaking the assassin for a legitimate herder of sheep, had attempted to direct him through gibbering and gestures toward greener pastures, but Ruby preferred to remain in the wastes where he squatted meditating on his sins. A twiggy character in a filthy tunic, with a clump of hair like a bird's nest, the boy shrugged his knobby shoulders and hied his flock toward the grassy heights. But he reappeared at odd intervals during the succeeding days so that Ruby suspected their meetings were not always accidental. With a broad grin proud of its broken teeth, a plaited ribbon dangling lewdly from his loincloth, he greeted his fellow shepherd with a merry "*Itbach al yahud.*" Death to the Jew. It was a salutation delivered with such hearty good humor that Ruby, who'd heard it often enough in other contexts, could only respond with a slightly puzzled, "Aleichem sholem." This became their customary exchange whenever they crossed paths.

Ruby assumed at first that the boy hailed from the mud-domed village of Kafr Qusra, which could be seen from the slopes of Tel Elohim, but soon he began to realize that the shepherd swore allegiance to no place on earth. He had a name, Iqbal bin Fat Fat, which Ruby had gleaned over the course of several visits, but though he babbled incessantly—a multitude of consonants trampling a handful of vowels—his unlikely moniker was the only solid detail the amateur herdsman was ever to learn of the boy's identity. He turned up unannounced and took for granted the Jew's unoffered hospitality, but while he was clearly a bit deranged—a mejdoub, he called himself, a born fool—Ruby began to look forward to their encounters. Their initial meeting had occurred during the fugitive period following the Baal Shatikah's prison escape, when he'd returned to the kibbutz after months of hiding out. He was still lying low, abstaining from the night patrols and tending to avoid the settlers as well—who were themselves not altogether happy to be hosting him, especially since his uncles of blessed memory were gone. So it surprised Ruby to discover that he welcomed the unscheduled visits of this quaint interloper; nor did it seem to matter that communication between them was so restricted, as the Arab apparently required no comprehension from his audience and the Jew had long since lost the habit of conversation.

They would sit together for hours, Ruby nodding at the weird modulations of Iqbal's chin music and sometimes sharing his water pipe. Their flocks never mingled; Iqbal's dog, Dalilah, saw to that. A nobler, curlier breed than Abimelech, she would weave among the lambs and ewes, encircling them in an invisible fold, though the snowy Arab flock would have shunned the Jewish bunch for their uncouthness in any case. It never occurred to Ruby to draw a moral from the situation any more than he was moved to speculate about the boy's origins: Iqbal was a denizen of the wilderness who had befriended the Jewish incendiary the way a jackal might approach a campfire to partake of the warmth. For the boy was very like a wild animal, or several animals, a mimic who spontaneously impersonated the behavior of whatever creature happened into their field of vision. If, say, a long-legged bustard flew overhead, the boy would rise on one leg flapping his arms and screeching hysterically; he would bay at the brindled wildcats and hyenas, who answered him with a forlorn plangency. Throwing back his burnoose, he might reveal the cowpie of his hair twisted into love locks plastered with butter, or lift his djellaba to withdraw from his sagging diaper a warehouse inventory of utensils and tools, which he offered for sale. In the heat of the day he would erect on the single pole of his shepherd's staff a haircloth tent whose shade he offered to share with the Jew.

His sack also contained, along with a waterskin and various spices, ingredients exceeding the uses of ordinary condiments, such as crows' wings, powdered porcupine quills, and pressed scorpion, which Ruby figured were employed in casting spells. At some point in the afternoon or evening the boy would gather his possessions and take up his crudely carved staff; Ruby would lift his rifle and the two of them would depart without ceremony in their separate directions. Often days, weeks, even months would elapse before they set eyes on each other again, upon which they would resume their chance acquaintance as if no time at all had intervened. But time did pass, and though the shepherd remained as unreconstructed as ever, Ruby noted that sparse hairs had begun to sprout over his tawny cheeks, and a knavish cast had entered his eye. Moreover, certain of his sheep had conceived the suspicious habit of nuzzling their backsides against him with a brazen immodesty.

The mongrel Abimelech, who barked at shadows and chased echoes, never bothered to signal the shepherd's approach. (He adored Dalilah and attempted to court her with acrobatics resembling rabid convulsions, though she spurned his overtures and left him to hump the sultry air.) Iqbal, however, always announced his own advent with the usual insults, most of which remained unintelligible to Ruby. But mostly Ruby was indifferent to the shepherd's language and satisfied to hunker beside him as he dredged a brazier from his bottomless sack for roasting gobbets of shashlik. Then the two of them would gnaw the leathery meat, their faces slathered with the grease, and afterward Iqbal, still unweaned, would suck the teat of his single goat until it staggered.

Once, as they sat among the saline bushes in a sandy stream bed, their sheep resting in the shade of the shallow chasm, the sun clouded over and a sudden storm came up. Even Iqbal, attuned though he was to every mood of the weather, was caught off guard. So torrential was the downpour that before the sheep could stir or the shepherds, languid from the afternoon's hashish, rouse themselves, a flash flood had filled the empty channel like the bursting of a dam. Struggling against the surging current, Ruby and Iqbal attempted to harry their animals to higher ground. Most found footholds among the rocks of the defile and were able to scramble to safety in advance of the rising trough, but a few were deluged by the instantaneous wall of water and carried away. At one point Ruby himself was swept off his feet by the turbulence, and though he didn't suppose himself in any danger, the shepherd plunged into the rushing conduit to rescue him. An aggravated Ruby found himself clutched by the beard, tugged from beneath the armpits, and dragged up the steep bank of what had become a roaring watercourse. But even then the boy did not let go his embrace (which was leavened now by an element of tenderness) until Ruby shoved him abruptly away, sitting up in time to see the incontinent old ram he'd been trying to save being swept downstream.

Not long after that the girl came to live at Tel Elohim. Then the shepherd discovered that he had been demoted in his friend's affections to something like the rank held by Abimelech — to whom Ruby occasionally tossed scraps though mainly the dog had to fend for itself. Soon the Jew was no longer alone and the company he kept was exclusive, so that even Iqbal, who had never been shy about intruding on his solitude, knew enough to steer clear of their dalliance. From time to time, however, Ruby was aware that the boy had not entirely vanished and every so often might catch sight of him standing storklike on a single leg in the distance, leaning pensively on his graven staff. After a while, however, he no longer looked out for the shepherd and had all but forgotten the existence of Iqbal bin Fat Fat.

Meanwhile Shprintze's pregnancy was the talk of the commune. For one thing, every pregnancy in the Yishuv was a participatory event and every expectant mother considered the property of the entire kibbutz, since the child she carried was destined to become another hero of labor. This was how the notion of a universal redeemer had been translated into the argot of the Zionist enterprise. That the child in question was also the fruit of an unsanctified union was of little consequence to most, but that it belonged to an individual whose status in the community was dubious at best, made it the more incumbent on the settlers to claim the mother and her offspring as their own. The women especially began to show an inordinate interest in Shprintze, a concern from which the girl retreated, sticking all the closer to the companion whose domicile she now shared. The tension between the misfit couple and the tribe to which they only marginally belonged increased throughout the months of the girl's gestation, during which she and the semi-retired assassin seldom left the vicinity of his firebrick hut. The hut itself had been somewhat transformed from its previously Spartan interior by the shelves Ruby built to display Shprintze's books. There were the Yid artifacts as well, the spice boxes and candelabra, that the girl had reclaimed from items the other survivors had discarded, which lent a certain coziness to the decor of what had previously been a monastic cell.

Contributing to that warmth (infernally whenever the Primus stove was lit) were the dishes that Shprintze served her man. But as cooking was for her a largely make-believe activity like her reading, the women of the settlement, anxious for the health of the unborn, had begun again to leave anonymous offerings on the doorstep. These usually consisted of dense tcholent, figgy compotes, and ragouts, though occasionally some more outré concoction might appear—such as boiled sheep's eyes in a camel's-urine marinade seasoned with spices found in no Jewish pantry. (Such reminders that the shepherd had not completely quit the scene were noted only in passing.) While Ruby viewed the commune's charity as an unbidden invasion, Shprintze appeared to accept it as her due, the propitiation of demons having, as she knew, a long tradition. Their domesticity was in any event something they both seemed to savor, and even Abimelech, who'd always valued his own independence, now stayed close to the hovel. Having come to acknowledge the girl in her delicate condition as his mistress, the dog established himself as the guardian of hearth and home.

At night by the light of a spirit lamp strafed by moths, they performed their ritual affinities. They read the tales about this one's headstrong daughter and that one's bumpkin son in search of their bashert, their fated one. During interludes they stepped out into the evening air, where Ruby would lift Shprintze's shift to bare her distended belly in a direct challenge to the waxing moon. Sometimes on the pallet that had replaced the folding cot that was too narrow for the both of them, the girl would walk the length and breadth of Ruby's nakedness with her fingers. She lingered over his scars, each of which had its origin in a different place, so that examining them was tantamount to making a tour of the Holy Land. And though the Baal Shatikah was half a stranger to Ruby now, the pressure of her fingers on his wounds revived each episode (in Nur Chams, Al-Qibilya, on the Damascus Road) with a sharpness that was a relief from the more excruciating pain of loving and being loved.

They never discussed what they would do when the baby came, so permanent a condition did Shprintze's tumescence seem. And while Ruby was constantly thumping her belly to test for ripeness, placing an ear to her extruded navel to hear the burbling beneath, while he rubbed her like a lamp containing a captive genie, he never expected that anything would really emerge. Of course, neither prospective parent had any education in these matters, nor was there a resident physician to advise them, but there was scarcely a woman who had not been schooled in midwifery. So, when the labor throes began and Shprintze gave herself up to wave upon wave of banshee shrieks, Ruby lost what was left of his pride and, leaving Abimelech to guard the girl, ran down the hill, calling to the women for help. They had apparently been waiting for just such an alarm. With them they brought provisions for almost every eventuality, though once they'd arrived at the hut on the ridge, the midwife-in-chief, a Rumanian immigrant with a nubbly frown, discovered the one thing they were missing. For there on the doorstep wrapped in a date frond was a gift: a taproot shaped like a seahorse, which the woman, sniffing before licking, determined to be a rare herbal parturifacient: "Der kishef!" she proclaimed. Magic! She had her assistants mash it to powder with a pestle, stir it into a glass of mint tea, and administer it to the caterwauling girl, who was soon after delivered of an infant with pipestem limbs and a gourdlike head—a peevish boy whom she and her demon lover proceeded to cherish beyond reason.

THERE WAS NEVER a specific moment when Ruby bowed out of military operations altogether. Rather, he had removed himself by degrees, until he was a warrior no more but only the shepherd of a flock of blighted sheep dwelling on the outskirts of a community that regarded him as extraneous. He still had his allies among the fresh breed of freedom fighters, young men in flared breeches and riding boots who had replaced their maimed and imprisoned forebears. They had been reared on tall tales of the Baal Shatikah's deadly expertise, and assured one another that when the time was ripe the old campaigner would rise up phoenixlike to deal the coup de grâce to Israel's foes. Whenever the opportunity arose, they attempted to curry favor with him, singing his praises within his earshot and entreating him to fill the vacuum left by the martyred Yair Stern, though Ruby seldom dignified their blandishments with a response. Moreover, the presence of Revisionists in their midst had always been a source of controversy among the settlers, who had never asked for their protection in the first place and were additionally irked at having to carry the dead weight of Ruben ben None. But after the birth of his son, when the women had rallied to the young mother's aid, things began to change.

The inveterately private couple still refrained from placing their offspring among the pool of infants in the children's house while they did the work of the collective, work they had in any case opted out of. But since Yudl's delivery and his subsequent cranky demands, the new parents had found it necessary to reintegrate themselves little by little into the society of the kibbutz. In exchange for pabulum, nappies, and the quinine-laced formula the baby required, Shprintze began to take her turn again among the mortals. With the squinch-faced infant dangling marsupial-like from a sling around her neck, she arranged the books in the recently established colony library, where she infiltrated the small Hebrew collection with her Yiddish texts. Lest his son be regarded a pariah like himself, Ruby offered his services for odd jobs, again displaying the talent for tinkering he'd inherited from his own starry-eyed papa. He devised a mechanical scarecrow to frighten away birds from the vineyard, used his skill at setting booby traps to blow a hole for a rainwater cistern, and recalling his sojourn among moonshiners designed a still for the manufacture of potato schnapps. In his absence his neglected flock strayed into alien pastures, where they were slaughtered by hostile neighbors to the dismay of nobody but Ruby himself, who silently mourned their sacrifice to higher priorities. No longer afraid of him, the colonists relaxed into a general impression that paternity had tamed the assassin: He was judged a reformed character whose past all somewhat self-righteously forgave. So when the circuit-riding rabbi traveled through the settlement on his sumpter nag, they felt confident enough to approach the regenerate Ruby about having his son circumcised. He had no reason to refuse provided he be allowed to guide the palsied old rabbi's knife—"like," observed a waggish onlooker, "cutting a wedding cake." The remark inspired the colonists to propose that, as one good turn called for another, the rabbi might as well go ahead and consecrate the mother and father's union. "They can stroke the prepuce," the same wag suggested, "till it spreads to a bridal canopy."

Since there was no time to advertise the spur-of-the-moment event, the wedding was a modest affair. Still, the few women in attendance insisted that, maiden or no, Shprintze should wear the communal bridal gown, which they altered then and there to fit her no longer so boyish frame. Also made available was a much recycled gold-filled wedding band, a decanter of plum brandy, and the machinist Kotik Gilboa playing "Rozhinkes mit mandlen" on his fiddle at the bride's request. The handful of IZL boys drew straws for the honor of standing up for the Baal Shatikah, and the ceremony — the old rabbi seemed anxious to wash his hands of it — was over in a matter of minutes. Ruby crushed the glass with his heel as if stomping a dormouse and, with the colicky Yudl squirming larvalike between them, kissed the bride. Then the witnesses toasted their health before dispersing, though one uninvited guest, tarrying with his dog behind a medlar at a distance of some hundred yards, continued to look on with an invidious eye.

However tentative, Ruby's reentry into the life of the settlement gave him an aura of accessibility, which made the young bravos of the revolutionary underground think he might now be fair game; and so they came calling. By this time the mood of the Yishuv had altered, and even the most accomodationist among the settlers were now in favor of hastening the departure of the British at any cost. The abuses of the centuries had culminated in such obscenities that enough was finally enough: Amalekites be blotted out, give us a home! For his part Ruby was so wracked by devotion to his wife and child that he could scarcely abide the thought of leaving them for even a day. But when the lads, some of whom had seen action in Europe in the Jewish Brigade and so could not be easily ignored, appealed for his assistance, he listened; though when they insisted that his participation in the next major tactical strike would be a boost to morale, he deprecated the idea: His soldiering days were over. But eventually they began to wear down his resistance, and in his new capacity as member in good standing of the Kibbutz Tel Elohim, Ruby was at last persuaded to yield just this once to their pleas.

This was during the Days of Awe, when the newlyweds ate apples and honey and attended Rosh Hashonah services in the sweatbox of the cinderblock chapel. Shprintze wore the toweling sling containing the baby, which Ruby had almost come to regard as an auxiliary appendage, almost as if mother and son were one flesh; and though the whiffy Yudl might have been an obstacle to their intimacy, his doting father found the contrary to be the case: He adored his wife and child as a single entity. While it amused him at first that the baby's unhappy face did seem to partake of the demonic, he now insisted with Shprintze that the boy appeared more normal every day. After the heat of the shul even the arid air of the biscuit-dry Galilean hills was refreshing, and the couple strolled along with the congregation down the gravel road to the irrigation well. Dividing a fistful of challah crumbs between herself and her husband, to the accompaniment of the baby who hadn't stopped bawling since his bris, Shprintze invited her man to perform the tashlikh ritual with her. This involved tossing the crumbs representing their sins of the past year into the well.

"Better," said Ruby, thinking of all the years prior to the last, "I should throw the whole of myself in." But Shprintze assured him it wouldn't matter anyway, since during the holy days when the Book of Life remained open, no one could die. Then it seemed as if the ritual they observed was their real life, while demon and demoness was something that Ruby and Shprintze only played at to add spice to their unpublic hours.

The action, planned for just before Yom Kippur, involved robbing a bank, which Ruby considered a purposeless exercise. The eroding British occupation, clearly on its last legs, had lately resorted to desperate measures: They attempted to enforce curfews after bombings and cordoned off various settlements, though nothing helped; the harassment of their troops and installations was unrelenting. Having realized that keeping the peace between Arabs and Jews—a plague on both their houses—was more trouble than it was worth, the occupiers were all but ready to pull up stakes and bugger off forever. But the directorate of Lehi or Palmach, or whatever high command the boys were taking their orders from these days, had decided that ordinary life should be disrupted at every instance in order to prove that the Brits had lost control. So one simmering September morning, having bid a guilty good-bye to his wife and child, Ruby set out for Tel Aviv with a carload of callow guerillas in a backfiring old canvas-roofed landaulet. The vehicle's smelly interior was crammed with lads singing "Hazak hazak venithazak, from strength to strength we grow stronger," until their older comrade, by the authority they'd vested in him, told them to please shut up.

After an interminable couple of hours they arrived in the city, where they proceeded to bungle the whole operation. The robbery of the Barclay's Bank in Nahalat Benjamin Street itself went off smoothly enough, but the aftermath was a disaster. It didn't help that the dauntless Baal Shatikah, curled up in a craven funk, had refused to leave the car. Giving up on him, three of the boys, themselves seasoned conspirators, tied bandannas over their faces, entered the art deco building with an empty suitcase, and emerged minutes later, as the alarm began to sound—two of them with weapons drawn while the third lugged the suitcase now bulging with piasters and pounds sterling. They jumped into the car and urged the driver to step on it, but the driver, a recent recruit from whose rabbity eyes the tears were streaming, may have been infected by the behavior of their celebrity passenger; because instead of heading along the prescribed escape route down Allenby, he became disoriented and steered the car into the nearby Carmel Market. He ploughed into a throng of shoppers at a Gazos stand, wounding several including a little girl in a hijab, whose legs were crushed beneath the screeching wheels. In the succeeding melee a mixed crowd of Arabs and Jews, united for once in their outrage, attacked the car (which was mired in produce) and dragged out its passengers. The boy in the watchcap hugging the suitcase to his chest, having received a boot to the gut, dropped his burden onto the pavement, where it burst open, releasing a blizzard of currency. Their anger instantly transformed to greed, the mob scrambled over one another in pursuit of the fluttering bills, and under cover of the commotion Ruby managed to make a getaway on foot. He took cover under the beach promenade among starfish and discarded "French yarmelkes," waiting for shame to overtake him, but instead felt only relief at having preserved himself for the sake of his family. After dark he stole from his hideout to catch a ride in a sherut packed with winery workers headed north from the port, arriving around midnight at the village of Qever Shimon from which he walked seven desolate kilometers to Tel Elohim.

Despite the early hour there were lights on in the long dining hall, and the short-wave radio, perhaps broadcasting news of the botched robbery, could also be heard. The kibbutzniks would be seated at their benches apportioning blame, and though Ruby wondered if other militia members had escaped the fracas—or had they been apprehended, beaten to death?—he crept past the hall in his anxiousness to return to his family. Trudging up the powdery slope, however, he found himself unable to hasten his steps, his legs teetering as if suddenly bowed with age. Ordinarily Abimelech, who seldom deigned to greet him, would be snoring beside Shprintze on the plank bed Ruby had constructed for his wife and himself, but tonight the dog was outside cavorting in front of the hut, performing the stunts he generally reserved for Dalilah. Ruby heard his son's hiccupping cries as he approached, which was nothing unusual, he was a fractious child; though upon entering the vine-knitted dwelling, he wondered that his wife could sleep through the sobbing of the kaddish at her breast. (Ruby had also built a cradle on rockers but the baby hardly slept in it.) He sat down in utter exhaustion on the mattress beside his bride, her features cameo-pale in the dim interior, and made to remove her arm from around the child. But when he touched it, he recoiled and sprang back to his feet, because the arm, scaly and cool, began to slide away from the bundled infant like a plump tourniquet unwinding and plopped onto the plywood floor. There, incandescently white, it lengthened and coiled and lengthened again as it slithered out the open door, where under a red moon in a lapis sky it grew dark and stiff as an axle. Then a slim figure with a sack slung over its shoulder, followed by a prancing dog, came forward from the shadows to lift the staff from the ground and, while Abimelech whimpered after them, pad swiftly away.

The autopsy was performed by a doctor called in from Haifa for the purpose. He pronounced what most had already assumed: that the young mother had died from a combination of symptoms—insults, said the doctor, to both her nervous and circulatory systems—consistent with the virulent bite of the adder native to that region. It never occurred to anyone that the death might have been due to happenstance, the diagnosis having satisfied all concerned that the Arabs of the district, notorious for employing venomous serpents to get even, were responsible. Given the bad blood over boundary disputes between Tel Elohim and the village of Kafr Qusra, the wonder was that no such homicides had taken place before. The couple of partisans who'd survived the bank debacle, anxious for a chance to redeem themselves, recommended an immediate reprisal which they called upon the Baal Shatikah to lead. Vengeance, they maintained, was the best medicine; it was the only cure for such mortal grief, and also (they insinuated) for the restoration of one's manly fortitude. But the Baal Shatikah was apparently not of their opinion. Declining both a memorial service and a plot in the newly inaugurated cemetery, Ruby buried Shprintze himself along with a storybook and the infant's empty sling at the foot of an oleander she'd planted outside the hut. As an afterthought he perforated Abimelech's heart with his icepick and dropped the dog into the grave beside the girl. Then the UN voted that a people should be allowed to become a nation, and the British began a pullout that left the Jews and Arabs (twins with different fathers) to settle things between themselves. Palestinians prepared to revolt while Arab armies started to mobilize on the borders of what would emerge as the state of Israel. But before the demons could come back to retrieve the boy (for he knew they would return for one of their own), Ruben Karp gathered up his son and took flight across the oceans to a ghetto in Memphis, Tennessee.

"When I got there," Ruby's grandson Bernie read to his girlfriend, "I dumped the kid in the lap of his grandma in her ice cream parlor on North Main Street, and told her I was a murderer. She told me she was a whore. I told her I used to be a Jew.

"'I said once the same thing to your papa,' she replied, dandling the fretful pisher whom she'd pacified with a cinnamon stick on her knee, 'and you know what he told me?'

"'What?' I asked.

"He said, 'I used to be a hunchback.'"

c. 1950 – 2002.

When Julius (né Yudl) Karp was still a child, just beginning to outgrow the crankiness of his coddled infancy, his grandmother Yokey, known in the Pinch as "that ice cream person," would recite to him his family's history:

"Yosl King of Cholera from Boibicz, who married Chava Babtcheh, her that died from giving birth to Salo that they called him Frostbissen"—pausing to catch her wheezy breath—"who married the sharptongued Basha Puah who begot in Lodz first the twins Yachneh and Yoyneh, who ran away to Palestine, then me,"—pause—"Jocheved, who begot in America with my poor husband Shmerl your father Ruben Karp, who was in the Yichud a holy terror before he got wed to his wife that was shlangbissen"—pause—"snakebit after already she begot you . . ."

A mannish creature with her cropped hair and coveralls, her chin whiskers and camelbacked spine, she informed little Julius of what he would have preferred not to know: that there was an umglik, a curse on the Family Karp that goaded them to extreme behavior. But as far back as he could remember, he'd determined that the curse would pass him over, maybe skip a generation, though God forbid it should be visited instead on his children. Not that he believed in curses. For even as a boy Julius Karp was on his way to becoming a forward-looking young man, and as such never saw much percentage in looking back. He grew to forget most of the names in his grandmother's catalog, just as he tended to forget his grandmother herself though she'd practically raised him. Neither did Julius retain any vivid memories of the apartment that he and his widowed father had shared with the mildly demented Grandma Yokey on a leafy street in midtown Memphis.

He was not an endearing man, Julius's father, no one would have called him that, but neither was he hard or cruel. Though his features were regular enough, if a bit chapfallen, his short frame solid and well knit, he made little impression on acquaintances and seemed devoid of any passion save his dedication to making a living. So conservative was he in his dress (everything steam-pressed and Sanforized) as to appear almost camouflaged, so self-effacing in his manner that he might have been about to disappear; and although Julius admired and even emulated his father's industry, there were times when he thought there was something rather calculated about his ordinariness—as if in performing the routine functions of a common merchant he were practicing some dark ritual. After his checkered stint in the Holy Land, he'd returned to the States a widower to raise his son in a less embattled environment. For a time he scooped sundaes in his mother's vest-pocket parlor, where Jocheved comported herself less like a soda jerk than a necromancer; but when that shop went the way of all the others on North Main Street, Ruben appealed to his uncle Marvin for a job. Though Marvin Karp had never approved of his nephew, the kid (now in his middle thirties) seemed chastened since his return from abroad, and as a favor to Ruben's mother Marvin took him on in his home appliance emporium, the new embodiment of his old general merchandise relocated from North Main to a shopping plaza out east. The business had always fared well, but owing in part to Ruben's knack with machinery, which helped secure its reputation for service and dependability, Karp's Appliance began to outdistance the competition. For while he was never especially personable with the customers, Ruben made himself readily available for installations and spot repairs, and stayed abreast of the latest advances in compact freezers, convection ovens, and blenders. Later, as the aging Marvin began to wean himself from business with a view toward retirement, he allowed Ruben to buy into a partnership; then retiring in earnest, he sold his own share of the establishment to his nephew. Karp's Appliance Showroom, while it wasn't quite the institution it would become after Julius took over, prospered under Ruben's management; it survived the general collapse of the city's economy following its wholesale abandonment by the white population, whose flight to the hinterlands left the inner city nearly a waste.

When, after a few incurious years of college, Julius accepted his father's invitation to come to work in the family business, it was clear from the start that the young man had a vocation. His outgoing personality was the antidote to Ruben's retiring nature, and their clientele responded favorably to his enthusiasm just as they did to the ads and jingles he cooked up, the numerous inventory sales he engineered. He also led the initiative in opening a discount annex that turned out to be nearly as lucrative as the flagship store. At first Julius had looked forward to working alongside his father, anxious to prove his mettle, but Ruben, while commending his son for his go-ahead attitude, remained the same benign but distant presence he'd been throughout the boy's life. Often the son felt ashamed of his father's subservience, of how passively he suffered a customer's unjust complaints, and wondered if his conduct might have less to do with decorum than faintness of heart. That assessment was further confounded by an incident that occurred during the lawless days following the murder of the man that the colored people regarded as a kind of black Moses, when there was rioting and looting all over town. Most of the mayhem was confined to the ghetto neighborhoods, but some of the looters ventured farther afield, if only to prove that nowhere was safe. This was the case on an afternoon when a car skidded into the lot of Karp's Appliance, its doors slamming shut, and Julius saw his ordinarily neutral father become strangely alert. Then, without explanation, the father hustled his son behind a checkout counter and bade him hunker down beside him, as two men burst into the otherwise empty store.

"Ain't nobody home," exclaimed one, and the other, "'Spose we got to wait on ourself." There was the sound of metal smashing merchandise, and Julius, who couldn't remember ever being in such close proximity to his father, sniffed a bad odor he associated with fear. Presently a flat-nosed man holding a mini-fridge on top of which lay a crowbar, a plastic pick stuck in his woolly hair, peered over the counter. "What we got here?" The other, in dark glasses and cradling a shotgun, came round to see: "Look like a pair of fascist insect." He stretched the pointy toe of his boot to prod a petrified Julius in the ribs, which was all it took to trigger an action that figured in no order of experience the youth had ever known. For his father was instantly upon the intruder, ignoring his weapon as he pummeled him to the ground, the rifle clattering across the floor as he fell. Then no sooner had he knocked down one than he lit into the other, who was pinned to the spot by the appliance he'd dropped on his foot. Having so savagely dispatched both vandals, Ruben Karp seemed not to know what to do with his leftover rage, and stood over them baying like a berserker, curling and uncurling his fingers as if strangling air, while the men dragged themselves bloodied and groaning from the store. After that the proprietor straightened the creases in his business suit and withdrew into a meekness that exceeded even his former demeanor. Julius, waiting to feel gratitude or awe, felt neither, but regarded his father from that moment with an increased wariness.

For all that, they were good years for Julius Karp, on the strength of which he married and started a family. Whey-faced and lethargic, his Yetta was perhaps not the most disarming girl, but aware that he was no prize himself (though his looks had improved since infancy from unpleasant to only slightly insipid), Julius was content to have found a bride who seemed to think that he would do as well as another. He was also pleased with his well-heeled in-laws, who had thrown in a suburban house to sweeten the deal. After the wedding there followed a prolonged honeymoon period during which husband and wife viewed history unfolding over their parallel TV trays. Together they witnessed a president resign in disgrace, though not before he had deputized the King (that is, Elvis) as an honorary member of the Secret Service. They watched the end of a war and the return home and subsequent death of Elvis Presley, prompting Julius to observe reverentially, "Our city is a place where Kings come to die." The event made him feel, as he had in his youth, that Memphis was the center of the world. It was around that time that his Grandma Yokey also expired, though Julius was nearly too preoccupied to notice. The old lady had been mostly an embarrassment anyway, what with her androgynous appearance and her maundering about being a container for her dead husband's soul. As far back as his childhood Julius was mortified to be seen with her in public, though daffyness aside she had managed his father's accounts with skill. Then her senescence caught up with the papery skin and mole gray hair she'd had for decades, and diagnosed with advanced dementia she was confined until her unminded end to the B'nai B'rith Home near Overton Park.

In the meantime, left alone on Hawthorne Street (from which he'd refused all these years to move, despite deepening pockets and the decay of the neighborhood around him), Ruben Karp surprised his son by accepting his perfunctory offer to occupy the guest bungalow behind Julius's home. His tastes being simple to the point of austerity, the old man, whose age like his mother's had exceeded his years, resisted any attempts on the part of his son and daughter-in-law to decorate his quarters, preferring to leave them as ascetically spare as a monk's cell. There was never any formal announcement of Ruben's retirement, but one day he simply ceased to show up for work and thereafter devoted his time to no one knew what. So excited was the family in any case over their daughter's first steps and the recent birth of a son that they practically forgot the old man's existence. The smell that ultimately led them to his remains—the coroner's report stated that the old man had effectively starved to death, though Julius never accepted the judgment; hadn't he always seen to it that the guest house had a well-stocked refrigerator and fully functional kitchen?—took weeks to fumigate. Among his scant belongings they found, on the night-stand beside the bed, an old icepick tucked into a limp ledger whose pages were strewn with a script that resembled an augur's tossed bones. There was a small shelf of disintegrating Yiddish books that Julius threw out and of course the grisly tenant of the Kelvinator freezer, which his father had transferred from the rear of Karp's Showroom when he came to live in the little house behind the house on Canary Cove.

Of the latter Julius seldom spared a thought. After all he had a family to raise and his position in the community to consolidate, his televised ad campaigns to manage. It was a good life in which he laid claim to the full complement of middle-class chattels, and wasn't there also some precept of the Jews that stated that a man was not a man without a wife and children? Though never observant, neither was Julius ashamed of his heritage. Regarding religious attendance as a more or less civic duty, he went to services with his family on the High Holidays. It was important to him that he not be perceived as in any way un-American, an unease that perhaps had its source in his having been born abroad. So while he purchased his annual share of Israel Bonds along with the other members of the Temple Brotherhood, he had no relation to the so-called Jewish homeland; his own place was here in the South, where he belonged to a number of fraternal organizations in whose fund-raising activities he par-ticipated with zeal. Much as he desired the renaissance of his ill-starred city, however, Julius thought it just as well that the great world not inter-fere overmuch in local affairs. That's why he was relieved when the relic from the deep freeze—notwithstanding the perversity of its defrosting—had adapted to the climate of these interesting times, and that its (his) message, while retaining its spiritual essence, did not contradict the basic values of the marketplace.

Nor had it seemed to upset the status quo when that message was translated into a profitable enterprise from which Julius Karp, as the rabbi's chief investor and financial consultant, had benefited as well. So much had he profited, in fact, that he'd begun to contemplate selling the Showroom in order to devote himself exclusively to the operations of the New House of Enlightenment. Lately, however, that venture had come under fire from the municipality. Hysterical rumors abounded and a stink had been raised in the editorial pages of *The Commercial Appeal*, whose bloodhounds demanded full disclosure of New House dealings — which, despite Sanford Grusom's facility for cooking books, were perfectly aboveboard. Nevertheless, Julius had started to wonder if, in getting involved with the recycled old huckster, he was perhaps in over his head, though his share in the revenues from the New House was simply too great to walk away from. Then there were the fringe benefits, which were hard to define, not the least of them being the tonic, almost joyful attitude that Julius's association with the rebbe had instilled in his wash-and-wear breast. To say nothing of the peace of mind that Mrs. Karp had found since coming under the rebbe's influence, in particular his Zen Judaism seminars. Truly, their relationship with Rabbi Eliezer ben Zephyr had opened a compelling new chapter in the annals of the Family Karp.

But now Sandy Grusom, Julius's trusted accountant, who had taken such an active role in promoting the House of Enlightenment, was seated on the opposite side of his desk advising his boss that the time had come to cut their losses.

"What losses?" Julius wondered, because the proof of the New House's bullish fortunes was winking at him in fiscal radiance from the computer screen. He swiveled the screen toward Grusom, a droopy-jowled fellow with a torso like an onion bulb, who swiveled it back without looking.

"The losses we're about to suffer when the shit hits the fan."

Julius knew his accountant for a cautious man who never spoke out of turn, but still in denial himself, he refused to believe that the rabbi's marvelous mumbo jumbo had had its day.

A week later the appliance maven was sitting in his office, still turning over the situation in his mind, when there came a knock at the open door. Shoving his glasses back onto the bridge of his nose, he saw in the doorway a slender, high-cheeked girl with particolored bangs like the teeth of a rainbow comb. She was wearing a braided military tunic like something out of a comic opera, drawing a bead on him with her forefinger as she accused him of being Bernie Karp's dad.

"Who wants to know?" he replied, wondering what this peculiar young person could have to do with him. Not by nature a suspicious type, however, he softened. "Okay, you got me dead to rights. What can I do for you?"

"Ain't you heard?"

"Guilty as charged," he added, still playful. "Heard what?"

She lurched uninvited into his office and plunked herself down in the only available chair, where she began to rock restlessly back and forth—this despite the chair's immobility. "The Mayor's been on TV," she announced a little breathlessly, studying the turquoise toenails at the tips of her sandal-shod feet. "He's ordered the House of Enlightenment shut down till further notice. Seems they mounted an investigation into the affairs of Rabbi ben Zephyr, whose place of bidness is s'posed to stay closed pending the findings." At which point she stopped rocking and stared up at Mr. Karp with heavily shadowed eyes.

This was troubling news indeed. The Mayor, Gaylord by name, a beetle-browed throwback to the apartheid South, had already been heard making veiled references to the New House's imprudent mixing of the races. But Julius couldn't get past the fact that the bearer of these ill tidings had yet to present her credentials.

"Do I know you?" he asked.

"A bunch of the Rabbi's followers," the girl went on, "hacksawed the chain across the front door, and now they're holed up inside the auditorium, which it is presently surrounded by cops. They want to arrest the lot of them, Rabbi included, for trespass and unlawful entry. The shit's done hit the fan."

"Is there an echo in here?" inquired Julius of the ceiling, loosening the knot of his tie. He wasn't sure what he found more disturbing, the news of the event itself or the instrument of its communication. "I repeat, who are you?"

With a hint of uncalled for defiance, Lou Ella stated her name, adding almost inaudibly, "I'm Bernie's girl."

"What's that?"

She repeated her avowal.

"Bernie? My son Bernie?"

"You maybe know another?"

"Don't get smart with me, young lady," snapped Julius more or less on principle, since reproach was never his strong suit. Then he tightened his tie again, musing out loud: "Bernie's got a girl?" It was a confidence he needed to digest at his leisure, but the girl went right on talking.

"He's playing with fire, your boy. He thinks he's some kind of a saint, which maybe he is, but that ain't the point."

"You're talking about my Bernie, the couch potato of Canary Cove?" But even as he said this, he was aware that the kid had changed, changed utterly, though he was damned if he knew exactly how.

"He's my Bernie now," murmured Lou Ella, straightening her spine for a proprietary instant before slumping again. "But mostly he don't belong to anyone, leastwise his own self. He ain't hardly a member of the human race no more. Do you know what a zaddik is?"

Julius assumed she was using some arcane teenage jargon. "Nooo," he tendered hesitantly.

"With all due respect, Mr. Karp, where you been?"

"Where *have* I been?" he wondered aloud. "Making a hard-earned buck is where." And if what she'd told him was true, then a goodly portion of that income was in serious jeopardy. But who was this little minx in her circus regalia to challenge him? "Let me get this straight," he said, matching her vexation with his own. "You're my son's girlfriend? Since when does Bernie have girlfriends?"

But Lou Ella had no intention of backtracking. "A zaddik is a kinda Jewish swami. He suffers for everybody. The dude's like in possession of all his mystical organs."

"Eh?"

"Ecstasy and him are like this. He can leave his body whenever he wants, sometimes even when he don't want, and rise up to glory or descend to the underworld to fetch back the soul of a person who died too soon. He's also known to escort the dead to the afterlife and only hangs around this world for the sake of his flock . . ."

All of which seemed neither here nor there to the home appliance merchant, who was growing more on edge by the moment. But despite the girl's unwelcome intrusion and the dire circumstance she'd come to impart, Julius found himself still dwelling on the news of his son's affair of the heart, which had given him an unexpected twinge. Maybe the kid was normal after all.

"Your common or garden zaddik," continued Lou, "can heal the sick too, which I ain't seen Bernie do yet, though he got my little sister, who's a might slow, to say her first word. Boykh, I think it was. He's pretty good for self-taught, though he insists on giving the rabbi credit for teaching him everything he knows."

"His girl," uttered Julius, squinting at the garish intruder over the rims of his glasses. "Who'da thunk it."

Lou Ella tilted her head, dangling an earring like a tiny tomahawk. "You still hung up on that? Well, if it makes you feel any better, we never done it, though it wadn't for want of trying."

Julius wasn't sure the information did make him feel better, but it was finally more than he needed to know. The girl had been in his office only minutes and already she'd led him far beyond his comfort zone. "Whoa," he said, hands raised like a holdup victim.

"Fact is," Lou was relentless, "if we was just regular sweethearts, I'da prolly lost interest in him by now. But, Lord help me, I got a soft spot for the shmegegi."

The unadorned declaration made the retailer doubly squeamish. "Why are you telling me all this?" he nearly shouted.

"'Cause I think I'm gonna lose him. That is," she conceded, "if I ever had him."

Julius considered calling security — did the Showroom have security? The girl was unstoppable.

"He's in trouble. He thinks he can save the rabbi, and he's gone to the New House to try and do I dunno what."

The thought of his laggard son venturing where angels feared to tread struck his father as absurd. "Shouldn't you both be in school?" it suddenly dawned on Julius to ask, though he himself was stunned by the irrelevance of the question.

"That place is a hornets' nest."

"School?"

"The New House! Ain't you been listening?"

He had, but enough was enough. "Well," said Julius, clearing his throat with a sound like a faltering transmission, "what do you expect me to do about it?"

Lou Ella glared at the agitated merchant with her fishiest eye, then let it go. In fact, she had entertained some fantasy in which she and Bernie's father joined forces to come to the aid of his son, even as Bernie rescued the rabbi from an uncertain fate. But there sat Julius Karp wearing the helpless expression of someone in the midst of taking a pratfall. Her lower lip trembled as she muttered, "Nothin', I guess."

"Then why drag me into this in the first place?"

"I just thought you oughta know. Also," she admitted, "I wanted to share the worry with somebody else." Feebly, "You know, like spread the wealth?"

"Okay, so now I'm worried. Are you happy?"

"No, but I'm a teensy bit relieved."

"Glad to hear it. So what happens now?"

She shrugged and rose from the chair, aeons older, turning with a sigh to slouch toward the office door. "Tragedy I s'pose."

As the girl made her melancholy exit without so much as a fare-thee-well, Julius was left stranded at his desk, harried by unbidden memories. So it seemed that the Karp family's affinity for untoward behavior had indeed leapfrogged the appliance merchant to bedevil his son. There was cold comfort in the knowledge: for the curse he had ducked all his life, in afflicting Bernie, had as good as circled back round to bite Julius in his own tush.

Autumn 2002.

He approached the New House of Enlightenment along a suburban street strewn with leaves and jackknifed squad cars flashing red lights. The tabernacle itself was surrounded by sawhorse barriers, onlookers from the neighborhood pressing against them as flak-jacketed police with bullhorns warned them to stay back. There were media vans, attendants fussing over broadcasters with perfect hair, pinning mikes the size of blood ticks to their lapels as they faced the cameras. Some enterprising children had set up a lemonade stand. The general air of expectancy seemed to Bernie, however, to have less in common with a crisis than the anticipation of a parade in which celebrities were due to appear. Maybe his own legend had preceded him and when he approached the barricades, explaining, "The rabbi is my teacher; I'm the one that discovered him," the crowds would part and the cops wave him through. But that wasn't likely. Besides, even if he was able to convince the authorities that he could be of assistance, they would no doubt attach such conditions that in the end he would be forced to betray the rabbi rather than rescue him. And rescue was what Bernie had in mind.

Having by now understood that his tenure as public guru had run its course, Rabbi ben Zephyr would have no choice but to accompany his onetime apprentice to some safe remove, where the holy man could again resume his original destiny as a hidden saint. But how to spirit the rebbe from the siege of the House of Enlightenment to some sanctuary beyond the reach of the law was a problem Bernie had yet to resolve, though he was confident that a solution would present itself when the time came. Meanwhile there was the more immediate problem of securing an audience with the old man in the first place. It occurred to him he might simply sidle through the police line, vault the barriers, and make a dash for the doors, but that would invite a doomed pursuit by the metro SWAT team, members of which were on hand for just such an event. And besides, Cholly Sidepocket, the rabbi's implacable bodyguard in his mirror glasses, chinchilla coat, and matching cap, had planted himself in front of the doors with folded arms, ready to repel anyone who dared to seek entry or take a bullet in the attempt. Bernie recalled a meditation of Shlomiel ben Hayyim of Dreznitz that rendered one invisible, but the technique had unpredictable side effects. Then a third option suggested itself, and making an abrupt about-face, the boy backtracked along the street of single-story ranch houses, their raked lawns anchored by bags of leaves tilting like fat kids in a sack race.

Behind him the voice over the megaphone, calling on the occupants of the New House to "Come out and save your sorry selves from future harm," was somewhat annulled by the bracing nip in the November air. In a block or two Bernie came to a place where the pavement was interrupted by a storm grate overarched by an inlet with cast-iron teeth, fixed into the lip of the curb like a snarl. Looking left and right, he sank to all fours and rolled his thin self between the iron teeth and the grate. He dropped some six feet into a shallow catchbasin full of sludge and standing water, stirring a swarm of drowsy mosquitoes and splashing ooze over his sneakers and jeans. From there he hauled himself into the mouth of a circular drainpipe through which, ducking his head, he proceeded at a simian stoop. It was dark in the pipe, but Bernie—veteran explorer (or so he told himself) of the obscurer reaches of the psyche—progressed with a blind assurance.

After a short incline, the tributary pipe spilled over a shelf into the storm drain proper, where he lowered himself into the deeper, broader conduit. But no sooner had he planted his feet on the sewer's pitched bank, unhunching his spine, than he lost his footing and slid down the slope on his backside into a trough the mixture of rainwater and raw sewage. Soaked and slimed to the skin, he made an attempt to rise only to slip again, his floundering efforts to regain his balance reverberating in the concrete tunnel. The outfall from the previous night's downpour had apparently backed up the passage, bringing with it a deposit of detritus that clogged the sewer like an unvoided intestine, and it took Bernie some moments to finally stand. Then, covered in muck as if he'd crawled from a primordial bog, he inched his way back up the slope to a less slippery purchase, where he cautiously began his forward progress again.

While the housing development above was of a fairly recent vintage, the sewer network beneath it seemed a holdover from some dark age. Unlike the sanitary system in Bernie's own neighborhood, which transported sewage efficiently toward flush tanks and treatment facilities, this cloaca-like passage appeared to have survived from a time when plagues of yellow jack were bred in miasmal sinks below the ground. Slowly Bernie's eyes, aided by tracers of light that penetrated the odd manhole cover, began to adjust to the gloom. There were other sources of illumination as well: sunlight slanting through the intermittent gratings, hanging pale-yellow parallelograms along the walls, whose fungus-laden masonry contributed to the atmosphere of a catacomb. Farther on, however, the floor of the tunnel itself began to come apart, breaking up like a fractured ice jam, where the stream of shmutz slopped over jagged concrete slabs into a cesspool. The pool, which contained the sediment of a wrecked civilization (TV chassis, dolls leaking electronic innards skittered over by rats as big as piglets), had spread to the width of a small lagoon; and beyond the lagoon the hydraulic cement of the sewer had given way to a pitch-black cavern like the mouth of Gehenna itself. It was a gaping blackness that seemed to beckon the feculent kid. Having memorized the coordinates in Rabbi Levi-Itzchok's *Way of the Righteous Transmigrant*, which mapped the soul's journey to infernal regions, Bernie was as much intrigued by subterranean as astral navigation, and had a powerful impulse to investigate. But wise to temptation, he realized he was peering into the darkness through the eyes of his nefesh, his spirit, which was inclined to see the mythic in the commonplace. He reminded himself that this was not the time for otherworldly spelunking; his first loyalty was to assiah, the literal world of action in which he still had urgent business to attend to.

He blinked, and the mouth of Gehenna reverted to a sewer tunnel, its ceiling invaded by plastic utility pipes and bundled cables. The cables hugged the wall for a dozen yards or so, then snaked around a corner into a downspout, which, as if following a thread through a labyrinth, Bernie squeezed himself into as well. Because the space was so tight, he had to slither on his belly through the narrow conduit, and while it contained only a minimal trickle of mildly contaminated water, he couldn't avoid being further dampened and soiled in the process. Then the spout dead-ended in a vertical shaft like a chimney flue, where the PVC pipes and wires veered upward alongside a rusty ladder that led to a metal grille at the top of the shaft. Bernie mounted the ladder and clambered toward the faint glow that filtered through the grille, which he dislodged once he'd reached it by pushing upward with his shoulder and hands. Then he hoisted himself into the basement of Rabbi ben Zephyr's institute. Here the cables branched around a light-studded panel of dials, switches, circuit breakers, and conductors that seemed to have blossomed directly from the tree of wires and pipes. So tall was the panel that it required climbing to a catwalk to gain access to its upper reaches, which included the main frame of a humming behemoth that Bernie assumed was a type of emergency generator, one that rendered the New House independent of the city's power grid.

It was ironic, then, that having negotiated a sulfurous nether precinct to get there, he should hesitate upon surfacing into such a well-lit place. Because something in this glittering display of man-made energy harnessed by the rabbi for the sake of his mercenary program caused Bernie to lose faith in his own wizardly prowess; as if, before that wall of technology, he were reduced again to the talentless lard-ass he'd been in that distant time before the Great Thaw. Who after all was Bernie Karp, caked head to toe in filth, to think he could snatch a corrupt old man from being (perhaps deservedly) crushed beneath the wheels of justice bearing down on him? Was he supposed to throw himself between the spokes?

"I am," Bernie had to remind himself aloud, "a wayfaring wonder whose origin is not known, and for me only the impossible has any appeal." Then having said it made it true. Wasting no more time, he located a spiral stair which he ascended with pinging steps and opened a door into the wide corridor of the main-floor concourse adjacent the gift shop that doubled as a museum.

Determined not to dawdle, he couldn't help observing that the shelves of books, baubles, and instructional CDs in their glass cases had been expanded to include various saint's relics: vials and ampules containing the bodily secretions of a tzaddik whose every emission was precious to his followers. In the center of the shop, mounted on a plinth, was an installation featuring the original caftan and ratty mink shtreimel that the Boibiczer Prodigy had worn during his frozen repose. This tattered raiment hung on a pair of crossed staves that loomed above a Kelvinator deep freeze (heaped with plastic sirloins and hams) like a mast on a boat. Bernie was then visited by a brief vision of restoring the rabbi to the freezer in which both of them might sail through caverns measureless to man down to the Gulf of Mexico, where they would fetch up on a tropical isle. Perhaps Lou could come too. When the vision passed, the boy's attention was drawn to a droning of voices, which grew in volume to a rolling din as he crossed the hall and opened the swinging doors. Poking his head into the great domed auditorium, he saw the large mixed gathering that swelled the galleries and lolled about the artificial turf in the arena where the rabbi's bima stood. Rather than the sobriety you might have expected of a besieged population waiting for the axe or the tear gas to fall, most appeared as relaxed as a grandstand crowd at a sporting event. While some sang hymns and chanted or meditated yoga-style, many were content to nod in time to the beat of different drummers over their iPods. There was a good deal of snacking, each according to his means: some munching bagels with a shmear, others fried chicken and deviled eggs, while others in designer running suits pulled squab, Camembert, and truffle paté from picnic hampers provided by gourmet markets; they drank bottled water and sparkling wine. At least one young couple were openly necking. Somewhere in their midst a single voice—Bernie spied a character in dark glasses balanced on a chair—was raised in a rallying cry, insisting that given the world's intolerance they ought all to take their own lives. "Let us die with dignity," he exhorted them, appropriating the Hebrew term for martyrdom, but no one looked to be paying him any attention. Nor did they seem to heed the muffled harangue from the loudspeaker outside, but carried on in their holiday mood as, presumably, they waited for their charismatic leader to appear.

Bernie, however, lacked their patience. He darted back across the corridor into the elevator's glass cubicle and rode to the top of the dome, where he crossed the slender steel bridge to the reinforced door. Then confronted by the door with its keypad combination, its peephole seconding the video camera angled above it, he thought twice before ringing the bell. What if they didn't let him in? Secure in his virtually impregnable quarters, the rabbi may have issued orders to admit no one, not even a boy who considered himself family. Bernie stood there wondering if there were perhaps a prayer he might invoke to crack the code of the electronic deadbolt, or maybe a password of the kind his Grandpa Ruby must have uttered outside the doors of speakeasies. Then the heavy door rolled open of its own accord; flew open, in fact, to allow the headlong exit of a lady Bernie recognized from his previous visit by her candy-floss wig. Pasting himself against the rail to keep from being run over by the woman in her tearful flight, he turned to watch her drop out of sight in the lift, then looked back toward the open portal to what he thought of as Rabbi ben Zephyr's bird's nest. It was empty but for the snake-haired technician in her pastel jumpsuit behaving at her console like a pilot in the cockpit of a plane going down. She was at once appealing frantically through the mouthpiece of her headset for assistance and hammering the computer keys in what may have been an SOS, her fingers raising a clatter like artillery. As he stood at the threshold, Bernie fought against being infected by her obvious panic, wondering if the police assault was already under way.

Unobserved by its sole occupant, Bernie had advanced far enough into the skybox to steal a peek into the rabbi's sleeping chamber, whose French doors had been left haphazardly ajar. Unable at first to trust what he saw, he rubbed his eyes with his fists, then squeezed them as if to drain their retinas of any lingering illusion. For there on the circular bed beneath the soft track lighting, an R&B singer crooning from an amp in the background, two women from among the rabbi's circle of votaries were kneeling, working strenuously over the supine body of the naked holy man. Also naked, the young one called Cosette with the whiplash braid and the older one with the chin tuck whose name Bernie couldn't recall were apparently trying to revive him. Cosette pumped the chicken bones of his arms, her pert breasts jiggling ornamentally with each effort, while her full-figured companion, quivering in every part, leaned above the rabbi and breathed into his mouth as if attempting to inflate a rubber raft. Both were performing their respective operations after a fashion that convinced the boy they had no idea what they were doing. Meanwhile the old man lay motionless, and if his virile member — trailing a condom like a stocking cap on a fireplug — were any indication, rigor mortis was already setting in.

Heart attack, stroke, kidney failure, let alone a multitude of collateral maladies, might have felled an old party well into his third century, especially one so renowned for his excesses. Nevertheless, as Bernie edged to within an arm's length of the disheveled bed, still unnoticed by the women, the rabbi seemed to be responding to their ministrations, his blanched eyelids fluttering open. "Please God, he's come back to us!" cried the older woman, getting hold of herself enough to remind him, "Rabbi, it's me, Rosalie," and to inquire, "are you comfortable?"

Then Bernie thought the old rascal might be looking past the women to wink at him with a sallow eye. "I make a livink," he said, and closed his eyes again.

Kneeling beside the bed, the boy must have exuded a nasty stench, because the women, despite their intense preoccupation, took note of him. Looking up to see what must have appeared to her as some pitch-bespattered devil from the abyss, Rosalie covered her breasts and let out a shriek, then leaning over the edge of the mattress to retch, tumbled after in a dead faint onto the floor. Cosette screamed, "Mama!" and bolted from the bed to help raise the sullied Rosalie to her feet, the two of them staggering out of the room in each other's arms.

Left alone with his rebbe, Bernie swallowed hard before speaking into the old man's bristly ear: "Rabbi, can you hear me?" And receiving an encouraging "Nu?" continued, "Don't you think it's time you returned to the path of righteousness?"

His voice the wheezy wedding of a rattle and a sigh, Rabbi Eliezer answered: "Farshtunkener boychik, don't make me laugh. There ain't no path; there's only the end of the road. What you call the path, it's just messing around."

Bernie considered the point, then concluded, "That's only your ego speaking," and reached over to peel off the flaccid condom.

"Ego shmego, so long as you got your health," replied the rabbi just this side of a whisper. "Listen, kiddo, when comes to earth even a angel, he must wear the garment of this world."

"Excuse me, Rabbi," Bernie couldn't help remarking, "but you're naked."

"So nobody's perfect."

"Rabbi," urged Bernie in the language of a desperate apostle, "let me get you out of here, and we'll do miracles. We can explore Ayn Sof, the

Big Nothingness, together; we can be glorious nothing, you and me, like before we were born."

"Psht," from the rabbi; "give a listen who thinks he's nothing," he said, beginning to cackle broadly at his own joke, laughing until he choked, the tundra of his face turning a deep shade of cyanine blue. Then his body began to convulse, his paltry torso and hips flapping like a shopworn standard until he stopped breathing altogether and was still.

Bernie's initial response to the sudden demise of the saint was denial, followed by jaw-dropping awe. It was his first encounter with actual physical death, and in some ways he thought it became the old bluffer, whose serenity recalled the original repose that Bernie had discovered him in before his thaw. Then the boy's preliminary reaction gave way to its polar opposite, an overriding impulse to disturb that peace. The blood of the generations that had made such sacrifices to preserve the Prodigy intact was building to a boil in his veins. Had he presided over the tzaddik's return to the world only to see him depart it in shame? Besides, Bernie found that he already missed the old man.

"I won't let you go!"

He knew he would have to act quickly, even as the Boibiczer's essence took flight from his spent anatomy. By now the authorities would have been alerted and at any moment cops and paramedics would burst upon the scene. In his mind Bernie had already done the deed; he'd made the transition and arrived at the destination through whose rheumy eyes he peered back at himself with abject longing. What he saw was a Bernie Karp who, though mantled head to toe in crud, was beloved of a girl and was a citizen of the sunlit world. How could he abandon himself when (it suddenly struck him) he wasn't even finished being young? Struggling against the temptation to stay, he concentrated on the image of "the lamp of darkness"; he attempted to meditate on a verse from Proverbs, "In all your ways know him," that was once a reliable trigger for launching him out of his skin. But it had been so long since he'd traveled that way and he'd acquired so much ballast in the interim. Bernie told himself the migration need not be permanent: The vessel he left behind might turn out to be proof against decomposition; it could even be frozen. He could return to his original self at his convenience, commute between one body and another, experiencing the best of at least two realities. All of which was finally beside the point, since he seemed to be stuck in the vessel he currently occupied. Of course, there was a surefire method of release, but that would be definitive; it would mean that in order to save the rabbi he would have to lose himself for good.

On the night table next to a plate of divinity sprinkled with confectioners' sugar (or was it cocaine?), Bernie spied a silver bucket containing a gallon jug of Manischewitz chilling in a niche chipped out of a king-size cube of ice. The steel pick used for the chipping was left sticking upright beside the bottle, and with a bravura gesture he leaned forward to yank it from the ice by its wooden handle. He raised the pick in front of him and heard a voice in his head pleading temporary insanity. "I can't do it by myself," he conceded. Then wiping his eyes, he took the tzaddik's stiffening fingers in his left hand and folded them around his right, the one that held the instrument, which — begging Lou's forgiveness — he plunged to the hilt into his own heart. A jolt as from a horse kicking through the skin of a drum shivered his chest, which exploded in a Pandora's box of pain. The blood spurted out like crude oil, further blackening the mud that daubed his jacket, and he no longer knew whether or not he remained on his knees. His nerves and sinews sang like live wires, his body demanding its right to relax into oblivion, his veiled eyes to survey the road to the Other Side — which passed through such picturesque vistas. Still he fought to complete the procedure in the seconds of consciousness left to him: A decision had to be made as to which of the rabbi's apertures was appropriate for the transference of Bernie's own immortal soul.

He'd already said so long to himself when he perceived through his dimming sight the old man's yet standing organ, which prompted the memory of a venerable Yiddish expression: "Er toyg nokh," as was said of libidinous elders: He's still good for it. This seemed providential enough, though nearly as great as his pain was his revulsion, which he dismissed as a residuum of the late Bernie Karp. Nevertheless, as he fell face-forward, holding his nose to keep his neshomah from escaping his nostrils, Bernie was relieved to recall an alternate text: "Mouth to mouth do I speak with him," as the Lord said of Moses, whom he awarded the death by kiss.

Later.

At the trial the rabbi showed no remorse, nor did he demonstrate any emotion readily identifiable to the mob that thronged the courtroom. Denied bail, which he'd never requested, he was trundled out of his cell at the Shelby County jail in a standard issue orange jumpsuit that ballooned about his broomstick frame. Guards led him mincing in his shackles behind the bar and seated him at a table beside his court-appointed counsel. From this vantage he viewed the proceedings with an expression of mild amusement, the way a sleepy child gazes into an aquarium. When asked at his arraignment how he pleaded, the old man, as if offered two equally delectable morsels, seemed unable to choose, and so an obligatory plea of not guilty was submitted. Hence the trial, during which Mr. Womack, the prosecuting attorney, a bald man of impressive girth whose every gesture seemed practiced, introduced a raft of evidence—largely fabricated but passionately maintained—to the effect that young Bernard Karp was the victim of a ritual murder. The boy had been degraded and defiled, made to perform unnatural acts, then murdered sacrificially so that his blood might be utilized in further satanic ceremonies. The prosecutor drew heavily on translations of old czarist documents called protocols to support his charges, and relished

describing in salacious detail the compromising situation in which the police had discovered the old man and the boy. A number of witnesses from
local law enforcement who'd been at the scene of the crime were on hand
to corroborate the prosecutor's characterization of the event.

The attorney for the defense, Mr. Frizell, an oily jackleg in mismatched
plaids going through motions for his minimal fee, took pains (small ones)
to point out that the prosecution's claims had been widely discredited since
the Middle Ages; that in any case the blood libel—and here he seemed to
contradict himself by giving credence to the very phenomenon he meant
to debunk—involved gentile victims, "Jew-on-Jew crime" being virtually
unheard of. But the imaginations of the jury, hand-picked for their ignorance, had already been ignited, and as the prosecution's case also included
the establishment beyond a reasonable doubt of motive and opportunity,
combined with a dramatic exhibition of the murder weapon itself, the verdict was a foregone conclusion. Rabbi Ezekiel ben Zephyr, old as he was
(though how old no one could say), was sentenced to life imprisonment for
actions so distasteful that the judge, the Honorable Schuyler Few, made a
show of spraying his mouth with antiseptic after speaking their name.

"By the authority vested in me by the state of Tennessee," pronounced
Judge Few, "I hereby sentence you the accused, Ezeekyul ben Zefire, to
be confined to the state correctional facility at Brushy Mountain for the
remainder of your natural life, with no recourse to parole." Later on, in
response to criticism of his failure to impose the death penalty, the judge
maintained that a slow death in prison was a crueller fate than the gas
chamber, which for the rabbi's people might be interpreted as a type of a
martyrdom. Still, there were those who detected a tincture of mercy.

The trial lasted only a week, in the course of which the media circus
was unrelenting. The austere, oak-paneled courtroom was packed every
day to capacity, the bailiffs hard pressed to silence a crowd sometimes
as unruly as spectators at a bearbaiting. Meanwhile the press had a field
day parsing every nuance of the case, the conservative papers weighing
in with a vengeance in favor of the rabbi's execution (some of the yel-

lower journals even suggesting the resurrection of a time-honored tradition involving lampposts and trees), while the liberal press, which had no local representation, derided the kangaroo atmosphere of the courtroom and deplored the rabbi's demonization, at the same time conceding that the accused might in fact be a demon. Nobody really questioned the old imposter's guilt. Though most of his followers distanced themselves from their leader after the murder, a steadfast few helped fill the pews and carried placards outside the courthouse reading FREE RABBI BEN ZEPHYR. Frequently interviewed by reporters, they mouthed the kind of gnomic catchphrases that lent substance to the belief that they were under some type of mind control.

The Family Karp were in daily attendance, a bench behind the attorneys' tables having been reserved for them throughout each phase of the trial. They sat, Julius and Yetta, stiffly during the proceedings, their faces gone slack from the effort of trying to sustain the proper balance of outrage and grief. Still in shock from the turn of events that had taken their only son in so terrible and untimely a fashion, they were nearly as crushed—God forgive them—by the rabbi's spectacular fall from grace. It was an attitude that neither could admit to the other. But while they tried their best on principle to abhor the old man, glaring daggers at the kippah—raffish as the dented cup of a black brassiere—that rode the back of his head, they fell short of invoking the rancor they sought. Despite the volumes of affection she expressed for her boy and her guilt over all the occasions she'd failed to declare it, Mrs. Karp confided to her husband in a moment of weakness that "the rabbi must have had his reasons"; and while he pretended he couldn't believe his ears, to his shame Julius secretly concurred. Their daughter, Madeline, was also present for a time, summoned from her career as artist's model to the funeral of her brother. A nuisance in life, her little brother had proved an even greater posthumous embarrassment owing to the public manner of his demise. But the girl nevertheless dutifully attended the funeral and stayed on for the commencement of the trial, even consenting to pose in all her pneumatic shapeliness for the newspaper photographers. After a few days, however, she became disgusted with her parents' inability to muster sufficient loathing for the defendant, and told them as much. When they responded that she should bite her tongue about things she didn't understand, she called them gross, and as the entire courtroom turned to watch her oscillating departure, sashayed again out of their lives.

Arrayed in a Zorroesque outfit complete with piratical headscarf that constituted her widow's weeds, Lou Ella Tuohy was there as well for every stage of the court case, sometimes with and sometimes without her baby sister of indeterminate age. She bagged school to attend and called in sick at the video store—whose hands-off proprietor told her not to worry; he would institute an honor system until she returned. Throughout the arguments and counterarguments, Lou sat in the gallery among reporters and curiosity seekers, snapping her gum and wondering exactly what had happened to shatter her world. Having never before seen the rabbi in person, she was intrigued despite herself by his benign appearance. A wizened old gargoyle with drooling eyes and yellow beard, sunken cheeks shot through with broken capillaries like purple spider webs, he nevertheless seemed possessed of a dormant vitality. Though stunned beyond apprehension by the ghastliness of what he had allegedly done, Lou—like the Karps, whom she'd thus far avoided—was unable to hate him with the fervency she felt he deserved. Her purpose was to mourn Bernie Karp with all her might, to miss him to the point of obliterating herself, but whenever she looked at the pacific old perp in chains, she was incapable of believing that Bernie was actually gone. This was identical to the feeling she'd had when viewing his cosmetically enhanced likeness in its open casket on the eve of his burial. So-called evidence aside (the evidence being patently a crock), she could conceive of no reason why a doddering holy man should want to murder her boyfriend. Would he even have had the wherewithal? What occurred at the New House on that calamitous November afternoon remained a mystery; the trial resolved nothing, and when the verdict was read and the rabbi hustled off toward his detention, it was *his* presence that she found herself missing, while she asked Bernie's forgiveness for her wicked inconstancy of heart.

Even before the trial, at the farcical funeral, Lou had failed to summon what she assumed was the appropriate degree of grief. Bernie's burial had taken place on a rainy morning in a treeless cemetery whose tombstones appeared to be marching lemminglike downhill toward the Interstate. Due to their proximity to the highway and the rain drumming the striped marquee, the small group of mourners huddled amid a crush of monuments caught only snatches of the rabbi's graveside eulogy. That was no great loss, since the rabbi from Congregation Felix Frankfurter had clearly not done his homework where the dead boy was concerned. He began predictably enough, his face severe beneath a snap-brim fedora, hands thrust into the pockets of his Burberry coat, by asserting that "the Lord has a plan," then seemed at a loss to say precisely what that plan might be. Swerving unexpectedly from convention, he began to speculate with an astonishing lack of compassion that "the boy must have been guilty of grievous sins in a past life to have been struck down so prematurely in this one." Those mourners who had bothered to follow his words—among them the quack psychologist and a few teachers from Tishimingo High, plus some parents who'd twisted the arms of their offspring who remembered the Karp kid (if at all) only for his narcolepsy—exchanged discomforted glances. They avoided making eye contact with the boy's family, who cupped their ears to hear what they thought they must surely have misunderstood. For the rabbi, changing tacks again, suggested that in any case young Bernard was well out of it "since this world is essentially God's bedpan. . . ." Were they witnessing the man's sudden loss of faith, or mind? In the event, as if having concluded that his voice had been hijacked by another, he clapped a hand over his mouth and remained silent. His thunderstruck expression was captured for all time by press photographers, who'd been standing by for every Bernie-related incident since the murder.

On what turned out to be the penultimate day of the trial the lawyer Frizell had called the rabbi himself to the witness stand. He'd previously summoned a parade of the rabbi's bochers (as they liked to call themselves) as character witnesses, though their loose-screw testimonies only helped to cement the prosecution's case. A rogues' gallery of real estate brokers, Hadassah ladies, auto mechanics, massage therapists, and soccer moms, they failed to impress the jury with their attempts to explain Rabbi ben Zephyr's theology of God as fun, and succeeded only in digging a deeper hole for the defense. Thus, in an act of desperation coupled with a perverse desire to steal a march on his shyster colleague, Mr. Frizell had Rabbi Eliezer hauled into the dock. In presenting his case, the attorney had downplayed the apocryphal tales surrounding the rabbi's origins, especially the one about his having been frozen for a century or more, but try as he might (and his efforts were never more than nominal) he'd yet to make a case for the old man as solid citizen. Here was his chance. It didn't help, though, that Eliezer's undocumented status compounded his unpopularity, and furthermore, once the rabbi was sworn in, his counsel seemed not to know how to question him, as even with regard to his name the old hoaxer was circumspect.

"For the record, you are Rabbi Ezekiel ben Zephyr, sometimes known as the Boy-bitcher Prodigy?"

"In a manner of speakink."

The lawyer thought it best to let it go. "And would you please tell the court in your own words what transpired between yourself and the deceased on the afternoon of November fourteenth?"

Said the rabbi, amiably, "That's the sixty-four-dollar question."

By then Mr. Frizell had understood his error: He should at the very least have coached his client regarding the content of his testimony beforehand. The lawyer smoothed his greasy salt-and-pepper hair (most of the salt being dandruff) with his hands, wiped his palms on his pants, and silently wished he'd left well enough alone. But now there was no turning back. "So would you mind telling the jury in your own words what occurred on the afternoon in question?"

"Well," the rabbi furrowed his brow, then seemed to brighten, his scratchy voice like a fiddle strung with electrical cord, "the last thing I remember, I was doing with Cosette and her mama a popular old-timey technique which by the received tradition is known as Manipulation of the Godhead—"

At that juncture the lawyer had begun to clear his throat with a rooster-like crowing, either by way of warning his client against the wrong turn his statement was taking or simply to drown out his words. "Let's start at the point when the young Mr. Karp entered your quarters," he interrupted.

"That I don't remember. Like I say, the last thing I remember is when Rosalie the mama—she's a little zaftig, Rosalie—on my face she sits while I'm beyn regel le-regel if you know what I mean with her daughter . . ." The courtroom, to gauge by its rumbling, knew precisely what he meant, the court reporter's fingers stumbling over a machine whose keys jammed like a crowd stampeding an exit.

Mr. Frizell tried to alert the old man with gestures that the court had heard enough of his smutty talk, but the rabbi seemed to have found his stride. "You see," he continued informatively, "as it is below, so is it above; it's a emb-a-lem, the holy zivvug, the sexual union from humans, for what happens in heaven. HaShem, when He sees what on earth we're doing, it gives to Him ideas. Then with His bride, His Shekhinah, He does the same, and is restored for a while the order in the universe. For a little while everybody got a extra soul—"

The hush the tzaddik's speech had induced in his audience was punctured by his attorney's shouted appeal to "Shut up!" with which the rabbi graciously complied. Facing the judge, the lawyer Frizell removed his glasses with their befogged lenses and announced, "No further questions, your honor." Then he bowed to the ladies and gentlemen of the jury and sat down again in careless defeat.

Judge Few, as if to break the spell that still held the courtroom, took a pecan from his robe and cracked it with his gavel, then said to Mr. Womack while chewing the nut, "Your witnesh, shir."

Mr. Womack hoisted his full-buttocked bulk from his chair and blew his nose in a monogrammed hankie whose contents he inspected closely like tea leaves, frowning at what he saw. He reminded the jury that reputable members of the psychiatric community had interviewed the rabbi and declared him competent to stand trial. Having made his point, he directed a steely stare at the rabbi, then turned back to the judge and said, "No questions, your honor."

In their closing remarks Mr. Womack recited again the litany of the rabbi's enormities, insisting that the jury had no choice but to find the defendant et cetera; whereas Mr. Frizell, almost devil-may-care in his final argument, said only that appearances can be deceiving. But despite the hostile atmosphere that had pervaded the proceedings from their outset, something had changed since Rabbi Eliezer had taken the stand. The press reported that his blasphemous and obscene testimony, rather than further antagonizing the courtroom, seemed to have inspired in the onlookers a curious sympathy. Schooled though they were in prejudice, the jury nevertheless took an inordinate amount of time to deliberate, the foreman reading their decision like an apology while pausing at intervals to mop his perspiring brow. But once the verdict was delivered, the sentence pronounced, and the old man ushered away, the whole episode receded into the fleeting diversion it had been all along, the attention of the citizenry having been redirected toward the issue of a world aflame.

IN THE TRANSPORT bus on the way to the state pen at Brushy Mountain, Cholly Sidepocket fought an urge to chew off his legs at the ankles in order to rid them of the irons he'd been made to wear. Now why was that? He'd done bids before; he knew the drill. He'd been in and out of joints since the gladiator schools of his youth, where, though he'd hardly shot a rack of pool since, he'd earned the street name that dogged him to this day. It was a foolish name, though no more foolish than the Two-Tones, Sheetrocks, and Sic Dawgs with which the other homies he'd run with were saddled. The handle had of course nothing to do with who he really was, which was the point, since Cholly had never had much to do with who he really was, at least not until he'd hooked up with the Old Man. Before that, the world was a place you visited like the bone yard in the prison compound, where the conjugal trailers were kept and the housebroken cons received their families. The world was the place where you peddled your crank, shacked up with your skank, as some wannabe rapper was chanting on the tier above; the place you did the crimes they fetched you back to do the time for, which you tried to do so that the time didn't do you. The system, once you were in it, was everywhere the same bad dream, the problem being that Cholly himself was different now.

Something had got switched on in him during his time with the Old Man, and he didn't think he could turn it off; he couldn't shut himself down like he'd done during his previous stretches. Before, despite his size and physique, Cholly'd been able to shrink himself, to fold up his soul like a doodle bug and secrete it in some part of his person where even he couldn't find it anymore. Because to show signs of humanity in the can was an invitation to the man to break you of those habits that distinguished you from the animals; and you could rest assured they had the means. So the best strategy was to beat them to it, to stupefy yourself, and sleepwalk through the years like some lumbering stiff. It was a condition that couldn't be faked, for even the most dimwitted hack could sniff out a human being. There had so far been no human beings in evidence at the Brushy Mountain Correctional Institution. Certainly none were at large when they marched Cholly through the monkey house on that first night of his incarceration, though the monkeys were all on view. Some did calesthenics or perused their short-eyes porn with a hand bobbing pistonlike in their lap; some flashed mirrors in an overt semaphore or peeped out through the bars at the new fish with bleary, tombstone eyes.

Familiar as it was, Cholly couldn't seem to get cozy in the double cell they'd assigned him during the mandatory six weeks' quarantine on the fish tier. He couldn't stand the company of the baby gangsta who wept all night in the bunk above his, a weeping interrupted only when the kid jerked himself off, which he did every hour or so. But rather than contemplate strangling him, the obvious solution, Cholly had the wack impulse to speak words of comfort, though he knew better, as sympathy was a sign of weakness and would come back to bite your ass in the form of some sucker hustle later on. So, between the sobs of his cellmate and the other animal sounds that swelled at dawn to an uproar like the Tower of Babel Zoo, Cholly wasn't sleeping too good. Then the day would begin again with its flimsy pretense of order, which collapsed with the least bit of pressure the way a maggoty carcass crumbles to powder at a touch; only, on A Block the powder was flammable. You had the monotony of chow runs, work runs, rec runs, and showers, the bug juice and special-programs calls, the law library or hospital if you could finesse them, visitations if you had any people left on the outside. But along the way you ran the gauntlet of cell soldiers and screws looking for an excuse to go off on you. There were jailhouse lawyers giving you advice you never asked for, entrepreneurs who ran regular commissaries out of their cages, peddling everything from hot electronics to shanks fashioned from Plexiglas or flint. You had the sad fucks of no known gender exiled to the untouchables table in the mess hall, the pay-him-no-minds shuffling about in their rubber flops, too far gone for the pigs to take notice of anymore, though the inmates, having no better diversion (the TVs in the common areas were unreliable), paid attention to one another, and no matter how forbidding your game face, you could bet that before the day was out some joker was going to get all up in your business. Cholly preferred to keep his business to himself.

He was a big man, Cholly, but that didn't discourage the gadflies and solicitors. Take for instance Daktari Brown, doing a twelve-year jolt for (as he claimed) smoking in the boys' room, who suggested that the new man might want to avail himself of his services. Wearing a kufi from beneath which his dreadlocks hung like stogies, Daktari ran a tattoo parlor out of his house, where he was as handy at etching the swastikas of the Aryan Nation as the pachuco crosses of the Raza Unidas and Bloods. Cholly curtly declined his offer, but Daktari, whose ambition was to leave his mark on all and sundry, was persistent, and one afternoon during gate time he prevailed on some power-lifters from the yard to jump Cholly Sidepocket and drag him into his cell. The following knock-down-drag-out raised an alarm that brought the screws running in their extraction gear with truncheons raised.

Coming to in a windowless box stinking of disinfectant, bare but for its stainless steel toilet and sink, the thin pallet and the light fixture that was never dimmed, Cholly wondered if this was what he'd wanted all along. Here he could maybe think straight, his aching head notwithstanding, and review the chain of events that had brought him to this sorry pass. But the truth was that the Special Housing Unit, for all its isolation, wasn't much quieter than the main line; you could still hear the jabbering of the monkeys with their catcalls and threats, their complaints that the CIA maintained a base of operations in their brain. Cholly didn't know if it was them or him that needed turning off. In the absence of his ostrichlike faculty, he was forced to listen to the noise that rattled the pipes the cons used as their "phone." From the hole it was hard to even recall the peace of mind he'd come to take for granted in the employ of the old Jew preacher man. Even now Cholly couldn't have said what it was about his attachment to that old rounder, with his string of bitches and dingbat disciples, that triggered the memories he seemed to have borrowed from someone else, some warrior he might have been had he not been himself. Had he not been brought up in foster homes where he proved himself unmanageable, and "industrial schools" from which he'd emerged with an arsenal of perfidious skills. Still it wasn't long, as he squired 'round the rabbi and watched his back, before Cholly had begun to think he might in fact be someone else, and that someone, he believed, did not belong in stir.

The voices he heard: Were they living men or only the ghosts of past deseg confinements, the jobbers whose names and gang devices were smeared in faded blood over the walls?

"Yo, Argo, holler atcha boy are you there."

"Franklin, dawg, that yo ebony ass?"

"Honey, if the SHU fit."

"Good one, dawg! Wha's crackin? Gimme the dily yo."

The only lulls in these disembodied dialogues came when the voices dummied up for a passing CO, or when a trustee delivered the sawdust loaves of affliction in their Styrofoam clamshells. But as soon as the coast was clear and their rations choked down — "Holla back" — the chatter would begin all over again. It continued in the chain-link exercise runs that the solitaries were released into for one hour out of every twenty-four.

"Y'all heard the back fence bout them niggahs up on Cee Block?"

"That the gorilla wing? Nothing but red eyes and booty bandits up there."

"Tha's what I'm sayin'. Tier Three, Block Cee, brothahs up there livin' ghetto fabulous."

"Dude, you in the O-zone? You done miss me with all that."

"Got a griot up there; suckah's tore-up-from-the-floor-up ugly, be teachin' em to catch theyself a ride without rock or reefer . . ."

Chinning himself on the bars of his cage to try and glimpse the mountains beyond the walls, Cholly was snapped back to where he was at by their noise, which elbowed his own thoughts clear out of his head. He resented the Old Man now for having given him a taste of possibilities, only to land him back in the drama by his antics. Still, time was he'd have laid down his life for that ragged-out old spieler, and probably would have had not the ladies come running bare-assed out the House of E screaming heart attack. Then Cholly'd left his post to see what was the matter and was instantly bushwhacked by SWATs; he was tossed in the county hoosgow doing dead time till his long-delayed trial, during which he was judged guilty of some imprecise charge and sentenced for an indeterminate term. He was sent off in a transport chain to a facility he'd only caught sight of from the window of the bus, which looked with its looming stone parapets surrounded by shrouded mountains like Dracula's castle. And all that time he'd been unable to get any news of the rabbi—heard only the rumor he'd been indicted for homicide or some such smack accusation that made no sense. In any case, here was Cholly back on the shelf, where his vintage anger festered under a hide that had once been so impenetrable. In the can your capacity for inspiring fear was your trump card, but in order to inspire it you had to feel it. Well, Cholly felt it now in spades. It threw salt in his game, the fear; it shook his control, and though he'd never even teased himself with the idea before, he began to entertain the possibility of escape.

Eventually removed from the hole and sent back to the general population, Cholly resolved to become a model citizen. He fell into lockstep with the prison routine, walked the tightrope between the man and the trash-talking toughs looking to make a reputation. He kept his own counsel and gave the screws no excuse for writing him up, resisted eyeballing them during the frisks and shakedowns. By forgoing trips to the commissary he amassed a small fortune in scrip, which he could use to bribe the COs who swapped it with the mules for drugs and smuggled loot. In this way Cholly accumulated favors he could call in along with the kites he floated for a release to labor details that might otherwise take years to obtain. Still, a season passed before he was given permission to work in one of the "shops." Cholly's was a concrete warehouse with huge fans expelling a hot elephants'-breath, where for eight hours a day he treated rubber gaskets by plopping them into a skillet of boiling water with a pair of tongs. Over time he graduated from vulcanizer to grease monkey in the small engine shop, and always he kept a weather eye open in his movements from building to building for some crack in the facility large enough for a big man to slip through. But Brushy appeared to Cholly Sidepocket to be seamless, its stone cell blocks hermetically sealed by center gates, end gates, and sally ports. Everywhere you looked there was hardware in the service of captivity: tiller-size brakes operating a multitude of deadlocks, systems of brass-handled levers protruding from their panels like organ stops. True, there were windows, unwashed in memory, through which nothing could be seen but the hazy outline of concertina wire and octagonal towers — and beyond them, what?

Sometime during the following fall, after considerable finagling, Cholly was promoted from the shops to the status of building tender. This was a porter primarily assigned to scut work, mopping and sweeping the trash-strewn galleries, emptying ashtrays in the dayrooms, carting dirty linen through a quarter mile of tunnels to the laundry. But while the work itself was menial, the porters were given virtual run of the facility, often entrusted with keys to secure parts of the prison and even access to inmate files. Instead of being cranked up by his greater liberty, however, Cholly felt sandbagged at every turn by his increased exposure to the type of incident that crippled your will. Plodding the prison corridors with his mop and pail, soap balls swinging from his waist, he was called upon almost daily to clean up the aftermath of routine atrocities. He scrubbed the "dressed out" cells on Six Wing, a kind of bedlam where the most depraved prisoners were housed, who flung their night soil about with gleeful abandon — that is, if they hadn't sewn up their assholes to keep from being sodomized. Once, on Six, Cholly saw a young fish being jocked by his cellmate, who'd stood his victim in a toilet while applying a charged wire to his parts. When he reported the event to the day-shift wing bull, the insouciant officer took a look and remarked wryly, "That'll sure cure yer rheumatiz."

A storm came up one afternoon in mid-winter — a violent thunderstorm mixed with snow. Cholly and a few other porters were sweeping garbage from the flats on C Block when Boss Wilcox, prodding Cholly in the small of the back with his quirt, sent him solo to the third-tier gallery, saying, "You don't need but to dry-mop it one time." As he trudged up the cast-iron spiral with the mop and bucket from which he'd become inseparable, Cholly, grown mightily tired of late, thought that his own clanking joints echoed the sound of the closing cell-block gates. These days he staggered like the dopers in their thorazine shuffle and wished that his mind were as muddled as theirs, because the only way to fly this miserable bid was blind. Meanwhile the storm that was buffeting the penitentiary challenged the din of the raucous population within, until a cannonade of thunder cracked open the dome of the firmament and the lights went out. Cholly paused on the pitch-dark stair in the momentary quiet, waiting for the generators to kick into gear and the power to return; there would be chaos in the house—already the cons were banging tin cans on the bars—if the power didn't return. But the blackout continued and the little heat the building retained had dissipated, as Cholly clumped the rest of the way in the dark up to Tier 3, where the entire gallery was illumined in a burnished glow.

Candles had been lit along the row of cells in which the prisoners, keeplocks all, were involved in a variety of unorthodox occupations. In the cell nearest Cholly an albino Negro with zebra stripes tatted over his hairless scalp was seated on his bunk, stringing an instrument that appeared to have been fashioned from half of a giant avocado. Next to him a Red Indian, a rainbow assortment of Sharpies poking out of his bandanna in lieu of a feather headdress, was sitting on the john with his pants around his ankles, limning the margins of a large open book. Next door to him a gawky yahoo with skin like cooked oatmeal—whom Cholly identified as a notorious pedophile—was hanging pink construction paper between curved cardboard struts, turning his cell into a diorama that depicted the ribbed belly of a beast. A brother in a conical cap decorated with stars and crescents poured pearl-colored gunk into a narrow flask and watched it slide around a helical tube of the type used to force-feed cons on a hunger strike. The tube was fixed to a syringe in which the fluid concluded as a drop of liquid gold. A bearded senior in a skullcap pounded shoe leather at an iron last; a splay-nosed gang potentate put the finishing touches on a pair of wings he'd carved from a block of ice, the ice apparently manufactured in his own dunker contraption assembled from scrounged odds and ends. Of course, whatever they created was only temporary; the goon squads would invade their cells and destroy what they didn't confiscate, a prospect that did nothing to dispel the rapt concentration with which each man bent to his craft. As spellbinding as their occupations, though, was the silence (of all but the wind) that seemed to neutralize the commotion from the other tiers, a silence so complete as to suggest it was itself a kind of contraband smuggled into the riotous big house.

Alien as it was, the atmosphere on Tier 3 impressed Cholly as a place he had experienced before, though perhaps not in his current life. Then slapping his brow, he turned around and revisited the cell where the old man, a filthy apron pulled over his work shirt and scrubs, sat laboring at his cobbler's bench, where the scent of leather and dye supplanted the usual urine-and-stiff-socks taint of the galleries. Becoming slowly aware of his observer, the old man lifted his smoke-gray head and exclaimed with a near toothless grin, "Cholly Sidepocket, mayn schwartze!" a puff of steam escaping his lips with every syllable.

Said Cholly regretfully, "I ain't belong to you no more."

The rabbi stood up and approached the bars with a buoyant, loping step; stir, it seemed, had done him a world of good. He was holding the grainy upper of the brogan he'd been working on by a tongue that lolled from its leather vamp. Then pointing to the floppy topsole with the wooden mallet in his other hand, he croaked, "This is the earth, and this," nudging the heel with a crooked pinkie, "is hashamayim, the world to come." Then he tapped with the mallet the bottom of the topsole that dangled its row of hobnails like a yawning jaw, joining it somewhat sloppily to the ill-made upper dripping latex cement like mayonnaise between crusts of bread.

"A shiddach!" he proclaimed with pride. "A match!"

At that Cholly felt the barrel vault of his chest give way and cave in. "Ol' man, you crazeh as evah," he managed through a single bearlike sob. The rabbi stuck a liver-spotted fist through the bars and bumped his knuckles against the black man's thick fingers, still wrapped around the handle of his mop. "Sprankle me, honey gee dawg," he piped, and having wrenched from his friend a lacerated chuckle, went on to explain: "Everyone that he enters here must abandon hope. But to those who hurt so hard they can't hope, is given to them a secret medicine. Shah," placing a bony finger to his lips, "if they knew this, the hopers, they will feel they have been cheated."

Back on his unit Cholly began to calculate the ways he might get himself transferred to C Block, Tier 3. He knew that the process could take time; he'd have to stay on the prowl, ride it out, maybe get up off a little info and tighten his game. But he also knew that, while you might age rapidly in the joint, and die a thousand deaths, time itself stood still. Time, so to speak, was on ice.

WHEN SHE WAS seated in a plastic chair at the rickety table across from the murderer, who was holding in either hand a red shoe, Lou Ella struggled to maintain her self-control. They were the ugliest shoes she had ever seen, a travesty of ruby slippers, bits of sequin sewn unevenly onto their heels and toes like the scales of a radioactive fish, globs of glue seeping between the counters and rubber soles. Though she judged herself a pretty tough cookie, the overnight trip across the state in a crowded bus (along with the burden of Sue Lily, who was no lightweight), the shakedown of her purse and then her person, and the shock of the dismal gray prison itself had taken their toll on Lou. Then, presented with the bogus old buzzard in his jailhouse getup, the beanie and outsize denims more foolish than stripes, she was suddenly overcome by fatigue, and the tears began to flow.

The rabbi caused the shoes into which he'd stuck his hands to tapdance on the tabletop. "What are you crying?" he wondered throatily. "How comes it everybody that they see me they got to shpritz tears?" he seemed to ask of the fluorescent lights.

She blew her nose in the pinafore of the unwieldy baby sister she was bouncing on her knee. "You tell me," she challenged, summoning a hostility she thought suitable to the occasion.

"For your dead lover you weep?" suggested the rabbi, sounding almost hopeful. Despite his ashen skin and runny eyes, the sulfury tangle of his beard, he looked none the worse for wear from his confinement; in fact, his moist eyes seemed almost to shine with a kind of crazed sympathy.

Lou Ella narrowed her eyes and stiffened, then snickered until the snot ran and she had to blow her nose again. "He wadn't never my lover. He wadn't but a crush." The vehemence of her outburst shocked her, though even more surprising was that the old dude actually looked hurt by her pronouncement. He nudged the tacky shoes tentatively in her direction.

"I made you," he offered, explaining that he'd begun to pursue a new hobby in prison.

A rogue impulse to apologize for having brought him nothing in return invaded her consciousness before she banished it, appalled. Then she inquired pointblank: "Why did you off him?" For there was no reason to postpone the question, having come all this way to ask it. But though she'd rehearsed it in her head innumerable times, it now sounded somehow misplaced.

But if not for this question, to which the rabbi (looking sheepish) had yet to respond, what was she doing in this godawful place? She seemed to be waiting for the old man to tell her, which wasn't logical; it was tantamount to having made the journey in order to find out why she'd made the journey. Lou ran a hand through her cropped magenta hair. Meanwhile the pitched voices in the Visiting Room, sweltering despite the seagreen film obscuring the windows, were so distracting that she could barely think. The room itself, with its sentinel vending machines and signs warning against inappropriate contact, defied any type of intimacy. At the adjoining table an obese woman in a flowered muumuu the size of a haymow leaned across to slap her son the convict silly after he'd attempted to sing her a yodeled rendition of "Mama Tried." At another table an inmate photographer snapped a Polaroid of a heavily medicated prisoner shackled to a restraint chair, next to which was parked a moribund old lady in a wheelchair with an oxygen tube up her nose. Infants swarming over the rails of their allotted play area had to be tossed back into their pen by patrolling officers in dress blues, while Sue Lily herself, ordinarily so passive, had begun to squirm and fidget in Lou Ella's lap.

"Boykh," she said in a nearly unprecedented ejaculation, becoming so unwieldy that Lou had to excuse herself and deposit the child in the turbulent playpen along with the others; and there she stood gripping the rail, a hair ribbon drooping over an unblinking eye, making ineffable noises that evoked a double-take from her big sister. When Lou Ella turned back to the rabbi, his simpering expression reinforced her conclusion that she'd made a grave mistake in coming here.

After all, Bernie Karp had been dead and buried these past two years and she was getting on with her life without him, wasn't she? A year out of high school already and although she'd been offered scholarships, advised by counselors what a shame it would be to waste a mind like hers, Lou had elected to stay home and work instead. Her baby sister had been diagnosed with some sluggish strain of autism and was being sent to a special day school that her mama, repeatedly passed over for a managerial post at Fed Ex, could ill afford. So Lou stayed on as a full-time employee at the video outlet whose absentee owner had neglected to convert his stock to DVDs, which meant that the store's already skeleton clientele had dwindled to a handful of irregulars. As a consequence, the girl had ample time to pursue her reading of Carlos Casteneda, Ekhart Tolle, and Emanuel Swedenborg, though in truth she hadn't done much reading lately. She preferred to view three handkerchief romances starring Ida Lupino or Loretta Young from the outlet's Adults Only section, though the films failed to move her either.

After the trial she'd thought, Now the grief will start, but it never did. There was the guilt, of course, due to the lack of grief, and there was the missing him; she did miss him, though she began to wonder why. After all, Bernie Karp was a very ethereal fellow with neither foot planted firmly on Mother Earth, and what had their hooking up been but a series of small frustrations ending in a large one? True, they'd shared certain common interests, but Lou was beyond all that now; she understood that to be alive was to be fettered to a dying planet where the only release was through some forbidden pleasure. "When's the tragedy begin?" she'd asked herself, but in place of it, in place of a blast of sorrow that might rupture the glacier in her breast, she felt only an enduring lassitude. Nothing seemed to matter much anymore. Restless in her isolation, she began to seek out the company of unsavory types, syrup heads and aspirin freaks among whom she earned the reputation of being an easy lay. Though she viewed her own bad behavior as a betrayal of her departed boyfriend, Lou found that remorse somehow sweetened the mischief. Was she so angry with him that she wanted to desecrate Bernie's memory? Well, yes. Yes, she fucking was. But she knew that anger wasn't the whole of her motivation, and after a time there was little satisfaction in bad behavior either.

One evening, despite her misgivings, she went to see Bernie's parents, though they'd made it abundantly clear at the trial that she represented associations they would rather not be reminded of. But time had passed and Mr. Karp had recouped his losses since the fall of the House of Enlightenment; he'd acquired an extra chin and an artificial tan which he displayed to good advantage in his TV ads. His wife, wearing a tangerine training suit, touted her enrollment in a Cardio Rebounding class (that involved weighted hula hoops and a mini-trampoline) in which she planned to sculpt her body to complement her blue-rinsed hair. Having apparently made a kind of peace with Bernie's slaying, they welcomed Lou Ella cordially, inviting her into their home, where they sat on a deep-cushioned sofa holding hands. Skeptical, Lou thought they were either making a show of congeniality or had maybe had themselves lobotomized.

When she'd weathered the shock of their friendly greeting, she asked them in all sincerity, "How do y'all cope?"

They trod on each other's answers, Mrs. Karp beginning again to praise the virtues of her exercise program while her husband claimed an absorption in business matters. Then a silence during which each, looking askance at the other, waited for their spouse to speak first, until both spoke simultaneously again.

"Pills," asserted Mrs. Karp, as her husband admitted, "We visit the rebbe." His wife gave him a subtle elbow to the kidneys, which he not so subtly returned. She swiveled toward him in a show of pique that just as quickly subsided, as she too confessed, "We visit the rebbe."

The girl was dumbfounded and said so. Begging their pardon, she asked how they could bring themselves to take solace in the man who had wasted their boy. The wife shrugged her own puzzlement, then offered a muddled adage about forgiveness being the spice of life, while her husband declared almost defiantly, "He's become like a second son to us."

Taking heart from his impenitence, Mrs. Karp added, though still a little shamefaced, that they had recently begun discussing adoption proceedings. Then she leaned forward to touch the girl's knee through the hole in her jeans. "You should go and see him," she ventured, as if recommending a good beautician.

Horrified, Lou Ella muttered thanks for their hospitality, declined an offer of pralines and tea, and left their house abruptly thereafter. But while she dismissed Mrs. Karp's advice out of hand (it was way weird), the conversation seemed to have awakened a latent impulse — because she did begin to conceive against all her better instincts a desire to visit Rabbi ben Zephyr herself. When the desire had grown to an urgency, she realized what should have been obvious all along: that she needed to go and ask him in person why he'd done what he'd done. What possible reason, she wondered for the umpteenth time, could he have had for icing her boyfriend? The answer would provide some "closure," wouldn't it, and wasn't closure what everyone wanted? Though Lou had the sneaking suspicion that what she really wanted was to open the whole can of worms again.

She'd had to travel all night on the bus from Memphis. That was the only way she could make the connection with the van that shuttled the families of inmates from the nearby town of Wartburg (a gas station and a rusted threshing machine among weeds) to the prison. She'd been surprised, when she contacted the prison authorities, to discover that she was already on the rabbi's visitors' list, since she and the murderer had never formally met, but this was the least of the mysteries surrounding Bernie's death. She informed her mother in the vaguest of terms of her projected trip, which got no more than a weary nod from Mrs. Tuohy, who complained she'd be stuck with Baby Sister all weekend. "Awrat," sighed Lou, "I'll carry her wi' me," though the truth was that she took comfort in the nearness of the mostly inanimate child. But when the searches began preliminary to the visit, she wished she'd left her little sister behind. It was bad enough, dreadful in fact, when the female guards began to strip-search Lou, making her remove her ballet skirt and tie-dyed underwear, snapping her thigh-highs and probing her private places under the supervision of a male CO. But that they performed a similar operation on Sue Lily, whom they handled like some big-boned glove puppet, was finally the limit. "We're out of here," she informed a matron, who ignored her, shepherding Lou and the oyster-eyed child into the hubbub of the visiting room.

Then she was seated before this poor excuse for an Ancient of Days, who offered her his cheesy red shoes, and suddenly the grief that had waited so long in abeyance chose that moment to well up and spill from her eyes. Across the table the rabbi gazed at her with a puppyish affection tinged with pity.

"Fuckwad," said Lou, incensed at his presumption, "you don't even know me."

He raised his bristly brows. "I know by you your pupik tattoo and the taste from your tongue that you burned it one time in your gleyzl chocolate in the Dixie Café," he said, leaning across the table so that a guard waved his baton between them to signal they should maintain the proper distance. "I know the journey of your soul from a guppy and the Island Mango air freshener you would spray in your room to hide the smell from the funny cigarette." He was leaning close again, his breath reeking of the lard cutlet he'd had for lunch, crumbs of which clung to his beard. "I know how you trim it, the poobick hair."

Lou cocked her head, transfixed, unable to tear her gaze from the fretted face that framed the old man's limpid eyes, the light therein beaming some species of molten moonshine. Involuntarily she stretched a hand over the table to rap on his forehead, scored with wrinkles like a musical staff, and when in response he nodded slowly in the affirmative, she recoiled in disbelief. "You stink of treyf," she accused, rummaging her brain for more ammunition to injure him with, resisting the fascination that wrung her heart. Shaking her head to rid it of nonsense, she repeated, "Why'd you rub him out?"

The rabbi extended the thoughtful blister of his lower lip. "Maybe I rubbed him in," he submitted. "To his neshomeh I gave it the liberty to take up a new what you call it . . . a crib?"

Crib? She hesitated. "What was wrong with his old one?"

"It was stuck tsvishn tsvay veltn—between this side and the other. So I set him aloose."

"Don't give me that bull," spat Lou, "I'm tired of all that hoodoo horse-shit. It's as phony comin' from you as it was from him." Though she wondered at that moment which "him" she referred to. "There ain't no world but this one and it's already half in the crapper."

"He was too much in it, the world," said the rabbi.

"He wadn't in it enough," declared Lou.

The old man let go a sigh like a groan with wings. "That too," he lamented, winking a watery eye, "that too."

Anger roiled in the girl, who saw herself in a scene from one of those noir flicks she watched at the video store, one in which Madeleine Carroll as the murder victim's moll removes a weapon from her purse to get even with his killer. But Lou's purse held only her makeup, some Goo Goo Clusters for Sue Lily, and a copy of *Zen and the Art of Motorcycle Maintenance*, and besides she had no wish to hurt him anymore. On the contrary, once her anger had fizzled she found that she was strangely relaxed in the killer's company, enjoying a tranquillity she told herself it was unforgiveable to succumb to. But the clamorous room no longer rattled her nerves; she might have been alone with him in, say, a parlor or the backseat of her mama's Malibu.

Just then there was a disturbance at one of the other tables. The administrative officer had bolted from the dais to back up a couple of guards who'd confronted a standing prisoner and his female visitor. The two of them were protesting their innocence—the con combative, his companion fussing with her beehive even as she shouted poisonous oaths—while a guard claimed that the photos in the album they'd been poring over were backed with pressed sheets of crystal meth. When the officer made to confiscate the album, the prisoner—ropy biceps, teardrop tats in the corner of an eye—tore out one of the pictures and stuffed it into his mouth, which brought down the wrath of the provoked COs. Voices were raised, batons deployed, canisters of irritant dust sprayed in a scuffle that commanded the attention of the entire room. Lou herself had turned toward the fracas, only to have her attention recalled to the table that the rabbi had abruptly shoved from between them. Then, with an audible crackling of joints or crinoline, he lifted the girl onto his lap. Why didn't she fight him? This was degrading, no? It was wrong in every category known to man: for there she sat in full view of the room astride the geezer's knobbly knees with her back against his whistling chest, feeling a sizeable lump in his pants. Buttons were sprung and the lump released, which nuzzled her rump beneath her flounced skirt like a small animal seeking shelter, which Lou felt curiously anxious to accommodate. It occurred to her that she had primped for this occasion—for this "rape," was it? The word hardly applied, though her underpants were pulled aside and her womb straight-upon filled, while the old perv gummed her earlobe whispering, "The Lord sm-m-mite thee, sweet m-maidl, with m-m-m-madness and astonishmum of heart."

"Awrat," Lou heard herself admit, "I'm sm-m-mitten," cracking up over the delirium of her willing surrender as the two of them took flight.

With eyes closed Lou Ella saw everything through her organs and pores, each facet of her anatomy featuring at least five senses. What they observed, once her lover had irrigated her insides with his luminous seed, were the toppled walls of the prison, the mountains and the pillowy clouds above them, the harum-scarum rooftops of the shtetls of Paradise. She heard from a playpen somewhere back on earth the warbling of her baby sister in the tongue of nightingales, whose language Lou understood perfectly.

ACKNOWLEDGMENTS

I would like to thank my agent, Liz Darhansoff, for her steadfastness; my editor, Chuck Adams, for his integrity; and the people at Algonquin for their good faith. I would also like to thank the John Simon Guggenheim Memorial Foundation for their generous support.